THE OUTLAWS

A Presidential Agent Novel

ALSO BY W. E. B. GRIFFIN

THE OUTLAWS

A Presidential Agent Novel

W. E. B. Griffin

and

William E. Butterworth IV

severn House

This first world edition published 2010
in Great Britain and in 2011 in the USA by
SEVERN HOUSE PUBLISHERS LTD of
9–15 High Street, Sutton, Surrey, England, SM1 1DF.
Trade paperback edition first published
in Great Britain and the USA 2011 by
SEVERN HOUSE PUBLISHERS LTD .

British Library Cataloguing in Publication Data

Griffin, W. E. B.
  The outlaws. -- (A presidential agent novel)
  1. Castillo, Charley (Fictitious character)--Fiction.
  2. Undercover operations--Fiction. 3. Biological weapons--
  Fiction. 4. Suspense fiction.
  I. Title II. Series
  813.5'4-dc22

ISBN-13: 978-0-7278-6929-6 (cased)

All Severn House titles are printed on acid-free paper.

Severn House Publishers support The Forest Stewardship Council [FSC],
the leading international forest certification organisation. All our titles that
are printed on Greenpeace-approved FSC-certified paper carry the FSC logo.

MIX
Paper from
responsible sources
FSC
www.fsc.org   FSC® C018575

Printed and bound in Great Britain by the
MPG Books Group, Bodmin, Cornwall.

26 July 1777

*The necessity of procuring good intelligence is apparent and
need not be further urged.*

George Washington
General and Commander in Chief
The Continental Army

FOR THE LATE

William E. Colby
An OSS Jedburgh First Lieutenant
who became director of the Central Intelligence Agency.

Aaron Bank
An OSS Jedburgh First Lieutenant
who became a colonel and the father of Special Forces.

William R. Corson
A legendary Marine intelligence officer
whom the KGB hated more than any other U.S. intelligence officer—
and not only because he wrote the definitive work on them.

★

FOR THE LIVING

Billy Waugh
A legendary Special Forces Command Sergeant Major
who retired and then went on to hunt down the infamous Carlos the Jackal.
Billy could have terminated Osama bin Laden in the early 1990s
but could not get permission to do so.
After fifty years in the business, Billy is still going after the bad guys.

René J. Défourneaux
A U.S. Army OSS Second Lieutenant attached to the British SOE
who jumped into Occupied France alone and later
became a legendary U.S. Army counterintelligence officer.

*When René Défourneaux was twenty, the odds against his living to be
old enough to vote were probably 100–1.*

*As I was writing this book, Colonel David Bennett, USA, notified
me that his uncle and my old friend René had passed after long service
to our country's intelligence community, both before and after his retirement.*

He died in bed. He was eighty-nine.

*Among the many attending his interment at Arlington National
Cemetery on 10 May 2010 were the sons of his friend Bill Colby.*

*René had a thousand stories to tell. My favorite was the one of being
decorated in the Pentagon with the Silver Star from the hands of the U.S.
Army Chief of Staff.*

*The citation described his extraordinary skill and great valor in
blowing up a bridge in France. René said he had never been anywhere
near that bridge, but had taken the medal because he had learned as a
second lieutenant never to argue with a four-star general.*

Johnny Reitzel
An Army Special Operations officer
who could have terminated the head terrorist
of the seized cruise ship *Achille Lauro* but could not get permission to do so.

Ralph Peters
A U.S. Army intelligence officer
who has written the best analysis of our war against terrorists.

and of our enemy that I have ever seen.

★

AND FOR THE NEW BREED

MARC L
A senior intelligence officer, despite his youth,
who reminds me of Bill Colby more and more each day.

FRANK L
A legendary Defense Intelligence Agency officer
who retired and now follows in Billy Waugh's footsteps.

OUR NATION OWES THESE PATRIOTS

A DEBT BEYOND REPAYMENT.

I

The small convoy—two battered Toyota pickups, a Ford F-150 pickup, and a Land Rover—had attracted little attention as it passed through Al-Ubayyid (estimated population around 310,000).

Al-Ubayyid was the nearest (seven kilometers) town to the El Obeid Airport, which was sometimes known as the Al-Ubayyid Airport. The town of Al-Ubayyid was sometimes known as El Obeid. In this remote corner of the world, what a village or an airport—or just about anything else—was called depended on who was talking.

The men were all armed with Kalashnikov rifles, and all bearded, and all were dressed in the long pastel-colored robes known as *jalabiya,* and wearing both *tagia* skullcaps and a length of cloth, called an *imma,* covering their heads.

The beds of the trucks each held one or two armed men. It was impossible to tell—even guess—what the cargo might be, as it was covered with a tarpaulin.

The convoy looked, in other words, very much like any other convoy passing through—or originating in—Al-Ubayyid on any given day. By whatever name, the town had been a transportation hub for nearly two centuries. First, there had been camel caravans. Then a rail line. Then roads—it's a nine-hour, five-hundred-kilometer trip from Khartoum—and finally, six kilometers south of town, the airport with a runway nearly a thousand meters long.

As it approached the airport, the convoy slowed and the headlights were turned off. It moved near to the end of the chainlink fence surrounding the airport and stopped, remaining on the road.

A dozen men—everyone but the drivers—quickly got out of the vehicles.

The man who had been in the front seat of the Land Rover went to the floodlight—not much of a floodlight, just a single fluorescent tube—on a pole at the end of the fencing and quickly shot it out with a burst from a .22 caliber submachine gun. The weapon was "suppressed," which meant that perhaps eighty percent of the noise a .22-long rifle cartridge would normally make was silenced.

He then quickly joined the others, who were in the process of quickly removing the immas and skullcaps from their heads and finally their long jalabiya robes. The discarded garments were then tossed into the Land Rover.

Under the jalabiya robes they had been wearing black form-fitting garments, something like underwear except these had attached hoods which, when they had been pulled in place, covered the head and most of the face.

Night-vision goggles and radio headsets were quickly put in place.

Next, they took from the Land Rover and the pickups black nylon versions of what was known in the U.S. and many other armies as "web equipment" and strapped it in place on their bodies.

The man with the .22 caliber submachine gun—the team leader—was joined by two other men equipped with special weapons. One was armed with a high-powered, suppressed sniper's rifle that was equipped with both night vision and laser sights. The other had a suppressed Uzi 9mm submachine gun.

The laws of physics are such that no high-powered weapon can ever be really suppressed, much less silenced. The best that could be said for the suppressed sniper's rifle was that when fired, it didn't make very much noise. The best that could be said for the Uzi was that when fired, it sounded like a suppressed Uzi submachine gun, which meant that it wasn't quite as noisy as an unsuppressed Uzi.

The sights on the sniper's rifle, which was a highly modified version of the Russian Dragunov SVD-S caliber 7.62 x 54R sniper's rifle, were state-of-the-art. When looking through the night-vision scope—which had replaced the standard glass optical scope—the marksman was able to see on the darkest of nights just about anything he needed to.

And by sliding a switch near the trigger, a small computer was turned on. A laser beam was activated. The computer determined how distant was the object on which sat the little red spot, and sent that message to the crosshairs on the sight. The result was that the shooter could be about ninety percent sure that—presuming he did everything else required of a marksman since the rifle was invented, such as having a good sight picture, firing from a stable position, taking a breath and letting half of it out before ever so carefully *squeezing* the trigger—the 147-grain bullet would strike his target within an inch or so of where the little red dot pinpointed.

The team leader made a somewhat imperious gesture, which caused another man—who had been standing by awaiting the order—to apply an enormous set of bolt cutters to the chainlink fence.

Within a minute, he had cut a gate in the fencing through which everyone could—and quickly did—easily pass.

The runway was about fifty meters wide. An inspection, which the team leader considered the most dangerous activity of this part of the operation, was required. A good leader, he had assumed this responsibility himself; he walked quickly in a crouch down the dotted line marking the center of the runway toward the small terminal building.

The man with the suppressed Uzi walked down the runway halfway between the dotted line and the left side, and the man with the sniper's rifle did the same thing on the right.

All the others made their way toward the terminal off the runway, about half on one side and half on the other. Most of them were now armed with the Mini Uzi, which is smaller than the Uzi and much larger than the Micro Uzi. The Kalashnikovs, as much a part of their try-to-pass-as-the-locals disguises as anything else, had joined the jalabiya robes and skullcaps in the Land Rover.

They had gone about halfway down the runway when a dog—a large dog, from the sound of him—began to bark. Or maybe it was the sound of *two* large dogs.

Everyone dropped flat.

The man with the Dragunov assumed the firing position, turned on the night sights, and peered down the runway.

He took his hand off the fore end and raised it with two fingers extended.

The team leader nodded.

The two shots didn't make very much noise, and there was no more barking.

The team leader considered his options.

It was possible that the shots had been heard, and equally possible that someone had come out of the terminal to see why the dogs were barking on the runway, or that they had come out—or were about to—to see why the barking dogs had stopped barking.

That meant the sooner they got to the terminal, the better.

But the problem of having to inspect the runway remained—that was the priority.

The team leader activated his microphone.

He spoke in Hungarian: "Trucks, lights out—repeat, lights out—to one hundred meters of the terminal. Hold for orders."

There was no need to give orders to the others; they would follow his example.

He got to his feet and resumed his inspection, this time at a fast trot, still crouched over.

The sniper and the man with the suppressed Uzi followed his example. The men off the runway, after a moment, followed their example.

They came to the dogs, lying in pools of blood where the animals had fallen, about a hundred meters from the terminal building.

The team leader could now see the flicker of fluorescent lights in the terminal building itself, and in the building beside it, which he knew housed the men—four to six—and their families—probably twice that many people—who both worked and lived at the airport.

And he could hear the exhaust of a small generator.

That was powerful enough to power the lights he saw now, and the two dozen or so fluorescent "floodlights" around the perimeter fence, but it wasn't powerful enough to power the runway lights.

He looked up at the control tower. There was no sign of lights, flickering fluorescent or otherwise.

Runway lighting would logically be on the same power as the control tower.

That meant he was going to have to find the much larger generator, see if he could start it, and see if there was enough diesel fuel to run it.

If he couldn't get the runway lights on, the whole operation would fail.

He spoke Hungarian into his microphone again: "Change of plans. Cleanup will have to wait until we get some of these people to show us the runway lights generator and get it started for us. Commence operations in sixty seconds from . . ." He waited until the sweep second hand on his wristwatch touched the luminescent spot at the top ". . . time."

The next stage of the operation went well. Not perfectly. No operation ever goes perfectly, and that is even more true, as the case was here, when the intelligence is dated or inadequate, and there has been no time for thorough rehearsals.

There had been several rehearsals, but there had been no time to build a replica of the airport and its buildings. And if there had been time, they had had only satellite photography, *old* satellite photography and thus not to be trusted, to provide the needed information.

They had improvised, using sticks and tape to represent the fence and the buildings, and guessing where the doors on the buildings would be.

But despite this, the team leader thought the operation had gone off—so far, at least—very well.

The man with the bolt cutters had opened the gates to the terminal area and to the tarmac. Then one two-man team had entered the terminal to make sure there were to be no surprises from there, and two teams of three men each had stormed and secured the building where the workers and their families lived.

The operator with the suppressed Uzi—who was the number two—had climbed up into the control tower.

The sniper—who was the number three—had gone first into the terminal building to make sure that team had missed nothing, and then into the living quarters, where he checked to see that everyone had been rounded up and securely manacled.

The operations scenario had used that term, but the "manacles" actually used to restrain the locals was a plastic version of the garrote.

The locals were frightened, of course, but none of them seemed on the edge of hysteria, which was often a problem with women and children.

Another potential problem, language, didn't arise. The team leader had been told to expect the locals might speak only the local languages, and the team had been issued hastily printed phrase books in Daza, Maba, Gulay, and Sara.

The trouble with phrase books was that while they permitted you to ask questions, they were not much help in translating the answers.

All four of the men the sniper had "manacled" in the living quarters spoke French. And so did most of the thirteen women and children, to judge by their faces and whispered conversations.

One of the men was a tower operator, and another was in charge of the generator. The former reported that the radios in the tower seemed to be operable, and that the runway lights could be turned on and off from the tower. The latter reported that if he had his hands free, he could have the generator started in three minutes.

The team leader signaled one of the operators to cut the plastic handcuffs from both. The sniper took the generator man to wherever the generator was, and the team leader took the tower operator to the tower.

He had just about reached the top of the ladder to the control tower when he heard the rumble of a diesel engine starting, and as he put his shoulders through the hole in the tower floor, the incandescent lightbulbs began to glow and then came on full.

There was a screeching sound from the roof as the rotating radar antenna began to turn.

All the avionic equipment in the tower was of American manufacture, and both the team leader and his number two were familiar with it. Nevertheless, the team leader ordered the control tower operator to get it running.

Dual radar monitors showed a target twenty miles distant at twelve thousand feet altitude. Just the target. No identification from a transponder.

"Light the runway," the team leader ordered.

The tower operator threw a number of switches on a panel under the desk which circled the room. As the sound of the diesel engine showed the addition of a load, the lights on the runway and two taxi strips leading from it glowed and then were fully illuminated.

Number two dialed in a frequency on one of the radios.

"Activate transponder," he said in Russian.

Thirty seconds later, a triangle appeared next to the target on the radar screen.

"I have you at twelve thousand, twenty miles. The field is lit. The runway is clear. Land to the south."

The target blip on the radar screen began moving toward the center of the screen. The numbers in a little box next to the transponder blip began to move downward quickly from 12000.

The team leader pointed to something under the desk.

The tower operator looked confused.

Impatiently, the team leader pointed again.

The tower operator dropped to his knees to get a better look at what was under the table that he was supposed to see.

The team leader put the muzzle of the .22 caliber submachine gun against the tower operator's neck at the base of his skull and pulled the trigger.

The short burst of fire made a *thump, thump* sound, and the tower operator fell slowly forward on his face. Then his legs went limp and his body completely collapsed.

There was no blood. As often happened, the soft lead .22 bullets did not have enough remaining velocity after penetrating the skull to pass through the other side. They simply ricocheted around the skull cavity, moving through soft brain tissue until they had lost all velocity. There might be some blood leakage around the eyes, the ears, and the nose, but there seldom was much and often not any.

A team member entered through the tower floor hole. The leader ordered: "Stay until the plane's on the ground. Then set these to twenty minutes."

"These" were four thermite grenades. Each had a radio-activated fuse, and, for redundancy, in case the radio detonation failed, a simple clock firing mechanism.

The team leader set the thermite grenades in place, two on the communications equipment, one on the radar, and the last on the spine of the tower operator near the entrance wounds made by the .22 rounds.

He took a last look around, and then spoke to his microphone. "Commence cleanup," he ordered. "Acknowledge."

Before the team leader had carefully climbed completely down the ladder, there was about thirty seconds of intense Uzi fire as the site was cleaned of the remaining three men and their women and children.

The firing made more noise than the team leader would have preferred, but the options would have been to either garrote the locals or cut their throats, and that was time-consuming, often a little more risky, and this way there was less chance of messy arterial blood to worry about.

As he watched one of his men carry a box of thermite grenades into the living quarters, the team leader heard a rushing noise, and a split second later, when he looked up, he could see two brilliant landing lights come on as the aircraft approached the field.

A moment later, he could see the aircraft itself.

It was an unusual-looking airplane, painted a nonreflective gray, ostensibly making it invisible to radar. That was a joke. As soon as they had turned on the radar just now, they had seen it twenty miles distant.

There were two jet engines mounted close together on top of the fuselage, where the wings joined the fuselage just behind and above the cockpit. This had made it necessary for the vertical fin and the horizontal stabilizers to be raised out of the way of the jet thrust. The tail of the aircraft was extraordinarily thin and tall, with the control surfaces mounted on the top.

The aircraft, a Tupolev Tu-934A, was not going to win any prizes for aesthetic beauty. But like the USAF A-10 Thunderbolt II—universally known as the Warthog—it did what it was designed to do and did so splendidly.

The Warthog's heavy armament busted up tanks and provided other close ground support. The Tupolev Tu-934A was designed to fly great distances at near the speed of sound carrying just about anything that could be loaded inside its rather ugly fuselage, and land and take off in amazingly short distances on very rough airfields—or no airfields at all.

It was also an amazingly quiet aircraft. The first the team leader had heard its powerful engines was the moment before touchdown when the pilot activated the thrust reversal system.

And even that died quickly as the aircraft reached braking speed on the landing roll and then stopped and turned around on the runway.

Number three, now holding illuminated wands, directed it as it taxied up the runway, and then signaled for it to turn.

Before it had completed that maneuver, a ramp began to lower from the rear of the fuselage.

"Bring up number one truck," the team leader ordered.

The Ford F-150 came across the tarmac and backed up to the opening ramp at the rear of the now-stopped aircraft.

A small, rubber-tracked front-loader rolled down the ramp. The driver and the four men riding on it were dressed in black coveralls.

The team leader saluted one of the newcomers, who returned it.

"Problems?" the operation commander asked in Russian.

"None so far, sir."

"Cleanup?"

"Completed, sir."

"Cargo inspected?"

"Yes, sir," the team leader lied. He had forgotten that detail.

"Well, then, let's get it aboard."

"Yes, sir."

Instead of a bucket, the front-loader had modified pallet arms. To the bottom of each arm had been welded two steel loops. From each loop hung a length of sturdy nylon strapping.

The other two men who had ridden off the aircraft on the rubber-tracked vehicle climbed into the bed of the F-150, removed the tarpaulin which had concealed its contents—two barrel-like objects of heavy plastic, dark blue in color, and looking not unlike beer kegs. They then removed the chocks and strapping which had been holding the rearmost barrel in place.

That done, they carefully directed the pallet arms over the bed of the truck until they were in position for the nylon strapping to be passed under the barrel and the fastener at the free end to be inserted into the loop on the bottom of the arm.

The strapping had lever-activated devices to tighten the strapping—and thus the barrel—against the underside of the pallet arm.

"Tight!" one of the men called out in Russian when that had been accomplished.

The front-loader backed away from the F-150, pivoted in its length, and then drove up the ramp into the aircraft.

The two men in the F-150's bed now removed the chocks and the strapping from the other barrel, and very carefully rolled it to the end of the bed.

By then the front-loader had backed off the ramp, turned again in its length, and was prepared to take the second barrel.

"Bring up truck two," the team leader ordered.

Truck two arrived as truck one started to drive off.

The procedure of taking the barrels from the trucks was repeated, exactly, for the two Toyota pickups. Truck four—the Land Rover—did not hold any of the barrels, but it held the discarded Kalashnikovs. These were carried aboard the aircraft.

"Set mechanical timers at ten minutes and board the aircraft," the team leader ordered.

"Check your memory to see that you have forgotten nothing," the operation commander ordered.

Thirty seconds later, the team leader replied, "I can think of nothing, sir."

The operation commander gestured for the team leader to get on the airplane. When he had trotted up the ramp, the operation commander almost casually strolled up the ramp, picked up a handset mounted on the bulkhead just inside, and ordered, "Get us out of here."

The ramp door immediately began to close.

When it was nearly closed, the aircraft began to move.

Thirty seconds later it was airborne.

The operation commander pulled off his masklike hood and looked at the team leader.

"Don't smile," he said. "Something always is forgotten, or goes wrong at the last minute, or both."

The team leader held up the radio transmitter which would detonate the thermite grenades.

The operation commander nodded. The team leader flicked the protective cover off the toggle switch and threw it.

[TWO]
The Oval Office
The White House
1600 Pennsylvania Avenue, N.W.
Washington, D.C.
0930 2 February 2007

The door opened and a Secret Service agent announced, "Ambassador Montvale, Mr. President."

Joshua Ezekiel Clendennen, who had acceded to the presidency of the United States on the sudden death—rupture of an undetected aneurism of the aorta—of the incumbent twelve days before, motioned for Montvale to be admitted.

President Clendennen was a short, pudgy, pale-skinned fifty-two-year-old Alabaman who kept his tiny ears hidden under a full head of silver hair.

Charles M. Montvale came through the door. He was a tall, elegantly tailored sixty-two-year-old whose silver mane was every bit as luxurious as the President's, but did not do much to conceal his ears.

Montvale's ears were the delight of the nation's political cartoonists. They seemed to be so very appropriate for a man who—after a long career of government service in which he had served as a deputy secretary of State, the secretary of the Treasury, and ambassador to the European Union—was now the United States director of National Intelligence.

The DNI was caricatured at least once a week—and sometimes more often—with his oversize ears pointed in the direction of Moscow or Teheran or Capitol Hill.

"Good morning, Mr. President," Montvale said.

"Can I offer you something, Charles?" the President asked, his Alabama drawl pronounced. "Have you had your breakfast?"

"Yes, thank you, sir, I have. Hours ago."

"Coffee, then?"

"Please."

The President's foot pressed a button under the desk.

"Would you bring us some coffee, please?"

He motioned for Montvale to take a seat on a couch facing a coffee table, and when Montvale had done so, Clendennen rose from behind his desk and walked to an armchair on the other side of the coffee table and sat down.

The coffee was delivered immediately by a steward under the watchful eye of the President's secretary.

"Thank you," the President said. "We can pour ourselves. And now, please, no calls, no messages, no interruptions."

"Yes, Mr. President."

"From anyone," the President added.

Montvale picked up the silver coffeepot, and said, "You take your coffee . . . ?"

"Black, thank you, Charles," the President said.

Montvale poured coffee for both.

The President sipped his, and then said, "You know what I have been thinking lately? When I've had time to think of anything?"

"No, sir."

"Harry Truman didn't know of the atomic bomb—Roosevelt never told him—until the day after Roosevelt died. General Groves walked in here—into this office—ran everybody out, and then told Truman that we had the atomic bomb. That we had two of them."

"I've heard that story, Mr. President," Montvale said.

"We had a somewhat similar circumstance here. The first I heard of the strike in the Congo was after it happened. When we already were at DefConOne."

Montvale didn't reply.

Clendennen went on: "And he never told me about this secret organization he had running. I heard about that only after he'd died. Secretary of State Natalie Cohen came in here, and said, 'Mr. President, there's something I think you should know.' That was the first I'd ever heard of the Analysis Operations Organization. They almost got us into a war, and I was never even told it existed."

Montvale sipped his coffee, then said, "It was called the 'Office of Organizational Analysis,' Mr. President. And it no longer exists."

"I wonder if I can believe that," the President said. "I wonder how soon someone else is going to come through that door and say, 'Mr. President, there's something you should know. . . .'"

"I think that's highly unlikely, Mr. President, and I can assure you that the Office of Organizational Analysis is gone. I was there when the President killed it."

"Maybe he should have sent a couple of squadrons of fighter-bombers, the way he did to the Congo, to destroy everything in a twenty-square-mile area, and to hell with collateral damage," the President said.

"Mr. President, I understand how you feel, even if I would have been inside the area of collateral damage."

"Tell me about Operations Analysis, Charles, and about you being there when our late President killed it."

"He set up the Office of Organizational Analysis in a Presidential Finding, Mr. President, when the deputy chief of mission in our embassy in Argentina was murdered."

"And put a lowly lieutenant colonel in charge?"

"At the time, Carlos Castillo was a major, Mr. President."

"And you and Natalie Cohen went along with this?"

"The Presidential Finding was issued over our objections, sir. And at the time, Natalie was the national security advisor, not secretary of State."

"Where did he find this Major Castillo? What is he, an Italian, a Mexican? Cuban? What?"

"A Texican, sir. His family has been in Texas since before the Alamo. He's a West Pointer—"

"I seem to recall that Lieutenant Colonel Oliver North, who almost got us into a war in Nicaragua, was an Annapolis graduate," the President interrupted. "What do they do at those service academies, Charles, have a required course, How to Start a War One-Oh-One?"

Montvale didn't respond directly. Instead, he said, "Castillo came to the President's attention over that stolen airliner. You remember that, Mr. President?"

"Vaguely."

"Well. An airliner, a Boeing 727, that had been sitting for a year in an airport in Luanda, Angola, suddenly disappeared. We—the intelligence community— were having a hard time finding it. Those things take time, something the President didn't always understand. And as you know, sir, the President was very close to the then–secretary of Homeland Security, Matt Hall. He talked to him about this, and either he or the secretary thought it would be a good idea to send someone to see which intelligence agency had learned what, and when they had learned it.

"Hall told the President that he had just the man for the assignment, Major Castillo, who was just back from Afghanistan, and working for him as an interpreter/aide."

"And?"

"To cut a long story short, Mr. President, Major Castillo not only located the missing aircraft but managed to steal it back from those who had stolen it, and flew it to MacDill Air Force Base—Central Command—in Tampa."

"I heard a little, very little, about that," the President said.

"The President decided, and I think he was right, that the less that came out about that incident, the better."

"And make sure to keep Clendennen out of the loop, right?" the President said, more than a little bitterly.

Montvale didn't respond directly. Instead, he said, "The people who stole the airplane planned to crash it into the Liberty Bell in Philadelphia. We would not have let that happen, but if the story had gotten out, the President believed there would have been panic."

President Clendennen considered that a moment, and then asked, "So where does the Finding fit in all this?"

"The wife of one of our diplomats in Argentina. The deputy chief of mission, J. Winslow Masterson—'Jack the Stack'?"

"I know who he was, Charles. Not only was he the basketball player who got himself run over by a beer truck, for which he collected a very large bundle, but he was the son of Winslow Masterson, who is arguably the richest black guy—scratch black—the richest guy in Mississippi. And they even—surprise, surprise—told me that Winslow's son had been killed."

"Yes, sir. First they kidnapped his wife. The minute the President heard about that, he sent Major Castillo down there. What Castillo was supposed to do was keep an eye on the investigation, and report directly to the President.

"By the time Castillo got to Buenos Aires, Masterson had eluded the State Department security people who had been guarding him, and gone to meet the kidnappers. They killed him in front of his wife, then doped her up and left her with the body."

"What was that all about?"

"We didn't know it at the time, but it was connected with the Iraqi oil-for-food scandal. Mrs. Masterson's brother was not only involved, but had stolen money from the thieves. They thought she would know where he was—she didn't; there was enormous friction between her husband and her brother—and they told her unless she told them where he was, they would kill her children."

"You didn't know this at the time?"

"No, sir. But when the President learned that Masterson had gotten away from his State Department guards, and had been assassinated, he went ballistic—"

"He had a slight tendency to do that, didn't he?" the President said sarcastically.

"—and got on the phone to the ambassador and told him that Castillo was now in charge of getting Mrs. Masterson and the children safely out of Argentina."

"And?"

"Which he did. The President send a Globemaster down there to bring Masterson's body and his family home. And when the plane got to the air base in Biloxi, Air Force One was sitting there waiting for it. And so was the Presidential Finding. The President had found that the national interest required the establishment of a clandestine unit to be known as the Office of Organizational Analysis, which was charged with locating and terminating those responsible for the assassination of J. Winslow Masterson. Major Carlos Castillo was named chief." He paused. "That's how it started, Mr. President."

"'Terminating' is that nice little euphemism for murder, right?"

"Yes, sir."

"Well, that explains, wouldn't you agree, Charles, why the President didn't feel I had to know about this? He knew I wouldn't stand for it. There's nothing in the Constitution that gives the President the authority to order the killing of anybody."

Montvale thought: *Well, he knew you wouldn't like it. But there is nothing you could have done about it if you had known, short of giving yourself the floor in the Senate and committing political suicide by betraying the man who had chosen you to be his Vice President.*

Being morally outraged is one thing.

Doing something about it at great cost to yourself is something else.

And if the story had come out, there's a hell of a lot of people who would have been delighted that the President had ordered the execution of the people who had murdered Jack the Stack in front of his wife. And even more who would have agreed that the murder of any American diplomat called for action, not complaints to the United Nations.

The only reason Clendennen said that is to cover his ass in case the story of OOA gets out.

"I never knew a thing about it. When DNI Montvale told me the story, after I had become President—he had been forbidden to tell me before—I was outraged! Ask Montvale just how outraged I was!"

"The security was very tight, Mr. President," Montvale said. "The access list, the people authorized to know about OOA, was not only very short, but extraordinarily tightly controlled."

"What does that mean?"

"There were only two people who could clear others for access to OOA information, Mr. President. Major Castillo and the President himself. I was made privy to it, of course, but I was forbidden to share what knowledge I had with anyone else—not even my deputy or my secretary—no matter how many Top Secret security clearances they had."

"That isn't surprising when you think about it, is it, Charles? When you are ordering murder, the fewer people who know about it, the better."

Montvale didn't reply.

"Just how many bodies did this Major Castillo leave scattered all over the world, Charles?" the President asked.

"I really don't know, Mr. President," Montvale said. "He reported only to the President."

"And now that there's a new President, don't you think it's time somebody asked him? Where is he?"

"I don't know, Mr. President."

"You're the DNI," the President snapped. "Shouldn't you know a little detail like that?"

"Mr. President, will you indulge me for a moment? I think it would be useful for you to know what happened vis-à-vis the Congo."

"I think a lot of people would find it useful to know what happened vis-à-vis the Congo."

"On Christmas Eve, Mr. President, there were several assassinations and attempted assassinations all over the world—"

"By Major Castillo? On Christmas Eve? Unbelievable!"

"No, sir. Directed against people with a connection to Lieutenant Colonel—by then he had been promoted—Castillo. A newspaper reporter in Germany, for one. An Argentine *gendarmería* officer, for another. A Secret Service agent on the vice presidential detail—"

"Which one?" the President again interrupted.

"His name is John M. Britton, if memory serves, Mr. President."

"Black guy," the former Vice President recalled. "Smart as hell. Funny, too. I liked him. I wondered what happened to him."

"Well, sir, immediately after the attempt on his life, he was of course taken off your protection detail."

"Why?"

"Sir, if someone was trying to kill Special Agent Britton and he was guarding you, standing beside you . . ."

The President stopped him with a gesture. He had the picture.

"What was Jack Britton's connection to Castillo?"

"Britton was a Philadelphia Police Department detective, working undercover in the Counterterrorism Bureau, when Castillo was running down the Philadelphia connection to the stolen airliner. Castillo recruited him for OOA."

"Then how did he wind up in the Secret Service on my protection detail?"

"I believe you know Supervisory Special Agent Tom McGuire, Mr. President?"

"He used to run the President's protection detail? Yeah, sure I know Tom. Don't tell me he has a connection with Castillo."

"The President assigned McGuire to OOA to act as liaison between the Secret Service and Castillo. He was impressed with Britton, and when Britton was no longer needed by Castillo and couldn't return to Philadelphia—his identity was now known to the terrorist community—McGuire recruited him for your protection detail."

"And?"

"Apparently, Special Agent Britton could not understand why an attempt on his life justified his being relieved from your protection detail and being assigned to a desk in Saint Louis. He said some inappropriate things to his supervisors. McGuire decided the best thing to do under the circumstances was send him back to OOA, and he did."

"Why did they—and who is 'they'?—try to kill Britton?"

"Castillo believed the assassinations and assassination attempts on all the people I mentioned were retaliatory actions ordered by Putin himself."

"I find it hard to accept that Vladimir Putin would order assassinations any more than I would," the President said. "But on the other hand, once we start murdering people, I think we would have to be very naïve or very stupid—how about 'stupidly naïve'?—to think the other side would not retaliate."

"Yes, sir. Well, Castillo was apparently delighted to have Britton back. He put him on an airplane and sent him and Mrs. Britton to Argentina to get them out of sight and then loaded some—most—of the others on his Gulfstream and flew to Europe."

"On his Gulfstream? He had access to an Air Force Gulfstream? Jesus Christ!"

"Yes, sir. He had access to an Air Force Gulfstream—and he had a document signed by the President that ordered any government agency to give him whatever assets he asked for."

The President shook his head in disbelief.

"But the Gulfstream on which he flew to Europe was a civilian aircraft, leased by OOA," Montvale said. "He kept it at Baltimore/Washington."

"Where did the money for that come from?"

"Mr. President, I wasn't in the loop. I just know he had the airplane."

The President exhaled audibly.

"And?" he asked.

"Well, according to Castillo, shortly after he arrived in Germany he was approached by two very senior SVR officers—"

"What's that?" the President interrupted.

"Sluzhba Vneshney Razvedki, the Russian Foreign Intelligence Service,"

Montvale explained. "The two officers were Colonel Dmitri Berezovsky, the SVR *rezident* in Berlin, and Lieutenant Colonel Svetlana Alekseeva, the SVR *rezident* in Copenhagen. They said they wanted to defect."

Montvale paused, and then went on. "I have to go off at a tangent here, Mr. President. At this time, our CIA station chief in Vienna, Miss Eleanor Dillworth, a highly respected longtime Clandestine Service officer, and her staff had for some time, and at considerable effort and expense, been working on the defection of Lieutenant Colonel Alekseeva and Colonel Berezovsky. These arrangements had gone so far as the preparation of a safe house in Maryland to house them while they were being debriefed."

"So why did they contact Castillo?"

"According to Castillo, they didn't trust Miss Dillworth. Castillo said when they came to him, they offered to defect to him in exchange for two million dollars and immediate transportation to Argentina on his plane. This whole transaction apparently took place on a train headed for Vienna. So he made the deal."

"Shouldn't he have gone to the nearest CIA officer, either this Miss Dillworth or some other CIA officer? Was he authorized to make a deal like that?"

"No, sir, he wasn't, and yes, sir, he should have immediately contacted either me or someone in the CIA."

"Incredible!"

"Yes, sir, it is," Montvale agreed. "When this came to my attention—Miss Dillworth reported to CIA Director Powell that the defection of Colonel Berezovsky and Lieutenant Colonel Alekseeva had blown up in her face and that she suspected the presence in Vienna of Castillo had something to do with it—"

"She knew about Castillo? Who he was?"

"By then, Mr. President, the existence of the OOA and the identity of its chief was not much of a secret within the intelligence community."

President Clendennen nodded and motioned for Montvale to go on.

"DCI Powell reported the situation to me. I immediately realized that something had to be done."

"So you went to the President?"

"At that stage, Mr. President, Colonel Castillo was the President's fair-haired boy. I decided the best thing to do was go to General Naylor."

"Naylor is a very good man," the President said. "Please don't tell me Naylor was involved with the OOA."

"Only in the sense that Castillo was a serving Army officer, and that General Naylor had recommended Castillo to the secretary of Homeland Security. There was a legality involved, too, Mr. President. So far as the Army was concerned,

Castillo was on temporary duty with the OOA from his regular assignment to the Special Operations Command. The Special Operations Command is under General Naylor's Central Command."

The President's face showed that he could easily have done without the clarification.

"And?" he said impatiently.

"Well, General Naylor, on being apprised of the situation, agreed with me that the situation had to be brought under control."

"By 'the situation,' you mean Castillo?"

"Yes, sir. And General Naylor and I were agreed that our first priority was to spare the President any embarrassment that Castillo's actions might cause. And the second priority was to get the two Russians into the hands of the CIA.

"After some thought, it was decided that the best thing to do with Castillo— and incidentally, the best thing for Castillo personally—was to have him retired honorably from the service. A board of officers was quickly convened at Walter Reed. After an examination of his record, it was decided that he was suffering as a result of his extensive combat service—his chest is covered with medals for valor in action—with post-traumatic stress disorder that has rendered him permanently psychologically unfit for continued active service and therefore he should be medically retired. The board awarded him a disability pension of twenty-five percent of his base pay.

"General Naylor appointed an officer, a full colonel, to present Lieutenant Colonel Castillo with the findings of the board. Taking him with me, I went to Argentina in a Gulfstream with the intention of bringing Castillo home and to place the defected Russians into the hands of the CIA. I took with me two members of my protection detail to guard the Russians, and, frankly, in case Castillo proved obstreperous."

"And did he prove to be 'obstreperous'?"

"Oh, yes, Mr. President. 'Obstreperous' doesn't half cover it. Our ambassador, Juan Manuel Silvio, told me that he hadn't heard Castillo was in Argentina, and that he had heard nothing about Colonel Berezovsky or Lieutenant Colonel Alekseeva.

"The words were no sooner out of his mouth—we were having lunch in a restaurant around the corner from the embassy—when Castillo walked in.

"I asked him where the Russians were. He said at the moment he didn't know, but if he did, he wouldn't tell me, because they had changed their minds about defecting.

"Letting that ride for the moment, I explained his position to him, and the colonel handed him the document he was to sign which would see him retired."

Montvale drained his coffee cup, put it beside the silver pot, then went on: "Castillo said, 'I will sign that when the President tells me to. And only then.'

"I told him that that was not an option, and pointed to the Secret Service agents, who were sitting at a nearby table. I informed him that I was prepared to arrest him, and hoped that wouldn't be necessary.

"He pointed to some men sitting at a table across the restaurant and said they were officers of the Gendarmería Nacional. He added that, at his signal, they would approach anyone coming near him, and demand their identification. They would not permit his arrest, he announced, and if the people approaching him happened to be armed, Ambassador Silvio would have to start thinking about how to get them out of jail, since the Secret Service has no authority in Argentina and is not permitted to go about armed.

"Castillo then said a restaurant was no place to discuss highly classified matters, and suggested we move to the embassy—presuming Ambassador Silvio would give his word that he would not be detained in the embassy."

"And what did the ambassador do?"

"He offered us the use of his office, and gave Castillo his word that he would not be detained if he entered the embassy. So we went to the embassy, where Castillo almost immediately told us what the Russians had told him about a chemical warfare laboratory-slash-factory in the Congo. And that he and everybody in OOA believed the Russians.

"I told him that the CIA had investigated those rumors and found them baseless. He then said, 'Well, the CIA is wrong again.'

"We then called DCI Powell at Langley, and raised the question to him about a germ warfare laboratory-slash-factory in the Congo. DCI Powell repeated what I had told Castillo. The rumors were baseless—what was there was a fish farm.

"To which Castillo replied that the CIA was wrong again, and that there was obviously no point in continuing the conversation.

"I gave him one more chance to turn the Russians over to me and to get on the Gulfstream. When he laughed at me, I turned to the ambassador and said that it was obvious Colonel Castillo was mentally unstable, and therefore, the ambassador could not be held to his word that Castillo could leave the embassy.

"The ambassador replied that the last orders he had had from the President vis-à-vis Colonel Castillo were that he was to provide whatever assistance Colonel Castillo asked for, and he didn't think that meant taking Castillo into custody.

"The ambassador then pushed the secure telephone to me, and said words to the effect that I was welcome to call the President to see if he could be persuaded to change his orders, but that if I made the call he would insist on telling the President that he could detect no sign of mental instability in Castillo— quite the opposite—and that in his personal opinion, I and the CIA were trying to throw Castillo under the bus because they had somehow botched the defection of the Russians and were trying to make Castillo the fall guy for their own incompetence."

"My God!" the President said.

"As I could think of nothing else to say," Montvale said, "I then returned to Washington."

"Let's call a spade a spade, Charles," the President said. "'As I could think of nothing else to say, *and I didn't want the President to know I had gone behind his back, at least until I had time to come up with a credible reason,* I then returned to Washington.'"

Montvale flushed, and realizing he had flushed, was furious, which made him flush even more deeply.

"The CIA does have a certain reputation for throwing people under the bus, doesn't it, Charles? Especially those people who have embarrassed it?"

Montvale decided to wait until he was sure he had his emotions under control before going on.

"Silvio was right, Charles, and you were wrong," the President said. "The President gave him an order, and he was obeying it. Disobeying it, getting around it, would have been damned near treason. And you were wrong to ask him."

"Mr. President, I was trying to protect the President," Montvale said.

"What you should have done was go to the President," Clendennen said. "It's as simple as that. You're the director of National Intelligence, Charles, not Benjamin Disraeli!"

"I realize now that I was wrong, Mr. President," Montvale said.

The President made another impatient gesture for Montvale to continue.

"The next time I saw Castillo was in Philadelphia. The President was giving a speech. I didn't know Castillo was coming. The last word I'd had on him was that he was in Las Vegas."

"In Las Vegas? Doing what?"

"I have no idea, Mr. President. I'm not even sure he *was* in Las Vegas. Anyway, Castillo showed up at the Four Seasons Hotel. The President gave him the opportunity to explain his incredible chemical warfare factory scenario. The President obviously didn't believe it any more than anyone else did, but Castillo still had enough remaining clout with him for the President to turn to DCI Powell and direct him to send somebody to the Congo.

"Castillo said, 'I've already got some people in the Congo, Mr. President.'

"The President said, 'Jesus Christ! Who?'

"And Castillo told him Colonel J. Porter Hamilton, and the President asked 'Who the hell is Colonel Hamilton?' and Powell, who was really surprised, blurted that Colonel Hamilton of the U.S. Army Medical Research Institute at Fort Detrick was the CIA's—for that matter, the nation's—preeminent expert on biological and chemical warfare."

"Are you telling me that Castillo, on his own authority—or no authority— actually sent an expert on biological warfare into the Congo?"

"Yes, sir, and not only that, he put him on the phone—actually a secure radio-telephone link—with the President right there in the Four Seasons."

"How the hell did he manage to do that?"

Montvale said: "I really have no idea, sir."

Montvale thought: *But I'll bet my last dime that Lieutenant General Bruce J. McNab of the Special Operations Command was in that operation up to that ridiculous mustache of his.*

Still, I'm not positive, and certainly can't prove it, so I'm not going to tell you.

I have been painfully cut off at the knees already today by you, Clendennen, and once a day is more than enough.

"And what did this expert say?"

"The phrase he used to describe what he found in the Congo, Mr. President, was 'an abomination before God.' He said that if it got out of control, it would be perhaps a thousand times more of a disaster than was Chernobyl, and urged the President to destroy the entire complex as soon as he could."

President Clendennen didn't reply.

"The mission was launched almost immediately, Mr. President, as you know."

"And we were at the brink of a nuclear exchange," President Clendennen said pointedly.

"That didn't happen, sir."

"I noticed," the President said, thickly sarcastic. "So, what happened to Castillo for rubbing the nose of the CIA in chemical-biological waste?"

"Right after the President ordered the secretary of Defense to immediately have an operation laid on to take out the Fish Farm, he told Castillo that OOA was dead, had never existed, and that what Castillo was to do was make himself scarce until his retirement parade, and after that to disappear from the face of the earth."

"And?"

"Castillo and the military personnel who had been assigned to OOA were retired at Fort Rucker, Alabama, with appropriate panoply on January thirty-first. There was a parade. Everyone was decorated. Castillo and a Delta Force warrant officer named Leverette, who took Colonel Hamilton into the Congo and then got him out, got their third Distinguished Service Medals.

"And then, in compliance with their orders, they got into the Gulfstream and disappeared from the face of the earth."

"You mean you don't know where any of these people are? You don't even know where Castillo is?"

"I know they went from Fort Rucker to Louis Armstrong International Airport in New Orleans, and from there to Cancún."

"And from Cancún?"

"I simply do not know, Mr. President."

"Find out. The next time I ask, be prepared to answer."

"Yes, Mr. President."

"And where are the Russians?"

"I don't know, Mr. President. I do know that the President told the DCI that the attempt to cause them to defect was to be called off, and that he was not even to look for them."

"Why the hell did he do that?"

"I would suggest, Mr. President, that it was because the information they provided about the Congo was true."

The President considered that, snorted, and then said, "Well, Charles, that seems to be it, doesn't it?"

"Yes, sir, it would seem so."

"Thank you for coming to see me. We'll be in touch."

[THREE]
Old Ebbitt Grill
675 15th Street, N.W.
Washington, D.C.
1530 2 February 2007

No one is ever really surprised when a first- or second-tier member of the Washington press corps walks into the Old Ebbitt looking for someone.

For one thing, the Old Ebbitt is just about equidistant between the White House—a block away at 1600 Pennsylvania Avenue—and the National Press Club—a block away at 529 14th Street, N.W. It's right down the street from the Hotel Washington, and maybe a three-minute walk from the Willard Hotel, whose lobby added the term "lobbyist" to the political/journalistic lexicon.

Furthermore, the Old Ebbitt's service, menu, ambiance, and stock of intoxicants was superb. The one thing on which all observers of the press corps agreed was that nothing appeals more to the gentlemen and ladies of the Fourth Estate than, say, a shrimp cocktail and a nice New York strip steak, plus a stiff drink, served promptly onto a table covered with crisp linen in a charming environment.

This is especially true if the journalist can reasonably expect that someone else—one of those trolling for a favorable relationship with the press lobbyists from the Willard, for example—would happily reach for the check.

Roscoe J. Danton—a tall, starting to get a little plump, thirty-eight-year-old who was employed by *The Washington Times-Post*—was, depending on to whom one might talk, either near the bottom of the list of first-tier journalists, or at the very top of the second tier.

Roscoe walked into the Old Ebbitt, nodded at the ever affable Tony the Maître d' at his stand, and walked on to the bar along the wall behind Tony. He continued slowly down it—toward the rear—and had gone perhaps halfway when he spotted the people he had agreed to meet.

They were two women, and they were sitting at a banquette. The one he had talked to said that he would have no trouble spotting them: "Look for two thirtyish blondes at one of the banquettes at the end of the bar."

The description, Roscoe decided, was not entirely accurate. While both were bleached blonde, one of them was far closer to fiftyish than thirtyish, and the younger one was on the cusp of fortyish.

But there being no other banquette holding two blondes, Roscoe walked to their table.

Roscoe began, "Excuse me—"

"Sit down, Mr. Danton," the older of the two immediately said.

The younger one patted the red leather next to her.

Roscoe Danton sat down.

"Whatever this is, I don't have much time," he announced. "There's a press conference at four-fifteen."

"This won't take long," the older one said. "And I really think it will be worth your time."

A waiter appeared.

The older woman signaled the waiter to bring what she and her companion were drinking, and then asked, "Mr. Danton?"

"What is that you're having?"

"A Bombay martini, no vegetables," she said.

"That should give me courage to face the mob," he said, smiled at the waiter, and told him, "The same for me, please."

The older woman waited until the waiter had left and then reached to the fluffy lace collar at her neck. She unbuttoned two buttons, put her hand inside, and withdrew a plastic card. It was attached with an alligator clip to what looked like a dog-tag chain. She pressed the clip, removed the card, more or less concealed it in her hand, and laid it flat on the tablecloth.

"Make sure the waiter doesn't see that, please," she said as she withdrew her hand.

Danton held his hand to at least partially conceal the card and took a good look at it.

The card bore the woman's photograph, the seal of the Central Intelligence Agency, a number, some stripes of various colors, and her name, Eleanor Dillworth.

It clearly was an employee identification card. Danton had enough experience at the CIA complex just across the Potomac River in Langley, Virginia, to know that while it was not one of the very coveted Any Area/Any Time cards worn by very senior CIA officers with as much élan as a four-star general wears his stars in the Pentagon, this one identified someone fairly high up in the hierarchy.

He met Miss Dillworth's eyes, and slid the card back across the table.

The younger blonde took a nearly identical card from her purse and laid it before Danton. It said her name was Patricia Davies Wilson.

"I told them I had lost that when I was fired," Mrs. Wilson said. "And kept it as a souvenir."

Danton met her eyes, too, but said nothing.

She took the card back, and put it in her purse.

"What's this all about?" he finally asked when his silence didn't elicit the response it was supposed to.

Miss Dillworth held up her finger as a signal to wait.

The waiter delivered three Bombay Sapphire gin martinis, no vegetables.

"That was quick, wasn't it?" Eleanor Dillworth asked.

"That's why I like to come here," Patricia Davies Wilson said.

The three took an appreciative sip of their cocktails.

"I was asking, 'What's this all about?'" Danton said.

"Disgruntled employees, Mr. Danton," Patricia Davies Wilson said.

"Who, as you know, sometimes become whistleblowers," Eleanor Dillworth said, and then asked, "Interested?"

"That would depend on what, or on whom, you're thinking of blowing the whistle," Danton replied.

"I was about to say the agency," Patricia Davies Wilson said. "But it goes beyond the agency."

"Where does it go beyond the agency?" Danton asked.

"Among other places, to the Oval Office."

"In that case, I'm fascinated," Danton said. "What have you got?"

"Have you ever heard of an intelligence officer-slash-special operator by the name of Carlos Castillo?" Eleanor Dillworth asked.

Danton shook his head.

"How about the Office of Organizational Analysis?"

He shook his head, and then asked, "In the CIA?"

Dillworth shook her head. "In the office of our late and not especially grieved-for President," she said.

"And apparently to be kept alive in the administration of our new and not-too-bright chief executive. But that's presuming Montvale has told him."

"What does this organization do? What has it done in the past?"

"If we told you, Mr. Danton, I don't think you would believe us," Eleanor Dillworth said.

Danton sipped his martini, and thought: *Probably not.*

Disgruntled employee whistleblowers almost invariably tell wild tales with little or no basis in fact.

He said: "I don't think I understand."

"You're going to have to learn this yourself," Patricia Wilson said. "We'll point you in the right direction, but you'll have to do the digging. That way you'll believe it."

"How do I know you know what you're talking about?" Danton challenged.

"Before I was recalled, I was the CIA's station chief in Vienna," Dillworth said. "I've been in—*was* in—the Clandestine Service for twenty-three years."

"Before that bastard got me fired," Patricia Wilson added, "I was the agency's regional director for Southwest Africa, everything from Nigeria to South Africa, including the Congo. You will recall the Congo is where World War Three was nearly started last month."

"'That bastard' is presumably this Mr. Costillo?"

"'Castillo,' with an 'a,'" she said. "And lieutenant colonel, not mister. He's in the Army."

"Okay," Danton said, "point me."

"You said you were going to the four-fifteen White House press conference," Dillworth said. "Ask Porky. Don't take no for an answer."

John David "Jack" Parker, the White House spokesman, was sometimes unkindly referred to—the forty-two-year-old Vermont native *was* a little on the far side of pleasingly plump—as Porky Parker. And sometimes, when his responses to questions tested the limits of credulity, some members of the Fourth Estate had been known to make *oink-oink* sounds from the back of the White House press room.

"Okay, I'll do it. How do I get in touch with you if I decide this goes any further?"

Eleanor Dillworth slid a small sheet of notebook paper across the table.

"If there's no answer, say you're Joe Smith and leave a number."

[FOUR]
The Press Room
The White House
1600 Pennsylvania Avenue, N.W.
Washington, D.C.
1715 2 February 2007

"Well, that's it, fellows," Jack Parker said. "We agreed that these would last one hour, and that's what the clock says."

Ignoring muted *oink-oink* sounds from the back of the room, he left the podium and headed for the door, where he was intercepted by Roscoe J. Danton of *The Washington Times-Post.*

"Aw, come on, Roscoe, this one-hour business was as much your idea as anybody else's."

"Well, screw you," Danton said, loud enough for other members of the Fourth Estate also bent on intercepting Porky to hear, and at the same time asking with a pointed finger and a raised eyebrow if he could go to Parker's office as soon as the area emptied.

Parker nodded, just barely perceptibly.

Danton went out onto the driveway and smoked a cigarette. Smoking was prohibited in the White House, the rule strictly enforced when anyone was watching. And then he went back into the White House.

"What do you need, Roscoe?" Parker asked.

"Tell me about the Office of Organizational Analysis and Colonel Carlos Costello. *Castillo.*"

Parker thought, shrugged, and said, "I draw a blank."

"Can you check?"

"Sure. In connection with what?"

"I have some almost certainly unreliable information that he and the Office of Organizational Analysis were involved in almost starting World War Three."

"One hears a lot of rumors like that about all kinds of people, doesn't one?" Parker said mockingly. "There was one going around that the Lambda Legal Foundation were the ones behind it; somebody told them they stone gays in the Congo."

"Shame on you!" Danton said. "Check it for me, will you?"

Parker nodded.

"Thanks."

[FIVE]
The City Room
The Washington Times-Post
1365 15th Street, N.W.
Washington, D.C.
2225 2 February 2007

Roscoe Danton's office was a small and cluttered glass-walled cubicle off the large room housing the "city desk." Two small exterior windows offered a clear view of a solid brick wall. He had wondered for years what was behind it.

His e-mail had just offered him Viagra at a discount and a guaranteed penis enlargement concoction. He was wondering whether he could get away with sending either or both offers to the executive editor without getting caught, when another e-mail arrived.

FROM: White House Press Office <parker@whpo.gov>

TO: Roscoe J. Danton <rjdanton@washtimespost.org>

SENT: 2 Feb 19:34:13 2007

SUBJECT: Costello/Castillo

Roscoe

   After you left, I had a memory tinkle about
Costello/Castillo and the Office of Organizational
Analysis, so I really tried—with almost no success—to
check it out.

   I found a phone number for an OOA in the Department
of Homeland Security with an office in the DHS Compound
in the Nebraska Avenue complex. When I called it, I got
a recorded message saying that it had been closed. So I
called DHS and they told me OOA had been closed, they
didn't know when. When I asked what it had done, they
helpfully told me my guess was as good as theirs, but
it probably had something to do with analyzing
operations.

   At this point, I suspected that you had been down
this route yourself before you dumped it on me.

   So I called the Pentagon. You would be astonished at
the number of lieutenant colonels named Castillo and
Costello there are/were in the Army. There is a retired
Lt Col Carlos Castillo, and he's interesting, but I
don't think he's the man you're looking for. This one
is a West Pointer to which institution he gained
entrance because his father, a nineteen-year-old
warrant officer helicopter pilot, posthumously received
the Medal of Honor in Vietnam.

The son followed in his father's footsteps, and before he had been out of WP a year had won the Distinguished Flying Cross flying an Apache in the First Desert War. He went from that to flying in the Special Operations Aviation Regiment, most recently in Afghanistan. He returned from there under interesting circumstances. First, he had acquired more medals for valor than Rambo, but was also a little over the edge. Specifically, it was alleged that he either had taken against orders, or stolen, a Black Hawk to undertake a nearly suicidal mission to rescue a pal of his who had been shot down. Nearly suicidal, because he got away with it.

Faced with the choice of giving him another medal or court-martialing him, the Army instead sent him home for psychiatric evaluation. The shrinks at Walter Reed determined that as a result of all his combat service, he suffered from post-traumatic stress disorder to the point where he would never be psychologically stable enough to return to active service. They medically retired him. His retirement checks are sent to Double-Bar-C Ranch, Midland, Texas.

I suggest this guy was unlikely to have tried to start World War III from the psychiatric ward at Walter Reed.

Sorry, Roscoe, this was the best I could do. If you get to the bottom of this, please let me know. My curiosity is now aroused.

Best,

Jack

The message gave Danton a number of things to think about. He would not have been surprised to receive a one-liner—*"Sorry. Nothing. Jack."*—and this one meant that Porky had spent a lot of time, of which he understandably had little, coming up with this answer.

Possibility One: His curiosity had been piqued and there had been time to do what he said he had done.

Possible but unlikely.

Possibility Two: This was a carefully thought-out ploy to get Danton off the track of a story which might, if it came out, embarrass the President, the White House, the department of State, or the Pentagon. Or all of the above.

Possible but unlikely. There was a hell of a risk, as Porky damned well knew, in intentionally misleading (a) The Washington Times-Post *and/or (b) Roscoe Danton personally.*

A short "Sorry. Nothing. Jack." e-mail maybe. But not a long message like this one. Including all the details of this Castillo character's military service.

So what do I do?

Forget it?

No. I smell something here.

The thing to do is find this Castillo character and talk to him; see if he has any idea why Meryl Streep and the other disgruntled whistleblower, whose thigh "accidentally" pressed against mine twice in the Old Ebbitt, are saying all these terrible things about him.

But only after I talk to Good Ol' Meryl and her pal, to see what else I can get out of them.

He tapped keys on his laptop, opened a new folder, named it "Castillo," and downloaded Porky's e-mail into it. Then he found the piece of paper on which Good Ol' Meryl had given him her phone number. He put this into the "Castillo" folder and entered it into his BlackBerry.

Then he pushed the CALL key.

II

La Casa en el Bosque
San Carlos de Bariloche
Patagonia
Río Negro Province, Argentina
1300 3 February 2007

"I believe in a democratic approach when having a meeting like this," Lieutenant Colonel Carlos G. Castillo, USA (Retired), announced. "And the way that will work is that I will tell you what's going to happen, and then everybody says 'Yes, sir.'"

It was summer in Argentina, and Castillo, a well-muscled, six-foot-two, one-hundred-ninety-pound, blue-eyed thirty-six-year-old with a full head of thick light brown hair, was wearing tennis whites.

There were groans from some of those gathered around an enormous circular table in the center of a huge hall. It could have been a movie set for a motion picture about King Arthur and the Knights of the Round Table. When this thought had occurred to Sandra Britton, Ph.D., Dr. Britton had thought Castillo could play Sir Lancelot.

Two people, one of each gender, gave Castillo the finger.

"We told quote unquote those people in Las Vegas that we would give them an answer in three weeks," Castillo said. "Three weeks is tomorrow."

"Go ahead, Ace. Let's get it over with," Edgar Delchamps said. He was a nondescript man in his late fifties. The oldest man in the room, he was wearing slacks with the cuffs rolled up and a dress shirt with the collar open.

"I would like to suggest that we appoint a chairman for this, and a secretary, and I recommend Mr. Yung for that," Castillo said.

"Cut the crap, Ace," Delchamps said. "Everyone knows you're calling the shots, but if you're going to make Two-Gun something, I more or less respectfully suggest you make him secretary-treasurer."

Men who have spent more than three decades in the Clandestine Service of the Central Intelligence Agency tend not to be impressed with Army officers who had yet to make it even to West Point while they themselves were matching wits with the KGB in Berlin and Vienna.

"Two-Gun, you're the secretary-treasurer," Castillo said to David William Yung, Jr.

Yung was a round-faced, five-foot-eight, thirty-six-year-old, hundred-fifty-pound Chinese-American whose family had immigrated to the United States in the 1840s. In addition to a law degree, he held a master's degree in business administration from the University of Pennsylvania, and was fluent in four languages, none of them Asian.

Before he had become a member of the OOA, he had been an FBI agent with a nearly legendary reputation for being able to trace the path of money around the world no matter how often it had been laundered.

Before his association with OOA, Yung had never—except at the Quantico FBI base pistol range—taken his service pistol from its holster. Within days of being drafted into the OOA, he had been in a gun battle and killed his first man.

But the "Two-Gun" appellation had nothing to do with that. That had come after Delchamps, who was not authorized at the time to be in possession of a firearm in Argentina, had Yung, whose diplomatic status at the time made him immune to Argentine law, smuggle his pistol across the border. Yung thus had two guns and was thereafter Two-Gun.

Two-Gun Yung signified his acceptance of his appointment by raising his balled fist thumbs up, and then opening up his laptop computer.

"First things first, Mr. Secretary-Treasurer," Castillo said. "Give us a thumbnail picture of the assets of the Lorimer Charitable and Benevolent Fund."

Two-Gun looked at his computer screen.

"This is all ballpark, you understand," he said. "You want the history?"

"Please," Castillo said.

"We started out with those sixteen million in bearer bonds from Shangri-La," Yung said.

Shangri-La was not the mythical kingdom but rather Estancia Shangri-La, in Tacuarembó Province, República Oriental del Uruguay. When Castillo had led an *ad hoc* team of special operators there to entice Dr. Jean-Paul Lorimer to allow himself to be repatriated, Lorimer was shot to death by mercenaries seeking to recover from him money he had stolen from the Iraqi oil-for-food scam, for which he had been the "bagman" in charge of paying off whomever had to be paid off.

His safe had contained sixteen million dollars' worth of what were in effect bearer bonds, which Castillo had taken with him to the U.S. When this was reported to the then-President of the United States, the chief executive managed to convey the impression—without coming right out in so many words—that justice would be well served if the bearer bonds were used to fund the OOA.

The following day, the Lorimer Charitable & Benevolent Fund came into being.

"Into which Charley dipped to the tune of seven and a half million to buy the Gulfstream," Yung went on. "Call that eight million by the time we fixed everything, and rented the hangar at Baltimore/Washington. Et cetera.

"That left eight, into which Charley dipped for another two point five million to buy the safe house in Alexandria. That left five point five million."

The house in Alexandria was used to house members of the Office of Organizational Analysis while they were in the Washington area, and also to conduct business of a nature that might have raised eyebrows had it been conducted in the OOA's official offices in the Department of Homeland Security compound in the Nebraska Avenue complex in the District of Columbia.

"To which," Two-Gun went on, "Mr. Philip J. Kenyon the Third of Midland, Texas, contributed forty-six point two million in exchange for his Stay Out of Jail card."

Mr. Kenyon had mistakenly believed his $46,255,000 in illicit profits from his participation in the Iraqi oil-for-food scam were safe from prying eyes in a bank in the Cayman Islands. He erred.

The deal he struck to keep himself out of federal prison for the rest of his natural life was to cooperate fully with the investigation, and to transfer the money from his bank account in the Cayman Islands to the account of the Lorimer Charitable & Benevolent Fund in the Riggs National Bank in Washington, D.C.

"There have been some other expenses, roughly totaling two million," Yung continued. "What we have left is about fifty point five million, give or take a couple of hundred thousand."

"That don't add up, Two-Gun," Edgar Delchamps challenged. "There shouldn't be that much; according to your figures, we've got two point something million more than we should have."

"There has been some income from our investments," Two-Gun said. "You didn't think I was going to leave all that money in our bank—our *banks* plural; there are seven—just drawing interest, did you?"

"Do we want to start counting nickels and dimes?" Colonel Castillo asked. "Or can we get to that later?"

"'*Nickels and dimes*'?" Sandra Britton, a slim, tall, sharp-featured black-skinned woman, parroted incredulously. "We really are the other side of Alice's Looking Glass, aren't we?"

Possibly proving that opposites attract, Dr. Britton, who had been a philologist on the faculty of Philadelphia's Temple University, was married to John M. Britton, formerly of the United States Secret Service and before that a detective working undercover in the Counterterrorism Bureau of the Philadelphia Police Department.

"I was going to suggest, Sandra," Charley Castillo said, "that we now turn to the question before us. *Questions* before us. One, do we just split all that money between us and go home—"

"How the hell can Jack and I go home?" Sandra interrupted. "Not only can I not face my peers at Temple after they learned that I was hauled off by the Secret Service—with sirens screaming—but the AALs turned our little house by the side of the road into the O.K. Corral."

Dr. Britton was making reference to an assassination attempt made on her and her husband during which their home and nearly new Mazda convertible were riddled by fire from Kalashnikov automatic assault weapons in the hands of native-born African-Americans who considered themselves converts to Islam and to whom Dr. Britton referred, perhaps politically incorrectly, as AALs, which stood for African-American Lunatics.

"If I may continue, Doctor?" Colonel Castillo asked.

Dr. Britton made a gesture with her left hand, raising it balled with the center finger extended vertically.

"I rephrase," Castillo said. "Do we just split that money between us and *go our separate ways*? Or do we stay together within what used to be the OOA and would now need a new name?"

"Call the question," Anthony "Tony" J. Santini said formally.

Santini, a somewhat swarthy, balding, short, heavyset man in his forties, until recently had been listed in the telephone book of the U.S. embassy in Buenos Aires as an assistant financial attaché. He had been, in fact, a Secret Service agent dispatched to Buenos Aires to, as he put it, "look for funny money." Before that, he had been a member of the vice presidential protection detail. He had been relieved of that assignment when he fell off the ice-covered running board of the vice-presidential limousine. He had been recruited for the OOA shortly after it had been established, to "locate and eliminate" the parties responsible for the murder of J. Winslow Masterson.

"Second the motion," Susanna Sieno said.

She was a trim, pale-freckled-skin redhead in a white blouse and blue jeans. She looked like she and the man sitting beside her—her husband, Paul—should be in a television commercial, where the handsome young husband comes home from the office and chastely kisses his charming young bride after she shows how easy it had been for her to polish their kitchen floor with Miracle Glow.

Actually, between the Sienos, they had more than four decades in the Clandestine Service of the CIA—Paul having served twenty-two years and Susanna just over twenty—which had been more than enough for the both of them to have elected to retire, which they had done ten days before.

"The motion having been made and seconded," Castillo said mock-formally, "the chair calls the question: 'Do we disband and split the money?' All in favor raise your hand and hold it up until Two-Gun counts."

"Okay," Castillo said a moment later, "now those opposed, raise your hands." Yung again looked around the table.

"I make it unanimously opposed," Yung said. "OOA lives!"

"OOA's dead," Castillo said. "The question now is, what do we do with the corpse?"

Delchamps said, "Sweaty, Dmitri—excuse me, *Tom*—and Alfredo didn't vote."

"I didn't think I had the right," Alfredo Munz, a stocky blond man in his forties, said.

Munz, at the time of Masterson's kidnapping, had been an Argentine Army colonel in command of SIDE, an organization combining the Argentine versions of the FBI and CIA. Embarrassed by the incident and needing a scapegoat, the interior ministry had, as a disgusted Charley Castillo had put it, "thrown Munz under the bus." Munz had been relieved of his command of SIDE and forced to retire. Castillo had immediately put him on the OOA payroll.

"Don't be silly," Castillo said. "You took a bullet for us. You're as much a part of us as anyone else."

Munz had been wounded during the Estancia Shangri-La operation.

"Hear, hear," Yung said.

"I didn't say the Argentine Kraut didn't have every right to vote," Delchamps said. "I simply stated that he, Sweaty, and Tom *didn't* vote."

"If I have a vote," Sweaty said, "I will vote however my Carlos votes."

"Sweaty," also in tennis whites, sat next to Castillo. She was a tall, dark-red-haired, stunningly beautiful woman, who had been christened Svetlana. Once associated with this group of Americans, "Svetlana" had quickly morphed to "Svet" then to "Sweaty."

Susanna's eyebrows rose in contempt, or perhaps contemptuous disbelief. In her long professional career, she had known many intelligence officers, and just about the best one she had ever encountered was Castillo.

The most incredibly stupid thing any spook had ever done was become genuinely emotionally involved with an enemy intelligence officer. Within twenty-four hours of Lieutenant Colonel C. G. Castillo having laid eyes on Lieutenant Colonel Svetlana Alekseeva of the Sluzhba Vneshney Razvedki—the SVR, the Russian Service for the Protection of the Constitutional System, renamed from "KGB"—on a Vienna-bound railroad train in Germany, she had walked out of his bedroom in a safe house outside Buenos Aires wearing his bathrobe and a smug smile, and calling him "my Carlos."

Dr. Britton smiled fondly at Sweaty when she referred to Castillo now as "my Carlos." She thought it was sweet. Sandra Britton knew there really was such a thing as Love at First Sight. She had married her husband two weeks after she had met him and now could not imagine life without him.

Their meeting had occurred shortly after midnight eight years before on North Broad Street in Philly when Jack had appeared out of nowhere to foil a miscreant bent on relieving her of her purse, watch, jewelry—and very possibly her virtue. In the process, the miscreant had suffered a broken arm, a dislocated shoulder, testicular trauma, and three lost teeth.

Britton had then firmly attached the miscreant to a fire hydrant with plastic handcuffs, loaded the nearly hysterical Dr. Britton in her car, and set off to find a pay telephone.

There were not many working pay telephones in that section of Philadelphia at that hour, and to call the police it had been necessary to go to Dr. Britton's apartment.

After Britton had called Police Emergency to report that the victim of an assault by unknown parties could be found at North Broad and Cecil B. Moore Avenue hugging a fire hydrant, one thing had led to another. Sandra made Jack breakfast the next morning, and they were married two weeks later.

"I don't think I have a vote," Tom Barlow said. "But if I do, I'll go along with however Sweaty's Carlos votes."

Barlow, a trim man of about Castillo's age and build, whose hair was nearly blond, and who bore a familial resemblance to Sweaty—he was in fact her brother—until very recently had been Colonel Dmitri Berezovsky, the SVR *rezident* in Berlin.

Castillo and Sweaty gave Barlow the finger.

"I would say the motion has been defeated," Yung said. "I didn't see any hands. And I have the proxies of Jake, Peg-Leg, the Gunnery Sergeant, Sparky, and Miller. They all like the idea of keeping OOA going."

Jake and Sparky were, respectively, Colonel Jacob S. Torine, USAF (Retired), and former Captain Richard Sparkman, USAF. Torine had been in on OOA since the beginning, when he had flown a Globemaster to Argentina to bring home the body of Jack the Stack Masterson, and his family. Torine had been quietly retired with all the other military members of OOA who had more than twenty years' service when OOA had shut down.

Sparkman, who on active duty had served under Torine on a number of black missions of the Air Force Special Operations Command, had been flying Washington political VIPs around in a Gulfstream and hating it when he heard (a) of OOA and (b) that Colonel Torine was involved. He made his way through the maze designed to keep OOA hidden in the bushes, found Torine, and volunteered to do whatever was asked, in whatever Torine was involved.

He had been accepted as much for having gotten through the maze as for being able to fill the near-desperate need OOA had for another pilot who (a) knew how to keep his mouth shut and (b) had a lot of Gulfstream time as pilot in command.

When OOA was shut down, Sparky didn't have the option of retiring, because he didn't have enough time in the service. He also realized that he really couldn't go back to the Air Force after having been tainted by his association with OOA. He knew the rest of his career in the Air Force would have been something along the lines of Assistant Procurement Officer, Hand-Held Fire-Extinguishing Devices.

He had resigned. There was an unspoken agreement that Sparky would go on the payroll as a Gulfstream pilot, details to be worked out later, presuming everybody was still out of jail.

Gunnery Sergeant Lester Bradley was in a similar situation. Another gunny, one in charge of the Marine guard detachment at the American embassy in Buenos Aires, had sent then-corporal Lester Bradley—a slight, five-foot-three, twenty-year-old Marine who could be spared most easily from more important duties—to drive an embassy GMC Yukon XL carrying two barrels of aviation fuel across the border to Uruguay.

Thirty-six hours later, the Yukon had been torched with a thermite grenade. Bradley, who had been left to "watch" the Yukon, had taken out—with head-shots firing offhand from a hundred meters—two mercenaries who had just killed Jean-Paul Lorimer, Ph.D., and then started shooting their Kalashnikovs at Castillo.

Inasmuch as Castillo thought it would be unwise to return Corporal Bradley to his embassy duties—where his gunnery sergeant would naturally be curious to learn under what circumstances the Yukon had been torched—he was impressed into the OOA on the spot.

The day that OOA ceased to exist, the President of the United States had asked Castillo, "Is there anything else I can do for you before you and your people start vanishing from the face of the earth?"

Castillo told him there were three things. First was that Corporal Bradley be promoted to gunnery sergeant before being honorably discharged "for the good of the service."

The second thing Castillo had asked of the President was that Colonel Berezovsky and Lieutenant Colonel Alekseeva be taken off the Interpol warrants outstanding for them. When they had disappeared from their posts in Berlin and Copenhagen with the obvious intention of defecting, the Russian government had said their motive had been to escape arrest and punishment for embezzlement.

The third thing Castillo asked was that he and everybody connected with him and OOA be taken off the FBI's "locate but do not detain" list.

The President had granted all three requests: "You have my word."

The first thing Castillo thought when he heard that the President had dropped dead was that his word had died with him. The chances that President Clendennen—especially with Director of National Intelligence Montvale whispering in his ear—would honor his predecessor's promises ranged from zero to zilch.

The retirements of Major H. Richard Miller, Jr., Avn, USA, who had been the OOA's chief of staff, and First Lieutenant Edmund "Peg-Leg" Lorimer, MI, USA, had posed no problem, although neither had twenty years of service.

Miller, a United States Military Academy classmate of Castillo's, had suffered grievous damage to his leg when his helicopter had been shot down in Afghanistan. Lorimer had lost a leg to an improvised explosive device in the same country. They would receive pensions for the rest of their lives.

As Castillo & Co. had begun to fulfill their part of the agreement with POTUS—disappearing from the face of the earth—they had made their way to Las Vegas, where they were the guests of Aloysius Francis Casey—president, chief executive officer, and chairman of the board of the AFC Corporation.

Castillo had first met Casey when Castillo had been a second lieutenant, freshly returned from the First Desert War working as aide-de-camp to just-promoted Brigadier General Bruce J. McNab at Fort Bragg when Casey showed up there. Casey announced that he had been the communications sergeant on a Special Forces A-Team in the Vietnam War and, further, told McNab and his aide-de-camp that he had done well after being discharged. Not only had Casey earned a Ph.D. from the Massachusetts Institute of Technology, but he had started up—and still owned more than ninety percent of—the AFC Corporation, which had become the world's leading developer and manufacturer of data transmission and encryption systems.

Aloysius Casey, Second Lieutenant Castillo had immediately seen, was not troubled with excessive modesty.

Casey said that he attributed his great success to Special Forces—specifically what he had learned about self-reliance and that there was no such thing as impossible.

And he said he had decided it was payback time. He was prepared to furnish Delta Force, free of charge, with his state-of-the-art communications and encryption equipment.

"It's three, four years ahead of anything anybody else has," Casey had announced. McNab had sent Castillo with Casey to Las Vegas—on AFC's Learjet— that same day to select what AFC equipment Delta Force could use immediately, and to brainstorm with Casey and his senior engineers on what advanced commo equipment Delta could use if somebody waved a magic wand and created it for them.

The latter devices had begun to arrive at Delta Force's stockade at Fort Bragg about two months later.

When OOA had been set up, Castillo had naturally turned to Casey—who now called him "Charley" rather than, as he had at first, "The Boy Wonder"— for communications and cryptographic equipment, and Casey had happily produced it.

When Charley had bought the Gulfstream, Casey had seemed a little annoyed that Charley had asked if Casey would equip it with the same equipment. Charley at the time had thought that maybe he had squeezed the golden goose a little too hard and vowed he would not be so greedy the next time.

When they got the Gulfstream back from the AFC hangar at Las Vegas's McCarran International Airport, it had not only the latest communications and encryption equipment installed, but an entirely new avionics configuration.

"I figured you needed it more than Boeing," Casey said.

His annoyance with Charley was because Castillo had been reluctant to ask for his support.

"For Christ's sake, Charley, you should have known better," Casey said.

The Gulfstream was again in Las Vegas, not for the installation of equipment, but to get it out of sight until a decision could be made about what to do with it.

Charley had flown the Gulfstream to Las Vegas the same day he had received his last order from the President: "You will go someplace where no one can find you, and you will not surface until your retirement parade. And after your retirement, I hope that you will fall off the face of the earth and no one will ever see you or hear from you again. Understood?"

Charley had said, "Yes, sir," and walked out of the room. After a quick stop at Baltimore/Washington International to pick up Major Dick Miller, he had flown to Las Vegas with newly promoted (verbal order, POTUS) and about to be discharged Gunnery Sergeant Lester Bradley and Mr. and Mrs. Jack Britton.

Immediately on arrival, Castillo had learned that providing equipment to Special Operations people free of charge had not been Aloysius Casey's only contribution to the national security of the nation.

Limousines met them at McCarran, and drove them to the Venetian Hotel and Casino, where they were shown to a private elevator which carried them to a duplex penthouse.

At the foot of a curving glass-stepped staircase which led to the lower floor, Castillo saw Dmitri Berezovsky—now equipped with a bona fide Uruguayan passport in the name of Tom Barlow—Sergeant Major Jack Davidson, Aloysius Francis Casey, and about a half-dozen men Castillo could not remember having seen before sitting on a circular couch that appeared to be upholstered with gold lamé.

Casey waved him down. Max, Castillo's hundred-plus-pound Bouvier des Flandres, immediately accepted the invitation, flew down the stairs four at a time, barked hello at the people he knew, and then began to help himself from one of the trays of hors d'oeuvres.

Not understanding what was going on, Castillo had gone down the stairs slowly. As he did, he realized that he did in fact recognize a few of the men. One of them was a legendary character who owned four—*Maybe five?*—of the more glitzy Las Vegas hotels.

But not this one, came a flash from Castillo's memory bank.

Another was a well-known, perhaps even famous, investment banker. And another had made an enormous fortune in data processing. Castillo had re-membered him because he was a Naval Academy graduate.

"Everybody pay attention," Casey had said, laughing. "You don't often get a chance to see Charley with a baffled look on his face."

"Okay, Aloysius, you have pulled my chain. What the hell is going on around here?"

"Colonel," the Naval Academy graduate said with a distinctive Southern accent, "what we are is a group of people who realize there are a number of things that the intelligence community doesn't do well, doesn't want to do, or for one reason or another can't do. We try to help, and we've got the assets—not only cash—to do so. We've been doing this for some time. And we're all agreed that now that you and your OOA associates are—how do I put this?—no longer gainfully employed—"

"How did you hear about that?" Castillo interrupted.

The Naval Academy graduate ignored the question.

"—you might want to come work for us."

"You've got the wrong guy," Castillo said simply. "The intel community hates me, and that's a nice way of describing it."

"Well, telling the DCI that his agency 'is a few very good people trying to stay afloat in a sea of left-wing bureaucrats' may not have been the best way to charm the director, even if I happen to know he agrees with you."

"Colonel," the man who owned the glitzy hotels said, "this is our proposal, in a few words: You keep your people together, keep them doing what they do so well, and on our side we'll decide how to get the information to where it will do the most good, and in a manner that will not rub the nose of the intelligence community in their own incompetence." He paused. "And the pay's pretty good."

"Right off the top of my head, no," Castillo said. "My orders from the President are—"

"To go someplace where no one can find you," the investment banker interrupted him, "until your retirement parade. And after that fall off the face of the earth. Something like that?"

How could he—they—possibly know about that?

Nobody had been in that room except the secretaries of State and Defense and the director of the CIA—the President had told Montvale to take a walk until he got his temper under control.

Does that mean these people have an in with any of them?

Or with all *of them?*

Of course it does.

Jesus H. Christ!

"I think we would have all been disappointed, Colonel," the Naval Academy graduate said, "if, right off the top of your head, you had jumped at the proposition. So how about this? Think it over. Talk to the others. In the meantime, stay here—no one can find you here, I can personally guarantee that—until your retirement parade. And then, after you fall off the face of the earth, call Aloysius from wherever that finds you, and tell him what you've all decided."

In compliance with his orders, Castillo had stayed out of sight at the Venetian—
it could not be called a hardship; Sweaty had been with him, and there is no
finer room service in the world than that offered by the Venetian—until very
early in the morning of his retirement parade.

Then he and Dick Miller had flown Sergeant Major Jack Davidson and
CWO5 Colin Leverette in the Gulfstream to Fort Rucker. After some initial
difficulty, they had been given permission to land. They had changed into Class
A uniforms in the plane.

There was some discussion among them about the wisdom under the circumstances of removing from their uniforms those items of insignia and qualification
which suggested they had some connection with Special Operations. But that
had been resolved by Mr. Leverette.

"Fuck 'em," Uncle Remus said. "This is the last time we're going to wear
the suit. Let's wear it all!"

There was a sea of red general officers' personal flags on the reviewing stand.
The four-star flag of General Allan Naylor, the Central Command commander,
stood in the center of them, beside the three-star flag of Lieutenant General
Bruce J. McNab, who commanded the Special Operations Command. There
were too many two- and one-star flags to be counted.

Among the two-star flags were those of Dick's father, Major General Richard
H. Miller, Sr. (Retired), and Major General Harold F. Wilson (Retired). General
Wilson, as a young officer during the Vietnam War, had been the co-pilot of
WOJG Jorge Alejandro Castillo—right up until Castillo, Charley's father, had
booted Wilson out of the Huey that would be shot down by enemy fire, ending
Castillo's life and finding him posthumously awarded the Medal of Honor.

The band played as it marched onto the parade ground before post headquarters, and those persons to be decorated marched front and center and were
decorated and the retirement orders were read and the band played again and
the troops passed in review.

And that was it.

They had been retired from the Army.

The four of them got into a waiting Dodge Caravan and were driven back
to Cairns Field.

Then, as Castillo was doing the walk-around and as Miller was returning from filing their flight plan, two Army Chevrolet sedans and two Army Dodge Caravans drove onto the tarmac in front of Base Operations.

General Allan Naylor got out of one of the sedans and Lieutenant General McNab got out of the other. Major General (Retired) Miller got out of one of the Caravans, and Major General (Retired) Wilson, and his grandson, Randolph Richardson III, got out of the other.

It was an awkward moment all around.

"I wanted to say goodbye and good luck," General Naylor said.

There was a chorus of "Thank you, sir."

"Well, I suppose if you castrate too many bulls," General McNab said, "you're going to get gored, sooner or later. Don't let the doorknob hit you in the ass on your way out."

General Naylor looked askance at General McNab.

General Miller took his son to one side for a private word.

General Wilson took his grandson and Castillo to one side for a private word. General Wilson had known all along that Castillo was the natural father of his grandson. The boy and Castillo had learned of their real relationship only recently.

"Sir," Randolph Richardson III asked, "where are you going?"

"Randy, I just don't know."

"Am I ever going to see you again?"

It took Castillo a moment to get rid of the lump in his throat.

"Absolutely, positively, and soon," he managed to say.

Randy put out his hand.

Castillo shook it.

Fuck it!

He embraced his son, felt his son hug him back, and then let him go.

He wanted to say something else but this time the lump in his throat wouldn't go away.

"Your mother's waiting lunch for us, Randy," General Wilson said, and led the boy back toward the Caravan.

Gulfstream 379 broke ground about four minutes later. It flew to Louis Armstrong International Airport in New Orleans, where it took on fuel and went through Customs and Immigration procedures, and then flew to the seaside resort city of Cancún on Mexico's Yucatán Peninsula.

Colonel Jake Torine and Captain Dick Sparkman, who had been retired that day from the USAF with considerably less panoply—each had received a FedEx package containing their retirement orders and their Distinguished Service Medals—were already there. Gunnery Sergeant Lester Bradley, USMC, had received a similar package from the Department of the Navy.

The Gulfstream refueled, Torine and Sparkman took off for Las Vegas, where the plane came to be parked in one of the AFC hangars until a decision about its future could be reached.

At the moment, Gulfstream 379 was leased "dry" from Gossinger Consultants, a wholly owned subsidiary of Gossinger Beteiligungsgesellschaft, G.m.b.H., of Fulda, Germany, which had bought the aircraft from Lopez Fruit and Vegetables Mexico, a wholly owned subsidiary of Castillo Agriculture, Inc., of San Antonio, Texas, whose president and chief executive officer was Fernando Lopez, and whose corporate officers included one Carlos Castillo.

That status would have to be changed, Two-Gun Yung had announced, no matter what decision was reached about the offer of "those people" in Las Vegas.

At Cancún Airport International several hours later, CWO5 Leverette (Retired) and Sergeant Major Davidson (Retired) boarded a Mexicana flight to Mexico City. There, Leverette, now traveling on a Honduran passport under another name, would board a Varig flight to São Paulo, Brazil, and Davidson, traveling under his own name on an Israeli passport, would board a Mexicana flight bound for Lima, Peru.

Castillo had watched the takeoff of the Mexicana flight to Mexico City from the tarmac on the cargo side of the Cancún airfield. Then he had climbed into a Peruaire 767 cargo plane.

The 767 had flown up that morning from Santiago, Chile, with a mixed cargo of Chilean seafood and Argentine beef, citrus fruits and vegetables. The food was destined for Cancún Provisions, Ltda., and would ultimately end in the kitchen of The Grand Cozumel Beach and Golf Resort, and in the galleys of cruise ships which called at Cancún.

PeruaireCargo, Cancún Provisions, Ltda., The Grand Cozumel Beach and Golf Resort, and at least four of the cruise ships were owned—through a maze of dummy corporations, genuine corporations, and other entities at least twice as obfuscatory as the ownership of Gulfstream 379—by a man named Aleksandr Pevsner.

In the late Union of Soviet Socialist Republics, Pevsner had been simultaneously a colonel in the Soviet Air Force and a colonel in the KGB, responsible for the security of Aeroflot worldwide.

When the KGB was faced with the problem of concealing its wealth—

hundreds of billions of dollars—from the people now running Russia, who were likely to put it in the state treasury, they decided that the wealth—much of it in gold and platinum—had to be hidden outside Russia.

And who better to do this than Colonel Aleksandr Pevsner? He knew people—many of them bankers—all over the world.

Pevsner resigned from the Air Force, bought several ex–Soviet Air Force cargo aircraft at distress prices, and soon began a profitable business flying Mercedes automobiles and other luxury goods into Moscow. The KGB's gold, platinum, precious stones, and sometimes cash—often contained in fuel barrels—left Moscow on the flights out.

For the latter service, Pevsner had been paid a commission of usually ten percent of the value. His relationship with the KGB—its First Chief Directorate now the SVR—had soured over time as the SVR had regained power under Vladimir Putin. The new SVR had decided that if Pevsner were eliminated, he could not tell anyone where their money had gone, and they might even get back some of the commissions they had paid him.

There had been a number of deaths, almost entirely of SVR agents, and Pevsner was now living with his wife and daughter in an enormous mansion on a several-thousand-hectare estate in the foothills of the Andes Mountains, protected by a security force Castillo called Pevsner's Private Army.

The mansion—which had been built during World War II—bore a remarkable similarity to Carinhall, Reichsmarschall Hermann Göring's estate in Germany. Not really joking, Pevsner and Castillo said it had probably been built by either admirers of the Number Two Nazi—or even *for* Göring—when the Nazi leadership was planning to keep Nazism alive under the Operation Phoenix program by fleeing to Argentina.

Castillo had met Pevsner—more accurately, Pevsner had arranged to meet Castillo—when Castillo thought Pevsner was a likely suspect in the disappearance of the 727 from Aeroporto Internacional Quatro de Fevereiro in Luanda, Angola.

Pevsner had learned of Castillo's suspicions from his chief of security, a former FBI agent. Castillo had been snatched from the men's room of the Hotel Sacher in Vienna and taken to the Vienna Woods at gunpoint.

On meeting Castillo, Pevsner decided the wisest path for him to follow was to help Castillo find the missing aircraft. He really didn't like to kill people unless it was absolutely necessary—incredibly, he was a devout Christian—and killing Castillo would certainly draw more American attention to him and his business enterprises.

The missing airplane was found with his help, and there was no sudden burst of activity by the Americans looking into Pevsner and his affairs.

But the real reason Pevsner was able to feel he had really made the right decision not to kill Castillo came when Pevsner was betrayed by the former FBI agent, who set up an assassination ambush in the basement garage of the Sheraton Pilar Hotel outside Buenos Aires.

The team of SVR assassins found themselves facing not only János, Pevsner's massive Hungarian bodyguard, but a number of members of the OOA, who had learned what was about to happen.

In the brief, if ferocious, firefight which ensued, János was seriously wounded and all four of the SVR would-be assassins had been killed. One of the Russians had been put down by Corporal Lester Bradley, USMC, with a headshot at thirty meters' distance from Lester's Model 1911A1 .45 ACP pistol.

That had, of course, made Aleksandr Pevsner think of Charley Castillo as a friend, but there had been another unexpected development. Shortly after they had been struck with Cupid's arrow, Sweaty had told her Carlos that the reason they had wanted to come to Argentina was because she and her brother had a relative living there. They were cousins. His mother and the mother of Sweaty and Tom were sisters. They didn't know where he was, and she hoped her Carlos would help her find him.

His name, Sweaty had said, was Aleksandr Pevsner.

Behind the flight deck of the PeruaireCargo 767 there was a small passenger area equipped with a table, a galley, and six seats which could be converted to beds at the press of a switch.

Castillo sat down beside Sweaty, and a stewardess showed him a bottle of Argentine champagne, her eyes asking if it met his pleasure. He nodded and she poured champagne for him and Sweaty and for Tom Barlow and Two-Gun.

"Randy came to my retirement parade," Castillo told Sweaty. "He asked if he was ever going to see me again."

"Oh, my poor Carlos," Sweaty said, and took his hand and kissed it.

Max, who seemed to understand his master was unhappy, put his paws on Castillo's shoulders and licked his face.

The PeruaireCargo 767 flew nonstop from Cancún to Santiago, Chile.

For some reason, the Chilean immigration and customs officials, who had a reputation for meeting all incoming aircraft before the doors were open, were not on the tarmac.

Castillo, Sweaty, Tom, Two-Gun, and Max were thus able to walk directly, and without attracting any attention, from the 767 to a Learjet 45 which was conveniently parked next to where the 767 had stopped. The Learjet began to taxi the instant the door had closed.

A short time later, it landed at the San Carlos de Bariloche airport in Argentina, just the other side of the Andes Mountains. Coincidentally, the Argentine immigration and customs authorities, like their brothers in Santiago, seemed not to have noticed the arrival of the Learjet. No one saw its passengers load into a Mercedes sedan and, led and trailed by Mercedes SUVs, drive off.

Forty-five minutes later, Charley was standing on the dock on the edge of the Casa en el Bosque property and looking out across Lake Nahuel Huapi.

"What are you thinking, my darling?" Sweaty asked, touching his cheek.

"That I just have, in compliance with orders, dropped off the face of the earth."

"Okay," Castillo said, "the motion to split the money and run having failed, we're still in business. But as what?"

"We're going to have to form a corporation," Two-Gun said.

"What are we going to call the corporation?" Castillo pursued.

"Do what Aloysius did. Use the initials," Sergeant Major (Retired) Davidson suggested. "The Lorimer Charitable and Benevolent Fund becomes the LCBF Corporation."

"Second the motion," CWO5 Colin Leverette (Retired) said. "And then when everybody agrees, I can go fishing."

He and Davidson had made their way to Bariloche the day before. Their passports had not attracted any unwelcome attention.

"Any objections?" Castillo asked, and then a moment later said, "Hearing none, the motion carries. It's now the LCBF Corporation. Or will be, when Two-Gun sets it up. Which brings us to Two-Gun."

"Uh-oh," Two-Gun said.

"I suggest we appoint Two-Gun, by any title he chooses to assume, and at a suitable wage, as our money and legal guy. I think we should hire Agnes to keep running administration and keep Dianne and Harold on at the house in Alexandria."

Mrs. Agnes Forbison, a very senior civil servant (GS-15, the highest pay grade) had been one of the first members of OOA, as its chief of administration.

Dianne and Harold Sanders were both retired special operators. They had been thinking of opening a bed-and-breakfast when Uncle Remus Leverette told them Castillo needed someone to run a safe house just outside Washington. They had jumped at the opportunity, and Castillo had jumped at the opportunity to have them. He'd been around the block with Harold on several occasions, and Dianne, in addition to being an absolutely marvelous cook, was also an absolutely marvelous cryptographer.

"Okay," Leverette then said, "after we approve that, can I go fishing?"

Castillo said, "Then there's the final question: What do we do about the offer from those people in Las Vegas?"

"I was afraid you'd bring that up, Ace," Delchamps said. "I have mixed feelings about that."

"We told them we'd let them know today," Castillo said.

"No, *they* told *us* to let them know by today," Delchamps said. "I'm not happy with them telling us anything."

"Call them up, Charley," Jack Britton said, "and tell them we're still thinking about it."

"Second the motion," Davidson said.

"Why not?" Castillo said. "The one thing we all have now is time on our hands. All the time in the world. Any objections?"

There were none and the motion carried.

"I'm going fishing," Leverette said, and grabbed his fly rod from where he'd left it on a table, then headed for the door.

[TWO]
Office of the Managing Editor
The Washington Times-Post
1365 15th Street, N.W.
Washington, D.C.
1605 3 February 2007

The managing editor's office was across the newsroom from Roscoe Danton's office, substantially larger and even more crowded. The exterior windows opened on 15th Street, and the interior windows overlooked the newsroom. The latter were equipped with venetian blinds, which were never opened.

Managing Editor Christopher J. Waldron had begun smoking cigars as a teenager and now, at age sixty-two, continued to smoke them in his office in defiance of the wishes of the management of *The Washington Times-Post* and the laws of the District of Columbia. His only capitulation to political correctness and the law had been the installation of an exhaust fan and a sign on his door in large red letters that said: KNOCK BEFORE ENTERING!!!!

This served, usually, to give him time to exhale and to place his cigar in a desk drawer before any visitor could enter and catch him *in flagrante delicto*, which, as he often pointed out, meant "while the crime is blazing."

There had been complaints made about his filthy habit, most of them from the female staff but also from those of the opposite and indeterminate genders, but to no avail. Chris Waldron was about the best managing editor around, and management knew it.

Roscoe Danton knocked on Waldron's door, waited for permission to enter, and, when that came, went in, closing the door behind him.

Chris Waldron reclaimed his cigar from the ashtray in his desk drawer and put it back in his mouth.

He raised his eyebrows to ask the question, *Well?*

Danton said, "I am fully aware that I am neither Woodward nor Bernstein, but—"

"Thank you for sharing that with me," Waldron interrupted.

"—but I have a gut feeling I'm onto a big story, maybe as big as Watergate, and I want to follow it wherever it goes."

"And I had such high hopes that you'd really stopped drinking," Waldron said, and then made two gestures which meant, *Sit down and tell me about it.*

"So what do we know about these two disgruntled employee whistleblowers?" Waldron asked.

"The younger one, Wilson, was an agricultural analyst at Langley before she got married to Wilson, who's a career bureaucrat over there. The gossip, which I haven't had time to check out, is that he's light on his feet. He needed to be married, and she needed somebody to push her career. Anyway, she managed to get herself sent through The Farm and into the Clandestine Service. They sent her to Angola, and then she got herself sent back to Langley. A combination of her husband's influence and her vast experience—eleven months in Angola—got her a job as regional director for Southwest Africa, everything from Nigeria to the South African border. She was where she wanted to be, back in Washington, with her foot on the ladder to greater things. She was not very popular with her peers."

"What got her fired?"

"According to her, this Colonel Castillo said terrible things about her behind her back about her handling of that 727 that was stolen. Remember that?"

Waldron nodded. "What sort of things?"

"She didn't tell me, not that she would have told me the truth. But anyway, that got her relieved from the Southwest Africa desk, and assigned to the Southern Cone desk—"

"The what?"

"Uruguay, Argentina, and Chile—otherwise known as the Southern Cone."

"From which she got fired?" Waldron asked, and when Danton nodded, asked, "Why?"

"I got this from a friend of mine who's close to the DCI and doesn't like her. Somebody sent the DCI a tape on which our pal C. Harry Whelan, Jr., proudly referred to her as his 'personal mole' in Langley."

C. Harry Whelan, Jr., was a prominent and powerful Washington-based columnist.

"That would do it, I guess. You check with Harry?"

Danton nodded.

"And did he admit knowing this lady?"

"More or less. When I called him, I said, 'Harry, I've been talking with Patricia Davies Wilson about you.' To which he replied, 'Don't believe a thing that lying bitch says.' Then I asked, 'Is it true somebody told the DCI she was your personal mole over there?' And Harry replied, 'Go fuck yourself, Roscoe,' and hung up."

"I can see where losing one's personal mole in the CIA might be a trifle annoying," Waldron said. "But—judging from what you've told me about this lady—might one suspect she is what our brothers in the legal profession call 'an unreliable witness'?"

"Oh, yeah," Roscoe agreed. "But the other one, Dillworth, is different."

"How different?"

"Well, for one thing, everybody I talked to liked her, said she was really good at what she did, and was sorry she got screwed."

"How did she, figuratively speaking of course, 'get screwed'?"

"She was the CIA station chief in Vienna. She had been working on getting a couple of heavy-hitter Russians to defect. Really heavy hitters, the SVR *rezident* in Berlin and the SVR *rezident* in Copenhagen, who happen to be brother and sister. Dillworth was so close to this coming off that she had had Langley send an airplane to Vienna, and had them prepare a safe house for them in Maryland."

"And it didn't come off?"

"Colonel Castillo showed up in Vienna, loaded them on his plane, and flew them to South America."

"She told you this?"

"No. What actually happened was that Dillworth said she wasn't going to tell me what had happened, because I wouldn't believe it. She said she would point me in the right direction, and let me find out myself; that way I would believe it."

"Is this Russian defectors story true?"

"There's an Interpol warrant out for"—Roscoe stopped and consulted his organizer, and then went on—"Dmitri Berezovsky and Svetlana Alekseeva, who the Russians say stole several million euros from their embassies in Germany and Denmark."

"And you *know* that Castillo took these Russians to South America? How do you know?"

"My friend who is close to the DCI and doesn't like Ambassador Montvale told me that Montvale told the DCI that he was going to South America to get the Russians. And that when he got down there, Castillo told him the Russians had changed their minds about defecting."

"And you believe this?"

"I believe my friend."

"So what happened is that when Castillo stole the Russians from Dillworth, blew her operation, the agency canned her?"

"That got Dillworth in a little hot water, I mean when the Russians didn't come in after she said they were, but what got her recalled was really interesting. Right after this, they found the SVR *rezident* in Vienna sitting in the backseat of a taxi outside our embassy. He had been strangled to death—they'd used a garrote—and on his chest was the calling card of Miss Eleanor Dillworth, counselor for consular affairs of the U.S. embassy."

"Curiouser and curiouser," Waldron said. "The agency thought she did it?"

"No. They don't know who did it. But that was enough to get her recalled from Vienna. *She* thinks Castillo did it. Or, really, had it done."

"Why? And for that matter, why did he take the Russians? To Argentina, you said? He was turned? We have another Aldrich Ames? This one a killer?"

Aldrich Hazen Ames was the Central Intelligence Agency counterintelligence officer convicted of selling out to the Soviet Union and later Russia.

"I just don't know, Chris. From what I've been able to find out about him, Castillo doesn't seem to be the traitor type, but I suppose the same thing was said about Ames until the FBI put him in handcuffs."

"And what have you been able to find out about him?"

"That he was retired at Fort Rucker, Alabama—and given a Distinguished Service Medal, his second, for unspecified distinguished service of a classified nature—on January thirty-first. He was medically retired, with a twenty-five percent disability as the result of a medical board at Walter Reed Army Hospital.

That's what I got from the Pentagon. When I went to Walter Reed to get an address, phone number, and next of kin from the post locator, he wasn't in it.

"A diligent search by another friend of mine revealed that he had never been a patient at Walter Reed. Never ever. Not once. Not even for a physical examination or to have his teeth cleaned."

"And being the suspicious paranoid person you are, you have decided that something's not kosher?"

"I suppose you could say that, yes."

"What do these women want?"

"Revenge."

"Is Dillworth willing to be quoted?"

"She assures me that she will speak freely from the witness box, if and when Castillo is hauled before Congress or some other body to be grilled, and until that happens, speak to no other member of the press but me. Ditto for Mrs. Patricia Davies Wilson."

"She has visions, in other words, of Senator Johns in some committee hearing room, with the TV cameras rolling, glaring at this Castillo character, and demanding to know, 'Colonel, did you strangle a Russian intelligence officer and leave him in a taxicab outside the U.S. embassy in Vienna in order to embarrass this fine civil servant, Miss Eleanor Dillworth? Answer yes or no.'"

Senator Homer Johns, Jr. (Democrat, New Hampshire), was chairman of the Senate Foreign Relations Committee and loved to be on TV.

Roscoe laughed, and added, "'Would you repeat the question, Senator?'"

Waldron laughed, then offered his own answer: "'Senator, I don't have much of a memory. I've been retired from the Army because I am psychologically unfit for service. I just don't recall.'"

"'Well, then, Colonel, did you or did you not steal two Russians from under Miss Dillworth's nose and fly them to Argentina?'"

Roscoe picked it up: "'Two Russians? Senator, I don't have much of a memory,' et cetera."

Waldron, still laughing, reached into another drawer of his desk and came out with two somewhat grimy glasses and a bottle of The Macallan twelve-year-old single malt Scotch whisky.

He poured.

"Nectar of the gods," he said. "Only for good little boys and naughty little girls."

They tapped glasses and took a sip.

"That's not going to happen, Roscoe," Waldron said, "unless we make it happen. And I'm not sure if we could, or even if we should."

"In other words, let it drop? I wondered why you brought out the good whisky."

"I didn't say that," Waldron said. "You open for some advice?"

Roscoe nodded.

"Don't tell anybody what you're doing, *anybody*. If there's anything to this, and I have a gut feeling there is, there are going to be ten people—ten powerful people—trying to keep it from coming out for every one who'd give you anything useful."

Roscoe nodded again.

"I can see egg on a lot of faces," Waldron said. "Including on the face of the new inhabitant of the Oval Office. He's in a lose-lose situation. If something like this was going on under his predecessor, and he didn't know about it, it'll look like he wasn't trusted. And if he indeed did know there was this James Bond outfit operating out of the Oval Office, stealing Russian defectors from the CIA, not to mention strangling Russians in Vienna, and doing all sorts of other interesting, if grossly illegal, things, why didn't he stop it?"

"So what do you want me to do?"

"One thought would be for you to go to beautiful Argentina and do a piece for the Sunday magazine. You could call it, 'Tacos and Tangos in the Southern Cone.'"

Roscoe nodded thoughtfully, then said, "Thank you."

"Watch your back, Roscoe. The kind of people who play these games kill nosy people."

[THREE]
U.S. Army Medical Research Institute
Fort Detrick, Maryland
0815 4 February 2007

There were three packages marked BIOLOGICAL HAZARD in the morning FedEx delivery. It was a rare morning when there wasn't at least one, and sometimes there were eight, ten, even a dozen.

This didn't mean that they were so routine that not much attention was paid to them.

Each package was taken separately into a small room in the rear of the guard post. There, the package—more accurately, the container, an oblong insulated metal box which easily could have contained cold beer were it not for the decalcomania plastered all over it—was laid on an examination table.

On the top was a black-edged yellow triangle, inside of which was the biological hazard indicator, three half-moons—not unlike those to be found on the tops of minarets of Muslim houses of worship—joined together at their closed ends over a circle. Below this, black letters on a yellow background spelled out DANGER! BIOLOGICAL HAZARD!

Beside this—in a red circle, not unlike a No Parking symbol—the silhouette of a walking man was bisected by a crossing red line. The message below this in white letters on a red background was AUTHORIZED PERSONNEL ONLY!

This was apparently intended to keep curious people from opening the container to have a look at the biological hazard. This would have been difficult, as the container was closed with four lengths of four-inch-wide plastic tape, two around the long end and two around the short. The tape application device had closed the tapes by melting the ends together. The only way to get into the container was by cutting the tape with a large knife. It would thus be just about impossible for anyone to have a look inside without anyone noticing.

Once the biological hazard package was laid on the table, it was examined by two score or more specially trained technicians. It was X-rayed, sniffed for leakage and the presence of chemicals which might explode, and tested for several other things, some of them classified.

Only after it had passed this inspection was the FedEx receipt signed. The package was then turned over to two armed security officers. Most of these at Fort Detrick were retired Army sergeants. One of them got behind the wheel of a battery-powered golf cart, and the other, after putting the container on the floor of the golf cart, got in and—there being no other place to put them—put his feet on the container.

At this point the driver checked the documentation to the final destination.

"Oh, shit," he said. "It's for Hamilton personally."

J. Porter Hamilton was the senior scientific officer of the U.S. Army Medical Research Institute. It was said that he spoke only to God and the commanding general of the U.S. Army Medical Research Institute, but only rarely deigned to do so to the latter.

Although he was triply entitled to be addressed as "Doctor"—he was a medical doctor, and also held a Ph.D. in biochemistry from Oxford and a Ph.D. in molecular physics from MIT—he preferred to be addressed as "Colonel." He had graduated from the United States Military Academy at West Point with the class of 1984 and thought of himself primarily as a soldier.

Colonel Hamilton had the reputation among the security force of being one really hard-nosed sonofabitch. This reputation was not pejorative, just a statement of the facts.

Colonel Hamilton—a very slim, very tall, ascetic-looking officer whose skin was deep flat black in color—showed the security guards where he wanted the biological hazard container placed on a table in his private laboratory.

After they'd left, he eyed the container curiously. It had been sent from the Daryl Laboratory in Miami, Florida. Just who they were didn't come to mind. They had paid a small fortune for overnight shipment, which also was unusual.

He went to a closet, took off his uniform tunic, and replaced it with a white laboratory coat. He then pulled on a pair of very expensive gloves which looked like normal latex gloves, but were not.

"Sergeant Dennis!" he called.

Dennis was a U.S. Army master sergeant, a burly red-faced Irishman from Baltimore who functioned as sort of a secretary to Colonel Hamilton. Hamilton had recruited him from the Walter Reed Army Medical Center.

Hamilton, doing what he thought of as his soldier's duty, often served on medical boards at Walter Reed dealing with wounded soldiers who wanted—or who did not want—medical retirement. Dennis had been one of the latter. He did not wish to be retired although he had lost his left leg below the knee and his right arm at the shoulder.

There was no way, Hamilton had decided, that Dennis could return to the infantry. On the other hand, there was no reason he could not make himself useful around Building 103 at Fort Detrick, if that was the option to being retired. He made the offer and when Dennis accepted, he'd asked, "Can you arrange that, Colonel?"

"I can arrange it, Sergeant Dennis. The chief of staff has directed the Army to provide whatever I think I need for my laboratory. Just think of yourself as a human Erlenmeyer flask."

Dennis appeared. "Sir?"

"What do we know of the Daryl Laboratory in Miami, Florida?"

"Never heard of it, sir."

"Good. I was afraid that I was suffering another senior moment. Right after we see what this is, find out who they are and why they sent me whatever this is."

"You want me to open it, Colonel?"

"I want you to cut the tape, thank you. I'll open it."

Dennis took a tactical folding knife from his pocket, fluidly flipped open the stainless-steel serrated blade, and expertly cut the plastic tape from the container.

Hamilton raised the lid.

Inside he found a second container. There was a large manila envelope taped to it, and addressed simply "Colonel Hamilton."

Hamilton picked up the envelope and took from it two eight-by-ten-inch color photographs of six barrel-like objects. They were of a heavy plastic, dark blue in color, and also looked somewhat like beer kegs. On the kegs was a copy of *The Miami Herald.* The date could not be read in the first shot, but in the second photograph, a close-up, it was clearly visible: February 3, 2007.

"My God!" Colonel Hamilton said softly.

"Jesus Christ, Colonel," Sergeant Dennis said, pointing. "Did you see that?"

Hamilton looked.

The envelope had covered a simple sign, and now it was visible: DANGER!!! BIOHAZARD LEVEL 4!!!

Of the four levels of biological hazards, one through four, the latter posed the greatest threat to human life from viruses and bacteria and had no vaccines or other treatments available.

Hamilton closed the lid on the container.

"Go to the closet and get two Level A hazmat suits."

"What the hell's going on?" Dennis asked.

"After we're in our suits," Hamilton said calmly.

Two minutes later, they had helped each other into the Level A hazmat suits. These offered the highest degree of protection against both direct and airborne chemical contact by providing the wearer with total encapsulation, including a self-contained breathing apparatus.

The suits donned by Colonel Hamilton and Master Sergeant Dennis also contained communications equipment that connected them "hands off" with each other, as well as to the post telephone system and to Hamilton's cellular telephone.

"Call the duty officer and tell him that I am declaring a potential Level Four Disaster," Hamilton said. "Have them prepare Level Four BioLab Two for immediate use. Have them send a Level Four truck here to move this container, personnel to wear Level A hazmat gear."

A Level Four BioLab—there were three at Fort Detrick—was, in a manner of speaking, a larger version of the Level A hazmat protective suit. It was completely self-contained, protected by multiple airlocks. It had a system of high-pressure showers to decontaminate personnel entering or leaving, a vacuum room, and an ultraviolet-light room. All air and water entering or leaving was decontaminated.

And of course "within the bubble" there was a laboratory designed to do everything and anything anyone could think of to any kind of a biologically hazardous material.

Colonel Hamilton then pressed a key that caused his cellular telephone to speed-dial a number.

The number was answered on the second ring, and Hamilton formally announced, "This is Colonel J. Porter Hamilton."

"Encryption Level One active," a metallic voice said three seconds later.

Hamilton then went on: "There was delivered to my laboratory about five minutes ago a container containing material described as BioHazard Level Four. There was also a photograph of some six plastic containers identical to those I brought out of the Congo. On them was lying a photo of yesterday's Miami newspaper. All of which leads me to strongly suspect that the attack on the laboratory-slash-factory did not—repeat *not*—destroy everything.

"I am having this container moved to a laboratory where I will be able to compare whatever is in the container with what I brought out of the Congo. This process will take me at least several hours.

"In the meantime, I suggest we proceed on the assumption that there are six containers of the most dangerous Congo material in the hands of only God knows whom.

"When I have completed my tests, I will inform the director of the CIA of my findings."

He broke the connection and then walked to the door and unlocked it for the hazmat transport people. He could hear the siren of the Level Four van coming toward Building 103.

III

[ONE]
Laboratory Four
The AFC Corporation—McCarran Facility
Las Vegas, Nevada
0835 4 February 2007

Laboratory Four was not visible to anyone looking across McCarran International Airport toward what had become the center of AFC's worldwide production and research-and-development activity.

This was because Laboratory Four was deep underground, beneath Hangar III, one of a row of enormous hangars each bearing the AFC logotype. It was also below Laboratories One, Two, and Three, which were closer to ground level as their numbers suggested, One being immediately beneath the hangar.

When Aloysius Francis Casey, AFC's chairman, had been a student at MIT, he had become friendly with a Korean-American student of architecture, who was something of an outcast because of his odd notion that with some exceptions—aircraft hangars being one—all industrial buildings, which would include laboratories, should be underground.

This had gotten J. Charles Who in as much trouble with the architectural faculty as had Casey's odd notions of data transmission and encryption had done the opposite of endearing him to the electrical engineering and mathematics faculties.

Years later, when Casey decided that he had had quite enough, thank you, of the politicians and weather of his native Massachusetts to last a lifetime, and wanted to move at least the laboratories and some of the manufacturing facilities elsewhere, he got in touch with his old school chum and sought his expertise.

Site selection was Problem One. Las Vegas had quickly risen to the head of the list of possibilities for a number of reasons including location, tax concessions to be granted by the state and local governments for bringing a laboratory/production facility with several thousand extremely well-paid and well-educated workers to Sin City, and the attractions of Sin City itself.

At Who's suggestion, just about everything would go to Vegas.

Charley Who, Ph.D. (MIT), AIA, had pointed out to Aloysius Casey, Ph.D. (MIT), that all work and no play would tend to make his extremely well-paid workers dull. It was hard to become bored in Las Vegas, whether one's interests lay in the cultural or the carnal, or a combination of both.

Construction had begun immediately and in earnest, starting with the laboratories that would be under Hangar III. They were something like the Bio-Labs at Fort Detrick in that they were as "pure" as they could be made. The air and water was filtered as it entered and was discharged. The humidity and temperature in the labs was whatever the particular labs required, and being below ground cut the cost of doing this to a tiny fraction of what it would have cost in a surface building. They were essentially soundproof. And, finally, the deeper underground that they were, the less they were affected by vibration, say a heavy truck driving by or the landing of a heavy airplane. Almost all of Aloysius's gadgets in development were very tiny and quite delicate. Much of the work on them was done using microscopes or their electronic equivalent. Vibration was the enemy.

What Casey was working on now in Laboratory Four, his personal lab—"My latest gadget," as he put it—was yet another improvement on a system he had developed for the gambling cops, or as they liked to portray themselves, "The security element of the gaming industry."

Many people try to cheat the casinos. Most are incredibly stupid. But a small number are the exact opposite: incredibly smart, imaginative, and resourceful. Both stupid and near-genius would-be thieves alike have to deal with the same problem: One has to be physically in a casino if one is to steal anything.

Surveillance cameras scan every inch of a casino floor, often from several angles, and the angles can be changed. The people watching these monitors know what to look for. If some dummy is seen stealing quarters from Grandma's bucket on a slot machine row, or some near-genius is engaged with three or more equally intelligent co-conspirators in a complex scheme to cheat the casino at a twenty-one table, they are seen. Security officers are sent to the slot machine or the twenty-one table. The would-be thieves and cheats are taken to an area where they are photographed, fingerprinted, counseled regarding the punishments involved for cheating a casino, and then shown the door.

The problem then becomes that stupid and near-genius alike tend to believe that if at first you don't succeed, one should try, try again. They come back, now disguised with a phony mustache or a wig and a change of clothing.

Specially trained security officers, who regularly review the photographs of caught crooks, stand at casino doors and roam the floors looking for familiar, if unwelcome, faces.

When Casey had first moved to Las Vegas, he had been very discreetly approached—the day he was welcomed into the Las Vegas Chamber of Gaming, Hospitality and Other Commerce—by a man who then owned three—and now owned five—of the more glitzy hotel/casinos in Sin City.

The man approached Casey at the urinal in the men's room of the Via Veneto Restaurant in Caligula's Palace Resort and Casino and said he wanted to thank him for what he was doing for the "boys in the stockade in Bragg."

"I don't know who or what the hell you're talking about," Casey had replied immediately.

But Casey of course knew full well who the boys in the stockade in Fort Bragg were—Delta Force; their base had once been the post stockade—and what he was doing for them—providing them with whatever they asked for, absolutely free of charge, or didn't ask for but got anyway because Casey thought it might be useful.

"Sure you do," the man had said. "The commo gear. It was very useful last week in Tunisia."

"How the hell did you find out about that?" Casey had blurted.

"We have sources all over."

"Who's 'we'?"

"Like you, people who happen to be in positions where we can help the good guys, and try quietly—very quietly—to do so. I'd like to talk to you about our group some time."

"These people have names?"

They were furnished.

"Give me a day or two to check these people out," Casey said, "then come to see me."

The first person Casey had tried to call was then-Major General Bruce J. McNab, who at the time commanded the Special Forces Center at Fort Bragg. He got instead then-Major Charley Castillo on the phone. Castillo did odd jobs for McNab—both had told Casey that—and he'd become one of Casey's favorite people since they'd first met.

And when Casey had asked, Castillo had flatly—almost indignantly—denied telling anyone about the Tunisian radios mentioned in the casino pisser and of ever even hearing of the man who claimed to own the glitzy Las Vegas hotels.

General McNab, however, when he came on the line, was so obfuscatory about both questions—even aware that the line was encrypted—that Casey promptly decided (a) McNab knew the guy who owned the three glitzy casinos; (b) had told the guy where the radios used in Tunisia had come from; (c) had more than likely suggested he could probably wheedle some out of Casey, which meant he knew and approved of what the guy was up to; and, thus, (d) didn't want Castillo to know about (a) through (c).

That had been surprising. For years, from the time during the First Desert War, when then-Second Lieutenant Castillo had gone to work for then-Colonel McNab, Casey had thought—*In fact I was told*—that Castillo was always privy to all of McNab's secrets.

Casey prided himself on his few friends, and on having no secrets from them. He had quickly solved the problem here by concluding that having no secrets did not mean you had to tell your friends everything you knew, but rather, if asked, to be wholly forthcoming.

If Castillo asked about these people in Las Vegas, he would tell him. If he didn't ask, he would not.

And, as quickly, he had decided if these people were okay in General McNab's book, they were okay—period.

Unless of course something happened that changed that.

Casey had called the man who owned the three glitzy hotels—and was in business discussions leading to the construction of the largest hotel in the world (7,550 rooms)—and told him he was in.

"What do these people need?" Casey asked.

He was told: secure telephones to connect them all.

While AFC had such devices sitting in his warehouse, these were not what he delivered to the people in Las Vegas. The secure telephones they used thereafter had encryption circuitry that could not be decrypted by even the legendary National Security Agency at Fort Meade, Maryland. Casey knew this because the NSA's equipment had come from AFC Corporation.

And after that, and after writing several very substantial checks to pay his share of what it had cost those people to do something that had to be done—but for one reason or another couldn't be done by the various intelligence agencies—Casey realized that he had become one of the group.

No one said anything to him. He didn't get a membership card.

He just knew.

He became friendly with the man who owned the glitzy hotels, and not only because one of his hotels had a restaurant to which lobsters and clams were flown in daily from Maine. The man who owned the hotels was from New Jersey. Politicians and high taxes, not the cuisine, had driven him from the Garden State. They took to taking together what they thought of as One of God's Better Meals—a dozen steamed clams and a pair of three-pound lobsters washed down with a couple of pitchers of beer—once or twice a week.

One day, en route to the restaurant, Casey had witnessed one of the gambling cops intently studying the face of the man who happened to be walking ahead of Casey.

"What's that all about?" Casey had asked his new friend the casino owner between their first pitcher of beer and the clams, and their lobsters and the second pitcher.

The problem of controlling undesirable incoming gamblers was explained.

"There has to be a better way to do that than having your gambling cops in everybody's face," Casey said. "Let me think about it."

The AFC prototype was delivered in three weeks, and operational a week after that. All the photographs of miscreants in the files were digitalized. Additional digital cameras were discreetly installed at the entrances in such positions that the only way to avoid having one's face captured by the system would be to arrive by parachute on the roof.

The computer software quickly and constantly attempted to cross-match images of casino patrons with the database of miscreants on the security servers. When a "hit" was made, the gambling cops could immediately take corrective action to protect the casino.

The owner was delighted, and ordered installation of the system in all his properties as quickly as this could be accomplished.

But Casey was just getting started. The first major improvement was to provide the gambling cops with a small communications device that looked like a telephone. When a "hit" was made, every security officer in the establishment was immediately furnished with both the digital image of Mr. Unwelcome—or Grandma Unwelcome; there were a surprising number of the latter—and the last known location of said miscreant.

It hadn't been hard for Casey to improve on that. Soon the miscreant's name, aliases, and other personal data, including why he or she was unwelcome, was flashed to the gambling cops as soon as there was a hit.

The next large—and expensive—step had required the replacement of the system computers with ones of much greater capacity and speed. The owner complained not a word when he got the bill. He thought of himself, after all, as a leader in the hospitality and gaming industry, and there was a price that had to be paid for that.

The system now made a hit when a *good* customer returned to the premises, presumably bringing more funds to pass into the casino's coffers through the croupier's slots. He was greeted as quickly and as warmly as possible, and depending on how bad his luck had been the last time, provided with complimentary accommodations, victuals, and spirits. Often, the gambling cops assigned to keep them happy were attractive members of the opposite gender.

Good Grandmother customers, interestingly enough, seemed to appreciate this courtesy more than most of the men.

The new system soon covered all of the hotels owned by the proprietor. And the database grew as guests' pertinent details—bank balances, credit reports, domestic problems, known associates, carnal preferences, that sort of thing—were added.

For a while, as he had been working on the system, Casey had thought it would have a sure market in other areas where management wanted to keep a close eye on people within its walls. Prisons, for example.

AFC's legal counsel had quickly disabused him of this pleasant notion. The ACLU would go ballistic, his lawyers warned, at what they would perceive as an outrageous violation of a felon's right to privacy while incarcerated. He would be the accused in a class action lawsuit that would probably cost him millions.

What Casey was doing when his cellular buzzed in the lab deep beneath Hangar III was conducting a sort of graduation ceremony for a pair of students who had just completed How This Works 101. He had just presented the graduates with what looked like fairly ordinary BlackBerrys or similar so-called smartphones.

Actually, by comparison, the capabilities of the CaseyBerry devices that Casey had given the two students made the BlackBerry look as state-of-the-art as the wood fire from which an Apache brave informs his squaw that he'll be a little late for supper by allowing puffs of smoke to rise.

The students were First Lieutenant Edmund "Peg-Leg" Lorimer, MI, USA (Retired), and former Gunnery Sergeant Lester Bradley, USMC.

When the Office of Organizational Analysis had been disbanded and its men and women ordered to vanish from the face of the earth, Casey had had a private word with Castillo about them.

Neither Bradley nor Lorimer had a family—perhaps more accurately: a family into whose arms they would be welcomed with joy—and neither had skills readily convertible to earning a decent living as a civilian. There was not much of a market for a one-legged Spanish/English/Portuguese interpreter, or for a five-foot-two, hundred-thirty-pound twenty-year-old who could give marksmanship instruction to Annie Oakley. Further, there was the problem that they, too, were expected to fall off the face of the earth and never be seen again.

Both men, Casey had told Castillo, had become skilled in the use of the state-of-the-art communications equipment that OOA had been using. Casey intended to keep providing similar equipment to Delta Force, and with some additional training, Bradley and Lorimer could assume responsibility for training Delta troopers to operate and maintain it.

So far as their falling off the face of the earth, Casey said, they would be hard to find in Las Vegas and next to impossible to find if they moved in with him at the home Charley Who had built for the Caseys on a very expensive piece of mountainside real estate that overlooked Las Vegas. Now that Mrs. Casey had finally succumbed to an especially nasty and painful carcinoma, there was nobody in the place but the Mexican couple who took care of Casey.

And to keep them busy when they weren't dealing with the equipment for Delta Force, or keeping an eye on the communications network used by those people, they would be welcomed—and well paid—by the gaming industry as experts in the digital photo recognition and data system.

Not thirty seconds after Casey had handed Lorimer and Bradley their new cell phones, vibration announced an incoming message on the peoples' circuit, and Casey thought he had inadvertently pressed the CHECK FUNCTIONING key.

But he checked the screen and saw that there was indeed an incoming message.

It's from Colonel Hamilton.

I wonder what the hell he wants.

When, inside his Level A hazmat gear, Colonel J. Porter Hamilton had pressed the TRANSMIT button for his cellular phone, and given his name, the following had happened:

An integral voice recognition circuit had determined that he was indeed Colonel J. Porter Hamilton and, at about the time a satellite link had been established between Hamilton and Las Vegas, had announced that Encryption Level One was now active.

By the time Hamilton spoke again to report the delivery of biohazardous material to his laboratory and what he planned to do about it, the cell phones in the hands of those people had vibrated to announce the arrival of an incoming call. Their cell phones automatically recorded the message, and then sent a message to Hamilton's phone that the message had been received and recorded.

He had then broken the connection.

When those called "answered" their telephones, either when the call was first made, or whenever they got around to it, they would hear the recorded message. A small green LED on the telephone would indicate that the caller was at that moment on the line. A red LED would indicate the caller was not.

Casey saw that the red LED was illuminated.

Hamilton's off-line.

I wonder what he wanted.

As he touched the ANSWER key, he saw that both Lester and Peg-Leg were doing the same thing.

Hamilton's message was played to them all.

"I wonder what the hell that's all about," Casey wondered out loud.

"He said, 'identical to what I brought out of the Congo,'" Peg-Leg said. "*What* did he bring out of the Congo?"

Both Peg-Leg and Aloysius looked at Lester, whose face was troubled.

"You know what Hamilton's talking about, Lester?" Casey asked.

Bradley looked even more uncomfortable.

Casey waited patiently, and was rewarded for his patience.

"Colonel Torine would, sir," Bradley said finally.

"How many times do I have to tell you to call me 'Aloysius'?" Casey said.

He pushed a button on his CaseyBerry.

"Jake? Aloysius," he said a moment later. "Got a minute? Can you come to my lab?"

"Captain Sparkman would know, too," Bradley said.

"Sparkman with you?" Casey said to his telephone, and a moment later, "Bring him, too."

Casey pushed another button and said, "Pass Torine and Sparkman," and then looked at Peg-Leg and Lester. "They're in the hangar."

He pointed upward.

Colonel Jacob Torine, USAF (Retired), and Mr. Richard Sparkman (formerly Captain USAF) got off the elevator ninety seconds later.

They were dressed almost identically in khaki trousers, polo shirts, and zipper jackets, and had large multibutton watches on their wrists. Their belts held cases for Ray-Ban sunglasses. They both had clear blue eyes. No one would ever guess that they were pilots.

"What's up?

"Listen to this," Casey said, and handed him his Caseyberry, and motioned for Lester to hand his to Sparkman.

Both listened to Colonel J. Porter Hamilton's message.

Sparkman's eyebrows rose in surprise.

Torine said, "Oh, shit!" and then asked, "When did you get this?"

"Just now."

"Not good news," Torine said. "What is the exact opposite of 'good news'?"

Casey said, "What's he talking about? What did he bring out of the Congo?"

Torine exhaled.

He looked around the laboratory.

"I don't suppose this place is bugged?"

Casey shook his head.

"We went over there in Delta's 727," Torine said. "It was painted in the color scheme of Sub-Saharan Airways—" He stopped. "Why am I telling you this? You know."

"Go on, Jake," Casey said.

"We landed at Kilimanjaro International in Tanzania. Uncle Remus and his crew went by truck to Bujumbura in Burundi. There's an airport at Bujumbura but Castillo decided we'd attract too much attention if we used it, particularly if we sat on the runway for a couple of days, maybe longer.

"Uncle Remus infiltrated Hamilton back into the Congo from Bujumbura. And then when Hamilton found what he found, and the shit hit the fan, we got a message from Uncle Remus to move the airplane to Bujumbura, yesterday, and have it prepared for immediate takeoff.

"We were there about three hours when Uncle Remus, his crew, and Hamilton showed up. They had with them a half-dozen of what looked like rubber beer kegs. Blue."

He demonstrated with his hands the size of the kegs.

"Uncle Remus asked me if we could fly to the States with the HALO compartment depressurized and open."

"I don't understand that," Lester said. "'HALO compartment'?"

"For 'High Altitude, Low Opening' parachute infiltration from up to forty thousand feet," Peg-Leg explained. "The rear half—the HALO compartment—of the fuselage can be sealed off from the rest of the fuselage, and then, where that rear stairway was, opened to the atmosphere."

"Got it," Lester said.

"I told him yes," Torine went on, "and Hamilton said, 'Thank God,' as if he meant it.

"I asked him what was going on, and he told me the beer barrels contained more dangerous material than I could imagine, and extraordinary precautions were in order; he would explain later. He asked me how cold the HALO compartment would get in flight, and I told him probably at least sixty degrees below zero, and he said, 'Thank God,' again and sounded like he meant it this time, too.

"Then he and Uncle Remus and his team loaded the barrels in the HALO compartment. When they came out, everybody stripped to the skin. They took a shower on the tarmac using the fire engine and some special soap and chemicals Hamilton had with him. Then they put on whatever clothing we had aboard, flight suits, some other clothing, and got in the front, and we took off.

"Before we had climbed out to cruising altitude, we got some company, a flight of F/A-18E Super Hornets from a carrier in the Indian Ocean. They stayed with us until we were over the Atlantic, where they handed us over to some Super Hornets flying off a carrier in the Atlantic.

"We headed for North Carolina—Pope Air Force at Fort Bragg. We were refueled in flight halfway across the Atlantic and when the refueling was over, we were handed over to a flight of Air Force F-16s who stayed with us until we got to Pope.

"When we got to Pope, we were directed to the Delta hangar, and immediately towed inside and the doors closed. Then maybe two dozen guys in science-fiction movie space suits swarmed all over the airplane. Some of them went into the HALO compartment and removed the barrels. I later learned they were sealed and then loaded aboard a Citation Three and flown to Washington.

"They took everybody off the airplane and gave us a bath. Unbelievable. Soap, chemicals, some kind of powder. It took half an hour. And then they held us—everybody but Hamilton and Uncle Remus; they went on the Citation with the barrels—for twenty-four hours for observation, gave us another bath, and finally let us go.

"General McNab was waiting for us—did I mention they held us in the hangar?—when they finally turned us loose. He gave us the standard speech about keeping this secret for the rest of our natural lives or suffer castration with a dull knife."

"What was in the barrels, Jake?" Casey asked softly. "Did Hamilton tell you?"

Torine nodded.

"He said two of them contained 'laboratory material' and the other four had 'tissue samples.' When I pressed him on that, he said that two of the barrels contained body parts from bodies he and Uncle Remus dug up near this place, and the other two held the bodies of two people, one black and one white, that Uncle Remus took down when they had to get into the laboratory. He said he needed them for autopsies."

"Jesus!" Casey said.

"And now we learn that not everything was destroyed," Sparkman said. "The word I got was there was nothing left standing or unburned in a twenty-square-mile area. What the hell is this all about?"

"I don't know," Casey admitted. "But I just had this thought: It doesn't matter to you guys. OOA is dead. You've fallen off the face of the earth. You're out of the loop. This has nothing to do with you."

"Why don't I believe that, Aloysius?" Torine asked softly.

"Probably because you're an old fart like me, and have learned that when things are as black as they can possibly get, they invariably get worse."

[TWO]
U.S. Army Medical Research Institute
Fort Detrick, Maryland
0905 4 February 2007

The declaration of a Potential Level Four Disaster at Fort Detrick by Colonel J. Porter Hamilton, MC, caused a series of standing operating procedures to kick in—something akin to a row of dominoes tumbling, one domino knocking over the one adjacent, but in this instance damned faster.

When Master Sergeant Dennis called the post duty officer, he actually called the garrison duty officer. On coming to work for Colonel Hamilton, Dennis had quickly learned that the colonel often had trouble with Army bureaucracy and that it was his job to provide the colonel with what he wanted, which often was not what he asked for.

The garrison duty officer immediately expressed doubt that Master Sergeant Dennis was actually asking for what he said he was.

"A Potential Level Four Disaster? You sure about that, Sergeant?"

"Yes, sir. Colonel Hamilton said he was declaring a Potential Level Four Disaster."

The garrison duty officer consulted his SOP dealing with disasters, and checked who was authorized to declare one.

There were three people who could on their own authority declare a Potential Level Four Disaster: the garrison commander, Colonel J. Porter Hamilton, and the garrison duty officer.

"Let me speak to Colonel Hamilton, Sergeant," the garrison duty officer said.

"He's on his phone, Major. Now, do you want to send a Level Four van over here, personnel in Level One hazmat suits, or should I call for it?"

"You have that authority?"

"Yes, sir. I do. And I have authority to have Level Four BioLab Two opened and on standby. You want me to do that, too, sir?"

"Why don't you do that, Sergeant, while I bring the garrison commander up to speed on this. And, Sergeant, see if you can have Colonel Hamilton call her."

"Yes, sir," Master Sergeant Dennis said.

The duty officer called the garrison commander.

"Major Lott, ma'am. Ma'am, we seem to have a problem."

"What kind of a problem?"

"Ma'am, Colonel Hamilton's sergeant just called and said the colonel wanted to declare a Potential Level Four Disaster."

There was a pause. Then the garrison commander said, "Let me make sure I understand the situation. You say Colonel Hamilton's sergeant called and told you Colonel Hamilton wants to declare a Potential Level Four Disaster? Is that it?"

"Yes, ma'am. That's it. I thought I'd better bring you up to speed on this, ma'am."

The garrison commander thought: *What you were supposed to do, you stupid sonofabitch, was sound the goddamned alarm sirens, get a Level Four van over to Hamilton, get a Level Four BioLab on emergency standby and then—and only then— call me.*

And you're a goddamn major?

Jesus H. Christ.

She said calmly: "Listen carefully. What I want you to do, Major, is first sound the alarm sirens. Then send a Level Four van to Colonel Hamilton's laboratory, and when you've done that, get a Level Four BioLab on emergency standby. Got all that?"

"Yes, ma'am."

"Then do it," the garrison commander said, and broke the connection.

Major Lott raised the cover of the alarm activation switch and then pressed on the switch. Sirens all over began to howl.

He then consulted the standing operating procedure to see what else was required of him to do—thus knocking over the first of the dominoes.

The provost marshal was notified. The first thing listed on his SOP was to lock down the fort. Nobody in. Nobody out. He did so. The second thing on his list was to notify the garrison medical facility to prepare for casualties. The third thing listed was to notify the Secret Service detachment on the base. He did so, and then continued to work down his list.

The first thing on the Secret Service Detachment SOP was to notify local law enforcement agencies. With Fort Detrick equidistant between Washington, D.C. (forty-five miles), and Baltimore, Maryland (forty-six miles), there was a large number of law enforcement agencies in that area, each of which was entitled to know of the problem at Fort Detrick.

The Secret Service agent instead first called his special agent in charge at the Department of Homeland Security at the Nebraska Avenue complex in the District of Columbia. He told him about the Potential Level Four Disaster, but had to confess that was all he knew.

"I'll handle it," the SAC said.

The Secret Service agent began calling the numbers on his list of law enforcement agencies to be notified.

The SAC at Homeland Security attempted to contact the secretary of Homeland Security but was told he was in Chicago with Mayor Daley. He then got the assistant secretary for enforcement on the telephone and told him about the Potential Level Four Disaster at Fort Detrick.

"I'll be damned," he said. "I'll handle it."

He contacted the garrison commander on a hotline.

"Assistant Homeland Security Secretary Andrews, Colonel," he said. "I understand you've got a little problem over there."

The garrison commander had by then spoken with Master Sergeant Dennis, who had told her about the container that had arrived with the morning FedEx shipment.

When she had told Andrews this, he said, "I'll take immediate action."

Andrews then called the SAC back, told him to get on the horn to his people at Detrick, and have them grab the container and not let anybody else near it.

"How's the quickest way for me to get there?" the assistant secretary asked.

"It would probably be quicker in one of our Yukons than trying to get a chopper, Mr. Secretary. I can have one at your door in ninety seconds."

"Do it."

Five and a half minutes later, a black Secret Service Yukon—red and blue lights flashing from behind its grille and with another magnet-based blue light flashing on the roof—skidded to a stop in front of the main building and picked up Assistant Secretary Andrews. The SAC was in the front seat, where the assistant secretary preferred to ride.

Andrews thought: *Ninety seconds, my ass.*

That took five minutes plus, and we need to roll.

"Get in the back," he said.

Only then did the assistant secretary remember he had had another option. He could have told the SAC to get out.

But it was too late. He took a seat in the second row and, siren screaming and lights flashing, they were on their way to the Potential Level Four Disaster at Fort Detrick.

[THREE]
Office of the Presidential Press Secretary
The White House
1600 Pennsylvania Avenue, N.W.
Washington, D.C.
1020 4 February 2007

There were a half-dozen television monitors mounted on the wall of John David "Porky" Parker's office, one for each of the major television networks, and the other three for the "major" cable news programs.

The sound of only one was on, the volume low but on.

Porky Parker was more or less addicted to watching/listening to Wolf News. Not because he liked it, but the opposite. He hated it. Wolf News gave him the most trouble. It seemed to be dedicated to the proposition that all politicians, from POTUS down, were scoundrels, mountebanks, and fools, and that it was Wolf News's noble duty to bring every proof—or suggestion—of this to the attention of the American people.

The problem was compounded for Porky by the fact that the people of Wolf News were very good at what they did, and with great skill went after the scoundrels, mountebanks, and fools regardless of political affiliation.

Wolf News used the fourth and final part of Gioacchino Antonio Rossini's (1792–1868) "William Tell Overture" to catch people's attention whenever there was "breaking news." Most people recognized the music as the theme for the *Lone Ranger* motion picture and television series.

That was happening now, and when Porky faintly heard the stirring music, he reached for the remote control as a Pavlovian reaction and raised his eyes to the screen. He had the sound turned up in time to see and hear the Wolf News anchor-on-duty proclaim, "There is breaking news! Wolf News is on top of it! Back in sixty seconds . . ."

There then followed a sixty-second commercial offering *The Wall Street Journal* delivered to one's home for only pennies a day.

Then the screen showed what looked like the scene of a major traffic accident. There were at least thirty police cars, all with their red and blue lights flashing. It had been taken from a helicopter. At the upper right corner of the screen, a message unnecessarily flashed, LIVE! LIVE! FROM A WOLF NEWS CHOPPER!

Porky was a second from muting the sound when the voice of the on-duty Wolf News anchor announced, "What we're looking at, from a Wolf News chopper, is the main gate of Fort Detrick, Maryland. We don't know, yet, what exactly is going on here. But we do know that the post has been closed down, nobody gets in or out, and that the director of the Central Intelligence Agency just choppered in and a 'senior official' of the Department of Homeland Security not yet identified just arrived in a vehicle with a screaming siren . . ."

In another Pavlovian reflex, Porky reached for his White House telephone and told the operator to get him the commanding general of Fort Detrick on a secure line.

"Colonel Russell."

"This is the White House switchboard. This line is secure. Mr. Parker wishes to speak with the commanding general."

"This is the garrison commander."

"Mr. Parker wishes to speak with the commanding general."

"We don't have a commanding general. I'm the senior officer, the garrison commander."

"One moment please."

"Colonel, this is John Parker, the President's press secretary."

"This is Colonel Florence Russell. What can I do for you, Mr. Parker?"

"What's going on down there?"

The garrison commander for a moment considered correcting the pompous political lackey with "What's going on *up* here, Porky. Fort Detrick is damn near due north of D.C. . . ." but instead said, "We have a Potential Level Four biological hazard disaster, Mr. Parker."

"What does that mean, exactly?"

"The operative word is 'potential.' We may have, repeat *may have*, a biological hazard disaster, Level Four. The most serious kind."

"What happened?"

"All I can tell you, Mr. Parker, is that our chief scientific officer, Colonel J. Porter Hamilton, has declared a Potential Level Four biological hazard disaster, and we have taken the necessary actions to deal with that."

"Colonel Russell, I repeat: What does that mean?"

"Per SOP, we have shut down the post, alerted the hospital, and notified the proper authorities. Until we hear from Colonel Hamilton, that's all we can do."

"May I speak with Colonel Hamilton, please?"

"I'm afraid that's not possible at the moment, Mr. Parker."

"Why not?"

"Colonel Hamilton is in Level Four BioLab Two."

"And there's no telephone in there?"

"There's a telephone. He's not answering it."

"Perhaps if you told him the White House is calling, he might change his mind."

"To do that, Mr. Parker, I would have to get him on the line. And he's not picking up."

"Can you tell me what he's doing?"

"I can tell you what I think he's doing. A package was delivered to him shortly before he declared the potential disaster. I think it's reasonable to presume he's examining the contents of that package."

"To what end, Colonel?"

"To see if what it contains justifies changing the current status from 'potential' to 'actual.' Or from 'Potential Level Four' to a lesser threat designation. We won't know until he tells us."

"The President, Colonel, is going to want to know."

"Colonel Hamilton is not answering the telephone in the laboratory, Mr. Parker."

"I understand DCI Powell is there."

"Yes, he is. Would you like to speak with him, Mr. Parker?"

"Not right now. Colonel, you understand that I'm going to have to tell the President that the only person who seems to know what's going on won't answer his telephone?"

"I suppose that's true," Colonel Russell said.

"I'll get back to you, Colonel," Parker said, and then feverishly tapped the switchhook in the telephone handset cradle to get the switchboard operator back on the line.

"Yes, Mr. Parker?"

"Get me DCI Powell."

"Powell."

"Mr. Parker is calling, Mr. Powell. The line is secure."

"Mr. Powell, John Parker. What the hell is going on over there?"

"John . . ." the director of Central Intelligence began, and then stopped. After a long moment, he resumed: "John, I was just about to call the President. I think it would be best if he decided what to tell you about this."

Parker heard the click that told him Powell had just broken the connection.

Porky Parker normally had unquestioned access to the President, anywhere, at any time. But now when he approached the door to the Oval Office, one of the two Secret Service men on duty put on an insincere smile and held up his hand to bar him.

The second Secret Service agent then opened the door, and called in, "Mr. President, Mr. Parker?"

Parker heard President Clendennen's impatient reply: "Not now."

Then he heard another male voice: "Mr. President, may I respectfully suggest that we're going to need Parker."

After a moment, Parker recognized the voice as that of Ambassador Charles M. Montvale, the director of National Intelligence.

There was a brief pause, and then Clendennen, even more impatiently, drawled, "All right. Let him in."

The Secret Service agent at the door waved Parker into the Oval Office.

The President was at his desk, slumped back in his high-backed blue leather-upholstered judge's chair. Ambassador Montvale was sitting in an armchair looking up at the wall-mounted television monitor. Secretary of State Natalie Cohen was sitting sideward on the couch facing Montvale, also looking at the television.

The President looked at Parker and pointed to the television. Parker moved to the opposite wall, leaned on it, and looked up at the television.

Surprising Parker not at all, the President was watching Wolf News.

There was a flashing banner across the bottom on the screen: BREAKING NEWS! BREAKING NEWS!

The Wolf News anchor-on-duty was sitting at his desk, facing C. Harry Whelan, Jr. A banner read: C. HARRY WHELAN, JR., WOLF NEWS DISTINGUISHED CONTRIBUTOR.

Whelan was answering a question, and although he hadn't heard it, Parker knew what the question was: "What's going on at Fort Detrick?"

"Well, of course I don't *know*, Steven," C. Harry Whelan, Jr., said, somewhat pontifically, "but it seems to me, with the director of Central Intelligence there—plus that unnamed senior official from Homeland Security—that the situation there, whatever it is, is under control. If I had to hazard a guess, I would say we have a case of high-level arf-arf."

"'Arf-arf,' Harry?"

"You don't know the term?" Whelan asked, surprised.

The anchor-on-duty shook his head.

"Well, far be it from me to suggest anything at all that would cast any aspersion whatever on my good friend, Central Intelligence Agency Director Jack Powell—or for that matter on the unidentified senior Homeland Security official—but, hypothetically speaking, if President Clendennen had two dogs— say, a Labrador and a cocker spaniel—and they started chasing their tails, the sound they would be making would be *arf-arf.*"

The camera paused for a moment on Mr. Whelan's face—he looked very pleased with himself—and then a picture of the front page of *The Wall Street Journal* replaced it and a voice-over deeply intoned, *"For only pennies a day . . ."*

The screen went black.

"I hate that sonofabitch," President Clendennen said.

A full thirty seconds later, Porky Parker broke the silence: "May I ask what's going on at Fort Detrick?"

President Clendennen glared at him.

Secretary of State Natalie Cohen came to his rescue.

"Mr. President, you're either going to have to make a statement, or have Jack make one in your name."

"That might prove to be difficult, Madam Secretary," President Clendennen said sarcastically, "as we don't seem to have the first goddamn clue about what's going on at Fort Detrick."

He let that sink in, and then went on: "And if what the DCI has just told me is true, I don't think we should broadcast that little gem from the White House."

"Mr. President, what exactly did DCI Powell say?" Ambassador Montvale asked.

"He said this colonel had gotten word to him that he 'strongly suspects' that the attack we made on the quote unquote Fish Farm in the Congo—the attack that brought us this close"—he held his thumb and index fingers perhaps a quarter of an inch apart—"to a nuclear exchange—did not kill all the fishes."

"You're talking about Colonel Hamilton, Mr. President?" Montvale asked.

The President nodded.

"How could he know that?"

"That's what Powell said; that he got a message to that effect from Hamilton."

"What does Hamilton say?"

"He's not answering his telephone," the President said bitterly, then picked up his telephone.

"Get me Powell," he ordered, and then, not twenty seconds later, said, "Is he still not answering his phone?"

There was a short reply.

"The minute he comes out of that laboratory, put him in your helicopter and bring him here."

He put the telephone handset into its cradle.

"And now we wait," Clendennen said. "The President of the United States, the secretary of State, and the director of National Intelligence wait for some lousy colonel to find time for us. . . ."

[FOUR]
U.S. Army Medical Research Institute
Fort Detrick, Maryland
1035 4 February 2007

Colonel J. Porter Hamilton, Medical Corps, U.S. Army, came through the outer portal of Level Four BioLab Two wearing only a bathrobe. The crest of the United States Military Academy was on the breast, and the legend WEST POINT was on the back.

He found in the room the garrison commander, the director of Central Intelligence, the assistant secretary of Homeland Security, the special agent in charge at the Department of Homeland Security, the Fort Detrick provost marshal, two Secret Service agents, and Master Sergeant Dennis.

"You'll have to pardon my appearance, Colonel Russell," Colonel Hamilton said.

"Not a problem, Colonel," Colonel Florence Russell replied.

Hamilton turned to DCI Powell, and said, "I can only surmise that those people relayed my message to you."

Powell nodded.

"Colonel, my name is Mason Andrews. I'm the assistant secretary of Homeland Security. I would be grateful—"

"First things first," Hamilton interrupted. "Sergeant Dennis, could I impose upon you to take your car and get me a uniform from my quarters? I'm afraid the keys to my car are in there, in my uniform."

"Way ahead of you, Colonel," Dennis said. "Fresh uniform's in the lobby. I'll go get it."

"Good man," Hamilton said. "Mr. Powell and I will be in the locker room."

He looked at Colonel Russell. "Colonel, would it offend you if I suggested that you come with us? You could turn your back while I dress."

"Not at all," she said.

"The President's really curious about what's going on here, Colonel," DCI Powell said. "He wants to see you at the White House. There's a helicopter—"

"Would you prefer to wait until we're at the White House?" Hamilton said. "I have to bring Colonel Russell up to speed on this before I go anywhere."

"I'll go with you and Colonel Russell," Powell said.

"So will I," Assistant Secretary Andrews said.

"I think not," Hamilton said.

"Excuse me?" Andrews bristled.

"I can tell you what you need to know right here: There is no immediate threat." He turned to the provost marshal, and added, "As soon as you can, you're to establish a guard around, one, where the package was originally examined; two, my office; and three, this building, to which no one is to enter without the specific approval of myself, Master Sergeant Dennis, or of course Colonel Russell. And you may lift the shut-down. Colonel Russell will have more details after we have spoken."

"Yes, sir," the provost marshal said.

"You had better impound the golf cart on which the package was moved— bring it and the two security people who drove it here. Dennis will see to their bath. Just a precaution. Better safe than sorry, I always say."

Master Sergeant Dennis came back into the room carrying a plastic bag in his prosthetic hand. He handed it to Hamilton.

"Good man," Hamilton said as he took it. Then he said, "Dennis, they are going to bring the golf cart and the security drivers here. See that they get a complete bath. Then do the same to the golf cart."

"Yes, sir."

"Colonel Russell, Mr. Powell, if you'll be good enough to come with me?"

"Am I correctly inferring, Colonel, that I was not included in that invitation?" Mason Andrews asked icily. He didn't wait for Hamilton to reply, and— obviously on the edge of losing his temper—went on: "Perhaps you didn't hear me, Colonel, when I told you that I am the assistant secretary of Homeland Security."

If he had intended to cow Hamilton, he failed.

"Mr. Secretary . . . or is it Mr. Assistant Secretary?" Hamilton replied. "I know that Mr. Powell is cleared for this sort of information. I don't know how much the President wants you to know. I am not about to risk the ire of the President by telling you any more than I already have."

Andrews flared: "Now, goddamn it, you listen to me, *Colonel*—"

"Mr. Andrews," DCI Powell interrupted, "why don't you let the President settle this? You're welcome to ride with us to the White House."

The assistant secretary of Homeland Security took a moment to get his temper under control.

"Perhaps that would be best," he said finally. "Thank you."

[FIVE]
The Oval Office
The White House
1600 Pennsylvania Avenue, N.W.
Washington, D.C.
1205 4 February 2007

"Thank you for coming so quickly, Colonel," President Clendennen said.

The sarcasm was lost on Hamilton.

"I came as quickly as I could, Mr. President," Hamilton said.

"I know. You were on Wolf. We all saw you both taking off from Fort Detrick and landing here. And we all saw C. Harry Whelan, Jr., tell his several million viewers he believes you were coming here to deliver the bad news. Please tell me he's wrong."

"Actually, Mr. President, it's a mixed bag. The news could be much, much worse."

"Well," Clendennen drawled, pronouncing the word *whale*, "tell me the good news."

"There is no cause for immediate alarm. I told Colonel Russell what was necessary for her to do, and that once she had done that, she could lift the shut-down. I have changed the Potential Level Four Biological Hazard Disaster to Level Two Biological Hazard Incident."

"What does that mean, exactly?"

"That, in my judgment, there is reason to believe that all Congo-X under my control is contained in a safe environment, and there is no immediate risk to the general public."

"'Congo-X'? What is that?"

"It is what I call this virus. Or organism. Or whatever it is. What I brought from the Congo just before the Fish Farm was attacked."

"Which is it, an organism or a virus?"

"I'm afraid I don't really know, sir. More than like a combination of both. An 'organismus,' perhaps. Or a 'virusism.' Those are terms I made up in the last week or ten days. There is no scientific terminology that I know of to describe Congo-X."

"Colonel," Press Secretary John D. Parker said, "did I understand you to say there is no immediate danger to the public?"

"I was speaking with the colonel, Parker," the President said unpleasantly.

"Mr. President, if the colonel can assure us that there is no immediate danger to the public, I think—to counter that comment of C. Harry Whelan, Jr., on Wolf News—you should make a statement to that effect. And as soon as possible. Immediately. We really have to control this before it gets out of hand."

The President glared at Parker.

"Mr. President," Ambassador Montvale put in, "I think Porky's right."

Parker glared at Montvale, which wasn't lost on the President.

"What do you think I should say, Porky?" Clendennen asked.

"Mr. President, if you make any statement, it carries great importance. I mean to suggest that it will give the impression that this situation is more serious than the colonel suggests it is."

"In other words, you want to make the statement?"

"That would be my recommendation, Mr. President."

"I agree with Porky," Ambassador Montvale said.

"That makes it twice, doesn't it?" the President asked, and then went on: "And what would you say, Parker?"

"Sir, something along the lines of this: 'There was an incident early this morning at Fort Detrick that has attracted a good deal of media attention. The President has just spoken with the chief scientific officer at Fort Detrick, who has assured him there is no cause for concern. What it was was the routine triggering of a safety system, erring on the side of caution. To repeat, there is no cause for concern.' Something like that, Mr. President."

The President was thoughtful for a long moment. Then he asked, "Read that back, please."

A female voice came over a loudspeaker and recited Parker's suggested statement.

"At the end of the first sentence, where it says 'has attracted a good deal of media attention,' strike that and change it to 'has apparently caused much of the media to start chasing its tail once again. *Arf-arf.*" The rest of it is fine. Type that up for Mr. Parker."

"Are you sure you want to do that, Mr. President?" Secretary of State Natalie Cohen asked.

The President ignored her, and gestured for Parker to leave the office. Then he turned to Hamilton.

"Okay, Colonel. Now let's have the bad news."

Hamilton inhaled audibly before he began to speak.

"I think we have to presume, Mr. President, that the attack on the establishment—the laboratory-slash-manufacturing facility—in the Congo was not successful. There is a quantity—I have no idea how much—of Congo-X in unknown hands."

"How do you know that?" the President asked, softly.

"Because a quantity of it—several kilograms, plus another several kilograms of infected tissue—was delivered to me at Fort Detrick this morning. It is identical to the Congo-X and the infected tissue I brought out of the Congo."

"Where did it come from?" the President asked, then interrupted himself: "No. Tell me what this stuff—Congo-X—is and what it does."

"I don't know what it *is*. I'm working on that. As to what it *does*, it causes disseminated intravascular coagulation, acronym DIC."

"And can you tell me what that means? In layman's terms?"

"DIC is a thrombohemorrhagic disorder characterized by primary thrombotic and secondary hemorrhagic diathesis, usually fatal."

"Try it again, Colonel," the President ordered, not unpleasantly, "and this time in layman's terms."

"Yes, sir. DIC is sometimes called consumptive coagulopathy, since excessive intravascular coagulation leads to consumption of platelets and nonenzymatic coagulation factors—"

The President interrupted Hamilton by holding up his hand and shaking his head.

"You might as well be speaking Greek, Colonel. Try it again, please, keeping in mind that you're dealing with a simple country boy from Alabama."

"Yes, sir," Hamilton said, paused in thought, and then announced, almost happily: "Sir, DIC causes coagulation to run amok."

"Coagulation, as in blood?"

Hamilton nodded.

"Go down that road, Colonel, and see where it takes us," the President said.

"Coagulation is the process, in this connection, which causes liquid human blood to turn into a soft, semisolid mass."

He looked at the President to see if the President was still with him.

The President responded by smiling encouragingly, and making a gesture with both hands for him to continue.

"If you think of the vascular system of the body, Mr. President, as a series of interconnected garden hoses, and of the heart as a pump that pushes blood through that system."

He paused to see if his student was still with him, and when the President nodded, went on: "Imagine, if you will, sir, that the blood is transformed into a very thick mud. The pump cannot push the mass through the vascular system. It is overwhelmed; it stops."

"And death occurs? By what a layman might call a heart attack?"

"That, too, Mr. President," Hamilton said.

"'That, too'?" the President parroted.

"The mud, the now-coagulated blood, then begins to attack the garden hose. As sort of a parasite. It feeds on it, so to speak."

"Eats it, you mean?"

Hamilton nodded. "And when it's finished, so to speak, with the vascular system, it begins to feed on the other tissues of the body. In some sort of unusual enzymatic manner, which I have so far been unable to pin down."

"You'd better run that past me again, Colonel," the President said. "'Enzymatic manner'?"

Hamilton considered for a moment the level of knowledge the President might have.

"Think of meat tenderizer, Mr. President. Do you know how that works?"

"I can't say that I do," Clendennen confessed.

"Meat—and that would of course include human flesh—is held together by a complex protein called collagen. This makes it quite tough to chew in the raw state."

"I've noticed," the President drawled dryly.

"Cooking destroys these proteins, making the meat chewable. But so does contact with certain enzymes, most commonly ones extracted from the papaya. These proteolytic enzymes break the peptide bonds between the amino acids found in complex proteins. Such as flesh."

"What you're saying is that Congo-X is some sort of meat tenderizer?" the President asked. "Why is that so dangerous?"

"Unlike the enzymatic tenderizers one finds in the supermarket, which lose their strength after attacking the peptide bonding between the amino acids of meat, the Congo-X enzymes—if they are indeed enzymes, and I am not yet prepared to make that call—seem to gather strength from the collagens they attack. In a manner of speaking, they are nurtured by it."

"What happens when they run out of meat?" the President asked, and then corrected himself: "Out of something to eat?"

Hamilton didn't answer directly.

"Grocery store tenderizer doesn't work on bones," he said. "Congo-X does. Whenever it finishes turning the meat into sort of a mush—perhaps strengthened by taking nutrition from that process—it attacks bones. They are turned into mush. When the entire process is completed, what is left is a semisolid residue, which then enters sort of a coma. Forgive the crudeness, Mr. President, but what remains bears a strong physical resemblance to what one might pass when suffering from diarrhea: a semisolid brown, or brownish black, mass."

"And what happens to that?"

"It apparently receives enough nutrients from the atmosphere to maintain life—I hesitate to use that term but I cannot think of another—for an indefinite period. If it is touched by flesh, the process begins again."

"The only way it is contagious, so to speak, is if there's physical contact with it? Is that what you're saying?"

"When it is in the dormant, coma stage, yes, sir. But when it is feeding, so to speak, on flesh, it gives off microscopic particles which, if inhaled, also start the degenerative process."

"How can it be killed?"

"My initial tests suggest the only way it can be killed is by thorough incineration at temperatures over a thousand degrees Centigrade. The residue, I am coming to believe, may then be encased in a nonporous container. Glass or some type of ceramic would work, I think, but there one would have the risk of the glass or ceramic breaking. Aluminum seems to form a satisfactory barrier. As a matter of fact, I used simple aluminum foil to isolate the material I brought out of the Congo; I had nothing else. And the Congo-X material that was sent to my laboratory today was wrapped in aluminum foil."

"Like a Christmas turkey?" President Clendennen asked.

"More like, I would say, Mr. President, cold cuts from a delicatessen. Very carefully, so there was little or no risk that the foil could be torn. The people who sent me the Congo-X obviously seem to know what they are doing."

"And who, would you guess, Colonel, were the people who sent you the Congo-X? More importantly, why do you think they did?"

"I've given that some thought, Mr. President," Hamilton said.

"And?"

The tone of impatience in the President's voice was clearly evident.

"They wanted us to know that the attack on the Fish Farm was unsuccessful," Hamilton said. "That they have Congo-X. We have to presume they know a great deal more about it than I have been able to learn in the few days I've had to work with it. They are making the point that the threat which existed before we learned of the Fish Farm and attempted to destroy it exists now."

"Why wouldn't they try to keep that secret, so they would have the element of surprise if they decide to use Congo-X on us?"

"That's the question to which I have given the most thought," Hamilton said. "It was self-evident that they wanted us to know we failed, and that they have Congo-X. The question is, why?"

"That's the question I asked, Colonel," the President said.

"I think they want something from us," Hamilton said, very seriously.

"And what, Colonel, do you think that might be?"

"I have no idea," Hamilton said. "Absolutely no idea."

President Clendennen looked around the Oval Office.

The Honorable Natalie Cohen, secretary of State; Ambassador Charles M. Montvale, director of National Intelligence; the Honorable John J. Powell, director of the Central Intelligence Agency; and the Honorable Mason Andrews, assistant secretary of the Department of Homeland Security, were sitting on the chairs and couches around a glass-topped coffee table. Not one had said a word during the "bad news" exchange between the President and Colonel Hamilton.

"Odd," Clendennen said to them. "I would have bet two bits to a doughnut that y'all would be falling all over yourselves to offer sage political advice and profound philosophical opinions concerning our little dilemma."

No one responded.

The President grunted, then announced: "One, I believe everything Colonel Hamilton has told us about this terrible substance. Two, we are not about to react to this threat the way my predecessor did. We bombed everything in a twenty-square-mile area of the Congo into small pieces and then incinerated the pieces. Since somebody still has enough of a supply of this stuff to share it with us, I think we have to concede that the only thing that bombing did was bring us within a cat's whisker of a nuclear exchange and give those people who don't like us much anyway good reason to like us even less.

"So what we're going to do now is proceed very carefully and only when we're absolutely sure of what we're doing. I will now entertain suggestions as to how we can do this." He paused, and then went on: "You first, Andrews."

There was no immediate reply.

"Well?" the President pursued, not very pleasantly.

"Mr. President," Mason Andrews said. "In addition to the obvious, I think we have—"

"What's the obvious?" the President interrupted.

"Well, we have to decide whether we are going to raise the threat level to orange, or perhaps red. I tend to think the latter."

"Not '*we* have to decide,'" the President said. "*I* have to decide. Somebody tell me why raising the threat level from yellow wouldn't cause more problems than it would solve."

He looked around the Oval Office. "Comments? Anyone?"

There were none.

"What else is obvious?" the President demanded.

"Well, sir, we have to find out who sent this stuff to the colonel," Andrews said.

"First of all, it wasn't sent to Colonel Hamilton," the President said. "It was sent to us. The government. Me, as President. Not to Colonel Hamilton. It was sent *through* him because these bastards somehow knew he was the only man around who would know what it was. And they knew he would tell me. Secondly, at this moment—and I realize this could change in the blink of an eye—there is no immediate threat. If these people wanted to start killing Americans, they would have already done so."

"Mr. President," Ambassador Montvale offered, "their intention might be to cause panic."

Clendennen nodded.

"That's what I'm thinking. And I'm not going to give them that. That's why the threat level stays at yellow."

The President was then silent, visibly in thought, for a long moment. Then he cocked his head to one side. A smile crossed his lips, as if to signify he was pleased with himself.

He said, "Fully aware that this is politically incorrect, I have just profiled the bastards who sent Colonel Hamilton the Congo-X. I have decided that the Congo-X was sent to the colonel by a foreign power, or at the direction of a foreign power or powers. And not, for example, by the Rotary Club of Enterprise, Alabama, or any sister or brother organization to which the Rotarians may be connected, however remotely."

Ambassador Montvale's eyes widened, and for a moment he seemed to be on the edge of saying something. In the end, he remained silent.

"The ramifications of this decision," the President went on, "are that finding out who these bastards are—and, it is to be hoped, what the hell this is all about—falls into what I think of as the CIA's area of responsibility, rather than that of the FBI or the Department of Homeland Security."

He looked at DCI Powell.

"Those are your marching orders, Jack. Get onto it. I will have the attorney general direct the FBI to assist you in any area in which you need help."

"Mr. President, with all respect," Mason Andrews said, "this crime, this threat to American security, took place on American soil! This situation is clearly within the purview of Homeland Sec—"

"What situation, Andrews?" the President interrupted him. "What threat to American security? No one has been hurt. What's happened is that a securely wrapped package of what the colonel has determined to be what he calls Congo-X was sent to Colonel Hamilton in a container clearly marked as a biological hazard.

"That's all. There has been no damage to anyone. Not even a threat of causing damage. If we had these people in handcuffs, there's nothing we could do to them because they haven't broken any laws that I can think of.

"What we are not, repeat *not*, going to do is go off half-cocked. For example, we are not going to resurrect my predecessor's private James Bond—what's his name? Costello?—and his band of assassins and give them carte blanche to roam the world to kill people. Or anything like that.

"What we are going to do is have Montvale—he *is* the director of National Intelligence—very quietly try to find out who the hell these bastards are and what they want. I think Colonel Hamilton is right about that. They want something. That means they will probably—almost certainly—contact Colonel Hamilton again.

"What that means, since we can't afford to have anything happen to him, is that Homeland Security is going to wrap the colonel in a Secret Service security blanket at least as thick as the one around me. That's your role in this, Andrews. That's your only role.

"And then we're going to wait for their next move. No action of any kind will be taken without my express approval."

The President met the eyes of everyone in the Oval Office, and then quietly asked, "Is there anyone who doesn't understand what I have just said?"

There were no replies.

"That will be all, thank you," the President said.

IV

The silver, two-month-old, top-of-the-line Mercedes-Benz S550 drove regally across the Szabadság híd, and on the other side of the Danube River turned left toward the Hotel Gellért, which was at the foot of the Gellért Hill.

Budapest, which began as two villages, Buda and Pest, on opposite sides of the Danube River, had a long and bloody history. Gellért Hill, for example, got its name from Saint Gerard Gellert, an Italian bishop from Venice whom the pagans ceremoniously murdered there in 1046 A.D. for trying to bring the natives to Jesus.

Buda and Pest were both destroyed by the Mongols, who invaded the area in 1241. The villages were rebuilt, only to suffer rape and ethnic cleansing when the Ottoman Turks came, conquering Pest in 1526 and Buda fifteen years later.

By the time the Szabadság híd was built in 1894–96, the villages had been combined into Budapest, and Hungary had become part of the Austro-Hungarian Empire. Emperor Franz Josef personally inserted the last rivet—a silver rivet—into the new bridge and then with imperial immodesty named the structure after himself.

The bridge itself was dropped—like all the other bridges across the Danube—into the river when the Russians and the Germans fought over Hungary during the Second World War. It was the first bridge rebuilt after the war by the Soviet-controlled government and named the Liberty Bridge. When the Russians were finally evicted, it became the Freedom Bridge.

The silver Mercedes-Benz turned off the road running alongside the Danube and onto the access road to the Hotel Gellért, then stopped.

Gustav, a barrel-chested man in his fifties who appeared to be a chauffeur but served as a bodyguard and more, got quickly out from behind the wheel and opened the rear passenger door.

A tall man, who looked to be in his midsixties, got out. He adjusted a broad-brimmed jet-black hat—one side of the brim down, the other rakishly up—and then turned back to the car, bending over, leaning into the car. When he came out, he had two Bouvier des Flandres dogs.

The larger, a bitch, was several times the size of a very large boxer. The other was her son, a puppy, on a leash. The puppy was about the size of a small boxer.

As the man had taken them from the car, another burly man in his sixties had gotten out the other side of the car, carrying an ermine-collared black leather overcoat.

The burly man's name was Sándor Tor. In his youth, Tor had done a hitch—rising to sergeant—in the French Foreign Legion. On his return to Budapest, he had become a policeman. He had been recruited into the ÁVH, the Államvédelmi Hatóság, Hungary's hated secret police, and again had risen to sergeant.

When the Russians had been driven from Budapest, and known members of the Államvédelmi Hatóság were being spat on and hung, Mussolini-style, en masse from any convenient streetlight, Tor had found sanctuary in the American embassy.

And only then had the CIA revealed to the new leaders of Hungary the identity of the man who had not only saved the lives of so many anti-Communists and resistance leaders—by warning them, via the CIA, that the ÁVH was onto them—but also had been one of the rare—and certainly the most reliable—sources of information about the inner workings of the ÁVH, which he'd gained at great risk to his life from his trusted position within the secret police.

Thus, the best that Sándor Tor could have hoped for had he been exposed was a quick death from ÁVH torture rather than a slow one.

Tor was decorated by the Hungarian government and appointed as inspector of police.

But that, despite having triumphed over the forces of evil, didn't turn out to be a movie scenario in which he lived happily ever after.

There were several facets of this. For one, his peers in the police, reasoning that if he had been keeping a record of the unsavory activities of the ÁVH, it was entirely likely that he would keep a record of theirs, both feared and shunned him.

And Tor didn't like being a cop without an agenda. He had done what he had done not only because he hated the Communists generally, but specifically because his mother and father and two brothers had been slowly strangled to death in the basement of the ÁVH headquarters at Andrássy út 60.

Getting back at the Communists was one thing; spending long hours trying to arrest burglars—for that matter, even murderers—was something else.

And his wife, Margo, had cancer. They had had no children.

He applied for early retirement and it was quickly granted.

Sitting around the apartment with nothing to do but watch cancer work its cruelty on Margo was difficult.

Then Tor heard of the return to Budapest of the German firm Gossinger Beteiligungsgesellschaft, G.m.b.H. The company's intention was to reclaim the properties—farms, a brewery, several vineyards, a newspaper business, and other assets—seized from them by the Communists.

He also heard they were looking for someone to head their security.

After he filled out an application form at Gossinger G.m.b.H's newly reopened downtown offices, he heard nothing for three weeks, and had decided that they weren't interested in his services.

Then there was a telephone call saying that if he was still interested, a car would pick him up in an hour, and take him for an interview. He almost didn't go; Margo had insisted and he went.

The car—a new, top-of-the-line Mercedes with Vienna plates—took him to the legendary Hotel Gellért, at Szent Gellért tér 1, overlooking the Danube River from the Gellért Hill.

Tor thought he would be interviewed, probably in the restaurant or the bar, by a personnel officer of the Gossinger organization. Instead, he was led to the elevator which carried him to a top floor apartment, overlooking the Danube, which apparently occupied that entire corner of the building.

An interior door opened and an enormous dog came out, walked to him, sniffed him, then sat down. Normally, Tor was not afraid of dogs. But this one frightened him. He thought it had to weigh well over fifty kilos. Even when the dog offered his paw, he thought carefully before squatting to take it.

"You come well recommended," said a voice in Hungarian with a Budapester accent. "Max usually shows his teeth to people he doesn't like. Often they wet their pants."

Tor had looked up to see a tall silver-haired man who seemed to be in his sixties standing in the doorway.

"My name is Eric Kocian," the man said. "Come in. We'll talk and have a drink."

He opened the door wide and waved Tor inside a spacious and well-furnished apartment.

Kocian walked to a sideboard and turned, holding a bottle in his hand.

"Wild Turkey Rare Breed all right with you?" he asked.

"I don't know what it is," Tor confessed.

"One of the very few things the Americans do superbly is make bourbon whisky. This is one of the better bourbon whiskys. My godson gave me a case for my seventy-seventh birthday."

Seventy-seventh birthday? Tor had thought. *My God, he's that old?*

"Sir, I don't know. I'm supposed to be interviewed for a job."

"And so you are. Don't you drink?"

"Yes, sir. I drink."

"Good. My experience has been you can't trust people who don't."

Kocian poured him a large, squarish glass half-full of the bourbon whisky. "This is what they call 'sipping whisky.' But if you want water and ice . . ." Kocian pointed to the sideboard.

"This is fine, thank you," Tor said.

"May I ask about your wife? How is she?"

How does he know about my Margo?

"Not very well, I'm afraid."

Kocian waved him into a leather-upholstered armchair and seated himself in an identical chair facing it.

"If you decide to take this position," Kocian announced, "she will be covered under our medical care program. Most German physicians are insufferably arrogant, and tend to regard their patients as laboratory specimens, but they seem to know what they're doing. Maybe they'll have answers you haven't been able to find here."

"Am I being offered the position?" Tor asked, on the cusp of incredulity.

"I have one or two other quick questions first," Kocian said.

"Quick questions? But you don't know anything about me."

"I know just about everything about you that interests me," Kocian said. "Are you still on the CIA's payroll?"

"I was never on their payroll," Tor said.

"That's not what I have been led to understand."

"I never took a cent. If I had been exposed, they promised to try to get Margo out of Hungary and give her some sort of pension, but . . ."

"You thought before the ÁVH arrested you, they would have arrested her for her value in your interrogation, so you didn't give it much thought?"

Tor nodded.

"I would have to have your word that you would no longer cooperate with the CIA in any way."

"I haven't talked to anyone in the CIA for over a year."

"That wasn't my question."

"I can promise you that," Tor said. "No cooperation with the CIA."

"Welcome to the executive ranks of Gossinger Beteiligungsgesellschaft, G.m.b.H."

"Just like that?" Tor asked, and then blurted, "We haven't even talked about what I'm going to do. Or how much—"

"What you are going to do is relieve me of keeping Hungarian fingers out of my cash box, prying eyes out of any part of our business, provide such other security as I deem necessary, and keep Otto Görner off my back. So far as compensation is concerned, I suggest that twice what you were being paid as an inspector would be a reasonable starting salary. There are of course some 'perks,' as my godson would say. Including an expense account and a car."

Tor knew that Otto Görner was the managing director of the Gossinger Beteiligungsgesellschaft, G.m.b.H., empire.

But who is this godson?

"You've mentioned your godson twice. Where does he fit in here?"

"His name is Karl Wilhelm von und zu Gossinger. You're a policeman. Is that enough of a clue for you?"

Tor chuckled.

"You know who Otto Görner is?"

Tor nodded.

"Otto has the odd notion that I have to be protected from myself and others, in particular the Russians. He has managed to convince my godson of this nonsense. It will be your job to convince both of them that you are doing so while at the same time making sure that whomever you charge with protecting me from the Russians and myself are invisible to me."

"Yes, sir."

"Let me top that off," Kocian said.

Tor looked at his glass and was surprised to see that it was nearly empty. He didn't remember taking one sip.

Sándor Tor had been director of security for Gossinger Beteiligungsgesellschaft, G.m.b.H. (Hungary), for six months when Margo died.

The doctors in Germany, with great regret, had been unable to do anything for her. When it was apparent the end was near, Margo asked to be returned from Berlin to Budapest so that she could die in her own bed.

Eric Kocian and a medical team from Telki Private Hospital—Budapest's best—were waiting with an ambulance at the Keleti Pályaudvar railway station. Staff from the kitchen of the Hotel Gellért was waiting at the Tor apartment.

Margo died at four in the morning the next day. At the time, her husband was asleep in a chair at one side of her bed and Eric Kocian was asleep in another chair on the other side of the bed.

Margo was buried the next day, beside Sándor's mother and father in the Farkasréti Cemetery in Buda (the western part of Budapest). Tor had found—not without great effort—where their Communist murderers had disposed of their bodies, and had them exhumed and reinterred in the Farkasréti Cemetery. He never learned what had happened to the bodies of his murdered brothers.

When Margo's crypt had been cemented closed, Eric Kocian had said, "You don't want to go back to your apartment. Come with me and we'll have a drink."

They had gone to the Hotel Gellért and stayed drunk together for four days.

Sometime during that period, Sándor had realized that while he might now be alone in the world except for his employer/friend Eric Kocian, Eric Kocian was similarly alone in the world, except for his godson, whom he apparently rarely saw, and his friend/employee Sándor Tor.

Early in the morning of their fifth day together, Sándor Tor led Eric Kocian to the thermal baths—built by the Romans—below the hotel where they soaked, had a massage, and soaked again. And then they had a haircut and shave.

At noon, they were at work.

Sándor returned only once to the apartment he had shared with Margo. He selected the furniture he wanted to keep, and had it moved to the Gellért, where Kocian had arranged an apartment for him on the floor below his own.

Sándor Tor draped the ermine-collared black leather overcoat over Eric Kocian's shoulders.

The bitch, who answered to the name Mädchen, headed for a row of shrubbery to meet the call of nature. Kocian led the puppy, named Max, to the shrubbery.

"You and Gustav go to bed," Kocian ordered. "I'll see you in the morning."

Tor got back in the Mercedes, which then carried him to the hotel entrance. When Gustav had parked the car—a spot near the door was reserved for it—he followed Tor into the hotel lobby. Gustav got on the elevator to check the apartment out before Kocian got there, and Tor walked to a column and stood behind it in a position from which he could watch Kocian enter the lobby and get on the elevator.

Kocian came through the door four minutes later and walked toward the elevator bank.

A tall, well-dressed man who had been sitting in an armchair reading the *Budapester Tages Zeitung* suddenly dropped the newspaper to the floor and walked quickly to where Kocian was waiting for the elevator.

Where in the name of the goddamn Virgin Mary and all the fucking saints did that sonofabitch come from?

Tor had almost made it to the bank of elevators when the door opened. Gustav saw him coming and stopped, then stepped back against the elevator's rear wall.

Kocian, Mädchen, and Max got on the elevator.

Tor followed.

"I thought I told you to go to bed," Kocian said.

Tor took a Micro Uzi from his under-the-arm holster, held it at his side, and then pushed the button which would send the elevator to the top floor.

"I mean Herr Kocian no harm," the tall, well-dressed man said in German, and then repeated it in Hungarian.

The elevator door closed, and the elevator began to rise.

"Pat him," Tor ordered, now raising the muzzle of the Micro Uzi.

Gustav quickly, but unhurriedly, thoroughly frisked the tall, well-dressed man.

"Nothing," Gustav said, referring to weapons. But he now held a Russian diplomatic passport, a Hungarian foreign ministry–issued diplomat's carnet (a plastic-sealed card about the size of a driver's license), and a business-size envelope.

He examined the carnet, saw that it read, COMMERCIAL COUNSELOR, RUS-SIAN EMBASSY, and then handed the carnet to Tor.

"Actually, I'm Colonel Vladlen Solomatin of the Sluzhba Vneshney Raz-vedki," the tall, well-dressed man then said in Hungarian, and for the third time said, "I mean Herr Kocian no harm."

"You're from the Sluzhba Vneshney Razvedki?" Kocian asked in Russian.

"It's the Foreign Intelligence Service of the Russian Federation," Colonel Solomatin said. "Yes, I am."

"I know what the SVR is, Colonel," Kocian said.

The elevator door opened.

Kocian looked over his shoulder to make sure there was no one in the land-ing foyer, and then backed out of the elevator, motioning for Solomatin to follow him.

"Put the elevator out of service," Kocian ordered.

"I mean you no harm, Herr Kocian," Solomatin said again.

"You keep saying that," Kocian replied. "What is it you do want from me, Colonel Vladlen Solomatin of the Sluzhba Vneshney Razvedki?"

"A service, sir. Your help in righting a great wrong."

"Specifically?"

Solomatin turned to the chauffeur, who was still holding Solomatin's diplomatic passport and the envelope. He reached for the envelope.

"May I?" he asked.

Gustav looked to Kocian for guidance. Kocian nodded, and Gustav allowed Solomatin to take the envelope.

Solomatin removed a letter from the envelope and extended them to Kocian.

"I am asking that you get this to Colonel Berezovsky. Or Lieutenant Colonel Alekseeva."

Kocian read the letter:

Sluzhba Vneshney Razvedki

1 February 2007

Yasenevo 11, Kolpachny
Moscow 0101000
Tel: Moscow 923 6213
Second Directorate
Colonel V. N. Solomatin

My Dear Cousin Dmitri:

   God's blessings and the warmest greetings to you, Lora, Sof'ya and Svetlana!!

I am very happy to be able to tell you that the committee has finally reached the only conclusions that they could in the circumstances:

(1) That the charges of embezzlement of state funds laid against you and Svetlana were without any basis in fact.

(2) That the late Colonel Evgeny Evgenyvich Alekseev, who laid the charges against you both, was at the time bereft of his senses, more than likely suffering from paranoia and had been so suffering for a considerable period of time, possibly as much as a year or even longer.

(3) That while it was clearly the responsibility of the both of you to bring your suspicions regarding Colonel Alekseev's instability to the attention of General Yakov Sirinov, your failure to do so in the circumstances, and your vacating your posts without authority, was understandable.

Other points made during the committee hearing by General Sirinov put to rest once and for all the allegation that you defected. "If they intended to defect," the general said, "they would not have left with only the clothing on their backs and what cash they had in their pockets. And if they had wound up in the hands of MI6 or the CIA, even involuntarily, you know our people would have told us."

At the conclusion of the committee hearing, General Sirinov was ordered to do whatever was necessary to locate you, make you aware of what has happened, and to bring you home.

He has delegated that responsibility to me, telling the committee that if he were you or Svetlana, the only person he would trust would be me. I have been given the authority to take any steps I consider necessary.

Embassies of the Russian Federation worldwide have been directed to provide you with whatever you need, including funds, and to facilitate your return to the Motherland.

> In this connection, when I suggested to General Sirinov that, considering what injustices had occurred, you and Svetlana might question even my motives, he said he would have no objection to your leaving Lora and Sof'ya wherever they may be for the time being, and directed me to provide funds for their support.
>
> They can join you here when you are satisfied that you have been welcomed home as loyal Russians.
>
> I really hope to see all of you here together soon.
>
> May God protect you both on your return journey!
>
> Your loving cousin,
> Vladlen

As Kocian handed the letter to Sándor Tor, he said, "I have no idea who either of these people are, Colonel."

"Please, Herr Kocian," Solomatin said. "I am really trying to help them; to right an injustice."

"Well," Kocian said dryly, "the Sluzhba Vneshney Razvedki does have a certain reputation for causing injustices. But this is the first I've ever heard of them trying to right any." He shook his head. "Sorry, Colonel, I can't help you."

"Herr Kocian, the last confirmed sighting of Colonel Berezovsky, his wife and daughter, and Lieutenant Colonel Svetlana Alekseeva was when they got on Lieutenant Colonel Castillo's airplane at Schwechat airfield in Vienna."

Kocian looked him in the eyes, and said, "Colonel Castillo? Someone else I never heard of."

"The colonel is sometimes still known by the name he was given at his christening, Karl Wilhelm von und zu Gossinger. Inasmuch as you stood as one of his godfathers, Herr Kocian, I find it hard to believe you've forgotten."

Kocian didn't respond.

"Herr Kocian, I swear before God and by all that's sacred to me that I am telling you the truth. And I am begging you to help me."

Kocian said nothing.

"Will you at least get the letter to Colonel Castillo?" Solomatin asked, plaintively.

After a long moment, Kocian said, "Gustav, please be good enough to escort Colonel Solomatin to his car. Give him back his passport and carnet."

"And the letter?" Gustav asked.

Kocian looked at the letter for a long moment, and then folded it and put it in his jacket pocket.

He walked toward the door to his apartment.

"Thank you, Herr Kocian. May God shower you with his blessings," Solomatin said.

Gustav motioned for him to get back on the elevator.

When Gustav walked into Kocian's apartment a half hour later, the old man was sitting in a Charles Eames chair with his feet on its footstool, holding a glass of whisky. Mädchen lay beside him. Max was sitting beside Tor, his head cocked as if to ask, "What the hell are you doing?"

Tor was sitting on a Louis XVI chair that looked to be of questionable strength to support his bulk. A section of a bookcase that lined that wall of Kocian's sitting room had been swung open, revealing a hidden compartment with a communications device on a custom-built shelf.

Tor had fed the communications device the letter Solomatin had given Kocian, and now took it from the device and walked to Kocian and handed it to him.

"There was no car outside," Gustav said. "I offered him a ride to wherever he wanted to go. He accepted, and said the Russian embassy. A Volkswagen with diplomatic plates got on my tail as we got off the Szabadság híd and followed us to Baiza. What I think is there were two cars, that one and another—or at least some Russian sonofabitch with a cell phone—here. They were waiting for us at the bridge."

"And what happened at Baiza?" Kocian asked, referencing the embassy of the Russian Federation at Baiza 35, Budapest.

"He got out of the car, and walked to the gate. The gate opened for him before he got there. They expected him. When I looked in the mirror, the Volkswagen that had been on my tail was gone."

Kocian waved the letter Solomatin had given him.

"Did you get a good look at this, Gustav?"

When Gustav shook his head, Kocian handed it to him, and Gustav read it.

"Well?" Kocian said.

Gustav shook his head again.

"I don't have a clue," he said. "Except, if I have to say this, it smells."

"You don't think the SVR forgives defectors?" Tor said sarcastically.

Gustav gestured toward the communications device. "What does Herr Gossinger think?"

"There is one flaw in that miraculous device," Kocian said. "It doesn't work unless the party you're calling answers, which my godson has not yet done." He paused, pointed to the telephone on the table near him, and said, "See if you can get him on the horn, Sándor. Try the house in Pilar."

Tor rose from his fragile-looking chair, walked to the couch by the phone, sat heavily down, then from memory punched in a long number on the keypad. He held the receiver to his ear.

"What time is it in Buenos Aires?" Kocian asked.

"It's after midnight here, so a little after eight," Tor said, then added, "It's ringing," and handed the receiver to Kocian.

Kocian reached over to the table and pushed the phone base's SPEAKER-PHONE button.

"¿Hola?" a male voice answered.

"With whom am I speaking?" Kocian asked in passable Spanish.

"Who are you calling?"

"I'm trying to get Carlos Castillo. He doesn't seem to be answering his other telephone . . ."

"You have the wrong number, Señor," the man said and broke the connection.

"Sonofabitch hung up on me!" Kocian said, handing the receiver back to Tor. Tor, turning away so that Kocian would not see his smile, punched in the number again, waited for the ring, and then hit the SPEAKERPHONE button.

"¿Hola?"

"My name is Eric Kocian, I need to speak to Carlos Castillo, and don't tell me I have the wrong damn number!"

"How are you, Herr Kocian?" the male voice said politely. "Sorry I didn't recognize your voice."

"I should have given you my name," Kocian said. "Paul Sieno, right?"

"Yes, sir."

"I thought I recognized your voice when you told me I had the wrong number," Kocian said. "Is Carlos handy?"

"Actually, sir, he's not."

"Where is he? Can you give me a better number?"

"I don't have one, sir."

"That's unusual, isn't it?"

"Charley's fly-fishing with his girlfriend in Patagonia, Herr Kocian."

"What did you say?"

"Charley went fishing with his girlfriend, Herr Kocian. In Patagonia. He left word not to bother him unless the sun went out."

"What if I told you this is very important, Paul? And what girlfriend would that be?"

"I can get word to him, Herr Kocian. Maybe tonight, and certainly by morning."

"And the girlfriend?"

There was a long pause, then Paul said, "Herr Kocian, if you don't know about Sweaty, I'm sorry, but you're not going to hear it from me."

"Are you telling me he's drunk and off in the woods with some floozy? Some floozy named Sweaty? That's what you said her name is, right? Sweaty?"

"Well, I can tell you he's probably not drunk, because Sweaty doesn't like him to drink too much. And that I can get word to him to call you, probably tonight, and certainly by morning. Your AFC's working, right?"

"As a matter of fact, Paul, my miraculous AFC communications device is not working at all. The reason I called on the telephone is because nobody we tried to call on it to find Carlos answered."

"Sir, we're not on twenty-four/seven anymore. Just once in the morning—oh-four-twenty-hundred Zulu time—and again in the afternoon at sixteen-twenty Zulu. I'm surprised no one told you."

"By Zulu, you mean Greenwich?"

"Yes, sir."

"Your AFC is working?"

"Yes, sir. I can have it up in a minute."

"There's a document I want Carlos to see. I want to send it in the highest encryption possible."

"Yes, sir, give me a minute to turn on my AFC."

"You can get it to him?"

"In the morning, maybe even tonight."

"I want you and Mrs. Sieno to have a look at it, to see if you can make more sense from it than I can. And tell Carlos what you think."

"Yes, sir."

"It's not addressed to Carlos, Paul. It's addressed to someone else. I don't want that party to see it until after Carlos does."

"This sounds important, Herr Kocian."

"I don't know. It may well be. Is Herr Delchamps available?"

"He's here, but he went out for dinner."

"Show this document to him, too, please, with the same caveat that I don't want the addressee to see it until Carlos has."

"Got it," Sieno said. And then, "There goes the AFC, Mr. Kocian. It shows you as online. I'm ready to receive. Send the message."

"It came through fine, Herr Kocian," Paul Sieno said over the encrypted AFC not quite two minutes later. "What the hell is it all about?"

"I don't know, Paul."

"Where did you get it?"

"A Russian who said he was Colonel Solomatin was waiting for me in the lobby of the Gellért when I came in about an hour ago."

"I will be damned! I'll have this in Charley's hands just as quick as I can."

"Thank you, Paul."

"Herr Kocian, I'm sorry I hung up on you before."

"No apology necessary. My best regards to Mrs. Sieno."

"Will do," Sieno said, then gave the AFC the order: "Break it down."

The green LED indicating the AFC was connected to another AFC device at Encryption Level One went out.

[TWO]
Club America
Miami International Airport, Concourse F
Miami, Florida
2205 4 February 2007

Roscoe J. Danton of *The Washington Times-Post* was not in a very good mood. Eagle-eyed officials of the Transportation Security Administration had detected a Colibri butane cigar lighter and a nearly new bottle of Boss cologne in his carry-on luggage and triumphantly seized both.

The discovery had then triggered a detailed examination of the rest of the contents of his carry-on luggage. This had uncovered a Bic butane cigarette lighter in his laptop case and three boxes of wooden matches from the Old Ebbitt Grill in his briefcase/overnight bag. Two small boxes of matches, he was told he should have known, was the limit.

With the proof before them that they had in their hands if not an Al Qaeda terrorist cleverly disguised as a thirty-eight-year-old Presbyterian from Chevy Chase, Maryland, then at the very least what they categorized as an "uncooperative traveler," the TSA officers had then thoroughly examined his person to make sure that he wasn't trying to conceal anything else—a rocket-propelled grenade launcher, for example—in his ear canal or another body orifice.

With no RPG or other potential weapon found, he was finally freed.

Danton—convinced that his near crimes and misdemeanors had probably caused him to miss Aerolíneas Argentinas Flight 1007, nonstop service to Buenos Aires—had then run all the way down Concourse F to Gate 17 hoping to be proven wrong. There he learned that "technical difficulties" of an unspecified nature were going to delay the departure of Flight 1007 for at least two hours.

As he walked the long way back down the concourse to the Club America, he recalled that C. Harry Whelan had called Miami International Airport "America's Token Third World Airport."

Say what you want about Harry—and there's a lot, all bad, to be said about Harry—but the sonofabitch does have a way with words.

Which is probably why he's always on Wolf News.

I wonder what they pay him for that?

Roscoe found a seat from which he could have a good view of one of the television sets hanging from the ceiling. Then he made three trips to the bar, ultimately returning to his seat with two glasses of Scotch whisky, a glass of water, a glass of ice cubes, a bowl of mixed nuts, and a bowl of potato chips. Then he settled in for the long wait.

When he looked up at the television, he saw C. Harry Whelan in conversation with Andy McClarren, the anything-but-amiable star of Wolf News's most popular program, *The Straight Scoop.*

The screen was split. On the right, McClarren and Whelan were shown sitting at a desk looking at a television monitor. On the left was what they were watching: at least two dozen police cars and ambulances, almost all with their emergency lights flashing, looking as if they were trying to get past some sort of gate.

A curved sign mounted over the gate read WELCOME TO FORT DETRICK.

Their passage was blocked by three U.S. Army HMMWVs, each mounting a .50 caliber machine gun. HMMWV stood for "high-mobility multipurpose wheeled vehicle." With the acronym a little hard to pronounce, the trucks were therefore commonly referred to as "Humvees."

"That was the scene earlier today at Fort Detrick, Harry," Andy McClarren said. "Can you give us the straight scoop on what the hell was going on?"

You're not supposed to say naughty words on television, Roscoe thought as he sipped his Scotch, *but I guess if you're Andy McClarren, host of the most-watched television news show, you can get away with a "hell" every once in a while.*

"A lot of arf-arf," Whelan said.

"What the hell does that mean?"

Careful, Andy. That's two "hell's," probably the most you can get away with. Three "hell's," like three small boxes of wooden matches, will see the federal government landing on you in righteous indignation.

"That's the sound—you've heard it—dogs make when chasing their tails."

"You said that earlier today, didn't you?"

"Yes, I did. To describe various senior bureaucrats rushing around, chasing their tails."

"And so did President Clendennen. Or his spokesman, What's-his-name."

"John David Parker," Whelan offered, "more or less fondly known as 'Porky.'"

"Okay. So, Porky said the press was playing arf-arf, too. Which meant they were chasing their tails, right?"

"And so they were. Andy, do you really want to know what I think went on over there?"

"I want the straight scoop," McClarren said. "That's what we call the show."

"Okay. Take notes. There will be a quiz," Whelan said. "You know, Andy, right, that the United States has vowed never to use biological weapons against our enemies?"

"Uh-huh."

"This was largely because Senator Homer Johns, the junior senator from New Hampshire, thinks that while it is perfectly all right to shoot our enemies, or drop a bomb on them, it is unspeakably evil to use poison gas or some kind of biological weapon on them."

"You think poison gas is okay, Harry?"

"I think poison gas and biological weapons are terrible," Whelan said. "But let's talk about poison gas. In World War One, the Germans used poison gas on us, and we used it on them. It was terrible. In World War Two, the Germans didn't use poison gas, and neither did we. You ever wonder why?"

"You're going to tell me, right?"

"Because between the two wars, the Army developed some really effective poison gas. When we got in the war, and American troops were sent to Europe, so were maybe a half-dozen ships loaded with the new poison gas. We got word to the Germans that we wouldn't use our poison gas first, but if they did, we were prepared to gas every last one of them. They got the message. Poison gas was never used."

"Interesting."

"Then science came up with biological weapons. Our Army, in my judgment wisely, began to experiment with biological weapons. This happened at an obscure little Army base called Fort Detrick. The idea was that if our enemies—we're talking about Russia here—knew we really had first-class biological weapons, they would be reluctant to use their biological weapons on us."

"Like the atom bomb?"

Harry Whelan nodded. "Like atomic bombs, Andy. We weren't nuked by the Russians because they knew that if they did, then Moscow would go up in a mushroom cloud. They called that 'mutual assured destruction.' The same theory was then applied to biological and chemical weapons.

"Then we had a President running for reelection. Senator Johns and his pals thought painting him as a dangerous warmonger would see their guy in the White House. When the incumbent President saw in the polls that this was working, he quickly announced that he was unilaterally taking the United States out of the chemical-biological warfare mutual destruction game. He announced we wouldn't use them, period, and ordered the destruction of all such weapons sitting around in ordnance warehouses.

"This saw him reelected. But Johns wouldn't let him forget his campaign promise. So the Army's biological warfare laboratories at Fort Detrick were closed and the fort became the home of the U.S. Army Medical Research and Matériel Command. What could be more opposite to biological warfare than medical research?

"Even Senator Johns was satisfied that the forces of virtue had triumphed, and we would never use evil biological warfare against our enemies.

"But Army medical research should, it seemed logical to assume, concern itself with what would happen to our soldiers—even our civilian population—should our enemies use biological warfare against us.

"With that in mind, the medical corps began to study the biological weapons in the Russian inventory. If they knew what the Russians were going to use against us, we could come up with antidotes, et cetera.

"How would we know what biological weapons the Russians had? Enter the CIA."

"Really?"

Harry Whelan nodded again. "They bribed the appropriate Russian scientists, and soon samples of the Russian biological inventory began to arrive at Fort Detrick for evaluation by the medical corps.

"Since it was the CIA's duty to evaluate the efficacy of enemy weapons, and since the best place to determine that was Fort Detrick, and since the medical corps was a little short of funds, the CIA thought it only fair that they pay for the investigation.

"This had the additional benefit—since CIA expenditures are classified—of keeping Senator Johns and his pals from learning what was going on. Getting the picture, Andy?"

"That's a hell of an accusation, Harry."

Whelan did not reply directly.

"And inasmuch as the CIA was interested in knowing how soon the United States could respond in kind to a biological attack, they asked the medical personnel at Fort Detrick to determine how the Russian biological weapons were manufactured, and to estimate how long it would take—should the un-thinkable happen—for us to get our manufacture of such up and running. Or even to compare the Russian biological weapons against our own from the bad old days—samples of our own had been retained for laboratory purposes—and see how long it would take to start to manufacture whichever seemed to be the most lethal."

"What you're suggesting, Harry," Andy McClarren said solemnly, "is that the CIA once again was engaged in doing things they're not supposed to. Once again doing things that the Congress had forbidden them to do."

"You sound like Senator Johns, Andy. And once again, you're both wrong. The CIA has the responsibility—given them by Congress—to find out as much as they can about our enemies' capabilities and intentions. That's what they were—are—doing at Fort Detrick. And thank God that they are."

"Give me a for-example, Harry," McClarren said, thickly sarcastic.

"How about a hypothetical, Andy?"

"Shoot."

"Let's suppose that the CIA, which really is not nearly as incompetent as you and people like Senator Johns think it is—or for that matter as incom-petent as the CIA *wants* people like you and Johns and our enemies to think it is—"

"Run that past me again, Harry," McClarren said.

"They call that 'disinformation,' Andy. The less competent our enemies think the CIA is, the less they worry about it. Can I get back to my hypothetical?"

"Why not?" McClarren said, visibly miffed.   •

"Let's say the CIA heard that the bad guys, say the Russians, were operating a secret biological weapons factory in some remote corner of the world—"

"You're talking about that *alleged* biological weapons factory in the Congo," McClarren challenged.

Whelan ignored the interruption.

He went on: "—and they looked into it and found that there was indeed a secret factory in that remote corner of the world."

"Making what?" McClarren challenged, more than a little nastily.

"They didn't know. So what they did was go to this remote corner of the world—"

"Why don't you just say the Congo, Harry?"

"If that makes you happy, Andy. Let's say, hypothetically speaking of course, that the incompetent CIA went to the Congo and, violating the laws of the sovereign state of the Republic of the Congo, broke into this factory and came out with samples of what the factory was producing—"

"Ha!" McClarren snorted.

"—and took it to Fort Detrick, where it was examined by the medical corps scientists. And that these scientists concluded that what the CIA had brought to them was really bad stuff. And let's say that the CIA took this intelligence to the President. Not this one, his predecessor.

"And let's say the President believed what the CIA was telling him. What he should have done was call in the secretary of State and tell her to go to the UN and demand an emergency meeting of the Security Council to deal with the problem.

"Now, let's say, for the purpose of this hypothetical for-example, that the President realized he—the country—was facing what they call a 'real and present danger.' And also that the minute he brought to the attention of the United Nations what the CIA had learned, the bad guys would learn we knew what they were up to.

"By the time the blue-helmet Keystone Kops of the UN went to the Congo to investigate these outrageous allegations—and this is presuming the Russians and/or the Chinese didn't use their veto against using the blue helmets—the factory would either have disappeared, or been converted to a fish farm."

"So he acted unilaterally?"

"And thank God he had the *cojones* to do so."

"And it doesn't bother you, Harry, that he had no right to do anything like that? We could have found ourselves in a war, a nuclear war! That takes an act of Congress!"

"You're dead wrong about that, too, Andy," Whelan said patronizingly, rather than argumentatively. Whether he did so without thinking about it, or with the intention of annoying—even angering—McClarren, it caused the latter reaction.

The one thing Andy McClarren could not stand, would not tolerate, was being patronized.

His face whitened and his lips grew thin.

"How so?" he asked very softly.

"Under the War Powers Act—I'm really surprised you don't know this, Andy; I thought everybody did—the President, as commander in chief, has the authority to use military force for up to thirty days whenever he feels it's necessary. He has to tell Congress he's done so and if they don't vote to support him within those thirty days, the President has to recall the troops. But for thirty days he can do whatever he wants. . . ."

Damn it! Andy McClarren thought as his face turned red. *The President does have that authority under the War Powers Act.*

Either this condescending smart-ass just set me up to make an ass of myself, or—worse—without any assistance from him, I just revealed my ignorance before three point five million viewers.

The only thing that can make this worse is for me to lose my temper.

Whelan went on: "So you see, Andy, in this hypothetical for-example we're talking about, the President did have the authority to do what he did."

McClarren knocked over one of the two microphones on the desk. They were props, rather than working microphones. But McClarren's three point five million viewers didn't know this.

McClarren thought: *Jesus! What can I do for an encore? Spill coffee in my lap?*

Whalen smiled at him sympathetically, and went on: "He didn't have to ask Congress for anything. The whole event was over in three days. What they call a *fait accompli*, Andy."

McClarren straightened the microphone, and then flashed Whelan a brilliant smile.

"I don't believe a word of that, Harry," he said.

"You weren't expected to," Whalen responded, every bit as condescendingly as before. "It was all *hypothetical*, Andy. All you were supposed to do was think about it."

"What I'm wondering is what all your hypothetical stuff has to do with all those police cars at the gate of Fort Detrick. Have you got the straight scoop on that, or just more hypothesis?"

He made "hypothesis" sound like a dirty word.

"Well, Andy, my gut feeling—my *hypothesis,* if you prefer—is that when Porky Parker made his statement, he was doing something he doesn't often do."

"Which was?"

"Porky was telling the truth, the whole truth, and nothing but the truth. There was some kind of accident in one of the laboratories. Somebody dropped an Erlenmeyer flask on the floor. Six white mice or a couple of monkeys escaped their cages. I have no idea what. *Something* happened. The material in those labs is really dangerous. They did what they were supposed to do: They declared a *potential*—operative word 'potential'—disaster. The post was closed down until the problem could be dealt with. When it was dealt with, they called off the emergency procedures.

"While all this was going on, the CIA and Homeland Security and every police force between here and Baltimore started chasing their tails—*arf-arf*—and when the ever-vigilant press got wind of this, they got in their helicopters and flew to Fort Detrick, where they chased *their* tails in the sky—*arf-arf*—until they were run off. If there was any danger to anyone at Fort Detrick today, it was from the clowns in the helicopters nearly running into each other. The Army scientists there know what they're doing."

"That could be, I suppose," Andy McClarren said very dubiously. "But what I would like to know is—"

Roscoe J. Danton saw the image of McClarren on the Club America TV replaced with an image of the logotype of Aerolíneas Argentinas and a notice announcing the immediate departure of Aerolíneas Argentinas Flight 1007, nonstop service to Buenos Aires from Gate 17.

"Christ," Danton complained out loud. "They told me it was delayed for at least two hours."

He stood up, and a firm believer in the adage that if one wastes not, one wants not, drained his drinks.

The Aerolíneas Argentinas announcement then was replaced first with the whirling globes of Wolf News, and then by the image of an aged former star of television advising people of at least sixty-two years of age of the many benefits of reverse mortgages.

Roscoe, who had been hoping to get another glimpse of the royally pissed-off Andy McClarren, said, "Shit!"

Then he hurriedly walked out of Club America.

V

[ONE]
United States—Mexico border near McAllen, Texas
0730 5 February 2007

"What the fuck is that?" United States Border Patrol agent Guillermo Amarilla inquired in Spanish of Senior Patrol Agent Hector Hernandez as the latter stepped hard on the brakes of their green Jeep station wagon.

The station wagon skidded on the rutted dirt road, coming to a stop at nearly a right angle. On one side of the road was a sugarcane field. On the other was waist-high brush. The brush extended for about one hundred fifty yards, ending at the bank of the Rio Grande. The demarcation line between the United States and the Estados Unidos Mexicanos was at the center of the river, which at that point was just over one hundred yards wide.

The dirt road, ten yards from where the Jeep had stopped, was blocked.

An oblong insulated metal box was sitting on a plank suspended between two plastic five-gallon jerrycans.

Nailed to the plank was a large sign hand-lettered ¡¡PELIGROSO!! and ¡¡DANGER!!

Amarilla and Hernandez, without speaking, were out of the vehicle in seconds. Both held Remington Model 870 12-gauge pump shotguns. Crouching beside the station wagon, Hernandez carefully examined the brush, and Amarilla the sugarcane field.

"Undocumented immigrants" sometimes vented their displeasure with Border Patrol agents' efficiency by ambushing Border Patrol vehicles.

Amarilla straightened up and continued looking.

After perhaps sixty seconds, he asked, "You hear anything?"

Hernandez shook his head, and stood erect.

"You think that's a wetback IED?" Amarilla asked.

Both men had done tours with their National Guard units in Iraq, and had experience with improvised explosive devices.

"It could be a fucking bomb, Guillermo."

"I don't see any wires," Amarilla said.

"You don't think a cell phone would work out here?"

Hernandez sought the answer to his own question by taking his cell phone out of his shirt pocket.

"Cell phones work out here," he announced.

"Maybe they left," Guillermo offered.

"And maybe they're waiting for us to get closer."

"Should I put a couple of loads in it and see what happens?"

"No. It could be full of cold beer. These fuckers would love to be able to tell the story of the dumb fucks from La Migra who shot up a cooler full of *cerveza.*"

Guillermo took a closer look at the container.

"It's got signs on it," he said.

He reached into the station wagon and came out with a battered pair of binoculars.

After a moment, he said, "It says, 'Danger: Biological Hazard.' What the fuck?"

He handed the binoculars to Hernandez, who took a close look.

He exhaled audibly, then reached for his cell phone and hit a speed-dial number.

"Hernandez here," he said into it. "I need a supervisor out here, right now, at mile thirty-three."

There was a response, to which Hernandez responded, "I'll tell him when he gets here. Just get a supervisor out here, now."

Ten minutes later, a Bell Ranger helicopter settled to the ground at mile thirty-three.

Two men got out. Both had wings pinned to their uniforms. One was a handsome man with a full head of gray hair and a neatly trimmed mustache. He had a gold oak leaf pinned to his uniform collar points. In the Army, it would be a major's insignia. Field Operations Supervisor Paul Peterson was known, more or less fondly, behind his back as "Our Gringo."

The second man, who had what would be an Army captain's "railroad tracks" pinned to his collar points, was Supervisory Border Patrol Agent Domingo García. He was known behind his back as "Hard Ass."

Both men walked to Hernandez and Amarilla, who were leaning against their Jeep station wagon.

"What have you got?" Hard Ass inquired not very pleasantly.

Hernandez pointed to the obstruction in the road, then handed the binoculars to Peterson.

Peterson peered through them and studied the obstruction. After a long moment, he said, "What in the fuck is that?"

[TWO]
Ministro Pistarini International Airport
Ezeiza
Buenos Aires Province, Argentina
1135 5 February 2007

At the same moment that Supervisory Border Patrol Agent Domingo "Hard Ass" García had put the binocs to his eyes—when it was 0835 in McAllen, Texas, it was 1135 in Buenos Aires—Roscoe J. Danton of *The Washington Times-Post* stepped off the ramp leading from Aerolíneas Argentinas Flight 1007. As he entered the Ezeiza terminal proper, he thought for a moment that he had accidentally gone through the wrong door. He found himself in a large duty-free store, complete with three quite lovely young women handing out product-touting brochures.

"Clever," he said, admiringly and out loud.

Someone down here has figured out a good way to get the traveling public into the duty-free store: place the store as the only passage between the arriving passenger ramp and the terminal.

But screw them. I won't buy a thing.

He started walking through the store.

Fifty feet into it, though, he had a change of heart. He had come to a display of Johnnie Walker Black Label Scotch whisky, and remembered what he had learned as a Boy Scout: "Be Prepared."

Three boxes of his favorite intoxicant were cellophane-wrapped together and offered at a price he quickly computed to be about half of what he paid in Washington, D.C.

He picked up one of the packages and went through the exit cash register, charging his purchase to his—actually, *The Washington Times-Post*'s—American Express corporate credit card. He examined his receipt carefully and was pleased. It read that he had charged $87.40 for unspecified merchandise in the store.

If it had said "three bottles Johnnie Walker Black Label Scotch," there would have been a note from Accounting reminding him that intoxicants could be charged to *The Washington Times-Post* only when connected to business entertaining, and as he had not identified on his expense report whom he had entertained, it was presumed that the whisky was for his personal consumption and therefore the $87.40 would be deducted from his next paycheck, and in the future, please do not charge personal items to the corporate credit card.

Accounting, he theorized, would probably give him the benefit of the doubt in this instance because it didn't *say* "whisky" and assume he had purchased, for example, items of personal hygiene, which were considered legitimate expenses when he was traveling.

Or maybe a battery for his—*The Washington Times-Post*'s—laptop computer.

He would not lie on his expense account. But he would take full advantage of the provisions regarding business travel in his employment contract.

He was entitled, for example, to first-class accommodations on airliners when traveling outside the continental United States on a flight lasting six hours or longer. On flights under six hours in length—say, Washington–London— his contract provided for business class.

It was for that reason that he had traveled on Aerolíneas Argentinas. When *The Washington Times-Post* Corporate Travel department had told him that only business class was available on Delta and American, he made them, per his contract, book him first-class seating on the Argentine carrier. His experience had taught him that once he accepted less than that to which he was entitled, the bastards in Corporate Travel henceforth would try to make it the rule.

Danton also was entitled by his contract, when on travel lasting more than twenty-four hours, to a hotel rated at four stars or better and, therein, a two-room suite rather than a simple room.

In the case of this trip, Corporate Travel had suggested they make a reservation for a two-room suite for him at the four-star-rated Plaza Hotel in Buenos Aires. The Plaza wasn't a *five*-star hotel but boasted that it contained the oldest restaurant in Buenos Aires, a world-famous bar, and was directly across Plaza San Martín from the Argentine foreign ministry. To Danton, that suggested that it wasn't going to be the Argentine version of a Marriott, and he had accepted Corporate Travel's recommendation.

Carrying the Johnnie Walker, he went through the immigration checkpoint without any trouble. His luggage, however, took so long to appear on the carousel that he became genuinely worried that it had been sent to Havana or Moscow. But it did finally show up, and he changed his suspicions toward the officers of the Transportation Security Administration back in Miami, who were, he thought, entirely capable of putting some clever chalk mark on his luggage signaling everyone in the know that it belonged to an "uncooperative traveler" and, if it couldn't be redirected to Moscow or Havana, then to the absolute end of whatever line it was in.

When the customs officials sifted through his suitcase and laptop briefcase with great care—and especially when they asked him if he was *sure* he was not trying to carry into the República Argentina more than ten thousand U.S. dollars in cash or negotiable securities or any amount of controlled substances—he was sure he saw the stealthy hand of the TSA at work.

Corporate Travel had told him that he should take a *remise* rather than a taxi from the airport to his hotel, explaining that Buenos Aires taxis were small and uncomfortable, and their drivers well-known for their skilled chicanery when dealing with foreigners. Remises, Travel had told him, which cost a little more, were private cars pressed into part-time service by their owners, who were more often than not the drivers. They could be hired only through an agent, who had kiosks in the terminal lobby.

The remise in which Roscoe was driven from Ezeiza international airport to Plaza San Martín and the Plaza Hotel was old, but clean and well cared for. And the driver delivered a lecture on Buenos Aires en route.

When the remise door was opened by a doorman wearing a gray frock coat and a silk top hat, and two bellmen stood ready to handle the baggage, Roscoe was in such a good mood that he handed the remise driver his American Express card and he told him to add a twenty-percent tip to the bill. Ten percent was Roscoe's norm, even on *The Washington Times-Post*'s dime.

The driver asked if Roscoe could possibly pay in cash, preferably dollars, explaining that not only did American Express charge ten percent but also took two weeks or a month to pay up. He then showed Roscoe the English language *Buenos Aires Herald*, on the front page of which was the current exchange rate: one U.S. dollar was worth 3.8 pesos.

"If you give me a one-hundred-dollar bill, I'll give you three hundred and ninety pesos," the remise driver offered.

Roscoe handed him the bill, and the driver counted out three hundred and ninety pesos into his hand, mostly in small bills.

Roscoe then got rid of most of the small bills by counting out two hundred pesos—the agreed-upon price—into the driver's hand. The driver thanked him, shook his hand, and said he hoped *el señor* would have a good time in Argentina.

Roscoe liked what he saw of the lobby of the Plaza—lots of polished marble and shiny brass—and when he got to reception, a smiling desk clerk told him they had his reservation, and slid a registration card across the marble to him.

On the top of it was printed, WELCOME TO THE MARRIOTT PLAZA HOTEL.
Shit, a Marriott!
Corporate Travel's done it to me again!
Roscoe had hated the Marriott hotel chain since the night he had been asked
to leave the bar in the Marriott Hotel next to the Washington Press Club after
he complained that it was absurd for the bartender to have shut him off after
only four drinks.

At the Plaza, though, he felt a lot better when the bellman took him to his
suite. It was very nice, large, and well furnished. And he could see Plaza San
Martín from its windows.

He took out the thick wad of pesos the remise driver had given him and
decided that generosity now would result in good service later. He did some
quick mental math and determined the peso equivalent of ten dollars, which
came to thirty-eight pesos, rounded this figure upward, and handed the bellman
forty pesos.

The bellman's face did not show much appreciation for his munificence.
Well, fuck you, Pedro! he thought as the bellman went out the door.
Ten bucks is a lot of money for carrying one small suitcase!
Roscoe then shaved, took a shower, and got dressed.

The clock radio beside the bed showed that it was just shy of two o'clock.
As he set his wristwatch to the local time, he thought it was entirely likely that
the U.S. embassy ran on an eight-to-four schedule, with an hour or so lunch
break starting at noon, and with any luck he could see commercial attaché
Alexander B. Darby as soon as he could get to the embassy.

Miss Eleanor Dillworth had told him that Darby was another CIA Clandestine Service officer, a good guy, and if anybody could point him toward the
shadowy and evil Colonel Castillo and his wicked companions, it was Darby.

Roscoe took out his laptop and opened it, intending to search the Internet
for the address and telephone number of the U.S. embassy, Buenos Aires.

No sooner had he found the plug to connect with the Internet and had
turned on the laptop than its screen flashed LOW BATTERY. He found the power
cord and the electrical socket. His male plug did not match the two round holes
in the electrical socket.

The concierge said he would send someone right up with an adapter plug.

Roscoe then tipped that bellman twenty pesos, thinking that the equivalent
of five bucks was a more than generous reward for bringing an adapter worth
no more than a buck.

This bellman, like the last one, did not seem at all overwhelmed by Roscoe's
generosity.

Roscoe shook his head as he plugged in the adapter. Ninety seconds later, he had the embassy's address—Avenida Colombia 4300—and its telephone number, both of which he entered into his pocket organizer.

"Embassy of the United States."
"Mr. Alexander B. Darby, please."
"There is no one here by that name, sir."
"He's the commercial counselor."
"There's no one here by that name, sir."
"Have you a press officer?"
"Yes, sir."
"May I speak with him, please?"
"It's a her, sir. Ms. Sylvia Grunblatt."
"Connect me with her, please."
"Ms. Grunblatt's line."
"Ms. Grunblatt, please. Roscoe—"
"Ms. Grunblatt's not available at the moment."
"When will she be available?"
"I'm afraid I don't know."
"May I leave a message?"
"Yes, of course."
"Please tell her Mr. Roscoe J. Danton of *The Washington Times-Post* is on his way to the embassy, and needs a few minutes of her valuable time. Got that?"
"Will you give it to me again, please? Slower?"

[THREE]
The Embassy of the United States of America
Avenida Colombia 4300
Buenos Aires, Argentina
1410 5 February 2007

It was a ten-minute drive from the Plaza Hotel to the American embassy.

The taxicab meter showed that the ride had cost fifteen pesos. Roscoe dug out his wad of pesos, handed the driver a twenty-peso note, and waited for his change.

Five pesos is too much of a tip.
Two pesos ought to be more than enough.

The driver looked at the twenty and then up at Roscoe. When Roscoe didn't respond, the driver waved his fingers in a "give me more" gesture.

Roscoe pointed to the meter.

The cab driver said, "Argentine pesos."

He then pointed to the note Roscoe had given him, and said, "Uruguay pesos."

He then held up his index finger, and went on: "One Argentine peso is"—he held up all his fingers—"five Uruguay pesos. You pay with Uruguay pesos, is one hundred Uruguay pesos."

Roscoe looked at his stack of pesos. They were indeed Uruguayan pesos.

That miserable sonofabitch remise driver screwed me!

He counted the Uruguayan pesos he had left. He didn't have enough to make up the additional eighty pesos the cab driver was demanding.

He took a one-hundred-dollar bill from his wallet.

The cab driver examined it very, very carefully, and then first handed Roscoe his twenty-peso Uruguayan note, and then three one-hundred-peso Argentine notes. He stuck the American hundred in his pocket.

Roscoe was still examining the Argentine currency, trying to remember what that sonofabitch remise driver had told him was the exchange rate, when the cab driver took one of the Argentine hundred-peso bills back. He then pointed to the meter, and counted out eighty-five Argentine pesos and laid them in Roscoe's hand.

Roscoe then remembered the exchange rate. It was supposed to be 3.8 Argentine pesos to the dollar, not 3.0.

"*Muchas gracias,*" the cab driver said, and drove off.

"Fuck, fuck, fuck," Roscoe said as he began walking toward the small building guarding access to the embassy grounds.

"My name is Roscoe Danton," he said to the rent-a-cop behind a thick glass window. "I'd like to see Mr. Alexander B. Darby, the commercial counselor."

"You got passport? American passport?" the rent-a-cop asked in a thick accent suggesting that he was not a fellow American.

Roscoe slid his passport through a slot below the window.

The rent-a-cop examined it carefully and then announced, "No Mr. Darby here."

"Then I'd like to see Miss—" *What the fuck was her name?* "—Miss Rosenblum. The press officer."

"No Miss Rosenblum. We got Miss Grunblatt, public affairs officer."

"Then her, please?"

"What your business with Miss Grunblatt?"

"I'm a journalist, a senior writer of *The Washington Times-Post.*"

"You got papers?"

Have I got papers?

You can bet your fat Argentine ass, Pedro, that I have papers.

One at a time, Roscoe took them from his wallet. First he slid through the opening below the window his Pentagon press pass, then his State Department press pass, and finally—the *ne plus ultra* of all press credentials—his White House press pass.

They failed to dazzle the rent-a-cop, even after he had studied each intently. But finally he picked up a telephone receiver, spoke briefly into it—Roscoe could not hear what he was saying—and then hung up.

He signaled for Roscoe to go through a sturdy translucent glass door.

Roscoe signaled for the return of his passport and press passes.

The rent-a-cop shook his head and announced, "When you come out, you get back."

Roscoe considered offering the observation that at the Pentagon, the State Department, and the White House they just looked at press passes and gave them back, but in the end decided it would probably be counterproductive.

He went through the translucent door, on the other side of which were two more rent-a-cops behind a counter, and another sturdy glass door, this one transparent, and through which he could see neatly trimmed grass around a pathway leading to the embassy building itself.

It's just as unbelievably ugly as the embassy in London, Roscoe decided.

Obviously designed by the same dropout from the University of Southern Arkansas School of Bunker and Warehouse Architecture.

The door would not open.

Roscoe looked back at the rent-a-cops.

One of them was pointing to the counter. The other was pointing to a sign on the wall:

NO ELECTRONIC OR INCENDIARY DEVICES BEYOND THIS POINT

Incendiary devices? Are they talking about cigar lighters?

"What in there?" one of the rent-a-cops demanded, pointing at Roscoe's laptop case.

"My laptop. I'm a journalist. I need it to take notes."

"Not past this point. You got cellular phone, organizer, butane lighter?"

"Guilty on all points."

"You got or not got?"

"I got," Roscoe said, and then put them on the counter.

"Keys set off wand," one of the rent-a-cops said. "You got keys, better you leave them, too."

Roscoe added his key chain to everything else.

One of the rent-a-cops came from behind the counter, waved the wand around Roscoe's body, and then gestured toward the glass door.

This time it opened.

A U.S. Marine in dress trousers and a stiffly starched open-collared khaki shirt was waiting for him outside the main entrance to the embassy building. He had a large revolver in a holster suspended from what looked like a patent-leather Sam Browne harness.

"Mr. Danton?"

"Thank God, an American!"

"Mr. Danton?"

"Roscoe Danton, an alumnus of the Parris Island School for Boys, at your service, Sergeant."

"If you will come with me, Mr. Danton?"

The sergeant led him into the building, through a magnetic detector, and down a corridor to the right.

He pointed to a wooden bench.

"If you will sit there, Mr. Danton, someone will attend to you shortly. Please do not leave this area."

Roscoe dutifully sat down. The Marine sergeant marched away.

There was a cork bulletin board on the opposing wall.

After perhaps thirty seconds, Roscoe, more from a desire to assert his journalist status than curiosity—he had been thinking, *Fuck you, Sergeant. I ain't in the Crotch no more; you can't order me around*—stood up and had a look at it.

Among the other items on display was the embassy *Daily Bulletin*. It contained the usual bullshit Roscoe expected to see, and at the end of it was: UNOFFICIAL: ITEMS FOR SALE.

His eyes flickered over it.

"Bingo!" he said aloud.

Immediately after an offer to sell a baby carriage "in like-new condition"—

Like-new condition? What did they do, turn the baby back in?—was an absolutely fascinating offer of something for sale:

> **2005 BMW.** Royal Blue. Excellent Shape. 54K miles.
> All papers in order for sale to US Diplomatic Personnel
> or Argentine Nationals. Priced for quick sale. Can be
> seen at 2330 O'Higgins. Ask doorman. Alex Darby. Phone
> 531-678-666.

Five seconds after Roscoe had read the offer, the paper on which it had been printed was off the wall and in his pocket.

He sat back down on the bench and trimmed his fingernails.

Maybe they have surveillance cameras.

Maybe they saw me tear that off.

If they did, so what?

"Mr. Danton, Ms. Grunblatt will see you now."

Sylvia Grunblatt was sitting behind a large, cluttered desk. She was not svelte, but neither was she unpleasingly plump. She had very intelligent eyes.

"What can the embassy of the United States do for Roscoe J. Danton of *The Washington Times-Post*?" she greeted him. "How about a cup of coffee for openers?"

"I would be in your debt," Roscoe said.

She poured coffee into a mug and handed it to him.

"Sugar? Canned cow?"

He shook his head.

"What brings you to the Paris of South America?" Grunblatt asked.

"I'm writing a feature with the working title, 'Tacos and Tango.'"

"Sure you are," she said. "What did you do, get demoted? I'm one of your fans, Mr. Danton, and you don't write features for the Sunday magazine."

"How about one with the lead, 'U.S. diplomats living really high on the taxpayer's dollar in the Paris of South America'?"

"If you were going to do that, you wouldn't tell me."

"I came down here to see Alex Darby," Roscoe said.

"Nobody here by that name," she said.

"You mean 'Nobody here by that name *now*,' right?"

"We had a commercial counselor by that name, but he's gone. Retired."

"When was that?"

"I don't seem to recall. I could find out for you, but then we would get into privacy issues, wouldn't we?"

"Or security issues. You know who cut his checks, Miss Grunblatt."

"One, it's *Ms.* Grunblatt—but you can call me Sylvia if 'Mizz' sticks in your craw."

"And you may call me Roscoe, Sylvia."

"And two, I have no idea what you're talking about. Mr. Darby was our commercial counselor. Who fed you that other wild notion?"

"Eleanor Dillworth, another longtime toiler in the Clandestine Service of the agency whose name we dare not speak."

"You know Eleanor, do you?"

"Eleanor came to me. Actually, she and her friend Patricia Davies Wilson came to me. Do you know Patricia?"

"I've heard the name somewhere. Eleanor came to you?"

"Both of them did. Whistles to their lips."

"And who—at whom—did they wish to blow their whistles?"

"They seem to feel the villain is an Army officer named Castillo. Major Charley Castillo."

"His Christian name is Carlos."

"You know him?"

She nodded, and said, "If he's the same man. He was sent down here when our consul general, J. Winslow Masterson, was kidnapped."

"Sent by who—whom?"

"Our late President. Who then, after Jack Masterson was killed, put him in charge of getting Masterson's family safely home."

"Tell me about Major Castillo," Danton said.

"Tell you what, Roscoe. You tell me what you think you know about Castillo and if I can, I'll tell you if you're right."

"Nice try, Sylvia."

"Excuse me?"

"If I tell you what I know about this guy, then you will know how close I am to learning what you don't want to tell me about him."

"Roscoe, I am a public affairs officer. It is my duty to answer any questions you might pose to the best of my ability. Providing of course that my answers would not include anything that is classified."

"You ever hear what C. Harry Whelan has to say about public affairs officers such as yourself?"

She shook her head.

"Quote: Their function is not the dissemination of information but rather the containment thereof. They really should be called 'misinformation officers.' End quote."

"Oh, God! He's onto us! There is nothing left for me to do but to go home and slit my wrists."

He chuckled.

Sylvia made the *time out* signal with her hands.

"Can we go off the record, Roscoe?"

"Briefly."

"What exactly did Eleanor tell you?"

"I presume that 'off the record' means that you're not going to send an urgent message to Foggy Bottom telling Natalie Cohen what Eleanor told me."

"Girl Scout's honor."

"Okay. Actually, she didn't tell me much. She said I wouldn't believe what an evil man this guy Castillo is unless I found out myself. What she did was suggest that Castillo had stolen two Russian defectors from her when she was in Vienna. And then pointed me at Alexander Darby."

Sylvia looked at him thoughtfully for a moment, and then said, "Eleanor and I go back a long time—"

"Meaning you have taken Darby's place as the resident spook?"

She shook her head and raised her right arm as if swearing to tell the truth, the whole truth, and nothing but the truth, so help her God.

"Meaning we go back a long time," she said. "Eleanor is very good at what she's done for all those years. If she says Charley Castillo stole two heavy Russian spooks from under her nose, that means there were two Russian spooks, and she believes Charley Castillo stole them."

"She said that it cost her her job."

"Stories like that are circulating, and I've heard them," Sylvia said. "What I can't figure is why Charley would do something like that unless someone— maybe even our late President—told him to. And I can't imagine why he brought them here."

"He brought Russian spooks here?"

"Ambassador Montvale thinks he did."

"How do you know that?"

"A friend of mine—you don't need to know who—was in the Río Alba— that's a restaurant around the corner, magnificent steaks; you ought to make an effort to eat there—at a table near my ambassador's. He was having lunch with Montvale. Castillo walked in. Montvale told him all would be forgiven if he gave him the Russians. Castillo told him to attempt a physiologically impossible act of self-reproduction. Montvale threatened to have him arrested; he had a couple of Secret Service guys with him. Castillo said if the Secret Service made a move, they would be arrested by a couple of Gendarmería Nacional—they're the local heavy cops—he had with him.

"The meeting adjourned to the embassy. I guess they were afraid someone might hear them talking. When the meeting was over, Montvale went to the airport without any Russians, got on his Citation Four, and flew back to Washington. Castillo walked out of the embassy and I haven't seen him since. Reminding you that we're off the record, my ambassador, who is a really good guy, thinks Castillo is a really good guy."

"Interesting."

"One more interesting thing: Right after we bombed whatever the hell it was we bombed in the Congo, a lot of people around here, including Alex Darby, suddenly decided to retire."

"What people?"

"No names. But a Secret Service guy, and a 'legal attaché,' which is diplomat-speak for FBI agent, and even a couple of people in our embassies in Asunción, Paraguay, and across the River Plate in Uruguay."

"Are you going to tell me where I can find Alexander Darby?"

"I don't know, and don't want to know, where he is. The last time I saw him was at Ezeiza."

"The airport?"

She nodded. "Alex is somebody else I've known for a long time. A really good guy. I drove him to the airport."

"He went home?"

She paused before replying: "Alex applied for, and was issued, a regular passport. I drove him to the airport. He left the country—went through immigration—on his diplomatic passport. Then he went back through the line and entered the country as a tourist on his regular passport. When he came out, he handed me—as an officer of the embassy—his dip's passport. Then I drove him to his apartment. I haven't seen him since."

"You going to tell me where that apartment is?"

"We're back on the record, Mr. Danton. I cannot of course violate Mr. Darby's privacy by giving you that information. I'm sure you understand."

"Of course. And thank you very much, Mizz Grunblatt."

"Anytime, Mr. Danton. We try to be of service."

"That's comforting."

"Did you ever hear what Winston Churchill said about journalists, Mr. Danton?"

"Can't say that I have."

"Churchill said, 'Journalists are the semiliterate cretins hired to fill the spaces between the advertisements.'"

"Oh, God! He's onto us! Now I suppose there's nothing left for me but to slash my wrists."

"That's a thought. Good morning, Mr. Danton."

[FOUR]
Apartment 32-B
O'Higgins 2330
Belgrano
Buenos Aires, Argentina
1505 5 February 2007

"I will miss the view," Alexander B. Darby—a small, plump man with a pencil-line mustache—said as he stood with Liam Duffy, Edgar Delchamps, and his wife, and gestured out the windows of the Darbys' apartment on the thirty-second floor. It occupied half of the top floor of the four-year-old building, high enough to overlook almost all of the other apartment buildings between O'Higgins and the River Plate.

"What you're supposed to be going to miss, you sonofabitch, is your loving wife and adorable children," Julia Darby—a trim woman who wore her black hair in a pageboy—said.

And was immediately sorry.

"Strike that, Alex," she added. "I was just lashing out at the fickle finger of fate."

"It's okay, honey. And I really don't think it will be for long."

"Hope springs eternal in the human breast," Julia said solemnly.

"And the movers never show up when they're supposed to," Edgar Delchamps said as solemnly.

The apartment showed signs that the movers were expected any moment. Cardboard boxes were stacked all over, and suitcases were arranged by the door.

"And it is always the cocktail hour somewhere in the world, so why not here and now?" Alex said.

Julia smiled at Edgar and Liam, and said, "Every once in a great while, he has a good idea. The embassy's glasses are in the cupboard, so all we have to do is find something to put in them."

"The booze is in the suitcase with the 'seven' stuck on it," Alex said, and looked at the suitcases by the door. "Which, of course, is the one on the bottom." He switched to Spanish. "Give me a hand, will you, Liam?"

Liam Duffy—a well-dressed, muscular, ruddy-faced blond man in his forties—looked to be what his name suggested, a true son of Erin. But he was in fact an Argentine whose family had migrated to Argentina more than a century before.

They went to the stack of suitcases, moved them around, and in about a minute Alex Darby was able to triumphantly raise a bottle of twelve-year-old Famous Grouse Malt Scotch whisky.

The house telephone rang.

Julia answered it.

"It's the concierge," she announced. "Somebody's here to look at the car."

"Tell him to show it to him," Alex said.

He walked into the kitchen carrying the whisky. Liam followed him.

Ninety seconds later, the telephone rang again, and again Julia answered it.

When Alex and Liam returned from the kitchen, Julia announced, "It's the movers."

"Which one?"

"His," Julia said, nodding at Duffy.

"Have them sent up," Alex said.

"I'm way ahead of you, my darling," Julia said as she reached for her glass.

Seconds later, the doorbell chimed, signaling there was someone in the elevator foyer.

Duffy went to the door and opened it, then waved three men into the apartment. They were all wearing business suits but there was something about them that suggested the military.

"The suitcases to the left of the doorway," Duffy said in Spanish. "Be very careful of the blue one with the number seven on it."

"*Sí, mí comandante,*" one of them said.

"Did they find a pilot for the Aero Commander?" Duffy asked.

"*Sí, mí general.* All is ready at Aeroparque Jorge Newbery."

"Whoopee!" Julia Darby said.

"And the people to stay with Familia Darby?" Duffy asked.

"In place, *mí comandante.*"

"Whoopee again," Julia said.

Duffy nodded at the men.

The doorbell rang again.

Duffy pulled it open.

A thirty-eight-year-old Presbyterian from Chevy Chase, Maryland, stood there.

"Mr. Darby?" Roscoe Danton asked.

"I'm Alex Darby. Come in."

Roscoe entered the apartment and offered his hand to him.

"Roscoe Danton," he said.

"That was a quick look at the BMW, wasn't it?" Darby asked.

"Actually, Mr. Darby, I'm not here about the car. I came to see you," Danton said. "I'm a journalist at *The Washington Times-Post*. Eleanor Dillworth sent me."

Darby's reaction was Pavlovian. One spook does not admit knowing another spook unless he knows whoever is asking the question has the right to know.

Spooks also believe that journalists should be told only that which is in the best interests of the spook to tell them.

"I'm afraid there's been a mistake," Darby said, politely. "I'm afraid I don't know a Miss Duckworth."

"Dillworth." Roscoe made the correction even as he intuited things were about to go wrong. "Eleanor Dillworth."

Comandante General Liam Duffy also experienced a Pavlovian reaction when he saw the look in Darby's eyes. He made a barely perceptible gesture with the index finger of his left hand.

The two men about to carry luggage from the apartment quickly set it down and moved quickly to each side of Roscoe Danton. The third man, who was already on the elevator landing, turned and came back into the apartment, looking to Duffy for guidance.

Duffy made another small gesture with his left hand, rubbing his thumb against his index finger. This gesture had two meanings, *money* and *papers*.

In this case, the third man intuited it meant papers. He walked to Danton and said, reasonably pleasantly, in English, "Papers, please, Señor."

"Excuse me?" Roscoe said.

Julia Darby looked annoyed rather than concerned.

"Gendarmería Nacional," the man said. "Documents, please, passport and other identity."

Roscoe wordlessly handed over his passport.

The third man made a *give me the rest* gesture.

Roscoe took out his wallet and started to look for his White House press pass.

The third man snatched the wallet from his fingers and handed it and the passport to Liam Duffy.

"My press passes are in there," Roscoe said. "Including my White House—"

Duffy silenced him with a raised hand, examined the passport and the contents of the wallet, and then handed all of it to Darby.

Then he made another gesture, patting his chest with both hands.

The two men standing beside him instantly started to pat down Roscoe, finally signaling that he was clean except for a wad of currency, a sheaf of papers, several ballpoint pens, a box of wooden matches, and two cigars. They handed everything to Duffy.

"How did you happen to come to this address, Mr. Danton?" Darby asked, courteously.

Roscoe decided to tell the truth.

"I saw the for-sale ad, for the BMW, in the daily bulletin at the embassy," he said. He pointed to the sheaf of papers.

"What were you doing at the embassy?"

"I went there to see if they could point me at you."

"Why would you want to be pointed at me?"

"I told you, Eleanor Dillworth said you would be helpful."

"In what way?"

"That you could point me toward Colonel Carlos Castillo."

"I know no one by that name. An Argentine Army officer?"

"An American officer, Mr. Darby," Roscoe replied, stopping himself at the last second from saying, *As you fucking well know.*

"I don't know what's going on here, Mr. Danton," Darby said. "But apparently someone has given you incorrect information. I'm sorry you've been inconvenienced. How did you get here?"

"In a taxi."

"Where are you staying?"

"The Plaza Hotel."

"Well, the least we can for you is give you a ride back there," Darby said. "We can do that, can't we, Liam?"

"Absolutely," Liam said.

"Nice to have met you, Mr. Danton," Darby said, and gestured toward the door.

"Likewise," Roscoe Danton snapped sarcastically. "And I'll pass on the free ride, thank you just the same."

Comandante General Liam Duffy locked eyes with Danton, and evenly said, "Let me explain something to you, Señor. There are some irregularities with your documents—"

"What kind of irregularities?" Danton interrupted angrily.

Duffy ignored him. He went on: "I'm sure they can be quickly cleared up. Possibly even today and certainly by the morning. Our usual procedure is taking people with irregular documents to our headquarters. Then we would notify the U.S. embassy and ask them to verify your documents. Sometimes, they can do that immediately. In the case of someone like yourself, a distinguished journalist, I'm sure they would go out of their way to hasten this procedure—"

"Call the public affairs officer," Danton interrupted again. "Sylvia Grunblatt. She knows who I am."

Duffy ignored him again. "—and by late today, or certainly by tomorrow morning, a consular officer would come by our headquarters, verify the legitimacy of your documents, which would then be returned to you and you could go about your business.

"But, in the meantime, you would be held. We can't, as I'm sure you understand, have people running around Buenos Aires with questionable documents. Now, partly because I am anxious to do everything I can for a prominent North American journalist such as you purport to be, and partly because Señor Darby feels sorry for you, what I'm willing to do is take you to your hotel and let you wait there. With the understanding, of course, that you would not leave the Plaza until your documents are checked and we return them to you. Believe me, Señor, the Plaza is far more comfortable a place to wait than the detention facilities at our headquarters."

Danton held up both hands at shoulder height.

"I surrender," he said. "The Plaza it is."

"*Comandante*, will you take this gentleman to the Plaza?"

"*Sí, mi comandante.*"

"What the hell was that all about?" Julia Darby asked.

"If I were still an officer of the Clandestine Service," Alex Darby replied, "I would hazard a guess that it has something to do with this."

He held up a copy of the letter Colonel Vladlen Solomatin had given to Eric Kocian in Budapest.

"If *I* were still an officer of the Clandestine Service," Edgar Delchamps said, "I would *know* not only what Roscoe Danton is up to, but also what Comrade Colonel Solomatin is up to."

"You think I'm wrong?" Liam Duffy asked.

"No. Vladimir Putin may very well have dispatched one of the Sluzhba

Vneshney Razvedki hit squads—or several of them—to whack us all," Delchamps said. "But I don't think Roscoe Danton is a deep-cover SVR asset who came out of his closet to do the deed. He's a pretty good journalist, actually."

"What was that about Eleanor pointing him at Alex? At Charley?" Julia asked. "Did he make that up?"

"I don't think so. Eleanor got fired when Charley stole her defectors. She's pissed. Understandably," Alex Darby said. "I think she'd like to watch as Charley was castrated with a dull knife."

"I don't think she likes me much either," Delchamps said.

"And you know why," Alex said.

"I don't," Julia said.

"Quickly changing the subject," Delchamps said, "I suggest we get the hell out of Dodge as quickly as possible. Just as soon as the movers come."

"I can leave somebody here to deal with the movers," Liam said.

"And Sylvia has the car keys—and the power of attorney—to sell the car," Darby said. "Moving Julia and the boys to the safe house in Pilar until it's time to go to Ezeiza seems to be the thing to do. Honey, will you go get the boys?"

"No," Julia said. "I'm a mommy. Mommies don't like it much when their sons look at them with loathing, disgust, and ice-cold hate. You go get them."

"It's not that bad, honey," Alex argued. "People who—hell, people who sell air conditioners get transferred, with little or no notice, all the time. Their children get jerked out of school. It's not the end of the world."

"You tell them that," she said.

"They'll like Saint Albans, once they get used to it," Alex said somewhat lamely.

"Why? Because you went there?" Julia challenged.

"No. Because Al Gore and Jesse Jackson, Jr., did," Alex said, and after a moment added, "I'll be right back. With my pitiful abused namesake and his pathetic little brother."

When the door to the elevator foyer had closed behind her husband, Julia asked, "What are you going to do, Edgar? Eventually, I mean."

Delchamps considered the question a long moment before replying.

"I don't know, Julia," he said. "Like Alex, this business of . . . of *selling air conditioners* . . . is all I know. What I won't be doing is hanging around the gate at Langley with the other dinosaurs telling spy stories."

"I didn't know what Alex did for a living until the night he proposed," Julia said. "And then he told me he was in research for the agency."

"They call that obfuscation," Delchamps said.

"You never got married, did you?"

He shook his head.

The telephone rang.

This time it was the embassy movers.

[FIVE]
The President's Study
The White House
1600 Pennsylvania Avenue, N.W.
Washington, D.C.
0935 5 February 2007

"What am I looking at, Charles?" President Joshua Ezekiel Clendennen inquired of Ambassador Charles M. Montvale, the director of National Intelligence.

Before Montvale could reply, the President thought he knew the answer to his question, and went on: "This is the—what should I call it?—the *package* that caused all the uproar at Fort Detrick yesterday, right? And why am I looking at this now, instead of yesterday?"

"These photographs were taken less than an hour ago, Mr. President," Montvale said. "On a dirt road one hundred fifty yards inside our border near McAllen, Texas."

The President looked at him, waiting for him to continue.

"A routine patrol by the Border Patrol found that sitting on the road at about half past seven, Texas time. The intel took some time to work its way up the chain of command. The Border Patrol agents who found it reported it to their superiors, who reported it—"

"I know how a chain of command works, Charles," the President interrupted.

"Homeland Security finally got it to me just minutes ago," Montvale said.

"Cut to the chase, for Christ's sake," the President snapped. "Is that another load of Congo-X or not?"

"We are proceeding on the assumption that it is, Mr. President, and working to confirm that, one way or the other—"

"What the hell does that mean?" the President interrupted again.

"As soon as this was brought to my attention, Mr. President, I contacted Colonel Hamilton at Fort Detrick. I was prepared to fly him out there."

"And is that what's happening?"

"No, sir. Colonel Hamilton felt that opening the beer cooler on-site would be ill-advised."

"'Beer cooler'?"

"Yes, sir. The outer container is an insulated box commonly used to keep beer or, for that matter, anything else cold. They're commonly available all over. The FBI has determined the one sent to Colonel Hamilton was purchased at a Sam's Club in Miami."

"I don't know why I'm allowing myself to go off on a tangent like this, but why don't you just call it an 'insulated box'?"

"Perhaps we should, sir. But the Congo-X at Fort Detrick was in a blue rubber barrel, resembling a beer barrel, in the insulated—"

"Okay, okay. I get it. So what's with Colonel Hamilton?"

"Colonel Hamilton said further that in addition to the risk posed by opening the insulated box on-site, to determine whether whatever it holds was Congo-X or not, he would have to take all sorts of various laboratory equipment—"

"So you're moving it to Detrick, right? Is that safe?"

"We believe it is the safest step we can take, sir."

"And that's under way?"

"Yes, sir. The insulated box will be—by now has been—taken to the Corpus Christi Naval Air Station in a Border Patrol helicopter. From there it will be—by now, is being—transported to Andrews Air Force Base here in a Navy C-20H. That's a Gulfstream Four, Mr. President."

"Thank you for the clarification, Charles," the President said sarcastically. "One can never know too many details like that. And when the beer cooler-slash-insulated box gets to Andrews? Is everything set up there to cause another public relations disaster, like the one we had yesterday?"

"An Army helicopter will be standing by at Andrews, sir, to fly the insulated container to Fort Detrick. It should not attract undue attention, sir."

"It better not."

"Mr. President, what caused the, the—"

"'Disaster' is probably the word you're looking for, Charles," the President said.

"—excitement at Fort Detrick yesterday was Colonel Hamilton declaring a Potential Level Four Biological Hazard Disaster. That probably won't happen today."

The President snorted, and then asked, "So what's going to happen when the insulated container from Texas is delivered to Hamilton?"

"He will determine whether the container contains more Congo-X."

"And if it does?"

"Excuse me?"

"If it does contain more of this noxious substance—now, that's an understatement, isn't it? 'Noxious substance'?—what is he going to do about that?"

"The colonel has been experimenting with high-temperature incineration as a means of destroying Congo-X. He has had some success, but he is not prepared to declare that the solution."

"So we then have several questions that need answering, don't we? One, what is this stuff? Two, how do we deal with it? More important, three, who's sending it to us? And, four, why are they sending it to us?"

"Yes, sir, that's true."

"And you have no answers?"

"I think we can safely presume, sir, that it was sent to us by the same people who were operating the 'fish farm' that we destroyed in the Congo."

"I think we can 'safely presume' that we didn't destroy everything that needed destroying in the Congo, can't we?"

"I'm afraid we have to proceed on that assumption, Mr. President."

"And you have no recommendations?"

"Sir?"

"It seems to me our options range from sending Natalie Cohen to Moscow and Teheran to get on her knees and beg for mercy all the way up to nuking both the Kremlin and wherever that unshaven little Iranian bastard hangs his hat in Teheran."

"There are more options than those extremes, Mr. President."

"Such as?"

"Sir, it seems to me that if whoever sent these two packages of Congo-X wanted to cause us harm, they would have already done so."

"That thought has also run through my mind," Clendennen said sarcastically.

"It would therefore follow they want something. What we have to do is learn what they want."

"Would you be surprised, Charles, if I told you that thought has also run through my mind?"

Montvale didn't reply.

"I want you to set up a meeting here at, say, five," the President said. "We'll brainstorm it. You, Natalie, the DCI, the FBI director, the secretary of Defense, the heads of Homeland Security and the DIA. And Colonel Hamilton, too. By then he'll probably know if this new stuff is more Congo-X or not. In any event, he can bring everybody up to speed on what he does know."

"Yes, sir. That's probably a good idea."

"I thought you might think so," President Clendennen said.

[SIX]
The Office of the Director of National Intelligence
Eisenhower Executive Office Building
17th Street and Pennsylvania Avenue, N.W.
Washington, D.C.
1010 5 February 2007

Truman C. Ellsworth, whose title was "executive assistant to the director of National Intelligence," learned only after having served in that position for three months that the title was most commonly used by members of the secretarial sorority to denote those women who were more than just secretaries. Those females who had, in other words, their own secretaries to do the typing, filing, and fetching of coffee.

By the time he found out, it was too late to do anything about it.

Ellsworth, a tall, silver-haired, rather elegant man in his fifties, had chosen the title himself when Charles M. Montvale had asked him to again leave his successful, even distinguished law practice in New York to work for him, as his deputy, in the newly created Directorate of National Intelligence.

He wouldn't have the title of deputy, Montvale explained, because there was already a deputy director of National Intelligence, whom Montvale privately described as "a connected cretin" who had been appointed by the President in the discharge of some political debt.

Montvale said he would make—and he quickly had made—it clear that Truman C. Ellsworth was number two in the Office of the Director of National Intelligence, and that any title would do. Ellsworth chose "executive assistant" because an executive is someone who executes and he was inarguably going to be Montvale's assistant.

In this role, while Charles M. Montvale sat on his office couch, Truman C. Ellsworth sat behind Montvale's desk and called first the secretary of State, Natalie Cohen, whom he knew socially well enough to address by her first name, and told her that the President had asked "the boss" to set up a five o'clock meeting at the White House to discuss "a new development in the Congo business."

She said she would of course be there.

Then Truman called, in turn, Wyatt Vanderpool, the secretary of Defense; John "Jack" Powell, the director of the Central Intelligence Agency; Mark Schmidt, the director of the Federal Bureau of Investigation; and Lieutenant General William W. Withers, U.S. Army, the commanding general of the Defense Intelligence Agency. He told them, somewhat more curtly, that "the ambassador" had told him to call them to summon them to a five P.M. brainstorming session at the White House vis-à-vis the new development in the Congo affair. He wasn't able to reach the secretary of Homeland Security, but he did get through to Assistant Secretary of Homeland Security Mason Andrews.

Ellsworth returned the telephone receiver to its cradle and reported as much to Ambassador Montvale: "I got through to everybody but DHS, Charles. I had to settle for Mason Andrews."

"I wish I had thought of this when you had Jack Powell on the line," Montvale said.

"Thought of what, Charles?"

"Castillo may be involved in this—probably is, in some way—and I have no idea where he is."

Ellsworth's eyebrows rose.

"I daresay that the colonel, retired, in compliance with his orders, has dropped off the face of the earth."

"I want to know where he is," Montvale said. "I forgot that the President told me the next time he asked, he expected me to be able to tell him where Castillo is."

"Well, you can tell Jack Powell to start looking for him when you see him at the White House."

"That's seven hours from now," Montvale said. "Get him on a secure line, please, Truman. I will speak with him."

Ellsworth reached for a red telephone on the desk, and said into it, "White House, will you please get DCI Powell on a secure line for Ambassador Montvale?"

VI

[ONE]
Estancia San Joaquín
Near San Martín de los Andes
Patagonia
Neuquén Province, Argentina
1645 5 February 2007

From the air, the landing strip at Estancia San Joaquín looked like a dirt road running along the Chimehuín River, which arguably was the best trout-fishing river in the world.

It was only when the manager of the estancia heard the Aero Commander—which he expected—overhead and threw a switch that the aeronautical function of the dirt road became obvious. The switch (a) caused lights marking both ends of the runway to rise from the ground and begin to flash, and (b) another hydraulic piston to rise, this one with a flashing arrow indicating the direction of the wind.

The sleek, twin-engined, high-wing airplane touched down and taxied to a large, thatched-roof farm building near the road. There, part of what looked like the wall of the farm building swung open and, as soon as the pilot shut down the engines, a half-dozen men pushed the aircraft into what was actually a hangar. There was a Bell Ranger helicopter parked inside.

The door/wall closed, the marking lights sank back into the ground, and the airfield again became a dirt road running along the tranquil Chimehuín River.

Edgar Delchamps was the first to emerge from the airplane.

Max ran to greet him, which he did by resting his paws on Delchamps's shoulder as he kissed him.

It was a long moment before the dog had enough and Delchamps could straighten up.

"Funny, I would never have taken you for a trout fisherman," Charley Castillo greeted him.

Castillo was wearing a yellow polo shirt, khaki trousers, a battered Stetson hat, and even more battered Western boots.

"Ha-ha," Delchamps responded.

Delchamps pointed to the helicopter and raised his eyebrows.

"Our host's," Castillo said. "Alek loans it to me from time to time, when I have something important to do, like going fishing."

Alex Darby came out of the airplane next, followed by Liam Duffy, and finally a man wearing a Gendarmería Nacional uniform and pilot's wings.

Darby and Castillo shook hands. Liam Duffy wrapped his arm around Castillo's shoulders and hugged him.

"Ace, your pal Alek wouldn't happen to be here, would he?" Delchamps asked.

"As a matter of fact, he is."

"Why do I think Alek is not here to fish?" Delchamps said.

"Because in a previous life, you were trained to be suspicious," Castillo replied. "You're going to have to adjust to our changed circumstances." When he saw the look on Delchamps's face, he went on: "But since you ask, at a few minutes after seven this morning, Alek and I were out on the beautiful Río Chimehuín catching our breakfast."

"Then Pevsner doesn't know about the letter?"

"Charley," Liam Duffy interrupted, nodding at the pilot. "We're going to have to get Primer Alférez Sanchez to the airport."

Primer Alférez, Alférez Sanchez, who had piloted the Aero Commander, was the equivalent of first lieutenant in the gendarmería. And Castillo saw his unhappy look.

He's thinking, "I'm being gotten rid of so I won't learn what's going on here."

And he's right to be pissed. Liam could have handled that better; the last thing we want is a pilot who knows more than he should harboring a grudge.

Duffy's sometimes the sort of commander whose officers loathe him.

"Sanchez, what did you think of the new avionics in that old bird?" Castillo asked, switching to Spanish, and smiling at the pilot.

"Fantastic!" the pilot replied. "All I had to do was take it off and land it. The navigation was entirely automatic, and when I dropped out of the cloud cover, I was lined up with the runway."

"We're working on that," Castillo said. "The idea is to eliminate pilots like you and me."

"I'm not sure I'd like that, señor."

"As I was just telling my friend here, one has to adjust to changed circumstances. I'm sorry there's no time to offer you a drink, but Aerolíneas Argentinas waits for no man, and if you don't get to the San Martín de los Andes airport in the next forty-five minutes . . ."

"I understand, señor," the pilot said, and then came to attention. "With your permission, *mi comandante?*"

Duffy nodded. The pilot saluted and Duffy returned it.

"Sanchez," Castillo said, "don't tell anyone about the avionics."

"*El comandante* made that clear on the way here, señor."

Delchamps waited until the pilot had left the hangar, and then said, "Tell me about the changed circumstances, Ace."

"I hardly know where to start," Castillo said.

"Try starting with telling me whether or not Pevsner has seen Solomatin's letter."

"Gladly," Castillo said. "Okay, starting at the beginning: Alek's man went on the net as scheduled at oh-four-twenty hundred Zulu."

"'Alek's man went on the net'? *Our* net?"

"I thought you knew that all of us are retired and have fallen off the face of the earth. We now have people to do things like going on the net at one-twenty in the morning."

Delchamps and Darby both shook their heads. This was unexpected.

"So Alek's guy," Castillo went on, "went on the net at oh-one-twenty local time. At oh-one-twenty-two, Colonel V. N. Solomatin's letter came through, five by five. At oh-one-twenty-five, Alek telephoned me here, waking me from the sleep of the innocent, to tell me he had a letter from Cousin Vladlen and that he wanted me to see it as soon as possible."

"Paul Sieno told me Kocian wanted to get the letter to you without anyone else seeing it."

"Don't anyone let Alek know you're surprised that he has seen it. We now have no secrets from Alek."

"Jesus Christ!" Delchamps said.

"So I told him that I'd fire up"—Castillo pointed to the Bell Ranger—"at first light, go pick him up, and he could show me Cousin Vladlen's letter. Or, better yet, bring him back here and he could have breakfast with Sweaty and me, we'd all read Cousin Vladlen's letter, and then go fishing to kill the time until you, Darby, and Duffy got here. Since that was the best idea he'd heard so far this week, Alek said that was fine, and he'd bring Tom Barlow along, since the letter was addressed to him in the first place."

"So Colonel Berezovsky is here, too?" Darby asked. "I wondered where he was."

"Aside from my belief that Colonel Dmitri Berezovsky has also fallen off the face of the earth," Castillo said, "I have no idea where he might be. *Tom Barlow*, however, is at the San Joaquín Lodge."

"And Sweaty has seen the letter, no doubt?"

"Certainly, Sweaty has seen it. How could I possibly not show it to her? Alek would have anyway."

Delchamps shook his head in resignation.

"Okay. Can we go now?"

"You don't want to know what else has happened?" Castillo asked.

"I'm afraid to ask."

"Well, we had another offer of employment from those people in Las Vegas," Castillo said.

"To do what?"

"It seems that someone sent Colonel Hamilton a rubber beer barrel full of whatever it was Hamilton brought out of the Congo . . ."

"Jesus H. Christ!" Darby exclaimed.

". . . and they wanted us to find out who did it and why."

"And?" Delchamps asked.

"I told them, sorry, we have all fallen off the face of the earth."

"What the hell is that all about?" Darby asked.

"It's none of our business," Castillo said.

"They were supposed to have destroyed everything in a twenty-mile area around that place in the Congo," Darby said.

"So they said," Castillo said.

"You think there's some sort of connection between that and Solomatin's letter?" Darby asked.

"I don't know, but you can count on Alek asking you that question."

He gestured toward an open rear door of the hangar. Two shiny olive-drab Land Rovers sat there.

"I think we can all get in one of those, can't we?" Castillo asked.

[TWO]

The Lodge at Estancia San Joaquín was a single-story stone masonry building on a small rise perhaps fifty feet above and one hundred yards from the Chimehuín River.

It had been designed to comfortably house, feed, and entertain trout fishermen from all over the world, never more than eight at a time, usually four or five, who were charged three thousand dollars a day. The furniture was simple and massive. The chairs and armchairs were generously padded with foam-filled leather cushions.

The wide windows of the great room offered a view of the Chimehuín River and the snow-capped Andes mountains. There was a well-stocked bar, a deer head with an enormous rack above the fireplace, a billiards table, a full book-case, and two fifty-six-inch flat-screen televisions mounted so one of them was visible from anywhere in the room.

There were four people in the great room—plus a bartender and a maid—when Castillo and the others walked in: Tom Barlow, his sister Susan, and Aleksandr Pevsner, a tall, dark-haired man—like Castillo and Barlow in his late thirties—whose eyes were large, blue, and extraordinarily bright. The fourth man was János, Pevsner's hulking bodyguard, of whom it was said that he was never farther away from Pevsner than was Max from Castillo.

There were fourteen Interpol warrants out for the arrest of Pevsner under his own name and the seven other identities he was known to use.

Barlow was dressed like Castillo, in khaki trousers and a polo shirt. Pevsner was similarly clothed, except that his polo shirt was silk and his trousers were fine linen. The men were at the billiards table.

Susan, who was leaning over a coffee table, fork poised to spear an oyster, was dressed like Castillo and her brother, except her polo shirt was linen and her khakis were shorts. Short shorts. Her clothing and posture left virtually nothing to the imagination about her bosom, legs, and the contours of her derriere.

"Funny," Edgar Delchamps said, "I would never have taken Sweaty for a fisherman."

Susan/Sweaty looked up from the platter of oysters, popped one in her mouth, smiled at Delchamps, and gave him the finger.

It was a gesture she had learned from Castillo and subsequently had used, with relish, frequently.

Pevsner carefully laid his cue on the billiards table, then walked to Del-champs, Darby, and Duffy, and wordlessly shook their hands. Tom Barlow waved at them.

"I'm sure you're hungry," Pevsner said. "I can have them prepare supper for you now. Or, if you'd rather, there's oysters and cold lobster to—what is it Charley says?—*munch on* to hold you until dinner."

"How the hell do you get oysters and lobster in the middle of Patagonia?" Darby said as he walked to the coffee table to examine what was on display.

"I have a small seafood business in Chile," Pevsner said.

That triggered a tidal wave of doubt and concern in Castillo, surprising him both by its intensity and the speed with which it hit him and then grew.

It started with his reaction to Pevsner's saying he had a "small seafood business in Chile."

A small seafood business, my ass, Castillo had thought sarcastically. *It's called Cancún Provisions, Limited, and it flies a Boeing 777-200LR full of seafood to Cancún every other day. The 777 is owned by Peruaire. And you own that, too.*

Was that natural modesty, Alek, or was the modesty a Pavlovian reflex of a former KGB colonel?

"Say as little as possible; deflect attention."

How much can I really trust Comrade Polkovnik Pevsner?

Right now he tells me I'm family. In love—intending to marry—his cousin Susan, formerly Podpolkovnik Svetlana Alekseeva of the SVR.

But how long will that last if whatever the hell is going on here threatens his wife and children or his way of life?

Most of the charges laid against him are bullshit.

But, on the other hand, I know he supervised the beating to death with an angle iron a man who betrayed him. Or used the angle iron himself. Probably the latter.

My friend Alek is not a nice man.

Edgar Delchamps neither likes nor trusts Alek, and has told me so bluntly. And I know I can trust Delchamps. He's been dealing with Russian spooks—successfully dealing with them—for nearly as long as I am old.

Castillo was as suddenly brought out of his unpleasant reverie as quickly as he had entered it.

There were soft fingers on his cheeks, the scent of perfume in his nostrils, and light blue eyes intently searching his.

"My darling," Sweaty asked. "What's the matter?"

"Nothing."

"You look like you'd seen a ghost!"

He shook his head, said, "I'm fine, baby." He put his hand on her back and felt her warmth though the linen shirt.

Sweaty rose on her toes and kissed him on the lips with great tenderness.

Edgar Delchamps's face showed signs of amused scorn.

Castillo gave him the finger with the hand that had been against Sweaty's back, and announced, "I need a drink."

He mimed to the bartender what he wanted. The bartender, a shaven-headed, barrel-chested man in his thirties, nodded and reached for a bottle of Wild Turkey bourbon. Castillo knew that the crisp white bartender's jacket concealed a Micro Uzi submachine gun.

The bartender was one of the nearly one hundred ex-members of the KGB or the SVR whom Pevsner had brought out of Russia to work for him. And from the looks of him, the bartender was probably ex-Spetsnaz.

There was the snap of fingers.

The bartender looked at Pevsner, who held up two fingers, and then pointed to two armchairs by the coffee table. The bartender nodded.

Pevsner waved Castillo toward the armchairs. Sweaty steered Castillo away from the armchair and to the couch and then sat beside him. Pevsner's face showed much the same amused scorn as Delchamps's face had. Castillo reacted by leaning over to Sweaty and kissing her.

Max walked to the coffee table, sniffed, decided he would pass on the seafood, and went and lay at Castillo's feet.

The bartender served the bourbon to Pevsner and Castillo, then looked to the others for orders. Sweaty shook her head. Delchamps ordered, in Russian, Scotch whisky on the rocks, two chunks only, and a glass of water on the side.

How did he know he's Russian?

Was that a way to find out?

The bartender looked at Darby and Duffy, and in English said, "What may I get for you, gentlemen?"

Pevsner looked genuinely amused, and he even made a little joke when everyone had their drinks and had taken seats around the plates of cold lobster chunks and oysters laid out on the coffee table.

"Well," Pevsner said. "Now that we're all here, whatever shall we chat about?"

Tom Barlow took the chair Pevsner had wanted Castillo to sit in, bringing with him an ice-covered bottle of vodka and a frozen glass.

"My call?" Delchamps asked.

Pevsner gestured for him to go on.

"Is that letter genuine?" Delchamps asked. "Is it really from Cousin Vladlen, or did Solomatin just sign what somebody put in front of him?"

"That's two questions, Edgar," Tom Barlow said. "Yes, I think the letter is genuine. And I think Cousin Vladlen wrote it. But he would have signed anything put in front of him by General Sirinov. Cousin Vladlen has built his career by doing whatever he is told to do."

"I know people like that in the agency," Delchamps said, smiling. "Is he really your cousin?"

"His father is our mother's brother," Barlow said, pointing at Sweaty.

"How come Cousin Vladlen didn't get burned when you and Sweaty took off?"

"General Sirinov may have believed him when he said he had no hint what Svetlana and I were planning. Vladlen's a respected *oprichnik*."

"A what?" Darby asked.

"That's right," Castillo said. "You weren't here for this history lesson, were you?"

"I don't know what you're talking about," Darby said.

"An 'oprichnik' is a member of the Oprichnina, the secret police state-within-the-state that goes back to Ivan the Terrible," Castillo said, and looked at Sweaty. "Did I get that right, sweetheart? Do I get a gold star to take home to Mommy?"

She smiled and shook her head resignedly.

"I'll explain it to you later, Alex," Castillo said.

"Tell me about General Sirinov," Delchamps said.

"General Yakov Sirinov runs the FSB and the SVR for Putin," Pevsner said.

"Putin as in Prime Minister Putin?"

"As in Prime Minister Vladimir Vladimirovich Putin, formerly president of the Russian Federation, and before that, polkovnik of the KGB, and before that . . ."

"Oh, *that* Putin," Delchamps said.

Castillo and Barlow chuckled.

"You think Putin's personally involved in this?" Castillo asked.

"Up to the nipples of his underdeveloped chest," Pevsner said.

"I'm getting the feeling you don't like him much," Delchamps said.

Pevsner chuckled.

"Is anyone interested in the possible scenario I've come up with?" Pevsner then said.

"Does a bear shit in the forest?" Delchamps asked in Russian.

"There's a lady present, Edgar," Castillo said.

"She's not a lady, she's an SVR podpolkovnik," Delchamps said.

Sweaty gave him the finger.

"A *former* lieutenant colonel of the Sluzhba Vneshney Razvedki," she corrected him. "Which has nothing to do with whether or not I'm a lady."

"I hate to tell you this, Sweaty, but it's a stretch to think of anyone—how do I put this delicately?—*consorting* with Ace here as being a lady."

Sweaty and Castillo both gave him the finger.

"Anyway," Delchamps said, "according to that letter, 'all is forgiven, come home.' That sounds as if someone still thinks of you as an SVR podpolkovnik in good standing."

"Alek, do they really think anyone is going to believe that letter?" Castillo asked. "That Tom and Sweaty are going to be 'welcomed home as loyal Russians'?"

"I am a loyal Russian," Svetlana said. "But loyal to Russia, not to Vladimir Vladimirovich Putin."

"That—loyalty, loyalty to Russia, or even loyalty to Vladimir Vladimirovich Putin personally—may be at the bottom of this," Pevsner said.

"What do you mean?"

"Putin wants Dmitri and Svetlana to come home."

"Is he stupid enough to think they'd be stupid enough to go back?" Castillo asked.

"No one who knows him—and I know Vladimir Vladimirovich very well—has ever suggested he's stupid," Pevsner replied. "And Dmitri . . . Tom . . . knows him even better than I do."

"I hate to use the word 'genius,'" Tom Barlow said, "but . . ."

"How about 'evil genius'?" Svetlana suggested.

"Why not?" Barlow said chuckling.

"So what is the evil genius up to?" Castillo asked.

"I wonder if you understand, Charley—at least as well as Edgar and Alek do—how important it is for the FSB and the SVR to appear both to the people and, more important, to its own members as all-powerful and without fault."

Castillo's temper flared.

But when he spoke, his voice was low and soft. Those who knew him knew that meant he was really angry.

"I don't even know what the Federal'naya Sluzhba Bezopasnosti and the Sluzhba Vneshney Razvedki are," he said, speaking Russian with a Saint Petersburg accent. "Perhaps before we go any further, someone will be kind enough to tell me."

"I hate to tell you this, Alek," Delchamps said in Russian, "but I think you just pissed Ace off."

After a moment, during which Pevsner looked carefully at Castillo, he said, "More important, Edgar, I once again underestimated my friend Charley. I tend to do that. It probably has something to do with his sophomoric sense of humor. No offense was intended, Charley."

"Offense taken, Polkovnik Pevsner," Castillo said. "In other words, screw you, friend Alek."

Pevsner shook his head, and smiled.

"Let me continue," Pevsner said. "Not long ago, all was right in the world of Vladimir Vladimirovich Putin. He had both finally taken over the KGB and its successor organizations and was president of the Russian Federation.

"He could start to restore the Russian Empire. With a good deal of help from me, he had managed to keep most of the KGB's money out of the hands of those misguided souls who thought it belonged to the people of Russia.

"He would have to deal with me, eventually, of course. I knew too much, and I had too much of what he considered the KGB's money. But that could wait—what does Charley say?—could 'sit on the back burner' until the right time came.

"He was so happy with the way things were going that when General Sirinov came to him with an idea to tweak the American lion's tail at little cost and with minimum risk—using a group of converts to Islam; there would be minimal Russian involvement—he told him to go ahead.

"What he was going to do was have the Muslims crash an airliner into the Liberty Bell in Philadelphia. There was an old American airplane sitting deserted on a runway in Angola. This plane would be stolen, equipped with additional fuel tanks, flown to Philadelphia, and . . ."

He made a diving gesture with his hand.

"I always thought he came up with that idea himself," Tom Barlow said.

"He could have," Pevsner said. "But Sirinov has the better imagination. It doesn't matter. I think of the both of them as one, as Putin-slash-Sirinov."

"Point taken," Barlow said.

"Enter friend Charley," Pevsner said, waving a hand in Castillo's direction. "A lowly U.S. Army major who, not having a clue about what was going on, jumped to the conclusion that the evil arms dealer Vasily Respin or the smuggler Alex Dondiemo or even the more mysterious and wicked Aleksandr Pevsner had stolen the 727 from the field at Luanda, Angola, for their criminal purposes and set out to reclaim it."

Everyone was aware that "Dondiemo" and "Respin" were two of the identities Pevsner used when he thought it was necessary.

"When this came to my attention through a man I had working for me and at that point trusted—Howard Kennedy—"

"That's the ex–FBI agent who was beaten to death by parties unknown in the Conrad Casino in Punta del Este?" Darby asked.

"That's the fellow. Kennedy looked into Major Castillo and reported what he had learned to me. Some of this—for example, that Major Charley Castillo was also Karl Wilhelm von und zu Gossinger, majority shareholder of the Gossinger Beteiligungsgesellschaft, G.m.b.H., empire and that he was working directly for the American President—made me rethink my original solution to the problem."

"Which was?" Delchamps asked.

"An Indian beauty mark," Pevsner replied matter-of-factly, tapping the center of his forehead with his index finger.

"That sometimes takes care of problems like that," Delchamps said.

"God wouldn't let you kill my Charley," Sweaty said seriously.

"Possibly. I never underestimate the power of divine intervention," Pevsner said. "But at the time, I thought it was just common sense. My primary motive was to avoid drawing attention to myself. But, now that I think about it, at the time, I *was* asking God's help to avoid taking anyone's life unnecessarily, so perhaps, Svetlana, you're right, and God was involved."

Charley smiled when he saw Alex Darby's face. It showed that he was having difficulty with Sweaty's and Pevsner's matter-of-fact references to the Almighty.

They don't sound much like godless Communists, do they, Alex? Maybe more like members of the Flaming Bush Church of Christ in Porter's Crossroads, Georgia?

"So," Pevsner went on, "I arranged to meet Charley in Vienna, to see if I could reason with him, come to some kind of understanding—"

"What you did, Alek," Castillo interrupted, "was have that sonofabitch Kennedy blindside me while I was taking a leak in the men's room of the Sacher Hotel bar. Then he dragged me, at gunpoint, up to the Cobenzl."

"Lovely spot," Delchamps said. "I know it well. Just hearing 'Cobenzl' makes me think of fair-haired mädchen and hear the romantic tinkle of the zither."

This earned him a look of mingled disbelief and annoyance from Pevsner.

After a moment, Pevsner said, "The moment I first saw Charley, I realized that it would be painful for me to have to give him a beauty spot. And, Svet, now that I think about, I did ask God to help me spare his life."

Darby was now really confused. He kept looking at Delchamps and Duffy to get their reaction to Pevsner's continued references to the Deity. But knowing of the genuine—if more than a little unusual—deep faith of Pevsner and the other Russians, their faces showed neither surprise or confusion.

"And that's the way it worked out," Pevsner went on. "Charley and I had a cigar and a little cognac watching night fall in Vienna, and then we went to dinner."

"At the Drei Hussars," Charley furnished. "Around the corner from the Opera House. By the time it was over, Alek and I were buddies."

Pevsner gave him an annoyed look.

"Charley," Pevsner continued, "said that he would do what he could with the President to call off the CIA and the FBI—they were then trying very hard to find me—if I would help him find the missing aircraft. I took a chance and trusted him.

"I admit that finding the missing 727 wasn't difficult for me. I operate a number of airplanes in sub-Saharan Africa, and all of my crews always keep their eyes open for things in which they think I might be interested.

"Cutting a long story short, Charley was able to take the 727 back from the Muslims before they could do any damage with it. And, as he said he would, he got the President to call off the FBI and the CIA.

"I did not know of General Sirinov's plan to tweak the American lion's tail, and Sirinov had no reason to suspect that I even knew Charley, much less that I was the one who had been instrumental in upsetting it.

"He did learn, of course, that Charley had flown the aircraft into MacDill Air Force Base in Florida. Charley was thus added to Sirinov's list of people to be dealt with when the opportunity presented itself.

"Next, friend Charley messed up another SVR operation. Sirinov sent a team—under Cuban Dirección General de Inteligencia Major Alejandro Vincenzo—to Lieutenant Colonel Yevgeny Komogorov, his FSB man in charge of operations in Argentina, Chile, and Uruguay, to eliminate a man who knew too much and had also made off with sixteen million dollars of the SVR's money. When that escapade was over, Vincenzo and his men were dead, and Charley had the sixteen million dollars.

"Since Komogorov needed somebody to blame for that disaster, he decided to blame it on me, reasoning that if I were dead, I couldn't protest my innocence. So he paid a large sum of money to my trusted assistant, the late Mr. Howard Kennedy, to arrange for me to be assassinated in the garage of the Sheraton Hotel in Pilar, outside Buenos Aires.

"When that was over, I was alive and Komogorov wasn't. Corporal Lester Bradley had put an Indian beauty spot on his right eye. The others on his team were taken out by others working for friend Charley. And Mr. Kennedy went to meet his maker shortly thereafter.

"All of this tended to reduce the all-powerful, faultless image of both the FSB and the SVR, which meant that the power of Sirinov and Vladimir Vladimirovich was becoming questionable.

"Sirinov decided to settle the matter once and for all. With a great deal of effort, Sirinov ordered the simultaneous assassinations of a man in Vienna known to be a longtime deep cover asset of the CIA; a reporter for one of Charley's newspapers who was asking the wrong questions about Russian involvement in the oil-for-food program; Liam Duffy, who had interrupted a previously successful SVR drug operation in Argentina and Paraguay; and—"

"So they're all connected," Alex Darby said.

"Oh, yes. Please let me finish," Pevsner said. "And the assassination of another of Charley's men, a policeman in Philadelphia, who knew the Muslims who planned to crash an airplane into the Liberty Bell were not smart enough to conceive of, much less try to execute, an operation like that by themselves and suspected the SVR was involved.

"When only the assassinations of the CIA asset in Vienna and of the journalist were successful, Sirinov had to report this failure to Putin. So far as Vladimir Vladimirovich is concerned, there is no such thing as a partial success. And Sirinov knew that the only thing worse than reporting a failure to Vladimir Vladimirovich was not having a credible plan to make things right.

"And he had one: Dmitri and Svetlana had been ordered to Vienna to participate in a conference of senior SVR officers. The cover was the presence in Vienna of Bartolomeo Rastrelli's wax statue of Peter the First, which the Hermitage had generously loaned to the Kunsthistorisches Museum.

"The *Tages Zeitung* journalist whom he had managed to eliminate was going to be buried with much ceremony in Marburg an der Lahn, Germany. There was no question that Eric Kocian and Otto Görner, managing director of Gossinger G.m.b.H. would be there. With a little bit of luck, so would Karl von und zu Gossinger, who was not only the owner of the Gossinger empire but Lieutenant Colonel Castillo, who had been causing the SVR so much trouble. All three—plus at least some of Charley's people who would be with him—could be eliminated at the same time.

"Tom's train would pass through Marburg on its way to Vienna. So Sirinov dispatched a team of Hungarians—ex–Államvédelmi Hatóság—to Marburg, with orders to report to Polkovnik Berezovsky. Sirinov knew Dmitri—*Tom*—could be counted upon to supervise their assassination assignment with his well-known skill for that sort of thing. And then catch the next train to Vienna.

"Well, that turned out to be an even greater disaster for General Sirinov, as we all know."

"Through God's infinite mercy," Svetlana said very seriously.

She crossed herself.

"Svet," Pevsner said seriously, "you may very possibly be right, but there's also the possibility that it was the incompetence of the CIA station chief in Vienna that saved Charley and Kocian from the ministrations of the Államvédelmi Hatóság."

"It was the hand of God," Svetlana said firmly.

"Possibly, Sweaty, it was the hand of God that contributed to Miss Eleanor Dillworth's incompetence," Delchamps said. "Same result, right?"

Svetlana looked at him coldly, not sure—but deeply suspecting—that he was being sarcastic.

"Eleanor is not incompetent," Alex Darby said loyally.

"Come on," Delchamps said. "She was incompetent in Vienna. The *rezident* there . . . what was his name?"

"Podpolkovnik Kiril Demidov," Barlow furnished. "He used to work for me."

"Demidov was onto Dillworth," Delchamps said firmly. "Maybe he didn't know it was Tom and Sweaty, but he knew that—Jesus Christ!—Dillworth had a plane sitting at Schwechat airfield ready to haul some defector, or defectors, away from the Kunsthistorisches Museum."

"You don't know that," Darby protested.

"I know that your pal Eleanor should have known that Demidov was going to take out the Kuhls. And once that happened, she didn't have a clue what to do next. I asked her. She said she was 'waiting for instructions from Langley.'"

"If I may continue, gentlemen?" Pevsner said a little impatiently.

"I didn't trust her, Edgar," Tom Barlow said, ignoring Pevsner. "I don't know if it was that I thought she wasn't professional or what."

"It was the hand of God," Svetlana insisted.

"But once I saw the picture in the *Frankfurter Rundschau* of Charley getting off his private jet," Barlow went on, "I decided that Svetlana and I were going to leave Europe on that aircraft if I had to give him Sirinov and all the ex–Államvédelmi Hatóság people."

"And from that moment, until we walked into Alek's house here, everything went smoothly," Svetlana said. "Does no one see the hand of God in that?"

"I do," Castillo said.

When Sweaty looked at him, he sang, *"Jesus loves me, this I know, for the Bible tells me so."*

"Don't mock God, Charley!" she snapped furiously and moved away from him on the couch.

"Well," Pevsner said, "Dmitri and Svetlana were not intercepted in Vienna, and that was the end of that. Except of course that Liam applied the Old Testament eye-for-an-eye principle to Lavrenti Tarasov and Evgeny Alekseev, who had come to Argentina in search of Tom and Svetlana."

"Not quite," Delchamps said. "Alex's good buddy, Miss Dillworth, sicced a reporter—a good one: Roscoe J. Danton of *The Washington Times-Post*—on Charley. He came to Alek's apartment just before we got out of there."

"A reporter? What did he want?" Castillo asked.

"He wanted you, Ace. He probably wants to know why you stole Sweaty and Tom out from under Miss Dillworth's nose. And if Dillworth told him about that, I wouldn't be at all surprised if she told him you left the Vienna *rezident*—what was his name? Demidov?—sitting in a taxi outside our embassy with an Államvédelmi Hatóság garrote around his neck, and her calling card on his chest."

"I had nothing to do with that, as you goddamn well know. The story going around is that some old company dinosaur did that."

"You sound like you think I had something to do with it," Delchamps said.

"Do I?" Castillo said sarcastically.

"Funny thing about those old company dinosaurs, Charley. You're too young of course to know much about them. But they really believe in what it says in the Old Testament about an eye for an eye, and if they do something like what happened to Demidov, they never, ever, 'fess up to it."

"Changing the subject just a little," Tom Barlow said. "I think we should throw this into the facts bearing on the problem: Just as soon as Sirinov and/or Vladimir Vladimirovich heard that the Americans had taken out the Fish Farm, they realized that information had to have come from me."

"You don't know that," Castillo argued.

"In our profession, Charley," Tom said, "we never *know* anything. All we ever have is a hypothesis—or many hypotheses—based on what we *think* we know."

"Touché," Castillo said.

"We all forget that at one time or another," Barlow said.

Castillo met his eyes, and thought, *That was kind of you, Tom.*

But all it did was remind everyone in this room that I am the least experienced spook in it.

Which, truth be told, I am.

"One of the things I was tasked to do in Berlin was make sure that the Fish Farm got whatever it needed," Barlow went on. "It's not hard to come up with a hypothesis that Sirinov and Vladimir Vladimirovich reasoned that since Polkovnik Berezovsky knew about the Fish Farm and it was destroyed shortly after Polkovnik Berezovsky defected to the Americans, whose CIA had looked into the matter and decided the factory was indeed a fish farm, Polkovnik Berezovsky told the Americans what it really was."

"You knew what the CIA thought?" Charley asked.

"Of course," Barlow said.

"You had . . . have . . . a mole?"

"Of course, but you don't need a mole to learn things like that," Barlow said. "Actually you can often learn more from a disgruntled worker who wouldn't think of betraying her country than from an asset on the payroll."

"Your pal Dillworth, for example, Alex," Delchamps said. "What is it they say, 'Hell hath no fury like a pissed-off female'?"

"Eleanor is a pro," Darby said, again showing his loyalty.

"She pointed Roscoe Danton at Charley," Delchamps argued. "What hypothesis does that suggest?"

Darby looked at Delchamps angrily, looked for a moment as if he were going to reply, but in the end said nothing.

Castillo said, "What's your hypothesis, Tom, about the stuff from the Congo suddenly showing up at Fort Detrick?"

"Well, it's clear it's got something to do with this," Barlow replied. "What, I don't know."

"It could have something to do with Vladimir Vladimirovich's ego," Pevsner said.

"He couldn't resist the temptation to let us know that we didn't wipe the Fish Farm off the face of the earth?" Delchamps offered.

Pevsner nodded.

"If he's got that stuff, he could have used it, and he didn't," Castillo said thoughtfully.

"So, what's next?" Delchamps said. "I buy that stick-it-up-your-ass motive, Alek, but I don't think that's all there is to it."

Pevsner nodded his agreement.

"So Charley has to tell those people in Las Vegas that he's changed his mind about working for them," Barlow said.

"Why would I want to do that?" Castillo replied. "The Office of Organizational Analysis no longer exists. I am in compliance with my orders to fall off the face of the earth and never be seen again. Sweaty and I are going to build a vine-covered cottage by the side of the road and live happily therein forever afterward."

"There goes that sophomoric sense of humor of yours again," Pevsner snapped.

"How so?" Castillo replied.

"Vladimir Vladimirovich is going to come after you. And Svetlana," Pevsner said. "You ought to read a little Mao Zedong. He wrote that 'the only real defense is active defense.'"

"Did he really?" Castillo said. "I wonder where he got that?"

"Probably from Sun-tzu," Svetlana said seriously. "That's where most people think Machiavelli got it."

"Sun-tzu?" Castillo asked. "That's the Chinaman who turned two hundred of the emperor's concubines into soldiers and won the war with them? I've always been an admirer of his."

"It was one hundred eighty concubines," Svetlana said. "He got their attention by beheading the first of them who thought it was funny and giggled, and then he beheaded the second one who giggled, and then so on down the line until he came to one who understood that what was going on was no laughing matter."

"Does anybody else think Sweaty's trying to make a point?" Delchamps asked innocently.

"Let me make a point, several points," Castillo said seriously. "One, as far as the intelligence community is concerned, I'm a pariah. So is everybody ever connected with the OOA. They hated us when we had the blessing of the President, and now hating us is politically correct. I'll bet right now both the company and the FBI—hell, all the alphabet agencies—have a 'locate but do not detain' bulletin out on us. They're not going to help us at all. Quite the opposite: If we start playing James Bond again, we'll find ourselves counting paint flecks on the wall at the Florence maximum security prison in Colorado.

"And, if I have to say this, we'll have less than zero help from anybody."

"I think you're wrong about that, Charley," Barlow said. "We know that—"

"Let me finish, Tom," Castillo said sharply. "Point two—probably the most important thing—is that any operation we might try to run would have to have a leader. And C. Castillo, Retired, cannot be that leader. What did President Johnson say? 'I shall not seek, nor will I accept . . .'"

"You're wrong about that, too, Ace," Delchamps said. "I for one won't go—and I don't think any of the others will—unless you're running the show. And we have to go, since the option to that is sitting around waiting for some SVR hit squad to whack us. And, Romeo, what about the fair Juliet? You're going to just sit around holding Sweaty's hand waiting for the hit squad to whack her? Worse, drag her back to Mother Russia?"

"You don't know how the others will feel," Castillo said, more than a little lamely.

"Hypothesis: They'll all go. Any questions?" Delchamps said.

"Count me in, Charley," Alex Darby said.

"I wouldn't know where to start," Castillo said.

"I'm not sure if you've ever heard this before," Barlow said. "But some people in our line of work think collecting as much intelligence as possible as quickly as possible is a good way to start."

"And how would I go about doing that?"

"That's what I started to say a moment ago," Barlow said. "You were there, Charley, in that suite in the Venetian Hotel in Las Vegas when those people as much as told us that the director of Central Intelligence is either one of them, or damn close to them."

"I don't remember that," Castillo said.

"The man who was a Naval Academy graduate quoted verbatim to you the unkind things you said to the DCI, something about the agency being 'a few very good people trying to stay afloat in a sea of left-wing bureaucrats.' Who do you think told him about that?"

"I remember now," Castillo said. "But I really had forgotten. That's not much of a recommendation, is it?"

"Charley, I said I'd take your orders," Delchamps said. "But . . . You saw *The Godfather*?"

"Yes, of course."

"Both Brando and the son—Pacino? De Niro? I never can keep them straight—had a consigliere. Think of me as Robert Duvall."

"Think of us both as Robert Duvall," Barlow said. "It was Al Pacino."

"I don't think so," Delchamps said.

"Can either of my consiglieri suggest how I can get in touch with those people?"

"Well, if you hadn't been gulping down all that Wild Turkey, I'd suggest you fly everybody to Carinhall in Alek's chopper. But since you have been soaking up the booze, I guess we'll have to drive over there and get on Casey's radio."

"No," Castillo said. "There's a Casey radio in the Aero Commander."

"It fits?" Delchamps asked, surprised.

"Aloysius's stuff is so miniaturized it's unbelievable," Castillo said. "But call your house, Alek, and tell your man to stand by. There's no printer in the airplane. And you'd better call down to the airstrip and have them push the plane from the hangar."

"Yes, sir, Podpolkovnik Castillo, sir," Svetlana said, and saluted him. Then she saw the look on his face. "My darling, I love it when you're in charge of things; it makes me feel comfortable and protected."

"It makes me think Ace's had too much to drink," Delchamps said.

"Aloysius, you think the offer from those people is still open?" Castillo asked.

Castillo was sitting in the pilot's seat of the Aero Commander. Delchamps was in the co-pilot's seat. Svetlana was kneeling in the aisle and her brother was leaning over her. Pevsner, Duffy, and Darby were sitting in the cabin. Max and János were standing watchfully outside by the nose of the airplane.

"I told them you'd change your mind," Casey said. "This thing sort of scares me, Charley. There was another beer keg of that stuff sitting on a road near the Mexican border in Texas this morning."

"Another one?" Castillo asked.

"Another one. They left it where the Border Patrol couldn't miss it. It's been taken to Colonel Hamilton at Fort Detrick. We're waiting to hear from him to tell us if it's exactly the same thing."

"Well, send me whatever intel you have, everything you can get your hands on. *Everything*, Aloysius."

"Done."

"What shape is the Gulfstream in?"

"Ready to go."

"Tell Jake to take it to Cancún. They'll expect him."

"You don't want him to pick you up down there?"

"No. I'll come commercial."

Svetlana was tugging at his sleeve.

She rubbed her thumb and forefinger together, mouthed *Money*, and then held up two fingers.

"Aloysius, I'm going to need some cash," Castillo said.

"No problem. How much?"

"Will those people stand still for two hundred thousand?"

"Where do you want it?"

Castillo was now aware Svetlana was shaking her head in what looked like incredulity but could have been disgust.

"Send it to Otto Görner and tell him to put it in my personal account."

"Otto will have it within the hour. Anything else?"

"That's all I can think of."

"Let me know," Aloysius Casey said. "And thanks, Charley. Break it down."

Castillo looked over his shoulder at Svetlana.

"You're going to tell me what I did wrong, aren't you, my love?"

"I meant two *million* dollars. Now those people are going to think they can hire you for an unimportant sum. The more people pay you, the more important *they* think you are."

"Well, my love, you'll have to excuse my naïveté. This is the first time I've signed on as a mercenary."

"Well, my darling, you'd better get used to it."

"What you'd better get used to, Ace," Delchamps said, "is thinking of Sweaty as Robert Duvall."

[THREE]
The Oval Office
The White House
1600 Pennsylvania Avenue, N.W.
Washington, D.C.
1715 5 February 2007

It had proven impossible to gather together all the people the President had wanted for the meeting. The secretary of Defense was in Europe at a NATO meeting, and the commanding general of the Defense Intelligence Agency had gone with him. The secretary of Homeland Security was in Chicago.

When Charles M. Montvale, the director of National Intelligence, and Colonel J. Porter Hamilton, MC, USA, walked into the Oval Office, the secretary of State, Natalie Cohen; John Powell, the director of the Central Intelligence Agency; and Mark Schmidt, the director of the Federal Bureau of Investigation, were sitting in chairs forming a rough semicircle facing the President's desk.

So were Assistant Secretary of Homeland Security Mason Andrews, standing in for the secretary, and General Allan B. Naylor, USA, commanding general of United States Central Command, who was representing both the secretary of Defense and the commanding general of the Defense Intelligence Agency. Presidential spokesman Jack "Porky" Parker sat at a small table—just large enough to hold his laptop computer—to one side of the President.

"I'm sorry to be late, Mr. President," Montvale said.

"It's my fault, Mr. President," Hamilton said. "I was engaged in some laboratory processes I couldn't interrupt."

"Not even for the commander in chief?" Clendennen asked unpleasantly.

"If I had stopped doing what I was doing when Mr. Montvale asked me to, it would have caused a two- or three-hour loss of time," Hamilton said. "I considered a fifteen- or twenty-minute delay in coming here the lesser of two evils."

"Until just now, Colonel, I wasn't aware that colonels were permitted to make decisions like that," Clendennen said sarcastically.

Hamilton didn't reply.

"What were you doing that you considered important enough to keep us all waiting for you to finish?" Clendennen asked.

"Actually, I had several processes working, Mr. President," Hamilton, uncowed, said. "The most important of them being the determination that

Congo-X and Congo-Y were chemically—perhaps I should say 'biologically'—identical—"

"What's Congo-Y?" the President interrupted.

"I have so labeled the material from the Mexican border."

"And are they? Identical?"

"That is my preliminary determination, Mr. President."

"Colonel, two questions," General Naylor announced.

"Sir?"

Clendennen didn't like having his questioning of Hamilton interrupted by anyone, and had his mouth open to announce *Excuse me, General, but I'm asking the questions* when he changed his mind.

Clendennen liked General Naylor, and had been pleased when he had shown up to stand in for the secretary of the Defense and Defense Intelligence Agency general. He knew he could always believe what Naylor told him. This was not true of the people he was standing in for: The secretary of Defense had assured President Clendennen that the infernal laboratory in the Congo had first been completely reduced to pebbles and then incinerated. Clendennen had never heard the DIA general mouth an unqualified statement.

"They're related, obviously," Naylor began. "First, do you know with reasonable certainty who developed this terrible substance? And, second, how would you say they intend to use it against us?"

"Sir, I have nothing to support this legally or scientifically, but something tells me the origins of this substance go back at least to World War Two and perhaps earlier than that."

"Go down that road," Clendennen ordered.

"During the Second World War, sir, both the Germans and the Japanese experimented with materials somewhat similar to Congo-X. That is to say, biological material that could be used as a weapon. The Japanese tested it in China on the civilian population and the Germans on concentration camp inmates."

"And did it work?" the President asked.

"All we have is anecdotal, Mr. President," Hamilton said. "There is a great deal of that, and all of it suggests that it was effective. There is strong reason to believe material similar to this was tested on American prisoners of war by the Japanese . . ."

"Do we know that, or don't we?" the President asked impatiently.

"A number of POWs were executed by the Japanese immediately after Hiroshima. Their bodies were cremated and the ashes disposed of at sea," Naylor said.

"Nice people," the President said.

"And there is further evidence, Mr. President, that the Chinese sent several hundred American POWs captured in the early days of the Korean war to Czechoslovakia, where they were subjected to biological material apparently similar to something like this. Again, no proof. We know the prisoners were sent to Czechoslovakia. But no bodies, not one, were ever recovered. We still have Graves Registration people looking."

"Why don't we know more about the chemicals, about whatever was used on the prisoners?"

"At the time, Mr. President," Naylor said, "the greatest threat was perceived to be the possibility the Russians would get their hands on German science vis-à-vis a nuclear weapon and rocketry. We were quite successful in doing so, but the effort necessary was at the expense of looking more deeply into what the Germans had been doing with biological weapons.

"In the Pacific, actually, we acquired what anecdotal information we have about the executed and cremated POWs primarily because MacArthur was passionately determined to locate, try, and hang as quickly as possible those Japanese officers responsible for the atrocities committed against our prisoners. They were, so to speak, just one more atrocity."

The President considered that for a moment.

"So, then what is your theory about this, Colonel Hamilton?" he asked.

Hamilton began: "It's pure conjecture, Mr. President—"

"I thought it might be," the President interrupted sarcastically, and gestured for Hamilton to continue.

Hamilton ignored the interruption and went on: "It is possible that, at the end of World War Two, the Russians came into possession of a substance much like Congo-X. They might even have acquired it from the Japanese; there was an interchange of technical information.

"They very likely acquired at the same time the German scientists working with this material, much as we took over Wernher von Braun, his rocket scientists, and the rockets themselves.

"If this is true—and even if it is not, and Russian scientists alone worked with it—it had to have become immediately apparent to them how incredibly dangerous it is."

"Why is it so 'incredibly dangerous'?" the President interrupted yet again.

Hamilton looked at Clendennen a long moment, then carefully said: "With respect, Mr. President, I believe I'm repeating myself, but: The Congo-X in my laboratory, when placed under certain conditions of temperature and humidity, gives off microscopic particles—airborne—which when inhaled into the lung of a warm-blooded mammal will, in a matter of days, begin to consume the flesh of the lung. Meanwhile, the infected body will also be giving off—breathing back into the air—these contaminated, infectious particles before the host has any indication that he's been infected.

"When I was in the Congo and saw the cadavers of animals and humans who had died of this infestation, I told the President—our late President—that the Fish Farm, should there be an accident, had the potential of becoming a greater risk to mankind than the nuclear meltdown at Chernobyl had posed."

"That's pretty strong, isn't it, Colonel?" the President asked.

"Now that I have some idea of the danger, Mr. President," Hamilton said, "that was a massive understatement."

"Is there a way to kill this material?" Naylor asked.

"I've had some success with incineration at temperatures over one thousand degrees centigrade," Hamilton said, looked at the President, and added: "That's about two thousand degrees Fahrenheit, Mr. President."

"I seem to recall the secretary of Defense telling me that the attack produced that kind of heat," the President said.

"Then where did the two separate packages of Congo-X come from?" Secretary of State Natalie Cohen asked.

"There're only two possibilities," Ambassador Montvale said. "The attack was not successful; everything was not incinerated and someone—I suspect the Russians—went in there and picked up what was missed. Or, the Russians all along had a stock of this stuff in Russia and that's what they're sending us."

"Why? What do they want?" Cohen asked.

"We're not even sure it's the Russians, are we?" Mark Schmidt, the director of the FBI, asked.

"Are we, Mr. Director of National Intelligence?" the President asked. "Are we sure who's been sending us the Congo-X?"

"Not at this time, Mr. President," Montvale replied.

"Have we the capability of sending someone into the Congo?" Assistant Secretary of Homeland Security Mason Andrew asked. "To do, in the greatest secrecy—what do they call it?—'damage assessment'?"

"Not anymore," Natalie Cohen said.

There was a long silence.

"Madam Secretary," the President asked finally, icily, "would I be wrong to think that you had a certain Colonel Costello in mind when you said that?"

She met his eyes.

"I had Lieutenant Colonel Carlos *Castillo* in mind, yes, sir," she said. "I was thinking that since he managed to successfully infiltrate Colonel Hamilton into the Congo and, more importantly, exfiltrate him—"

"Weren't you listening, Madam Secretary, when I said that in this administration there will be no private bands of special operators? I thought I had made that perfectly clear. Castillo and his men have been dispersed. He was ordered by my predecessor to—the phrase he used was 'fall off the face of the earth, never to be seen again.' I never want to hear his name mentioned again, much less to see him. Is everybody clear on that, absolutely clear?"

"Yes, Mr. President," Secretary Cohen said.

There was a murmur as everyone responded at once: "Yes, sir." "Yes, Mr. President." "Absolutely clear, Mr. President."

"Mr. President, there may be a problem in that area," Porky Parker said.

The President looked at him in surprise, perhaps even shock. The President thought he had made it absolutely clear to Parker that the spokesman's role in meetings like this was to listen, period.

"What did you say, Jack?" the President asked softly.

"Mr. President, Roscoe Danton of *The Washington Times-Post* is looking for Colonel Castillo."

"How do you know that?"

"He came to me, sir."

"And what did you tell him?"

"I told him I had no idea where he was," Parker said.

"Charles?"

"Sir?" Montvale replied.

"Where is Castillo?"

"I don't know, Mr. President."

"I told you the next time I asked that question, I would expect an answer."

"I'm working on it, Mr. President, but so far without any results."

"Wonderful! It's so nice to know that whenever I want to know something, all I have to do is ask my director of National Intelligence!"

There was another thirty-second silence, and then the President went on: "Far be it from me to try to tell the director of National Intelligence how to do his job, but I have just had this probably useless thought: If Roscoe Danton is looking for Colonel Castillo, perhaps he has an idea where he is. Has anyone thought of that? Where's Danton?"

There was no reply.

"Find out for me, Charles, will you, please?"

"I'll get right on it, Mr. President," Montvale said.

[FOUR]
The Office of the Director of National Intelligence
Eisenhower Executive Office Building
17th Street and Pennsylvania Avenue, N.W.
Washington, D.C.
1805 5 February 2007

"I can't think of anything else to do, can you?" Ambassador Montvale asked Truman C. Ellsworth, his executive assistant.

When Ellsworth had called *The Washington Times-Post* for Roscoe J. Danton, they refused to tell him where he was. They said they would contact Danton and tell him Ambassador Montvale wanted to speak with him. Ellsworth finally called the publisher, Bradley Benjamin III, and told him what had happened, and asked for his help. Mr. Benjamin told him that what he had already been offered was all he was going to get, and please give Ambassador Montvale his best regards.

Since both Truman C. Ellsworth and Charles M. Montvale would swear— because they believed it—that they were incapable of letting anger, or a bruised ego, interfere in the slightest with their judgment, or the execution of their offices, what happened next was attributed to the fervor with which they chose to meet the President's request to locate Mr. Roscoe J. Danton.

The National Security Agency at Fort Meade, Maryland, was directed as the highest priority to acquire and relay to the ambassador's office any traffic by telephone, or over the Internet, containing Mr. Danton's name.

The Department of Homeland Security was directed to search the flight manifests of every passenger airliner taking off from either Reagan International Airport or Dulles International Airport during the past forty-eight hours for the name of Roscoe J. Danton, and if found to immediately report his destination and time of arrival thereat.

The Secret Service was ordered to obtain the residential address of Mr. Roscoe J. Danton and to place such premises under around-the-clock surveillance and to immediately report any sighting of Mr. Danton. They were further ordered to send agents to the National Press Club to see if any clue to his whereabouts could be obtained.

The cooperation of the FBI was sought and obtained to put out an immediate "locate but do not detain" bulletin on Mr. Danton.

"I just had an idea," Mr. Ellsworth said when asked if he could think of anything else that could be done.

He told the White House operator get *The Washington Times-Post* for him again, this time the Corporate Travel department.

Montvale's eyebrows rose, but he didn't comment.

"Hello, Corporate Travel?" Ellsworth then said. "Yes, hi. Brad Benjamin just told me you would know where I can find Roscoe Danton."

Not sixty seconds after that, he said, "Got it. Thank you," hung up the phone, and turned to Ambassador Montvale and reported, "Danton went to Buenos Aires. They made a reservation for him at the Marriott Plaza."

"The *Marriott* Plaza?" Montvale replied, obviously surprised.

"That's what they told me. You want me to put in a call to our ambassador?"

"I wouldn't believe that sonofabitch if he told me what day it is."

"The CIA station chief, then?"

"Get me John Powell. I'll have the DCI call the station chief and tell him I'll be calling."

Ellsworth told the White House operator to connect the director of National Intelligence with the director of Central Intelligence on a secure line and then pushed the LOUDSPEAKER button and handed the receiver to Montvale.

"Jack, Charles M. Montvale. I want you to give me the name of the station chief in Buenos Aires, and something about him, and then call him and tell him I'll be calling on an errand for the President."

"Hang on a second, Charles," Powell replied.

He came back on the line ninety seconds later.

"Got a little problem, Charles. We had a really good man there, Alex Darby, but he went out the door with Castillo. A kid just out of The Farm has been filling in for Darby, until Bob Lowe, another good man, can clear his desk in Mexico City. I don't know if Lowe made it down there yet."

"Well, please call the kid, and tell him I'll be calling."

"Clendennen."

"Charles M. Montvale, Mr. President. I've located Mr. Danton. He's in the Marriott Plaza Hotel in Buenos Aires."

"That would suggest he knows where Colonel Castillo is, wouldn't you say?"

"That's a strong possibility, Mr. President."

"I presume your next call will be to the ambassador down there."

"I was thinking of calling the CIA station chief, Mr. President."

"Okay, your call. That might be best, now that I think of it."

"There's a small problem there, Mr. President. The acting station chief is a young man just out of agency training. John Powell just told me that the man he's sending down there to replace the former station chief, who, sir, fell off the face of the earth with Castillo, has not reported for duty."

"So what are you planning to do?"

"I thought I would send Truman Ellsworth down there, sir. Just as soon as he can get to Andrews."

"I dislike micromanagement, Charles, as you know. But if I were in your shoes, I would go down there myself. Take What's-his-name with you if you like."

"Yes, sir. That's probably the right thing to do."

"It would be better if someone of your stature were the person to suggest to Costello that he would be ill-advised to get anywhere near our little problem. You understand me?"

"Yes, sir."

"Keep me advised," President Clendennen said, and Montvale heard the click that signaled the commander in chief had terminated the call.

"I'll call Andrews and have the plane ready," Truman Ellsworth said.

Their presidential mission began in a two-GMC-Yukon convoy from the Executive Office Building. The first Secret-Service-agent-driven, black-tinted-window Yukon held the driver; the two Secret Service agents assigned to protect Montvale; and the two assigned to protect Ellsworth. The second Yukon carried Montvale and Ellsworth and everyone's luggage.

On the way to Andrews Air Force Base, Montvale and Ellsworth consoled themselves for having to travel all the way down to Argentina by agreeing that it wouldn't be that bad a trip. The C-37A—the Air Force designation for the Gulfstream V—on which they would fly was just about as nice an airplane as airplanes came.

It had a range greater than the 5,100-odd miles between Washington and Buenos Aires, and could cruise nonstop at Mach 0.80, or a little faster than five hundred miles per hour. There was room for eight passengers, which meant that Montvale and Ellsworth—rank hath its privileges—could make the most of the journey spread out on bed-size couches. Or they could sit up on the couches and have a drink or two from the portable bar in one of the Secret Service agent's luggage.

And they were sure to get one of the two Gulfstream Vs at Andrews: Ellsworth had made a point of telling the commanding officer of the presidential flight detachment that he and Montvale were traveling at the direct personal order of President Clendennen.

That, however, did not come to pass.

At Andrews, they learned that one of the two Gulfstream V jets had carried Mrs. Sue-Ellen Clendennen to Montgomery, Alabama, where the First Lady's mother was sick in hospital.

Both Montvale and Ellsworth habitually took a look at the reports of the presidential security detail. They therefore knew the President's mother-in-law was not in a hospital *per se* but rather an "assisted-living facility" and that her being sick therein was a sort of code which meant the old lady had once again eluded her caretakers and acquired a stock of intoxicants.

That was moot. They knew they were outranked by the First Lady. And the second Gulfstream V at Andrews was not available to them either, as it was being held for possible use by someone else who outranked them, the Speaker of the House of Representatives, who could be counted upon to throw a female fit of monumental proportions if a Gulfstream V was not immediately available to take her to her home in Palm Beach if she suddenly felt the urge to go there.

That left only a C-20A—what the Air Force called the Gulfstream III— from the half-dozen kept by the Air Force for VIP transport at Andrews for their flight to Buenos Aires. While just about as fast as a C-37A, the C-20A is a somewhat smaller aircraft with a maximum range of about thirty-seven hundred miles. That meant that not only was a fuel stop necessary en route to Buenos Aires, but that the couches on which Montvale and Ellsworth would attempt to sleep were neither as wide nor as comfortable as those on the Gulfstream V would have been.

They had finally gotten off the ground at Andrews just before midnight. Flight time was a few minutes under twelve hours. The fuel stop added another hour and forty-five minutes. There was a one-hour difference between time in Washington and in Buenos Aires. They would arrive, if there were no problems, at Jorge Newbery Airport in Buenos Aires at about one in the afternoon.

VII

[ONE]
Estancia San Joaquín
Near San Martín de los Andes
Patagonia
Neuquén Province, Argentina
2130 5 February 2007

Aleksandr Pevsner took a sip of his after-dinner brandy, then took a puff on his after-dinner cigar, and then pointed the cigar at Castillo.

Castillo also had a cigar, but no brandy. In the morning he was going to have to fly the Bell Ranger to the airport at San Carlos de Bariloche, where, Pevsner had decided earlier, his Learjet would be waiting to fly them over the Andes to El Tepual International Airport in Puerto Montt, Chile. They would travel to Cozumel on a Peruaire cargo plane carrying foodstuffs for the cruise ship trade and Pevsner's Grand Cozumel Beach & Golf Resort. Castillo would have to do that twice; there wasn't room in the helicopter to fly everybody at once.

"I have been thinking, friend Charley . . ." Pevsner announced.

"Uh-oh," Castillo replied.

Pevsner shook his head in resignation, and then went on: "Two things: First, I think it would be useful if I went to Cozumel with you. I have contacts in Mexico that might be useful, and if you're going to use the Beach and Golf as a base, certain arrangements will have to be made. Comments?"

"Makes sense," Tom Barlow said.

"I agree," Svetlana said.

"Pay attention, Marlon Brando," Delchamps said. "Your consiglieri have been heard from."

"This meets with your approval, Charley?"

"Who am I to argue with my consiglieri?"

But I wonder what you would have said if I had said, "That's a lousy idea."

"Second, I've been thinking that it would be best if you flew the Aero Commander to Puerto Montt. That would both save us time in the morning, and we would be less conspicuous. The latter depends, of course, on whether you can fly that airplane over the Andes. Can you?"

"Quick answer, no," Castillo replied. "The Commander's cabin is not pressurized, and the service ceiling is about thirteen thousand feet. There are lots of rock-filled clouds in the Andes much higher than that."

"Actually, the average height is about thirteen thousand feet," Pevsner said. "Could you fly around the peaks?"

"Probably," Castillo said. "I'd have to look at the charts, and I don't have any charts."

"János, call down to the hangar and have them bring the necessary aerial charts," Pevsner ordered. "And when you've finished that, call the house and have our luggage prepared."

"If, after I look at the charts and decide I can fly around the peaks, I'd still have to make two flights," Castillo said. "We can't get everybody in the Commander at once. Have you considered that?"

"You'd have to make two flights in the Lear, too. Taking the little airplane still makes more sense," Svetlana said.

"Concur," Tom Barlow said.

"There they go again!" Delchamps said. "What would you do without them whispering sage advice in your ear, Don Carlos?"

Tom Barlow chuckled. Svetlana gave him the finger.

[TWO]
El Tepual International Airport
Puerto Montt, Chile
0830 6 February 2007

The first flight in the Aero Commander from Estancia San Joaquín through the Andes mountains had carried Alek Pevsner—who had said he wanted to make sure things went smoothly in Puerto Montt—plus János, Tom Barlow, Sweaty, and of course Max.

The Casey avionics worked perfectly, and everyone but the pilot seemed to enjoy the flight. In the early light of day, the snow-capped Andes were incredibly beautiful. The pilot spent much time during the flight—whenever the altimeter showed that he was at or just over thirteen thousand feet—remembering that the U.S. Army had taught him that at any altitude over twelve thousand feet, the pilot's brain is denied the oxygen it needs.

Despite its grandiose title, El Tepual International was just about completely deserted when they landed. There was no Peruaire cargo jet in sight; just three Chevrolet Suburbans whose drivers looked more Slavic than one would expect of Chileans.

Svetlana immediately exercised her female right to change her mind and announced she would return to Estancia San Joaquín with Castillo to pick up Alex Darby and Edgar Delchamps.

That could be because my lover can't bear to be even briefly separated from me.

But on the other hand it could be because former Podpolkovnik Svetlana Alek-seeva of the SVR thinks she had better keep an eye on the crazy American to make sure that he doesn't do something stupid.

The second flight went smoothly, and this time the pilot elected to fly more closely to the terrain, rather than trying to attain as much altitude as he could.

And when he turned on final approach, he saw that there was another air-craft on the tarmac: a Peruaire Boeing 777-200LR.

Jesus, that's one great big beautiful sonofabitch!

When he taxied up close to it, feeling like one of the little people Gulliver had encountered in his travels, he saw that a swarm of workers had just about finished loading it with refrigerated containers.

What was the Triple-Seven freighter's revenue payload?

I think Alek said just over a hundred tons—one hundred twelve tons, was what he said.

Jesus, that's a lot of seafood and beef!

Ten minutes after he landed at El Tepual, he was strapped into one of the ten seats in the passenger compartment just behind the 777's cockpit.

The plane began to taxi and when it turned onto the main runway, the pilot simply advanced the throttles and it began the takeoff roll.

One of Marlon Brando's consiglieri caught his hand with one of hers and crossed herself with the other.

[THREE]
Jorge Newbery International Airport
Buenos Aires, Argentina
1305 6 February 2007

As the Gulfstream III carrying Ambassador Montvale and his party had made its approach to the airport, Montvale had remembered that the last time he had met with the sonofabitch in Argentina, Lieutenant Colonel C. G. Castillo had pointed out to him that inasmuch as they were in a foreign and sovereign nation, his Secret Service security detail did not enjoy diplomatic immunity and therefore had no right to bear arms, and were thus liable to be arrested for doing so.

He elected not to mention this to anyone. If there was a problem, Ambassador Juan Manuel Silvio would have to deal with it. And deal with it, he would have to: *I'm here at the direct order of the President of the United States. I look forward to making that point to that slick bastard and pal of Castillo's.*

Before the Gulfstream III had reached the end of its landing roll, Jorge Newbery ground control directed it to the commercial side of the airfield on the bank of the River Plate.

There they were met by Argentine immigration and customs officers and two members of the staff of the United States embassy. They were passed through both bureaucratic procedures quickly and without incident. Importantly, no Argentine official searched the persons of anyone, which neutralized the problem of his armed security detail, at least for the moment.

There were two diplomats from the American embassy on hand to meet the Gulfstream. One introduced himself as Colonel C. C. "Call me CC" Downs, the military attaché. He said he was there to take care of the crew. There were three crew members: the male pilot, a major; the male co-pilot, a captain; and a stout woman wearing the chevrons of a senior master sergeant. She had delivered a stewardess-type speech about the safety features of the C-20A, ordered everybody to fasten their seat belts, and then taken a seat, from which she had arisen only once to announce that intoxicants were prohibited aboard Air Force C-20A aircraft and if the Secret Service agent in the process of pouring Scotch into glasses for the Montvale party continued to do so, she would have to make an official report to her superiors.

"CC" said he would take care of the crew, and that Mr. Spears would know how to contact them when their services were required. He then loaded the crew into an embassy's Yukon and drove off.

Mr. I. Ronald Spears was carried on the books as an assistant consular officer but was in fact the acting CIA station chief for Buenos Aires. He had assumed that duty following the unexpected retirement of Alexander W. Darby.

The director of the Central Intelligence Agency had first planned to replace Darby with Paul Sieno, the CIA station chief in Paraguay, only to learn that Sieno, too, had suddenly retired, presumably to join Lieutenant Colonel Castillo in his disappearance from the face of the earth, and was therefore not available. Next, the CIA station chief in Mexico City, Robert T. Lowe, had been ordered to Buenos Aires to replace Darby, but he was still in the process of clearing his desk in Mexico City.

I. Ronald Spears was twenty-four years old, looked to be about nineteen, and had graduated from CIA training four months before.

Apparently unaware that the director of National Intelligence and his deputy each had Secret Service protection details, Spears had brought to the airport a single embassy Yukon, into which the four Secret Service agents, Montvale, Ellsworth, and their luggage could be loaded only with great difficulty.

Spears lost no time somewhat smugly telling Ambassador Montvale that he had "taken the liberty" of changing the reservations Ambassador Montvale had requested. The ambassador and his party would now be housed in the Alvear Palace Hotel, rather than the Marriott Plaza, as Spears had learned that the former was "much classier" than the latter.

With great effort, Montvale did not say what he wanted to say. Instead, he asked, "Do you happen to know, Spears, if Mr. Danton is in the Marriott Plaza?"

"Mr. *who*, Ambassador Montvale?"

At that point, Montvale remembered that he had asked Jack Powell, the DCI, only to tell the acting station chief that he was going to Buenos Aires, and had not asked him to tell the acting station chief to start looking for either Roscoe J. Danton or Lieutenant Colonel Castillo.

"My first order of business is to see the ambassador," Montvale then announced. "So we'll go to the embassy first."

The pleasure of envisioning that confrontation—"*Mr. Ambassador, I am here at the personal order of the President*"—was quickly shattered when Spears told him that the ambassador and most of his staff would be out of town until the next day.

I shouldn't be surprised by that. The moment that sonofabitch heard I was coming down here, Silvio got on his horse, and galloped his miserable ass out of town.

"Certainly someone's minding the store, right, Spears?"

"Yes, sir. Mizz Sylvia Grunblatt has the duty."

"And she is?"

"The embassy press officer, Mr. Ambassador."

Roscoe J. Danton is either still in the Marriott Plaza, or he isn't. And even if the press officer can't tell me where to find Castillo, she might know where that station chief—Darby—is, and Darby can lead me to Castillo.

At the very least, this female has the authority to order up another vehicle and driver. Riding around Buenos Aires in a stuffed-to-the-gills Yukon is simply not acceptable.

"Take me to see Miss Grun . . . whatever you said her name is," Montvale ordered.

"*Grunblatt*, Mr. Ambassador. Mizz Sylvia Grunblatt."

"Miss Grunblatt, the President has sent Mr. Ellsworth and me down here to have a word with Lieutenant Colonel C. G. Castillo. Do you know who I mean?"

"Yes, I do, Mr. Montvale."

"Do you happen to know where I can find him?"

"I'm afraid not," Grunblatt said. "There's been a journalist—a good one, Roscoe J. Danton, of *The Washington Times-Post*—down here looking for him, too. What's that all about?"

"You said *has been*? May I infer that Mr. Danton is no longer here?"

"The last I heard, he was in the Marriott Plaza."

"What about Alexander Darby, Miss Grunblatt?"

"If you don't mind, Mr. Montvale, I prefer 'Ms.'"

After a perceptible pause, the director of National Intelligence said, "Excuse me, Mizz Grunblatt."

"What did you mean, Mr. Montvale, when you asked, 'What about Alexander Darby?' I assume you know he resigned."

"I don't suppose it would surprise an experienced foreign service officer such as yourself, Mizz Grunblatt, if I told you Mr. Darby had duties beyond those of commercial attaché?"

"If you're asking did I know that Alex was a spook, yes, I did. I've known that he was in the agency's Clandestine Service since we served in Rome, and that's . . . oh, twenty years ago."

"And do you know where he is now, by any chance, Mizz Grunblatt?"

"Haven't a clue. The last time I saw him was at Ezeiza. The airport."

"He was going where, do you know?"

"What he did, Mr. Montvale, was go through the departing Argentina immigration procedure on his diplomatic passport, and then he turned right around and came back, so to speak, into Argentina on his regular passport. He then gave me—as an embassy officer—his diplomatic passport and carnet. Then I drove him here to the embassy, where he got out of my car, and got in a taxi."

"Then he's still in Argentina. Would you know where?"

"I didn't say that he's still here. I don't know if he is or not. I know his wife and children aren't here any longer; I put them on a plane to the States."

"But not Mr. Darby?"

"No. Not Mr. Darby. I don't know where Alex is."

"Do you happen to know where Mrs. Darby was going?"

"I do. And I'll give you the address once you tell me you're acting in an official capacity."

"I've already done that."

"That's right, you have," Grunblatt said.

She picked up a pen and wrote an address on a piece of notepaper and handed it to him.

Montvale glanced at it, saw that it meant nothing to him, then handed it to one of his Secret Service men.

"Hang on to that."

"Yes, sir."

The Secret Service agent looked at it, and then said, "Mr. Ambassador, I know what this is, this 7200 West Boulevard Drive. It's the Alexandria house Colonel Castillo and the others had. I drew the duty there a couple of times when it was under Secret Service protection."

"Mizz Grunblatt, I'm going to have to get on a secure line to the Secret Service in Washington."

Grunblatt considered that a moment, then said, "Yes, I can arrange that for you. I presume you'd prefer to talk from a secure location?"

You're damned right I would.

There's absolutely no reason for you to hear what I'm going to say.

"Could that be arranged?"

"It'll take me a minute or two to set it up," she said. "You'll have to go to the commo room."

"I understand. Thank you very much."

"Not a problem," Grunblatt said as she pushed herself out of her chair.

"And while I'm on the phone, Mizz Grunblatt, do you suppose you could rustle up another car for me? All we have is a Yukon, and we're stuffed into it like sardines."

"The call I can do. The car I can't. All of our vehicles are out of town with the ambassador. Tomorrow afternoon, if he returns as scheduled, it should be no problem at all."

Is that Cuban sonofabitch capable of that? Taking all the cars with him, so that I have to ride around town like a fish in a can?

"Secret Service, Claudeen."

"This is the State Department switchboard. I have Ambassador Montvale on a secure line for the senior agent on duty."

"Hold one, please, for Supervisory Special Agent McGuire."

"It will be a moment, Ambassador Montvale."

"Not a problem."

Montvale knew Supervisory Special Agent Thomas McGuire. He had once been in charge of the presidential protection detail.

A good man.

More important, he knows who I am.

"McGuire."

"Tom, this is Charles M. Montvale."

"Good afternoon, Mr. Ambassador. How are you, sir?"

"Much better now that I've got you on the phone, Tom. I need someone with a grasp of the situation."

"What situation is that, sir?"

"There are two facets of it, Tom. I'm sure you know what happened to the Office of Organizational Analysis?"

"That's not much of a secret, sir."

"And you've heard, I'm sure, about what's been going on in the last few days at Fort Detrick?"

"Yes, sir."

"Well, I'm in Buenos Aires. The President sent Mr. Ellsworth and me down here to locate Colonel Castillo to make sure he understands that he is not to go anywhere near that problem. I am to personally relay that presidential order to Castillo, once I find him."

"Castillo's in Argentina, sir?"

"I don't know where he is. But I've come across a lead. One of the members of the now-disbanded OOA was an agency officer named Alexander W. Darby. He retired when Castillo got the boot. Now, I can't find him. But I have reason to believe his wife . . . Got a pencil . . . ?"

"Yes, sir."

". . . is in a house at seventy-two hundred West Boulevard Drive in Alexandria."

"Isn't that the place we used to protect?"

"Yes, it is. That's what I meant by your having a grasp of the situation. Now, what I want you to do is send a couple of your best men out there—better yet, go yourself—and see if Darby is there, and if he's not, ask his wife if she knows where he is. I'm sure Darby knows where Castillo is."

"Have you got a first name on the wife, sir?"

Call her "Mrs. Darby," you Irish moron!

"No, I'm afraid not."

"Well, then I'll just call her Mrs. Darby."

"That'll work. Now, Tom, there is a possibility that she might deny he is there, and another possibility, slight but real, that Castillo himself might be there, and even a remote possibility that two Russians we're looking for—former SVR Colonel Dmitri Berezovsky and former SVR Lieutenant Colonel Svetlana Alekseeva—may also be in that house. Castillo is just arrogant enough, wouldn't you agree, to try to hide himself, and the Russians, in plain sight, so to speak."

"Would you spell those Russian names for me, please?"

Montvale did so. Then added: "So, do a really thorough job of searching the place."

"Yes, sir. And what do I do if I find these people?"

"If you find Darby"—*you Irish moron*—"you find out from him where Castillo and the Russians are. If you find Castillo or the Russians, you detain them, and immediately notify the President, or his chief of staff."

"Yes, sir. And whom do I see at Justice for the warrants, sir?"

"What warrants?"

"The search warrant for the premises, and the arrest warrants for Castillo and these Russians."

"You don't need a warrant"—*you cretin*—"you're acting on the authority of the President."

"Yes, sir. I understand. And from whom do I get that, sir?"

"Get what?"

"The presidential authority."

"I just gave it to you."

"Sir, it has to be in writing. I would suppose if I'm to act on the authority of the President, President Clendennen would have to sign it himself."

Well, what did I expect? McGuire is part of the Washington bureaucratic establishment.

You don't rise in that—for that matter, stay in that—unless you have mastered the fine art of covering your ass.

"Tom, I'm not sure if President Clendennen would be available to do that at this time. So here's what I want you to do. Just go out there with enough of your people to place the premises under around-the-clock surveillance—discreet surveillance. This situation requires, as I'm sure you understand, the greatest discretion."

"Yes, sir. I understand."

"Do you happen to know either Darby or his wife, Tom?"

"I've met them, sir."

"Then could you just knock at the door, unofficially, and tell Mrs. Darby you were in the neighborhood and took a chance to see if Darby was at home?"

"That would work, sir. And if he is?"

"Then you tell him that you're looking for Colonel Castillo; that you have a message for Castillo from me that has to be personally delivered."

"Yes, sir. And if he directs me to Colonel Castillo—I mean, if I find him—then what do I do?"

"You don't actually have to talk to him, Tom. Just locate him. Put him under really tight surveillance. Then call my office and tell them to get word to me that you've found Colonel Castillo. I'll take it from there."

"Yes, sir. I'll get right on it."

"Good man! I can't tell you how pleased I am that you were on duty, Tom. I know I can rely on you."

"Thank you, sir. I'll do my best."

There may be just about a dime's worth of silver in this black cloud. Darby might be at the house in Alexandria. He might know where Castillo is. And he might tell McGuire.

Montvale found I. Ronald Spears waiting for him outside the communications room.

"Get in touch with that Air Force colonel, Spears. Tell him to keep the pilots off the booze. Something has come up that might require my immediate return to Washington."

"Yes, sir."

"Do that immediately after you drop me off at the hotel."

"Yes, sir."

[FOUR]
7200 West Boulevard Drive
Alexandria, Virginia
1525 6 February 2007

Dianne Sanders, a grandmotherly type in her early fifties, was wearing an apron over her dress when she answered the chimes.

"Well, hello, Mr. McGuire. What brings you to our door?"

"I'm hoping Mrs. Darby is here," Tom McGuire said.

"Can I wonder why you might hope that? Or would that be impolite?"

"Come on, Dianne," McGuire said.

"I'll see if Mrs. Darby is at home. If you'll please wait?"

"Lock up the liquor," Mrs. Julia Darby said thirty seconds later. "The Secret Service is here."

She walked up to McGuire, and said, "I'm not sure if I'm glad to see you or not. But I'll give you a kiss anyway."

She stood on her toes and kissed his cheek.

"Are you here socially or otherwise, Tom?" she asked.

"Otherwise, I'm afraid."

"Uh-oh."

"Why did I suspect that?" Dianne Sanders asked.

"I have been ordered here by Ambassador Montvale to see if Alex is here, and if not, to ask you to tell me where he is."

"Did he say why he was curious?"

"He hopes Alex will point him to Charley Castillo. He says he has a message for him."

"Why didn't he come himself?"

"He called me from Buenos Aires."

"Ah-ha! The plot deepens," Julia Darby said.

"Is Alex here?"

She shook her head.

"Can you point me either to him or Charley?"

"The question is not whether I can, but whether I will. If I pointed at somebody, you would feel duty-bound to tell Montvale, right?"

"Yes, I would."

"I cannot tell a lie, especially to a senior officer of the United States Secret Service," she said. She then took a moment to orient herself and pointed in the general direction of South America. "To the best of my knowledge and belief, both of them are somewhere down there."

"Your cooperation is deeply appreciated. You were pointing at South America, right?"

"In that general direction, yes."

"Can you . . . *will* you be more specific?"

She shook her head.

"Not even if I told you that Ambassador Montvale told me he's acting for President Clendennen?"

"*Especially* if you told me that."

"One final question, Julia. You're not concealing two ex–SVR officers on the premises, are you?"

"I *will* answer that question. No, I am not."

"And you wouldn't know where such people would be, either, right?"

Julia Darby again pointed toward South America.

"They could be down that way," she said. "But on the other hand, maybe not. Those SVR people are slippery, you know."

He chuckled.

"Is my interrogation over, or is there anything else you'd like to know?" Julia Darby asked.

"This interview is concluded, Mrs. Darby. Thank you for your cooperation."

"I'm always willing to cooperate with the Secret Service, Mr. McGuire. It's my duty as a patriotic citizen." Julia smiled warmly, then said: "Dianne and I were about to have a Bloody Mary. Would you like one?"

He hesitated.

"Come on, Tom. The interrogation is over. I swear Montvale will never know."

He smiled. "Why not?"

"Let's go in the kitchen," Julia said. "Dianne is baking brownies for the boys. I was never much in the kitchen department, but I do make great Bloody Marys."

In the kitchen, McGuire asked Dianne Sanders, "Where's Harold?"

"My husband is shopping. He shops. I cook. Should be back anytime now."

Dianne Sanders had spent most of her working career as a cryptographer and later as a highly respected cryptographic analyst. Harold, her husband, had been a Delta Force special operator until he developed heart disease and had been medically retired.

For a while he had been what he described as a "camp follower," taking care of their house while Dianne stayed on active duty. That hadn't worked, and eventually—*Hell, with both our retirements we can live pretty damned well*—Dianne had retired, too.

That hadn't worked either.

They both had been climbing the walls of their garden apartment in Fayetteville, North Carolina, when CWO5 Colin Leverette, aka Uncle Remus, who had been around the block many times with Harold, asked them if they would be interested in running a safe house for Charley Castillo outside Washington. Harold had been around just as many blocks with Castillo as he had with Uncle Remus, and the Sanderses had jumped at the chance to get out of the garden apartment.

Julia Darby made Bloody Marys and handed them to Tom and Dianne.

"Take a sip of that, and then go back on duty," she said.

He did so, and said, "Okay."

"Ask me how Alex is," Julia said.

"Okay. How's Alex?"

"I hope that miserable sonofabitch and his hot-pants, large-breasted, twenty-year-old Argentine girlfriend freeze together in Ushuaia," she said.

"Where or what is Ushuaia?"

"It's the southernmost city in Argentina, way at the end. Coldest place I've ever been, including the personnel office at Langley."

"You don't expect me to believe that about Alex, do you?"

"I don't care if you believe it or not, but I hope Charles M. Montvale does. I'd love to hear that he's running around down there freezing *his* ass looking for Alex."

Tom McGuire grinned.

"You have always been an evil woman, Julia," he said admiringly, and tapped his Bloody Mary against hers. "How do you spell 'Ushuaia'?"

[FIVE]
Penthouse B
The Grand Cozumel Beach & Golf Resort
Cozumel
Quintana Roo, Mexico
1805 6 February 2007

En route to Cozumel—somewhere over Peru—a dozing Castillo woke to find Sweaty's head resting on his neck. Upon smelling her perfume, he realized with more than a little pleasure that there was going to be enough time between their arrival in Cozumel and dinner for what the French—who sometimes do things with a certain style—called a *cinq à sept*.

He dozed off again considering this pleasant possibility, to be wakened perhaps an hour after that by one of the pilots of the Boeing 777 offering him a very nice luncheon plate fresh from the microwave.

Sweaty already had hers.

Castillo waited until the pilot had moved away, then asked her in French: "*Ma chère*, what does 'a five-to-seven' mean to you?"

"Five to seven means what it sounds like," she replied in Russian. "I have no idea what *a* five-to-seven means."

"Just as soon as we get to our room in the hotel, I'll show you a"—he pronounced the term phonetically—"sank-ah-set."

She kissed his cheek. "But I have other plans for you just as soon as we get to our room in the hotel, my darling."

Svetlana then removed any doubt he might have had that there was a certain sexual overtone to her remark by quickly groping him.

It was not to be.

When they got to Penthouse B, they were not alone. Everybody who had been on the plane was with them.

"We had to move some guests," Alek Pevsner explained. "That shouldn't take long. I always like to know who's in the room next to mine."

"How long is 'long'?" Castillo asked. "As in 'shouldn't take long'?"

Pevsner ignored him and went to the bar and reached for a bottle of bourbon. Alex Darby opened a sliding glass door and inhaled appreciatively.

"The final death blow to my marriage will come when my wife hears I'm in a penthouse in Cozumel by the Sea," he announced, "while she is in the snow and slush of Washington, trying to find some roof over her and our abused children."

"Is that good or bad?" Delchamps asked.

Max pushed Darby out of his way, having seen Penthouse B's swimming pool, which had obviously been put there for his use. He immediately decided that a quick dip after the long flight was just what he needed.

A Bouvier des Flandres is a large animal and can cause a substantial splash when diving into a pool.

The splash reached Darby.

Everyone laughed.

Pevsner went to a bathroom and returned with a towel for Darby.

By then Max, having enough aquatic activity, had climbed out of the pool and was now standing on the edge of the pool shaking the water from his body. The fur of a Bouvier des Flandres can hold an astonishing amount of water. Pevsner's shirt and trousers had received a good deal of flying water, and there were drops all over his face, which was now pale with anger and tight-lipped.

Everyone waited for Pevsner's explosion. When it didn't come, Castillo poured gasoline on the smoldering embers.

"Well, it was high time you had a bath," Castillo offered. "And Max was just being helpful."

Pevsner looked at him and then said, "I have just had a horrible thought."

"I can't wait to hear what that is," Castillo replied.

"Those adorable puppies you gave my Elena and Dmitri's Sof'ya are going to turn into uncontrollable beasts like that."

Pevsner took another look at his drenched trousers, and announced, "Believe it or not, this place makes it clear on all the advertising that it is not a pet-friendly hotel."

"I hear that they make exceptions for friends of the owner," Castillo said.

"Sometimes the owner is sorry he has certain friends," Pevsner said as he patted his clothing with a towel.

"Sweaty, I think he means me," Castillo said. "Say something rude to him."

"Why doesn't everybody get out of here so that I can have a shower?" Sweaty said.

"Methinks the lady has carnal desires on our leader's body," Delchamps said.

Throwing water on that topic, Pevsner said, "Colonel Torine and the others are on their way from the airport."

"They just got here?" Castillo asked.

"The manager just told me. I told him to send them here when they arrive," Pevsner said, and glanced at Svetlana. "While we're waiting for rooms."

"Further delaying Svet's bath and the satisfaction of her other desires," Tom Barlow said. "Now she will say something rude."

"Very probably," Pevsner said, and smiled warmly at her and Castillo.

Castillo thought: *My God! Aleksandr Pevsner, you're good!*

I've known you long and well enough to know when you're really pissed off, and the last time I saw you this pissed was when you learned that Howard Kennedy had betrayed you.

If you could, you'd happily throw Max off the balcony, à la Ivan the Terrible, who Svetlana told me threw dogs off the Kremlin walls so he could watch them try to walk on broken legs.

But right now, you need all the help you can get to protect you and your family from Putin and the SVR—which means you think that's a real threat, which is nice to know—and you can't afford to piss me off—which means you think I have what you don't have and can't do without, which is also nice to know—so you smile warmly at the uncontrollable beast's owner and his girlfriend as if you agree that he's an adorable puppy and you didn't mind getting soaked at all.

They call that professional control, and it's one facet of character I don't have and really wish I did.

Ten minutes later, the doorbell chimed, and when Alex Darby answered it, seven former members of the now-defunct Office of Organizational Analysis—two more than Castillo expected—walked in.

They were Colonel Jake Torine, USAF (Retired); former USAF Captain Richard Sparkman; former USMC Gunnery Sergeant Lester Bradley; Major

H. Richard Miller, Jr., USA (Retired); First Lieutenant Edmund Lorimer, MI (Retired); Chief Warrant Officer (Five) Colin Leverette (Retired); and former FBI Special Agent David William Yung, Jr.

"I knew in my bones that there would be no rest for the weary," Leverette greeted him. "How they hanging, Charley?"

Colin Leverette was an enormous black man, a legendary Special Operations man, known to his close friends—and only his close friends—as Uncle Remus.

"You and Two-Gun got yourselves kicked out of Uruguay, did you?" Castillo said, and turned to Torine. "You actually went to Uruguay to pick them up? Wasn't that a little out of your way?"

"It was a supply run, Charley," Torine said, and then, seeing the confusion on Castillo's face, added, "about which, I gather, you didn't know?"

"I'm always the last to know anything, Jake. You know that."

"We went down there with a planeload of the newest Casey radios," Torine said. "That's not precise. We went down there with a *bunch* of the newest Casey radios. You won't believe how small the new ones are. And they don't need the DirecTV dish antenna."

Leverette said, "Colonel Torine was kind enough to take pity on us when we met him in Montevideo and told him that unless he took us with him, we couldn't get here in less than seventy-two hours."

"He was weeping piteously," Torine said. "He said you needed him."

"To do what, Uncle Remus?" Castillo asked.

"To get you out of whatever trouble you're in," Leverette said.

"And your excuse, Two-Gun?" Castillo asked.

"I came to deliver this," Yung said, and handed Castillo a small package.

"What's this?"

"Two hundred thousand in used—therefore nonsequentially numbered—hundreds, fresh from the cashier's cage at the Venetian," Yung said. "When Casey told me you'd asked for the money, I told him to give it in cash to Jake. It would have been too easy to trace if it went into and out of your personal German account."

"I don't recall asking for volunteers," Castillo said.

"Oh, come on, Charley," Leverette said. "Come and let Uncle Remus give you a great big kiss."

"Screw you," Castillo said.

Moving with astonishing speed for his bulk, Leverette walked quickly to Castillo, wrapped his massive arms around him, which pinned Castillo's arms to his sides, and then proceeded to wetly kiss both of Castillo's cheeks and then his forehead.

Castillo saw that Pevsner was smiling.

That's a genuine smile.

Because Uncle Remus is kissing me?

Or because he's really happy to see the reinforcements?

Leverette finally turned Castillo free.

"Now," Leverette announced, "just as soon as I have a little something to cut the dust of the trail, we will see what Charley's problem is, and set about solving it. I already have the essential ingredient." He dug in his pocket and came out triumphantly with a small bottle. "Peychaud's bitters. I never leave home without it. I shall also require rye whisky—*good* rye whisky—some simple syrup, absinthe, lemons, ice, and a suitable vessel in which to assemble the above."

"I feel better already," Castillo said.

"What is he talking about?" Pevsner asked.

"A Sazerac," Castillo said.

"And what is a Sazerac?" Tom Barlow asked.

"Nectar of the gods," Leverette said. "God's reward to the worthy."

He examined the stock of intoxicants in the bar, finally coming up triumphantly with a bottle of Van Winkle Family Reserve rye in his left hand and a bottle of Wild Turkey rye in his right.

"These will do nicely, but I can't find any syrup, absinthe, or lemons. Presumably, there is room service?"

"Lester," Castillo ordered, "get on the horn and tell room service that Mr. Pevsner requires immediately what Uncle Remus just said."

"Yes, sir," Bradley said, and started for the telephone.

"You're all going to sit around and get drunk, is that the idea?" Pevsner asked unpleasantly. "We have a serious problem and—"

Leverette interrupted him. "Charley, I hate to tell you this, but I'm starting to dislike your Russian buddy. Again."

"Me, too," Edgar Delchamps said.

"Who do you think you're talking to?" Pevsner demanded angrily.

"Somebody who thinks he's Ivan the Terrible, Jr.?" Leverette asked innocently.

Castillo laughed, but even as he did, he realized that was not the wise thing to do.

"Not one more word from anybody!" Svetlana snapped. "Not one!"

Everyone looked at her in surprise.

Castillo and Leverette had much the same thought at the same moment, but Leverette was the first to say it out loud: "Be careful," he said in Russian. "Sweaty just put on her podpolkovnik's hat."

"You'd better be careful," Castillo said. "That's way over your word limit. What Podpolkovnik Alekseeva said was 'Not one more word.'"

"I said from anybody and that includes you," Svetlana snapped. "For God's sake, Charley, you're in command. Act like a commander!"

Everyone looked at Castillo to see what his reaction to that would be.

His first reaction was a sudden realization: *This is getting out of control. And the commander is in large measure responsible.*

Sweaty's right about that.

His next reaction was: *On the other hand, Sweaty should not have snapped at the commander like that, telling him to act like a commander.*

One of the problems of having women subordinates is that one cannot jump all over their asses when they deserve it.

Especially when said female subordinate is sharing one's bed.

This sort of situation was not dealt with in Problems of Leadership 101 at West Point, nor anywhere else since I've been in the Army.

Correction: During the time I was in the Army.

So, what are you going to do now, General MacArthur, so that everyone can see you are in fact acting like you're in command?

Confidently in command.

There's a hell of a difference between being in command, and being confidently in command.

And those being commanded damned well know it.

You better think of something, and quick!

Colin Leverette came to his rescue.

"I know what," Leverette said. "Let's start all over."

"What?" Svetlana asked.

"No, Mr. Pevsner," Leverette went on, "we are not all going to sit around and get drunk. We're going to have one—possibly two—Sazerac cocktails, and then we're going to get down to business."

Pevsner didn't respond.

Castillo looked between them, and thought: *I believe Uncle Remus just saved my ass.*

What is that, for the two hundred and eleventh time?

"That was your cue, Mr. Pevsner," Delchamps said, "to say, 'I should not have said what I did. Please forgive me.'"

Pevsner looked at him incredulously.

"It's a question of command, Aleksandr," Tom Barlow said, his tone making it clear that now he was wearing his polkovnik's hat. "If Charley, the commander, doesn't object to something, you have no right to. Now, ask Uncle Remus to forgive your runaway mouth."

"You have just earned my permission, Podpolkovnik Berezovsky," Leverette said, "to call me Uncle Remus."

Now, everyone looked at Pevsner.

"Uncle Remus is waiting, Mr. Pevsner," Delchamps said after a long moment.

After another long moment, Pevsner smiled, and said, "If an apology for saying something I should not have said is the price for one of Mr. Leverette's cocktails, I happily pay it."

Castillo had another unpleasant series of rapid thoughts:

Well, Pevsner caved, and quicker than I thought he would.

Problem solved.

Wait a minute! Aleksandr Pevsner—unlike me—never says anything until he thinks it through.

He knew the apology meant he understood he can't question me.

But what about the first crack he made?

Was that an attempt to put himself in charge?

If we'd caved, that would have put him in a position to question—question hell, disapprove—of anything.

Alek, you sonofabitch!

His chain of thought was interrupted by the arrival of the butler—not a bellman; penthouses A and B shared the full-time services of an around-the-clock butler—bearing simple syrup, absinthe, a bowl of ice, a bowl of lemon twists, and a tray of old-fashioned glasses.

"The first thing we will do—actually, Lester will do," Leverette announced, "is fill the glasses with ice. This will chill them while I go through the rest of the process. Now, how many are we going to need?"

Everyone expressed the desire to have a Sazerac.

Leverette arranged all the old-fashioned glasses in two rows.

"You understand, Sweaty," he said, "that one of my Sazeracs has been known to turn a nun into a nymphomaniac?"

"I'll take my chances. Stop talking and make the damned drink."

"First, we muddle the syrup and the Peychaud bitters together," Leverette announced. "When I've done that, we will carefully measure three ounces of rye per drink and a carefully measured amount of ice into the mixing vessel."

He picked up a champagne cooler, and quickly rinsed it in the sink of the wet bar.

"This will serve nicely as a mixing vessel," he said, and then demonstrated that his notion of a carefully measured three ounces of rye and ice per drink was to upend the bottle of Wild Turkey over the champagne cooler and empty it. He shook it to get the last drop, then repeated the process with the bottle of Van Winkle Family Reserve. He then added four handfuls of ice cubes.

He stirred the mixture around with one of the empty bottles.

"You'll notice that I did not shake, but rather stirred. I learned that from Double-Oh-Seven," he said, then looked at Bradley. "Lester, dump the ice."

Lester emptied into the sink the melting ice from all the glasses.

"I will now pour the absinthe, and Lester will swirl. I know he will do a good job of swirling because I taught him myself."

Leverette then picked up the bottle of absinthe, and ran it very quickly over the lines of glasses in one motion. This put perhaps a teaspoon of the absinthe in each glass.

Lester then picked up each glass, swirled the absinthe around, and then dumped the absinthe into the sink.

Leverette picked up the champagne cooler. Lester picked up a silver strainer and held it to the lip of the champagne cooler to hold back the ice cubes as Leverette poured the chilled liquid content of the cooler into the glasses.

"There is a slight excess," Leverette announced as he looked into the cooler. "Stick this in the fridge, Lester. 'Waste not, want not,' as my saintly mother was always saying."

Leverette then picked up handfuls of the lemon twists and squeezed them in his massive hands, which added not more than two drops of the essence into each glass.

"Finished!" he announced triumphantly.

He handed one to Castillo and another to Pevsner. He handed a third to Sweaty, and took a fourth with him as he walked to the couch.

He raised his glass to Pevsner, took an appreciative sip, and then asked, "And what do you think, Mr. Pevsner?"

Pevsner sipped his cocktail.

"Unusual," Pevsner said. "But very good."

"I will pretend that I don't know the only reason you said that is because you knew I would tear off both of your arms and one leg if you hadn't, and will accept that as a compliment."

"You're insane," Pevsner said with a smile.

"Genius is often mistakenly identified as insanity," Leverette said. "I'm surprised you didn't know that. Now, shall we deal with our problem?"

He came to attention, gestured at Castillo, and gave the Nazi salute.

"*Mein Führer,* you have the floor."

Pevsner's eyes rolled in disbelief.

Castillo rose from his chair, walked to the bar, and leaned his back against it.

"Two-Gun," he began, "I think you'd better take notes."

Yung gave him a thumbs-up, then reached for his laptop computer.

"To bring everybody up to speed," Castillo began, "let's start with what we do know. First, somebody sent Colonel Hamilton a barrel of Congo-X. Then, in Budapest, Colonel Vladlen Solomatin of the Sluzhba Vneshney Razvedki handed Eric Kocian a letter asking him to get it to Tom Barlow. The letter said, in essence, 'Come home. All is forgiven.' I think it's likely the two actions are related."

"About as likely as the sun will come up tomorrow," Svetlana said.

She waited for a chuckle. When she didn't get one, she looked at Castillo.

"We won't *know,*" Castillo said, "about the sun rising until tomorrow morning, will we, Svet? Until then, it's just *likely* that it will. And the way this works, Svet, is that no one offers an opinion, clever or otherwise, until I ask for it. Got it?"

Her face colored and her eyes flared angrily, but she didn't reply.

Well, Commander Casanova, guess who's not going to get laid tonight?

Castillo took a sip of his drink, then went on: "Let's start with the Congo-X. Where did it come from? That raises the question, 'Did we destroy it all in the attacks on the Fish Farm or not?' Colin?"

"Sir, I respectfully suggest Colonel Torine can answer that better than I can," Leverette said.

"Jake?" Castillo asked.

Torine nodded. "Charley, you know as well as I do, except for nukes, there is no such thing as total destruction of anything by high explosive or incendiary saturation bombing. The question then becomes: 'How much was not destroyed?' And I suggest Colin can answer that better than I can. He (a) was there, and (b) he's done a lot of damage assessment."

Castillo motioned with his hand toward Leverette.

"The Fish Farm was a collection of concrete block buildings, none of them over three stories, most of them just one," Leverette said. "The few I got into had basements, and I saw a half-dozen buried and half-buried steel-door revetments—like ammo bunkers. Let's say the bombs and the incendiaries took out ninety-five percent of everything."

"Jake?" Castillo said.

Torine nodded his agreement. "Leaving five percent," he said.

"Until we run into a stone wall, let's try this scenario," Castillo said. "Five percent of the Congo-X in barrels survived the bombing. Let's say that's six barrels. Two of them got to the States. How and by what means? Tom?"

"I'm sure one of the first things Sirinov did after the bombing—"

Alex Darby interrupted: "General Yakov Sirinov, who runs the SVR for Putin?"

Barlow nodded, and went on: "What he did was send in a Vympel Spetsnaz team for damage assessment and to see if anyone was still alive."

Castillo said, "Can we presume (a) the Spetsnaz made it into the Fish Farm, and (b) while they were there found—more important, took control of—the six barrels of Congo-X?"

"If Tom is talking about Spetsgruppa V," Leverette said, and looked at Barlow.

Barlow nodded. He said, "Also known as the Vega Group of KGB Directorate B."

"The Russian Delta Force, Charley," Leverette said. "They're damned good."

"It is because they are so good that they were selected to provide security for the Congo operation," Barlow said. "I was surprised that you didn't encounter at least one or two of them, Uncle Remus, when you were there."

Leverette met his eyes for a moment.

"Quickly changing the subject," Leverette said, making it clear there had been a confrontation with at least one or two Spetsnaz special operators and that they had lost. "So they found the six barrels of Congo-X. What did they do with it?"

"This is conjecture," Barlow said, "based on my knowledge of how Sirinov's mind works. The Spetsnaz were parachuted onto the site from a great height, probably from a specially adapted Ilyushin Il-96 passenger transport on a flight path duly reported to aviation authorities. The parachutists would not have opened their canopies until they were quite close to the ground, so they would appear only momentarily, if at all, on radar screens."

"That's what we call HALO," Castillo said. "High-altitude, low-opening."

"Copyright, Billy Waugh," Leverette said.

Castillo, Torine, and Peg-Leg Lorimer chuckled or smiled or both.

"Excuse me?" Barlow said.

"The first guy to do that was Billy Waugh, a friend of ours," Leverette explained.

Castillo said, "Okay, back to the question of now that Spetsnaz has six beer barrels full of Congo-X, what do they do with it?"

"They would have to truck it out," Barlow said. "But since—using Uncle

Remus's ninety-five percent destruction factor—there would be no trucks, at least not as many as would be needed, left at the Fish Farm, I don't know how they could have done that."

"They leave the Fish Farm area and steal some trucks," Castillo said. "And then truck it out. But where to?"

"Any field where a Tupolev Tu-934A can get in," Jake Torine said. "And that wouldn't have to be much of a field."

"You know about the Tu-934, Jake?" Tom asked.

"I've never seen one but, oh yeah, I know about it," Torine said.

"I don't," Castillo said.

"Ugly bird," Torine said. "Can carry about as much as a Caribou. Cruises at about Mach point nine. Helluva range, midair refuelable, and it's state-of-the-Russian-art stealth. And it can land and take off from a polo field. The story I get is that the agency will pay a hundred twenty-five million for one of them."

"You do know about it," Barlow said, raising his drink in a toast, demonstrating he was clearly impressed.

Torine returned the gesture, and they both sipped their Sazeracs.

"Okay, picking up the scenario," Castillo said. "The Spetsnaz load their six barrels of Congo-X onto their stolen trucks and drive it to some dirt runway in the middle of Africa, and then load it and themselves onto this . . . what was it?"

"Tupolev Tu-934A," Torine furnished.

". . . which then takes off and flies at Mach point nine to where? To Russia?" Castillo pursued.

"No. They don't want Congo-X in Russia. They know how dangerous it is," Svetlana said. "They remember Chernobyl. That's why the Fish Farm was in the Congo."

"Could this airplane make it across the Atlantic?"

"Sure. With an en-route refueling, it could fly anywhere," Torine said.

"Where's anywhere? Cuba? Mexico?"

"Distance-wise, sure," Barlow said. "But politically . . ."

"They'd spot it on radar, right?" Castillo said.

"Charley, it has stealth technology," Torine said. "And even if it didn't, it could fly under the radar."

"So why not Cuba, Tom?" Castillo asked.

"The Castro brothers would be too expensive," Barlow said. "Both in terms of cash and letting them in on the secret. More the latter. Sirinov doesn't like to be obligated to anybody."

"Then right into Mexico," Edgar Delchamps said. "Getting it across the border into the States would be easy."

"I think we could say getting it across the border *was* easy," Castillo said. "But I have a gut feeling Mexico is not—was not—the final stop."

Alex Darby then said, "Drop off the Congo-X and enough people to get two barrels of this stuff into the States via Mexico, then fly the rest of it on to . . . where?"

"Venezuela," Delchamps suggested. "Hugo Chávez is in love with Communism, and has yet to be burned by the Russians, as the Castros were burned. And, God knows, Fat Little Hugo is no rocket scientist. Sirinov could easily have put him in his pocket."

Barlow pointed at Delchamps, and said, "You're on it, Edgar."

"Okay, then. Now what?" Leverette said. "We've located the Congo-X in Venezuela. What do we do about it?"

"We start to prove—or disprove—the scenario," Castillo said. "First step in that will be when we get from Aloysius the intel he's going to get from the DCI."

"You don't *know* that's who's giving him the intel he's promised to send, my darling," Svet said.

Castillo, at the last split second, kept himself from saying something loving and kind—for example, *What part of "Don't offer a goddamn opinion unless I ask for it" didn't you understand, my precious?*

Instead, he said: "Who else could it be?"

Svetlana replied, "The value of the intel we get from Casey is only as reliable as the source, and we don't *know* it's coming from the CIA, do we? So I suggest we take what Casey sends us with a grain of salt."

"She got you, Ace," Delchamps said. "Listen to your consigliere."

"Yeah, she did," Castillo admitted. "Okay, Sweaty: Give us your take on the 'Come home, all is forgiven' letter from Cousin Vladlen."

"You haven't figured that out? It is meant to let your government off the hook, my darling. It'll come out that we've returned to Russia—"

Castillo interrupted, "What do you mean, 'we've returned to Russia'?"

"You asked me a question: Let me finish answering it," Svetlana said. "Maybe I should have said *if* we return to Russia and it comes out—and it would—then your government couldn't be accused of cruelly and heartlessly sending us home to the prison on Lubyanka Square. Your press will get that letter. It says 'All is forgiven.' Your government can then say all they did when they loaded us aboard an Aeroflot airplane was help us go home to our loving family."

"Score another one for Sweaty," Delchamps said.

"The U.S. government is not going to put you on an Aeroflot plane," Castillo said.

"You better hope, Ace," Delchamps said.

"Over my dead body," Castillo said.

"Thank you, my darling," Svetlana said. "I will pray that it doesn't come to that."

"Me, too," Tom Barlow said. "May I offer a suggestion, Charley?"

"Sure."

"Before we get whatever Casey is going to send us, why don't we all, independently, try to find fault with our scenario?"

Castillo nodded. "Sure. Good idea."

"And while we're all doing that, independently come up with a scenario on how to deal with this?"

"Another good idea," Castillo said.

"Are we going to try to grab this stuff in Venezuela?" Lorimer asked.

"What I would like to do is grab that Tupolev Tu-934A in Venezuela," Torine said.

Everyone was quiet for a long moment.

Then Pevsner said: "I'll check, but I think everybody's rooms should be ready by now. Shall we meet here in, say, an hour and have another of Leverette's cocktails and then dinner?"

VIII

There was nothing unusual about the GMC Yukon XL that turned off State Highway 304 into the gas station. Indeed, there were two near twins—three, if one wished to count a Chevrolet Suburban—already at the pump islands.

The driver of the arriving Yukon pulled up beside one of the pumps, got out, and fed the pump a credit card. Other doors opened and three men—all dressed in plaid woolen jackets—got out and walked quickly toward the men's room, suggesting to a casual witness that it had been a long time between pit stops.

A Chrysler Grand Caravan turned off State Highway 203 and drove right up to the men's room door. The van's sliding door opened and three men—also in plaid woolen jackets and also apparently feeling the urgent call of nature—hurried into the restroom.

A minute or so later, the first of the men came out of the restroom, and got into either the Yukon or the Grand Caravan. In two minutes everybody was out of the men's room. The Caravan backed up and stopped at a pump. The Yukon driver walked quickly to the men's room.

By the time he came out, the driver of the Caravan had topped off his tank and returned to the wheel. By the time the Yukon driver got behind his wheel, the Caravan was out of the station. Ninety seconds later, so was the Yukon.

If anyone had been watching it was unlikely that they would have noticed that one of the men who had gone to the restroom from the Yukon had gotten into the Grand Caravan when he came out and that one of the Caravan passengers had gone to the Yukon when he came out of the men's room.

The man in the front passenger seat of the Grand Caravan turned and offered the man who had just gotten in a silver flask.

"What is it they say about 'beware of Russians passing the bottle'?" A. Franklin Lammelle, deputy director of the Central Intelligence Agency, asked. "And it's a little early for vodka, even for me."

"It's not vodka, Frank. It's Rémy Martin," Cultural Counselor Sergei Murov of the Washington embassy of the Russian Federation replied.

"In that case, Sergei, I will have a little taste," Lammelle said, and reached for the flask. He held it up in a toast, and said, "Here's to Winston Churchill, who always began his day with a taste of fine cognac."

Both men were stocky, in their midforties, fair-skinned, and wore small, rimless spectacles. Murov had a little more remaining hair than Lammelle. They could have been cousins.

Murov was the SVR's Washington *rezident.* Lammelle knew this, and Murov knew that Lammelle had known that since the Russians had proposed Murov to be their embassy's cultural counselor.

Ten minutes later, the convoy turned onto Piney Point Farm Lane. A quarter of a mile down the lane, ten-foot-high chainlink fences became visible behind the vegetation on both sides of the road. On the fencing, at fifty-foot intervals, there were signs: PRIVATE PROPERTY! TRESPASSERS WILL BE PROSECUTED!

Finally, the Caravan came to the first of two chainlink fence gates across the road. Outside the outer gate there was a black Ford sedan with MARYLAND STATE POLICE lettered on the body. Two state troopers in two-tone brown uniforms sat in the front seats. When the Caravan came a stop, one got out of the passenger door and carefully examined the minivan, but made no attempt to do anything else. The three SUV's parked on either side of the lane.

The outer gate swung open, and a man in a police-type private security guard uniform inside the second gate motioned for the Caravan to advance. When the van had done so, the outer gate closed behind it. The security guard came from behind the second gate, walked to the Caravan, and opened the sliding door.

When he was satisfied that there was no one in the vehicle determined to trespass on what—like the Russian embassy itself—was legally as much the territory of the Russian Federation as was the Lubyanka Square headquarters of the KGB in downtown Moscow, he signaled for the interior gate to be opened.

Frank Lammelle knew a great deal about what was known as the "Russian dacha on the Eastern Shore." Some of what he knew, he had known for as long as he had been in the CIA. Back in the bad old days when Russia had been the Union of Soviet Socialist Republics, young Frank Lammelle of the Clandestine Service had thought it was ironic that the ambassador of the USSR spent his weekends in a house built by John J. Raskob, almost a caricature of a capitalist. Raskob had been simultaneously vice president of General Motors and E. I. du Pont de Nemours and Company—which owned forty-three percent of GM—and had ordered the construction of the Empire State Building in New York City with the mandate to the architect that it be taller than the Chrysler Building.

Raskob's three-floor brick mansion had not been quite large enough to house him and his thirteen children, so he had built another one just about as large for them and his guests, who included such people as Walter Chrysler, Henry Ford, and Thomas Edison.

The Soviet government had bought both houses from Raskob's heirs in 1972 and later enlarged the estate by swapping land the Americans wanted in Moscow for land adjacent to the Maryland property.

The Russians then further improved the property by importing from Finland fourteen small "rental" houses for the use of embassy employees.

Some of what Lammelle knew about the Russian dacha on the Eastern Shore he had learned more recently. At five-thirty that morning, he had met with J. Stanley Waters, the CIA's deputy director for operations, and several of his deputies in The Bubble at CIA headquarters in Langley. Only the people in The Bubble—plus of course DCI Jack Powell—knew that Lammelle had accepted Sergei Murov's invitation to go boating in Maryland.

The meeting had been called both to guess the reason Murov wanted to talk to Lammelle—probably it had something to do with Congo-X, but no one was sure—and to prepare Lammelle for it.

To that end, the latest—just taken—satellite photos of the compound were shown. "Photos" was probably a misnomer, as these were satellite motion pictures. The infrared and other sensors showed life in only four of the rental cottages, including the two known to house the Russians' communications center. The analysts agreed there was no significant change from the data taken over the past week.

The NSA at Fort Meade reported they had been unable to pull anything of interest from the ether—that is, any reference to Lammelle, Murov, or a meeting between the two—and that the level of traffic between Moscow, the dacha, the embassy in Washington, and the Russian Mission to the United Nations in New York City was normal. Nothing had been sent either in a code, or by any technical means the Russians erroneously believed had not been detected or cracked at Fort Meade.

The FBI liaison officer reported that the FBI agents tracking Murov had seen nothing out of the ordinary in his behavior, and that the FBI agents on-site— one of the two state troopers stationed around the clock at the gate was always an FBI special agent—had similarly seen nothing of special interest.

Lammelle had closed the meeting with a reminder that the visit had to be kept a secret. Secrecy was important because Senator Homer Johns (Democrat, New Hampshire), the chairman of the Senate Foreign Relations Committee, who loved to be on TV and despised the CIA, would—should he learn of the meeting—love nothing better than to call DCI Powell to ask about the meeting, then quickly leak the secret to CNN and/or C. Harry Whelan, Jr., the syndicated columnist, who didn't like the CIA either.

There were three Mercedes-Benz automobiles lined up in the circular drive before the three-story brick mansion: a CLS 550 sedan—the pilot car—then an elegant twin-turbo V12 CL600—obviously the ambassador's vehicle—and then another CLS 550—the chase car.

The precautions are necessary, Lammelle thought, *not to protect the ambassador from the Americans, but from his fellow Russians.*

Chechen rebel leader Doku Umarov would be delighted to sacrifice a half-dozen of his associates if that was the price for taking out the ambassador.

"It looks as if the boss is about to go to work," Murov said. "Why don't we say hello?"

This is not a coincidence, Lammelle decided. *The ambassador probably waited until the gate reported their arrival before he came out of the house.*

Obviously, he wants me to know that he knows I'm here, and, as important, to know that he knows Murov invited me.

"What a pleasure to see you, Mr. Lammelle," the ambassador said, offering his hand.

He was a ruddy-faced, somewhat chubby fifty-five-year-old.

"It's always a pleasure to see you, Mr. Ambassador," Lammelle said.

"Sergei tells me you're going boating," the ambassador said.

"That's not exactly true, Mr. Ambassador. Going out on the river in February may be sport for a Siberian, but for an American it's insanity."

The ambassador laughed.

"What I thought I would do, Mr. Ambassador, is look through a window in the hunting lodge and watch Sergei turn to ice."

"I'm not a Siberian, Frank. I was born and raised in Saint Petersburg," Murov said.

Which at the time was called Leningrad, wasn't it, Sergei?

"In that case, I suggest we both look out the windows of the hunting lodge at the frigid waters."

The ambassador laughed again, and laid his hand on Lammelle's arm.

"If I have to say this, the door here is always open to you."

"That's very gracious of you, Mr. Ambassador."

"Perhaps if you're still here when I get back, we can have a drink," the ambassador said, and then gestured for his chauffeur to open the door of the Mercedes.

"I don't think that's likely, but thank you, Mr. Ambassador."

"Give my best regards to the President and Mr. Powell when you see them, please."

"I'll be happy to do so, Mr. Ambassador."

And say "Hi!" to Vladimir Vladimirovich Putin for me, please, Mr. Ambassador, when you get the chance.

"I thought we'd have breakfast in the hunting lodge, rather than in the house, if that's all right with you, Frank," Murov said as they watched the ambassadorial convoy of three luxury cars roll away.

"Fine with me, Sergei," Lammelle said.

Murov waved him back into the Caravan for the short ride to the hunting lodge, which was a small outbuilding that had been converted into a party room. There was a table that could seat a dozen people. A small kitchen was hidden behind a half-wall on which was a mural of two old-time sailors—one Russian and the other American—smiling warmly at each other as they tapped foam-topped beer mugs with one another.

Lammelle thought: *In the professional judgment of our best counterintelligence people, somewhere on that mural and on that oh-so-charmingly-rustic chandelier with the beer mugs overhead and God only knows where else are skillfully concealed motion picture camera lenses and state-of-the-Russian-art microphones. All recording for later analysis every syllable I utter and every movement and facial expression I make.*

And as much as I would love to roll my eyes and grimace for the cameras before giving them the international signal for "Up yours, Ivan," I can't do that.

Doing so would violate the rules of proper spook deportment, and we can't have that!

Unless we play by the rules, we would never learn anything from one another.

Murov waved Lammelle into one of the two places set at the table, and a cook—a burly Russian man—immediately produced coffee mugs and set a bottle of Rémy Martin and two snifters on the table.

That's really a little insulting, Sergei, if you thought I was going to oblige you by getting sauced and then run my mouth.

Or it could simply be standard procedure: "Put the booze out. The worse that can happen is that the American won't touch it."

"I asked Cyril to make eggs Benedict," Murov said. "That all right with you, Frank?"

"Sounds fine," Lammelle said, "but looking the gift horse in the teeth, can we get on with this? I really have to get back to the office."

"Just as soon as he lays the eggs Benedict before us, I'll ask Cyril to leave us."

"I hardly know where to begin," Murov said as he finished his breakfast.

The hell you don't.

Item two on your thoughtfully prepared agenda—item one being put out the Rémy Martin—was to suggest you don't know what you're talking about and simply are going to have to wing it and thus be at my mercy.

"How about this?" Murov went on. "I think there are certain areas where cooperation between us would be mutually advantageous."

"Does that mean, Sergei, that I have something you want, and you hope that what you're going to offer me will be enough to convince me I should give it to you?"

Murov considered that a moment, then shrugged, smiled, and nodded.

"You can always see right through me, Frank, can't you?"

"Only when you want me to, Sergei. If you don't want me to . . ."

"I know how to neutralize Congo-X," Murov said.

Now, that's interesting!

Starting with: How does he know that we're calling it Congo-X?

"I didn't know you had assets in Fort Detrick. Now I'll have to tell the counterintelligence guy there to slit his wrists."

"I have people all over. Almost as many as you do, Frank."

"Did your assets tell you that we've already just about figured out how to neutralize Congo-X?"

"They told me Colonel Hamilton has had some preliminary success," Murov said.

I don't think there's an SVR agent inside Detrick.

What I think we have is some misguided noble soul, a tree-hugger—or a half-dozen of them—who is making his—or their—contribution to world peace and brotherhood among men by feeding anything they think is another proof of our innate evilness to the Russians, who are no longer godless Communists, and thus no longer a threat.

The proof of how good they are now is that when they reburied the tsar and his family in Moscow, Vladimir Vladimirovich Putin was there on his knees. Somehow that photograph of that born-again Christian made front-page news all over the world.

"Just for the sake of conversation, Sergei, what have I got that you want?"

"Colonel Dmitri Berezovsky and Lieutenant Colonel Svetlana Alekseeva."

"Since you have assets all over, Sergei, I'm really surprised you don't know that we don't have either of them, and never have had."

"But in a manner of speaking, Frank, if you have someone who has anything—a bottle of Rémy Martin, for example—wouldn't it be fair to say you also have that bottle of cognac?"

"If you're suggesting I have someone who has your two defectors, I don't. And I think you know that, Sergei."

"What about Lieutenant Colonel Carlos Castillo? Doesn't he have Berezovsky and Alekseeva? And since that name has come up, he wants Colonel Castillo, too."

"Who 'he,' Sergei? Who 'wants Colonel Castillo, too'?"

Murov smiled, but now his eyes were cold.

"Frank, we never lie to one another," Murov said.

True. But we obfuscate as well as we know how—and we're both good at it—all the time.

"So far, that's been the case, Sergei," Lammelle said.

"That being the case, you're not going to deny that Berezovsky and Alekseeva left Vienna on Castillo's airplane, are you?"

"Several people I know have told me that, so I'm prepared to believe it. But I don't know it for a fact."

"Or that Castillo works for you?"

"It's my turn to ask a question. You didn't answer my last question: Who 'he' that wants Castillo?"

Murov took a moment to organize his thoughts, and then asked, "How much of the history of the SVR do you know, Frank?"

"Not nearly as much as I should," Lammelle said. "I know that the Sluzhba

Vneshney Razvedki used to be the First Directorate of the KGB, and there's a story going around that the reason it's so powerful is because, in addition to his other duties to the Russian Federation, Vladimir Putin runs it."

"You do know how to go for the jugular, don't you, Frank?"

"Excuse me?"

"My question was: How much of the history of the SVR do you know?"

"Putin doesn't run it? For a moment there, I was beginning to think that Putin was he who wants Castillo, too."

"Once more, Frank: How much of the history of the SVR do you know?"

"Why don't you tell me, Sergei, what you think I should know about it?"

Murov looked at him carefully and pursed his lips as he framed his reply.

Finally, he asked, "Would you be surprised to learn that its history goes back beyond the Special Section of the Cheka? Back beyond the Revolution?"

"I don't know. I never gave that much thought."

"Where do you think the Cheka came from?"

"I know it really became important in 1917—1918?—when Felix Dzerzhinsky took it over."

"Did you ever hear that Dzerzhinsky was an oprichnik?"

"I don't know what that is. But I have heard that Dzerzhinsky had been locked up and nearly starved to death by the Bolsheviks until just before he was given the Cheka."

"That's what you and I would now call 'disinformation,' Frank. I think it unlikely that he ever spent a day behind bars. Dzerzhinsky was in fact an oprichnik."

"And I told you I don't know what that means."

"I'm about to tell you. In 1565, Ivan the Terrible moved out of Moscow, taking with him a thousand households he'd selected from the nobility, senior military officers, merchants, and even some serfs. Then he announced he was abdicating.

"The people left behind were terrified. Ivan the Terrible was really a terrible man, but those who would replace him were as bad, and before one of them rose to the top, there would be chaos."

Where the hell is he going with this history lesson?

"So they begged Ivan to reconsider, to remain the tsar. He told them what that would take: the establishment of something, a 'separate state' called the 'Oprichnina,' within Russia. The Oprichnina would be made up of certain districts and cities, and the revenue from these places would be used to support Ivan and his oprichniki.

"To make the point that it would be unwise to challenge this new idea, Ivan first had Philip, the Metropolitan of Moscow—who had said the Oprichnina was un-Christian—strangled to death. Then Ivan moved to Great Novgorod, Russia's second-largest city, where the people had complained about having to support the new state-within-the-state.

"There he killed all the men and male children, raped all the women, seized all the crops and livestock, and leveled every building. No one ever questioned the Oprichnina again."

"Not once, in the next—what?—four hundred fifty give-or-take years?"

Murov ignored the sarcasm, and went on: "In 1825, after Tsar Nicholas the First put down the Decembrist Revolution, he realized the revolution would have succeeded had it not been for the assistance—more important, the intelligence— provided by trusted elements of the Oprichnina, so he made them into a separate state within the separate state. He called this the Third Section, or sometimes the Special Section.

"When the Bolsheviks, Mensheviks, and, finally, the Communists took over, Lenin, on December 20, 1917, formed from the tsar's Special Section what was officially The All-Russian Extraordinary Commission for Combating Counterrevolution and Sabotage, but commonly known by its acronym as the Cheka. He placed an aristocrat named Felix Dzerzhinsky in charge."

"The tsar's secret police became the Cheka under an *aristocrat* named Dzerzhinsky?" Lammelle asked incredulously.

Murov nodded.

"Dzerzhinsky's father had been one of the more important grand dukes under the tsar. One of the oprichniki. There were no more grand dukes, of course—or any 'nobility.' But there was the Oprichnina, and Dzerzhinsky was one of them.

"He apparently decided he could best serve Russia by serving Lenin. The family still lives on the estates they had under the tsar. That's the point of this history lesson, Frank. To make sure you understand how important the Oprichnina remains even today."

"I guess you wouldn't know all these fascinating details if you weren't one of them, huh, Sergei?" Lammelle said, more than a little sarcastically.

Murov either missed the sarcasm or chose to ignore it.

"My family has been intelligence officers serving the Motherland for more than three hundred years," Murov said with quiet pride. "We have served in the Special Section, the Cheka, the OGPU, the NKVD, the KGB, and now the SVR."

"And Vladimir Vladimirovich Putin is one of you, too, I suppose?"

"I've answered your question truthfully. Now answer mine: You're not going to deny that Colonel Castillo works for you, are you?"

"*Lieutenant* Colonel Castillo does not now, nor has he ever, worked for the agency. That's the truth, Sergei."

"But you're—how do I put this?—in touch?"

Lammelle shook his head. "No."

"Do you know where he is?"

Lammelle shook his head again. "No, but if I can find out, I'm going to warn him that Putin's after him."

"I didn't say that."

"You didn't have to," Lammelle said. "Are you going to tell me what that's all about? Why does Putin want his head?"

"I didn't say President Putin is in any way involved in this, Frank."

Of course you didn't.

Those cameras and microphones also are recording everything you say, aren't they?

"Okay. Let me rephrase. Why does He Who Wants Castillo want him? And please don't tell me 'wants' isn't shorthand for 'wants eliminated.'"

"There are several reasons, most of which—probably all of which—have occurred to you. For one thing, Colonel Castillo has left a great many bodies behind him in his travels around the world. Do I make my point?"

"That accusation would be a good deal more credible, Sergei, if you put names to the bodies," Lammelle said.

"If you insist," Murov said. "I suppose the first was Major Alejandro Vincenzo of the Cuban Dirección General de Inteligencia. You're not going to deny Castillo was involved in that, are you?"

"As I understand that story, that was self-defense," Lammelle said.

"Whatever the circumstances, Vincenzo and half a dozen others were shot to death in Uruguay by a commando team under Colonel Castillo."

"There was a confrontation and Vincenzo lost. Sometimes that happens in our line of work, Sergei. The good guys don't always win."

Murov smiled.

"That comment can be interpreted in two ways, Frank, depending on who one thinks are the good guys."

"I suppose it could."

"In any event, Vincenzo's death was an embarrassment to General Sirinov, who had to explain it to the Cubans."

"General who?"

"Contrary to your beliefs, General Yakov Sirinov is the man in charge of the FSB and the SVR."

"You mean he runs them for Mr. Putin?"

"President Putin has nothing to do with either the FSB or the SVR."

"You keep telling me that."

Not because you believe it, or expect me to believe it, but because the cameras are rolling.

Murov met Lammelle's eyes for a moment, but did not reply directly, instead saying, "Podpolkovnik Kiril Demidov."

"Is Podpolkovnik Demidov somebody else Podpolkovnik Castillo is supposed to have killed?"

Murov smiled and shook his head.

"All right, Frank, *Lieutenant Colonel* Demidov was a lifelong friend of mine."

"Another member of the oprichniki?"

Murov nodded. "More important, his family and that of General Sirinov were close—more than close, distant cousins, that sort of thing—and even more important than that, close to other powerful people."

"Like he whose name we're not mentioning, who wants Castillo eliminated?"

Murov nodded.

"Vienna is not nearly as important a post as it once was, but when Kiril was named *rezident* there, there were those who said he was too young and did not have the experience he should have."

"But they didn't complain, right, because that might annoy he whose name we are not mentioning who arranged his appointment?"

Murov shrugged in admission.

"Well, I hate to tell you this, Sergei, but I happen to know that Lieutenant Colonel Castillo was nowhere near Vienna when someone strangled your friend and left him in a taxi in front of our embassy."

"We're back to my analogy about who controls the brandy bottle," Murov said. "And the other bodies had names, too: Lieutenant Colonel Yevgeny Komogorov, for one."

Lammelle said, "There was a story going around that he was the FSB man for Argentina, Chile, and Uruguay. The story I heard about what happened to him was that he made the mistake of trying to assassinate Aleksandr Pevsner."

"And then there was Lavrenti Tarasov and Evgeny Alekseev, whose bodies were found near the airport in Buenos Aires. Evgeny was another old friend of mine. I'm sure you know that he was Podpolkovnik Svetlana Alekseeva's husband."

"Why would you think I would know that?"

"Because you're the deputy director of the CIA," Murov said coldly.

"Do I detect a subtle tone of disapproval in your voice, Sergei?" Lammelle said.

"How about disappointment? I really hoped we could have a serious discussion and resolve our problem. As professionals."

"As a professional, Sergei, I find it hard to believe that you thought we could have a serious discussion when what I'm hearing from you strikes me as nonsense."

"Nonsense?"

"Right now I don't have a clear picture of the long-term implications of Congo-X turning up at Fort Detrick and on the U.S.–Mexico border. If you wanted to hurt someone with it, you would have. If you *had* hurt someone, that *could have* led anywhere, right up to a nuclear exchange. If you *do* hurt something that hurts us badly, for example, killing as many people as the ragheads taking down the World Trade Center towers killed, then the missiles *will* fly. We didn't know whom to nuke after 9/11. But if something happens involving Congo-X, we know just where to go: Lubyanka Square, Moscow, and you damned well know it.

"And what you're suggesting here is that you're willing to risk a nuclear exchange unless we turn over to you three people, a colonel and two lieutenant colonels! You're right, Sergei, that's not nonsense. It's not even a clumsy attempt at blackmail. What it is, is pure bullshit!"

Murov looked at him for a moment, then reached for the bottle of Rémy Martin cognac. He poured two inches of it into one of the snifters, and then looked at Lammelle.

"Why not?" Lammelle said. "Not only are the gloves off, but I'm about to walk out of here."

Murov poured cognac into another snifter, then handed it to Lammelle.

They touched glasses.

"Mud in your eye," Murov said.

"Up yours, Sergei," Lammelle said unpleasantly.

"I used the word 'disappointed' a moment ago, Frank. And I am. I'm disappointed that you don't really understand power."

"And what don't I understand about it?"

"In your government, your leader, your President, doesn't really have absolute power. There are things he simply cannot do because he wants to. In other governments—Cuba, for example, North Korea, Venezuela, and one or two others—the leader can do anything that pleases him. Anything."

Lammelle felt a chill at the base of his neck.

"Russia wouldn't be one of those other countries, would it?"

"Of course not. We are a democracy now. Our president and other officials must—and always do—follow the law and the will of the people."

Lammelle took a healthy swallow—half of the cognac in the glass—and felt the warmth move through his body.

"That's utter bullshit, too," he said.

"I'll tell you what's going to happen now, Frank," Murov said. "You're going to go back to Langley and report this conversation to Jack Powell. And he will be as unbelieving as you were. This will evolve into anger. And then you'll go to the President. And he will be as unbelieving as you were and Jack Powell will be. And then he will become angry. Fortunately—for all of us—President Clendennen is not nearly as impulsive as his predecessor. He will think things over carefully, and in the end he will tell you to call me back and say that you will do whatever you can to resolve this problem. As you yourself pointed out, in the balance, the lives of a colonel and two lieutenant colonels aren't really worth all that much."

"Fuck you, Sergei."

"I'll have the car brought around," Murov said, and reached for a telephone.

"Let me call first," Lammelle said, and Murov slid the telephone to him.

Lammelle punched in a number from memory.

"It's time to pick up the dry cleaning," he said a moment later, and then hung up.

He slid the telephone back to Murov.

"Don't bother to make note of the number," he said. "In ten minutes, it will be out of service."

"You didn't have to tell me that, Frank," Murov said, and then punched in a number and said, in Russian, "My guest will be leaving."

Murov walked him to the Caravan.

When Lammelle was in the front passenger seat, Murov motioned for him to roll down the window. Lammelle found the switch, but the window remained up.

"Unlock his fucking window," Murov called nastily in Russian.

Lammelle tried the switch again, and this time the window went down.

"Well?" Lammelle asked.

"Frank, the problem people like you and me have is that sometimes we have to do things we don't like at all. I took no pleasure in what happened between us today. There was no feeling of 'Score one for our side.'"

Lammelle met his eyes, but said nothing. He found the switch, put the window up, and then in English said, "Okay, let's go."

[TWO]
The President's Study
The White House
1600 Pennsylvania Avenue, N.W.
Washington, D.C.
1225 7 February 2007

"Fascinating," President Joshua Ezekiel Clendennen said when Deputy DCI Frank Lammelle had delivered his report on what had happened that morning in the Russian dacha. "How much are we supposed to believe?"

He turned in his high-backed blue leather judge's chair and pointed at Secretary of State Natalie Cohen.

"I think Frank can answer that better than I can, Mr. President," Cohen said. "He was there."

"I'll rephrase, Madam Secretary," Clendennen said, a long way from pleasantly. "Presuming Mr. Lammelle told us the truth and nothing but, how much of what this Russian told him can we believe? Make that two questions: How much of what the Russian told Lammelle are we expected to believe, and, two, how much can we believe?"

If she felt insulted, it didn't show on her face or in her tone of voice.

"Mr. President, I always like to start with what we do know. In this case, we know the Russians were involved with the bio-chem laboratory in the Congo. And since they know we call this substance Congo-X, and that some of it was delivered to Fort Detrick and some left for us to find on the Mexican border, I suggest that it is safe to presume they have more of it. The threat, therefore, is real."

"Natalie, we don't know that," DCI Jack Powell said. "For all we know, the stuff they sent us may be all they have. This whole thing may be a bluff."

"I asked her, Jack," the President said. "You'll get your chance."

"I think, Mr. President," Cohen said, "to respond to your questions directly, that they expect us to believe everything they told Frank, and I think we should."

Clendennen grunted, then looked at Powell.

"Okay, Jack, your chance," the President said. "Do these bastards have more of this stuff, or not?"

"Off the top of my head, Mr. President, I would say they have at least a little more, enough of it so they can leave us a couple more samples."

"And that's all they have?"

"Mr. President, we leveled and then burned everything in a twenty-mile radius of the Fish Farm. Either we somehow missed this, or they had some of it in a laboratory in Russia. Or someplace else. My gut tells me there's not much of Congo-X anywhere."

"But we don't know that, do we?" Clendennen asked.

"No, sir, we don't."

"Why would Putin do something like this?" Clendennen wondered aloud.

"Was that a question, Mr. President?" Mark Schmidt, the director of the FBI, asked.

"Does that mean you have an answer?"

"No, sir. Just that I've been thinking about motive."

"Well, out with it."

"For one thing, we humiliated the Russians when we took out the Fish Farm," Schmidt said. "For another, Castillo and his people—"

"My predecessors' loose cannon and his merry band of outlaws humiliated the Russians?" the President interrupted, sarcastically incredulous.

"Yes, sir. Castillo and his people have not only humiliated the Russians—which is to say Putin—all over Europe and South America but—according to what the Russian told Frank—has killed a lot of them. I think it's credible that Putin did know some of them personally, and wants revenge."

"Madam Secretary?" the President asked.

Natalie Cohen nodded her agreement with Schmidt's theory.

"And he could well be reasoning that we really don't want a confrontation when that could be avoided by returning their two defectors. We can't give him Castillo, of course—"

"Why can't we?" the President asked.

"Jesus Christ!" Lammelle exclaimed.

"Let's go down that road," Clendennen said. "No. Of course we can't give him Colonel Castillo or any of his people. As much as I might want to. But we can go along with that notion . . ."

"Let me go on the record here," Natalie Cohen said. "I will not be part of any agreement which will turn over the two defectors, much less Colonel Castillo or any of his people, to the Russians."

"Duly noted," President Clendennen said. "Let me finish, please. I said we can let the Russians *think* we're willing to give them all three of them. So far as the Russians are concerned, we weren't responsible for their defection."

"Castillo flew them out of Vienna on his plane, Mr. President," Powell said. "And if he hadn't, we had a plane waiting at Schwechat to do the same thing."

"If they had gotten on a plane sent by the CIA, Mr. Powell," the President said coldly, "we would have some sort of moral obligation to protect them. They didn't. Castillo was not acting on behalf of the U.S. government when he flew them to South America. Therefore, we have no such moral obligation."

"I don't agree with that at all, Mr. President," Powell said.

"I don't care, Mr. Powell, if you agree with it or not. I'm telling you that's the way it is."

He let that sink in for a moment, and then went on: "Madam Secretary, I want you to call in the Argentine ambassador and tell him that it has come to our attention that there are two people in his country illegally . . . what are their names?"

"Presumably, Mr. President, you are referring to Dmitri Berezovsky and Svetlana Alekseeva," she said.

". . . for whom Interpol has issued warrants alleging the embezzlement of several millions of dollars."

"Excuse me, Mr. President," Mark Schmidt said. "Interpol has canceled those warrants at the request of the Russian Federation. Three days ago. Berezovsky and Alekseeva are no longer fugitives."

"You're sure?" the President said.

"Yes, sir. I'm sure."

"Well, so much for that idea," the President said. "That would have been easier. We'll have to come up with something else. So here's what we're going to do: Lammelle, get in touch with your Russian and tell him he has a deal."

"Am I to tell him the deal includes Colonel Castillo?"

"Yes. I told you I was not about to turn over an American to those Russian bastards, but if they think I am, so much the better for us."

"Yes, sir."

That sonofabitch is lying through his teeth. He'd happily turn Castillo over to the Russians, or anyone else, if it would get him out of this mess.

"The next step is to locate the Russians. You think they're in Argentina?"

"I have no idea where they are, Mr. President," DCI Powell said.

"Well, I want them found and I want them found quickly. Do whatever has to be done. Send as many people down there—or to anywhere else you think they might be—and find them. Run down the people who used to work for Castillo. See if they know where the Russians are. And Castillo is."

"Yes, sir."

"This is a no-brainer, Mr. Powell. If we can get these Russian bastards to keep that stuff out of the country, and all it costs us is giving them back two traitors, that's a price I can live with. I've always thought that people who change sides are despicable."

"Even if the side they change from is despicable, Mr. President?" Natalie Cohen asked.

"I'm going to pretend I didn't hear you say that, Madam Secretary," the President of the United States said.

[THREE]
Penthouse B
The Grand Cozumel Beach & Golf Resort
Cozumel
Quintana Roo, Mexico
1310 7 February 2007

A good deal of conversation and thought had not shot many holes in the scenario of what was probably going on, but on the other hand it also hadn't done much to confirm it.

Neither had "all the agency intel" that Casey had furnished. The CIA's analysts also seemed to feel the Congo-X sent to Fort Detrick and left for the Border Patrol to find on the Mexican border had most probably come from the Fish Farm in the Congo. But they had no idea how it had been moved from Africa to the United States, and apparently had not considered that the Tupolev Tu-934A might have been involved.

Castillo had called Casey and asked him to see if his source could find anything about Tupolevs moving anywhere, and again asked him to send any intel, no matter how unimportant or unrelated it might seem.

The only thing to do was wait for something to happen. Everybody was frustrated, but everybody also knew that sitting around with your finger in your ear—or other body orifice—waiting for something to happen was what intelligence gathering was really all about.

So everybody but Castillo, Svetlana, Pevsner, and Tom Barlow had gone deep-sea fishing on a forty-two-foot Bertram owned by the Grand Cozumel Beach & Golf Resort.

Castillo had seen everybody's departure as an opportunity. But Tom Barlow had come to the penthouse and asked if he wanted to play chess before he could take advantage of the opportunity. Castillo no more wanted to play chess than he wanted to lunch on raw iguana, but the alternative was saying, "No, thanks, as I'm planning to spend the morning increasing my carnal knowledge of your sister."

When the door chime went off, they were playing chess, and Svetlana—in a bikini—was taking in the sun on a chaise longue by the pool, with Max lying beside her.

The latter went to answer the door.

Aleksandr Pevsner, János, and another man were standing there.

Before Pevsner knew what was happening, Max put his paws on Pevsner's shoulders and licked his face.

"Look at that!" Tom Barlow called happily. "Max loves you, Alek."

And then he recognized the man with Pevsner and exclaimed, "I'll be damned!"

The man with Pevsner was plump, ruddy-faced, and in his early fifties. His short-sleeved blue shirt had wings and epaulets with the four stripes of a captain on it.

"Well, my God, look who's all grown up and wearing lipstick! And not much else," the man said, and spread his arms.

"Uncle Nicolai!" Svetlana cried happily and ran into his arms.

Castillo watched, then thought: *Well, that explains that. Another relative.*

But what is Uncle Nicolai doing here?

Tom Barlow was now waiting patiently for his chance to exchange hugs with Uncle Nicolai. When it came, the two embraced and enthusiastically pounded each other's back.

"Aleksandr said you were in Johannesburg," Svetlana said.

"I spend a good deal of time there," Uncle Nicolai said. He looked at Charley and offered his hand. In fluent, just slightly accented English, he said, "I'm Nicolai Tarasov."

"Charley Castillo."

"Who has captured Svetlana's heart. Alek told me."

"So what brings you to Cozumel by the Sea, Uncle Nicolai?" Castillo asked.

Tarasov avoided the question.

"Alek and I go back to our days with Aeroflot," Tarasov said. "When I tried without much success to teach him to fly Ilyushin Il-96s."

Castillo felt his temper turn on.

"Why don't you want to tell me what brings you to Cozumel by the Sea, Uncle Nicolai?" he repeated, then added: "Somehow I don't think this is a happy coincidence and that you're all going to sit around eating fried chicken and telling stories about Grandma."

"Why are you going out of your way to be unpleasant, Charley?" Svetlana asked.

Castillo switched to Russian: "Because Cousin Alek"—he pointed at

Pevsner—"can't seem to get it through his thick Russian skull that since I'm running this operation, it's not nice to spring surprises on me. Like Uncle Nicolai just happening to drop in from Johannesburg to say hi."

"You speak Russian very well; you sound like you're from Saint Petersburg," Tarasov said. "Aleksandr told me you did. Just after he told me to be very, very careful not to underestimate you."

"I still don't have an answer," Castillo said.

"Just for the record, Charley," Tom Barlow said, "I'm as surprised to see Nicolai as you are."

"Goodbye, Uncle Nicolai," Castillo said, motioning toward the door. "The next time you're in town, make sure you call."

"Now, wait just a minute, Charley!" Pevsner flared.

"Why do I have to spend all my time making peace between you two?" Svetlana asked.

"Maybe because Alek the Terrible has trouble understanding I don't recognize him as the tsar," Charley said.

Both Barlow and Tarasov chuckled.

Pevsner gave them both an icy glare.

"'Alek the Terrible'?" Tarasov quoted. "I like that."

"I got in touch with Nicolai to see what he could contribute to our scenario," Pevsner said after a moment.

"And can he?" Castillo challenged, and then looked at Tarasov. "Can you?"

"I'm trying to run down something I heard, about an incident that took place at the El Obeid Airport in Sudan," Tarasov said. "That may take a little time. And I think there's at least a good chance that if a Tupolev Tu-934A was used in this operation, I know where they landed in Mexico."

"What took place in Sudan?"

"They found a lot of dead people at the burned-down airport," Tarasov said. "From what little I know so far, it sounds like something that one of Yakov Sirinov's Vega Groups would do. No witnesses."

"And the airport in Mexico?"

"Laguna el Guaje," Tarasov said. "In Coahuila State."

"Laguna el Guaje mean anything to you, Charley?" Pevsner asked.

Castillo shook his head.

"It's sort of the Mexican version of Groom Dry Lake Test Facility," Nicolai explained. "Far fewer aircraft, and different secrets."

Castillo knew that Groom Lake, on the vast Nellis Air Force Base near Las Vegas, was rumored to be where—in Area 51 thereon—the CIA was holding little green men from Mars, or elsewhere in the universe. He hadn't seen any of them when he had been to Area 51, but he had seen some very interesting experimental aircraft.

"I have never heard of either what you just said or Area 51," Castillo said. "But if I had, and talked to you about it, I'd have to kill you."

Nicolai laughed out loud and punched Castillo's shoulder.

"I like him, Alek," he said.

"Don't speak too soon," Pevsner said.

"Why do you think that might be the place?" Castillo said.

"Because we use it from time to time," Tarasov said.

And what do you use it for, from time to time?

Moving cocaine around?

"How do we find out?"

"A man who you should know is going to meet us there," Pevsner said.

"And how do we get there?"

"Fly," Tarasov said. "It should take us about an hour."

"Two of the three pilots who can fly our Gulfstream are deep-sea fishing. It may take some time to get them back here. And when they get here, they'll probably be half in the bag. They didn't expect to go flying. And I really don't like flying that airplane by myself."

"But you could if you had to, right? I hear you're quite a pilot." He paused, then added: "Schwechat–Ezeiza via Africa is a *long* way to go in a G-Three unless you really know how to fly a Gulfstream."

"Flattery will get you nowhere, Uncle Nicolai. Goodbye, Uncle Nicolai," Castillo said.

Tarasov seemed unaffected by Castillo's belligerence.

"Actually, Colonel Castillo," he said, "I have an airplane. I just picked up a Cessna Citation Mustang at the factory in Wichita. That's what I was doing when Aleksandr called, getting checked out in it."

"And now you're going to fly it to Johannesburg, right?" Castillo said sarcastically. "I hope you know how to swim. The specs I saw on the Mustang gave it a range of about eleven hundred nautical miles, and the last time I looked, the Atlantic Ocean was a lot wider than that."

"He's not going to fly it to South Africa," Pevsner said. "The casino here bought the Mustang to replace the Lear it uses to pick up good casino customers and bring them to Cozumel."

The last I heard, Cessna was happy not only to deliver a plane like that to the customer, but also to have whoever delivered it teach the new owner or his pilot how to fly it.

And since you own the casino, please forgive me for wondering what almost certainly illegal services this new Mustang will render to you when it's not hauling high-rollers around.

What's behind all this bullshit?

You know, but you don't like to think about it.

Fuck it. Get it out in the open.

"Alek, listen to me carefully," Castillo said. "Whatever we do to solve our current problem, we are not going to get involved with the drug trade or anybody in it."

"Friend Charley, you listen carefully to me," Pevsner said, icily furious. "I am not, and never have been, involved with the drug trade."

Castillo considered that a moment, and then realized: *I'll be a sonofabitch if I don't believe him!*

Why? Because I want to?

"Why do I keep waiting for you to say 'but'?" Castillo asked.

"Aleksandr, I think you should answer Charley's question, and fully," Svetlana said.

Pevsner glared at her.

"Svet took the words from my mouth, Alek," Tom Barlow said. "Not only is he entitled to an answer, but the last thing we need right now is Charley questioning your motives."

"I'm not used to sharing the details of my business operations with anybody," Pevsner said. "I told you I am not, and never have been, involved with the drug trade. That should be enough."

"I keep waiting for the rest of the sentence beginning with 'but,'" Castillo said.

"Colonel Castillo," Tarasov said, "let me try to explain: Once a month—sometimes three weeks, sometimes five—certain businessmen—most often Mexican, Venezuelan, and Colombian, but sometimes from other places—want to visit Switzerland, or Liechtenstein, or Moscow, without this coming to anyone's attention.

"We pick them up at Laguna el Guaje. It's always two of them. Each has two suitcases, one of them full of currency, usually American dollars, but sometimes euros or other hard currency. But only cash, no drugs."

"How do you know that?"

"Because we open them to count the cash, which determines the fare, which is five percent of the cash. We bring them here, where they travel to El Tepual International Airport at Puerto Montt, Chile, aboard a Peruaire aircraft returning from a foodstuff delivery here. At El Tepual, they transfer to an aircraft—

depending on their final destination—of either Cape Town Air Cargo or Air Bulgaria—"

"Both of which the tsar here owns?" Castillo asked.

"The tsar or one of the more charming of the tsar's grand dukes," Tarasov said. "To finish, the aircraft is carrying a cargo of that magnificent Chilean seafood and often Argentinean beef to feed the affluent hungry of Europe. Getting the picture? Any questions?"

"Oh, yeah," Castillo said. "And the first one that comes to mind is: Are all you Russian expatriate businessmen really related? Aren't you worried that you'll corrupt the gene pool?"

Tarasov laughed. "I'm starting to understand you, Colonel Castillo. You say things designed to startle or outrage. People who are startled or outraged tend to say things they hadn't planned to say. Alek was right to warn me not to go with my first impression of you, which—by your design, of course—is intended to make people prone to underestimate you.

"Got me all figured out, have you, Uncle Nicolai? Tell me about the gene pool."

"We're not really related, except very distantly. Our families have been close, however, for many years."

"Do I see the Oprichnina raising its ugly head?" Castillo asked.

"Why ugly?" Tarasov said. "Did what you may have heard of the Oprichnina make you think that?" He turned to Pevsner. "How much did you tell the colonel about the separate state, Alek?"

"What I didn't tell him, Svetlana did," Pevsner said.

"And what Svet didn't tell him, Nicolai, I did," Tom Barlow said, and then turned to Castillo. "Charley, when Alek first left Russia and bought the first Antonov An-22 and went into business, the man who flew it out of Russia was an ex–Aeroflot pilot and Air Force polkovnik named Nicolai Tarasov."

"And we have been in business together since then," Tarasov said. "Does this satisfy your curiosity, Colonel Castillo, or have you other questions?"

This could all be bullshit, which I am, in my naïveté, swallowing whole.

On the other hand, my gut tells me it's not.

"Just one," Castillo said. "Are you going to check me out in the Mustang on our way back and forth to Area 51?"

"It would be my pleasure," Tarasov said.

"Can I go like this?" Sweaty asked, twirling in her bikini.

Castillo saw in Pevsner's eyes that he was considering discouraging her notion, and wondered why, and then that Pevsner had decided she could—or even should—go, and wondered about that, too.

"You can go as naked as a jaybird, as far as I'm concerned," Pevsner said, "but you probably would be more comfortable in a dress."

"Your dog thinks he's going," Tarasov said, pointing at Max, who was sitting on his haunches by the door.

And again Castillo saw something in Pevsner's eyes, this time that Max going was a good idea. He wondered about that, too.

"Max goes just about everywhere with Charley, Nicolai," Pevsner said.

There were two Yukons with darkened windows waiting for them in the basement garage of the luxury hotel, and two men standing by, each not making much of an effort to conceal the Mini Uzis under their loose, flowered shirts.

Castillo wondered if all the security was routine, and then considered for the first time that if the Russians were successful in getting Svetlana and Tom back to Russia, they would probably—almost certainly; indeed Pevsner had said so—be coming after Pevsner.

And if that's true, they will also be coming after Tarasov.

I'll have to keep that in mind.

And continue to wonder when Alek will decide that if throwing me—and possibly even Tom and Sweaty—under the bus is the price of protecting his family and his businesses, then so be it.

Am I paranoid to consider the possibility that that's what may be happening right now? When we get to this mysterious airfield, is there going to be a team of General Yakov Sirinov's Spetsnaz special operators waiting for us, to load us on the Tupolev Tu-934A and fly us off to Mother Russia?

That would solve everyone's problems.

No. That's your imagination running away with you.

Scenario two: The crew of the Bertram terminates all the fishermen and tosses their suitably weighted bodies overboard to feed the fishes.

That would get rid of everybody else who knows too much about the affairs of Aleksandr Pevsner.

And nobody knows—except Pevsner and his private army of ex–Spetsnaz special operators—that any of us have ever been near Sunny Cozumel by the Sea.

Come to think of it, there was no real reason we couldn't have passed through customs under our own names, or the names on the new passports we got in Argentina.

You are being paranoid, and you know it.

On the other hand, you have had paranoid theories before, and on more than several occasions, acting on them has saved your ass.

The Yukon convoy drove directly to the airport, and then through a gate which opened for them as they approached, then onto the tarmac and up beside a Cessna Citation Mustang.

There were two pickup trucks parked close to the airplane. An air-conditioning unit was mounted in the back of one, with a foot-wide flexible tube feeding cold air through the door. The other held a ground power generator.

As soon as the doors of the Yukons opened, the air-conditioning hose was pulled out of the door.

Max knew his role in the departure procedure: He trotted up to the nose gear, sniffed, then raised his right rear leg.

"Does he do that often?" Tarasov asked.

"Religiously," Castillo said.

"You want to do the walk-around with me?" Tarasov said.

Castillo would have done the walk-around without an invitation—no pilot trusts any other pilot to do properly what has to be done—but he intuited Tarasov's invitation was more than courtesy, and even more that it wasn't something a pilot about to give instruction would do.

"Max, go with Sweaty," Castillo ordered in Hungarian, and the dog went to the stair door and politely waited for Svetlana to board, then leapt aboard himself, pushing Pevsner aside as he did.

Castillo's suspicion deepened when Tarasov said, "Why don't you come with us, Dmitri?" and was confirmed when they came to the rear end of the port engine, which could not be seen from inside the airplane.

"Colonel," Tarasov asked, "are you armed?"

"No," Castillo admitted. "Should I be?"

"Dmitri?"

Tom Barlow shook his head.

Tarasov squatted beside his Jeppesen case, opened it and came out with two pistols. Castillo was surprised to see that both were the officer's model—a cut-down version—of the Colt 1911A1 .45 ACP semiautomatic pistol.

They held five cartridges—rather than seven rounds—in the magazines in their shortened grips. The slides and barrels had been similarly shortened. They had once been made from standard pistols by gunsmiths at the Frankford Arsenal for issue only to general officers but later became commercially available.

That's my weapon of choice, Castillo thought.

I wonder where Uncle Nicolai got them. And if by coincidence, or because he's aware that they're about the best people shooter around.

"I'm sure you know how to use one of these," Tarasov said to Charley, and handed him one of the pistols. Then he turned to Barlow. "Dmitri?"

Barlow took the extended pistol, said, "They work like the regular ones, right?" and proceeded to quickly check the pistol to see if there was a round in the chamber. There was. He ejected the magazine, then worked the action, which ejected the round in the chamber. He caught it in the air, said, "Lester showed me how to do that," put it back in the magazine, shoved the magazine back in the pistol, and worked the action. It was now ready to fire.

"Am I going to need this, Nicolai?" he asked.

"I hope not. But Alek said to give them to you, and he always has his reasons. Try not to let Svetlana know you have them."

"Why not?" Castillo challenged.

"I think Alek wants the people we're going to talk to think she's somebody's girlfriend."

"Why?" Castillo pursued.

"If somebody brings his girlfriend to a meeting with people like these, it means either that he's not afraid of them, or stupid, and these people know that whatever he is, Alek is not stupid."

"Neither is Sweaty. If she's going to play a role, she should know what's expected of her."

"You want to tell Alek that?" Tarasov asked.

"My immediate reaction to that is an angry 'Hell, yes, I'll tell him.' But since I tend to get in trouble when I react angrily, let me think about it."

"In the meantime, why don't we get aboard?" Tarasov asked.

The small cabin of the jet was crowded. Castillo and Tarasov had to step carefully around Max, who was sprawled in the aisle, to get to the cockpit.

"Would you like to follow me through?" Tarasov asked when Castillo slipped into the co-pilot's seat.

"You fly, I'll watch," Castillo said.

"Good. You're cautious. Follow me through start-up, and have a look at the panel. It's a very nice little airplane. The latest Garmin, the G1000," he said, pointing at the panel. "When we're ready to go, you can have it. It handles beautifully, and will not try to get away from you, which cannot be said of the G-Three."

"And we're going GPS?" Castillo asked, nodding at the Garmin's screen.

"Very few navigation aids where we're going," the pilot said, smiling, "and we'll be flying, I hope, under the radar."

Tarasov threw the master buss switch, and then reached for the engine start control.

"Starting number one," he announced, and then turned to Charley: "Get on the radio and tell Cancún Area Control that we're going on a four-hour VFR low-level sightseeing ride, with a fuel stop at Santa Elena."

IX

[ONE]
Aboard Cessna Mustang N0099S
North Latitude 27.742, West Longitude 103.285
1425 7 February 2007

"You're not going to find an approach chart in there," Nicolai Tarasov said to Castillo, who had just gone into Tarasov's Jeppesen case searching for exactly that.

"I don't even see a runway on these," Castillo replied. "How do we know where to land? And how do we know there won't be boulders on it?"

"Presuming there's no water in the lake—and it usually is dry—you can land practically anywhere. Your Instructor Pilot will show you physical features used to locate the best place to land."

"And if an IP's not handy?"

"That's the idea, Colonel. If you don't know where to land, you shouldn't try. There won't be any boulders, but you're liable to find large tree trunks in your way. Your IP will show where there are no tree trunks."

"Meaning there are people here who remove them?"

Tarasov nodded, then said, "May I call you 'Charley'? Or 'Carlos'?"

"I wish you would—'Carlos'—as I ain't a colonel no more."

"Once a colonel, Carlos, always a colonel," Tarasov said. "Put it into a shallow descent on this course. Go into a low-level pass to make sure there really are no dead trees on the runway, and then you can land."

"What about the wind?"

"When they hear us coming, a wind sock will miraculously appear next to the runway."

"I gather there is no Laguna el Guaje tower?"

"That's the idea, Carlos. Since there is no tower, curious ears cannot overhear it clearing aircraft in and out of here."

The "physical feature" Tarasov pointed out was a sprawling ranch house and some outlying buildings on the high terrain next to the lake.

"Immediately down the hill you should see—there it is—the wind sock," Tarasov said. "Usually there are negligible crosswinds. Just land into the wind, remembering, of course, to lower the wheels first."

"I have a tendency to forget that," Castillo said as he began a one-hundred-eighty-degree turn.

"Wheels coming down," Tarasov said a moment later, "and down and locked."

And a moment after that, Castillo greased the Cessna Mustang onto the lake bed.

"Not too bad a landing for a beginner," Tarasov said. "After another, say, twenty hours of my masterful instruction, I might be prepared to sign you off to fly this aircraft."

Castillo gave him the finger. Tarasov smiled at him.

"What now?" Castillo asked.

"Taxi back toward the house. You'll see sort of a hangar."

What Castillo saw just over a minute later was "sort of a hangar" dug into the side of the hill lining the dry lake bottom. It was invisible from the air, and to him as he landed, but now an enormous dirt-colored tarpaulin had been raised out of the way, revealing a cavelike area in which Castillo could see a Learjet.

A burly man in khakis walked out of the opening, holding wands and motioning him to taxi inside. An Uzi hung around his shoulder and when Castillo turned the nose, he could see three other men similarly dressed and armed.

"They don't look very friendly," Castillo said.

"They're not," Tarasov said.

Castillo turned the Mustang nose out and shut down the engines.

"Now what?" he asked.

"Now it gets interesting," Tarasov said as he unfastened his harness. Charley followed suit, and when he stood up, saw that Max and Pevsner were standing by the door.

"Maybe you better tell Max to stay onboard," Pevsner said. "Those people are liable to shoot first and ask questions later."

The best defense is usually a good offense.

"Maybe I should get off first," Castillo said, and reached for the opening mechanism.

When the stair door dropped in place, he jumped to the ground.

The men with the Uzis moved toward the airplane.

"Good afternoon," Castillo said in Spanish. "My dog is about to get off the airplane. If anyone looks like he's even thinking about pointing a weapon at him, I'll stick it up his ass, before I kill him."

The men stopped moving toward him.

He snapped his fingers and Max jumped easily to the ground. Castillo pointed to the nose gear. Max headed for it. He would have anyway, but the men with the Uzis didn't know that, and they were as much impressed with the obedient, well-trained dog as they were with his size.

"Okay, Alek," Castillo called. "You're next. This is your show."

János came down the doorstairs, followed by Pevsner, then Tom Barlow, and finally Svetlana.

The men's faces made it clear that she surprised them even more than the dog.

"*El Señor* García-Romero is presumably here?" Pevsner asked, more than a little arrogantly.

There was a faint flash from Castillo's memory bank: *I know that name.*

Héctor García-Romero headed a law firm which maintained offices in Mexico City, San Antonio, and New York.

Among its clients was Lopez Fruit and Vegetables Mexico, a wholly owned subsidiary of Castillo Agriculture, Inc., of San Antonio, Texas, whose honorary chairman of the board was Doña Alicia Castillo, whose president and chief executive officer was Fernando Lopez, Charley's cousin, and whose officers included Carlos Castillo.

This can't be my Tío Héctor. What the hell would he be doing here at a thug-guarded secret airfield that might as well have a sign reading WELCOME TO DRUG CARTEL INTERNATIONAL AIRPORT?

And there are probably two hundred ninety-seven thousand and six Mexicans named García-Romero.

"*Sí, señor.* In the house."

"Then what are we standing around here for?"

"Excuse me, señor, but we must check to see if you are armed."

"That's none of your business," Pevsner snapped. "Now, get on the telephone and tell Señor García-Romero that I am here with a pistol in each hand."

One of the men considered that briefly, then turned, and walked quickly deeper into the cave. The remaining three men eyed everyone, except for Svetlana, warily. In Svetlana's case, the adjective was "lustfully."

In under a minute, the man who had walked away came back.

"If you will be good enough to come with me, señor?"

In the back of the cave, incongruously modern and high-tech against the gray stone into which it had been cut, was a stainless-steel-framed elevator door.

Carefully staying out of Max's way, the men ushered them onto the elevator, but did not get on it. The door closed and just as Pevsner reached for a button with an UP arrow on it, the elevator began to rise.

A Haydn string quartet came over speakers.

The door opened.

Four people were waiting for them, three of them much better dressed than the guards in the cave, but just as obviously guards. The fourth was a superbly tailored, portly, silver-haired man in his sixties.

I will be goddamned.

"Please accept my apologies for the misunderstanding down there," Héctor García-Romero said, and then he took a closer look at Castillo.

"Holy Mother of God, is that really you, Carlitos?"

"It's been a long time, Tío Héctor," Castillo said.

"What did you call him?" Svetlana asked.

"Carlitos," Héctor García-Romero said. "It means 'Little Carlos.'"

"That's sweet!" Svetlana said.

"I have known him since he was this tall," García-Romero said, holding his hand flat a few inches below the level of his shoulder. "You were what, Carlitos, eleven?"

"Twelve," Castillo said.

"I saw Doña Alicia ten days ago in San Antonio," García-Romero said. "She said you were in Hungary with Billy Kocian."

"I was."

And now we're both in the VIP Lounge of Drug Cartel International Airport in the middle of the Mexican desert.

What the hell are you doing here, Tío Héctor?

"I had no idea you knew Señor Pevsner," García-Romero said.

"Likewise," Castillo said. "And I've been wondering what sort of business you do together."

"Carlitos's grandfather was one of my dearest friends," García-Romero said. "If he had one flaw, it was his habit of asking indelicate questions. Carlitos has apparently inherited that, along with his more desirable character traits."

"Why don't you answer the indelicate question?" Castillo asked.

"Why don't we all go sit in the great room, have a little snack, and a little something to drink, and then we can sort this out?" García-Romero said, and waved them into the house.

An elaborate buffet had been laid out on an enormous low table. Silver coolers held wine, champagne, and beer bottles, and there was an array of whisky bottles at the end of the table.

Max went immediately to examine them, and with great delicacy, helped himself to a wafer topped with salami and cheese. And then helped himself to another.

"I thought Doña Alicia was exaggerating when she told me how big your dog is," García-Romero said.

"And what did Doña Alicia tell you about me?" Svetlana asked.

"That Carlitos had brought a girl to the Double-Bar-C Ranch she really hoped would be the one with whom he would finally settle down and start a family."

"That's the plan," Svetlana said.

"And that's about all she told me," García-Romero said.

"Héctor," Pevsner said, "Svetlana and I are cousins."

"And this gentleman?" García-Romero asked, indicating Tom Barlow.

"Dmitri and Svetlana are brother and sister," Pevsner said.

"And Carlitos fits in how?"

"We think of him as family," Pevsner said.

"He *is* family," Svetlana corrected him.

"And I have always thought of Carlitos and his cousin Fernando as my nephews," García-Romero said.

"So, in a manner of speaking," Pevsner said, "we're all family."

"Above the sound of the violins softly playing 'Ave Maria,'" Castillo said, "I keep hearing a soft voice asking, 'Charley, who the hell do these two think they're fooling?'"

"Excuse me?" García-Romero asked.

"You heard me, Héctor," Castillo said. "How come I never saw you surrounded by thugs with Uzis before?"

"They're necessary security, Carlos," García-Romero said.

"To protect you from whom?"

"You're a Mexican, a Mexican-American. You know there's a criminal element here."

"I'm a Texican, and you goddamned well know the difference between a Mexican-American and a Texican."

García-Romero did not answer.

"I saw surveillance cameras in that cave downstairs," Castillo said. "What I want from you now, Tío Héctor, *right now*, is to see the tapes of the Tupolev Tu-934A when it was here."

He could see in García-Romero's eyes that that had struck a chord.

"The what?" García-Romero asked.

"The Russian airplane," Castillo qualified. "And please don't tell me you don't know what I'm talking about. I've had about all the bullshit I can take."

García-Romero looked at Castillo and then at Pevsner.

"You know about that? Is that why you're here?"

"Why don't you show us the tapes, Héctor?" Pevsner replied.

"I was going to show them to you anyway," García-Romero said.

"Mommy, I was only trying to see how many cookies were in the jar. That's the only reason I had my hand in it. I wasn't going to eat any of them. And that's the truth."

"Let's go, Héctor," Castillo said. "Where are they?"

"In the security office," García-Romero said. "It's on the upper floor."

He gestured toward the center of the building, and then led everybody out of the great room into the foyer, and then up a wide, tiled stairway to an upper floor.

The security room was at the end of a corridor to the right.

García-Romero didn't even try to work the handle, instead pulling down the cover of a keypad and then punching in a code. And even then he didn't try to open the door.

"I wondered what kind of an airplane that was," he said. "I'd never seen one before."

There was the sound of a bolt being drawn, and then the door was opened by a man in khakis. He had a pistol in a shoulder holster.

"We want to see the tapes of that strange airplane," García-Romero said.

"Shall I bring them to the great room, Don Héctor?"

"No," Castillo said. "We'll look at them here."

The man looked at Castillo in surprise, and then at García-Romero for guidance.

García-Romero courteously waved Svetlana ahead of him through the door, and then motioned for the others to follow.

Inside, there was a desk and chairs and a cot, and another door. That was opened only after another punching of a keypad—this one mounted in sight beside the door—and the sliding of another bolt.

Inside the interior room there was a wall holding more than a dozen monitors. A man sat at a table watching them. There was room and chairs for two more people at the table.

Castillo looked at the monitors. He was not surprised to see that it was a first-class installation, which covered just about everything in and around the house, the "airfield," and the cave. And he was pleased to see a battery of recorders; that meant that whatever had happened when the Tupolev Tu-934A had been at Drug Cartel International had been recorded and would be available.

"We want to see whatever the cameras picked up when that strange airplane was here," García-Romero said. "So I suspect we had better start with the arrival of the cars from the Russian embassy."

The man who had opened the door for them went to a rack, quickly found what he was looking for, and inserted it into a slot of the desk.

"It will be on Monitor Fourteen, Don Héctor," he said.

"What cars from the Russian embassy?" Pevsner demanded a split second before Castillo had finished opening his mouth to ask the same thing.

"There were three," García-Romero said, "two Ford sport—"

He stopped and pointed to Monitor Fourteen.

The monitor showed two enormous black Ford Expeditions and a Mercedes sedan being waved past khaki-clad guards at a gate across a dirt road.

"Aleksandr, I was told that the aircraft would be on the ground here just long enough for the people from the Russian embassy to take the two crates from it," García-Romero said.

"Héctor, anything you have to tell anybody about this, you tell me," Castillo said. "Alek is not the tsar of this operation, I am."

Pevsner's face whitened but he didn't say anything.

"Are you going to tell me what 'this operation' is all about, Carlos?" García-Romero asked.

"Probably not. Who told you about the Tupolev coming and the involvement of the Russian embassy?"

García-Romero hesitated before replying, then said, "Valentin Borzakovsky."

"Who's he?"

García-Romero hesitated again.

"He's a businessman who lives in Venezuela."

"What kind of a businessman? FSB or drug cartel?"

"I don't think I like the question, or your tone, Carlos," García-Romero said.

"Probably both, Carlos," Nicolai Tarasov answered Castillo. "He's one of the people we often fly out of here. And then back in here."

"With suitcases full of money?"

Tarasov nodded, smiled, and added, "On the way out. He always comes back empty-handed."

Monitor Fourteen now showed the cave. The Expeditions and the Mercedes were driving into it.

Then it showed the sky, the camera obviously looking for an aircraft.

Or cameras, plural, Castillo thought as the view which had shown some terrain changed to one showing only the sky.

How do they know to expect it?

He looked around the control room and found a radar screen.

I wouldn't want to make an instrument landing using that, but that's not what it's intended for. That's just to let the authorities of Drug Cartel International know that an aircraft has entered their area.

There was a blip on the radar screen.

I wonder how far away that airplane is. How far and how high.

Monitor Fourteen showed a dot in the sky that quickly grew into an airplane.

Castillo looked at Tarasov to see if he had seen it. Tarasov nodded.

Castillo went back to the screen. The airplane had now grown an enormous vertical stabilizer and engines above the fuselage.

Castillo looked at Tarasov again.

Tarasov nodded and mouthed, "Tu-934A."

That's one weird-looking airplane. If I had ever seen one—even a picture of one—I would have remembered.

Monitor Fourteen showed the weird-looking airplane coming in low for a landing.

"I'd never seen an airplane like that before," García-Romero said.

Well, the Russians certainly didn't show it off at the Paris Air Show. That's a Special Operations special.

That it exists can't be kept a secret but the fewer people who know anything else about it, the better.

The landing roll looked normal, until all of a sudden it decelerated at an amazing rate until it was almost at a complete stop and then turned.

He must have spotted the cave.

Proof of that came when Monitor Fourteen showed the Tu-934A coming into the cave, and the camouflaged tarpaulin being lowered into place once the plane was inside.

The rear door of the Mercedes opened and a man in a business suit walked toward the Tu-934A.

The monitor pulled in on his face.

"Well, hello, Pavel," Tom Barlow said.

"Who is he?" Castillo asked.

"Pavel Koslov," Svetlana said. "The Mexico City *rezident*."

"And that means this is important, and probably that there's somebody notorious on the plane," Barlow said.

Monitor Fourteen showed the ramp at the rear of the Tu-934A's fuselage lowering. Before it quite touched the ground, two men in rather tight, hooded black coveralls, their faces masked, and carrying Kalashnikov rifles, trotted down it and looked the area over.

One of them made a *come on* gesture and two more similarly dressed and armed men came down the ramp.

"We call people who dress up like that 'ninjas,'" Castillo said. "What do you call them, Sweaty?"

"Spetsnaz."

Another man, in the black coveralls but not wearing a mask, came down the ramp. The camera moved in for a close-up.

"And a very good afternoon to you, General," Barlow said. "I trust the general had a pleasant flight?"

"That's General Yakov Vladimirovich Sirinov," Svetlana said. "Which tells us that Vladimir Vladimirovich Putin is indeed behind all this."

"Behind all what?" García-Romero asked. "May I ask?"

"Right now, Tío Héctor . . ." Castillo began and then stopped when another man, this one in a business suit, came down the ramp, and again the camera moved in for a close-up.

"That's Valentin Borzakovsky," García-Romero said.

"Why do I think he didn't just come from Venezuela?" Castillo asked.

"A fuel stop at friendly José Martí International Airport?" Tarasov said.

"I'd bet Ciego de Ávila," Castillo said. "They wouldn't want the Tu-934A to be seen at José Martí."

"You're right, that's more likely," Tarasov said.

"Where Whatsisname . . . Bora-something?"

"Borzakovsky, Valentin Borzakovsky," Svetlana furnished, a touch of impatience or resignation in her voice.

". . . where he boarded FSB Airlines Flight 007, one-stop—here at Drug Cartel International—service to Maiquetía International Airport in the People's Democratic Republic of Venezuela."

Tarasov and Barlow chuckled.

Barlow then said: "I don't think Hugo Chávez would want the Tu-934A . . . I rephrase: I don't think *General Sirinov* would want—as much as Hugo would want it to put it on display—the Tu-934A to be seen at Maiquetía. Maybe the Santo Domingo Air Base?"

"More likely La Orchila," Svetlana said. "That's on an island. And it's a pretty decent air base. The runways will take a 747, and Chávez has moved all the civilians off the island."

"Which would add to the security," Barlow agreed.

"If you Russians have no ambitions in the Caribbean, how come you know so much about all the military airfields?"

"Charley, my darling, Alek is right," Svetlana said. "You really have a sophomoric sense of humor."

"My precious, I'll bet you don't even know what a sophomore is."

"The term probably has its roots, my precious darling, in one of the late sophist *Dialogues of Plato*, but what it means is 'tricky and superficially plausible,' so therefore a sophomore is someone who is tricky and superficial, with emphasis on superficial. Does the shoe fit?"

"Not at all, my precious beloved darling. A sophomore is a second-year student at a college or university. You really should try to be sure of your facts before you open your adorable mouth to challenge your intellectual betters."

Svetlana made a gesture to Charley involving the use of the index fingers on both hands held in upward position.

Tom Barlow laughed out loud.

"You will pay for that, Charley," he said.

"Look what's coming down the ramp," Tarasov said.

Monitor Fourteen showed a tracked front-loader rolling off the Tu-934A's ramp. Two blue plastic vessels, looking not unlike beer kegs, were suspended from its arms.

It moved to the rear of one of the Expeditions and, under the watchful eyes of General Sirinov and one of the ninjas, was carefully loaded into it.

Then it moved to the second Expedition, where the process was repeated.

General Sirinov held a brief conversation with the man who had helped him supervise the loading of the barrels; Pavel Koslov, the Mexico City *rezident*; and Valentin Borzakovsky, the Venezuelan "businessman."

Then they all shook hands, except for the ninja, who first saluted and then shook hands. Koslov got back in his Mercedes and immediately drove off. Borzakovsky and the ninja and two others got in one of the Expeditions, and four of the ninjas in the other.

The Expeditions drove off.

Monitor Fourteen showed first the Mercedes, and then, a minute later, the Expeditions moving up a road in the hill surrounding the dry lake.

"They're wearing their ninja suits?" Castillo thought out loud.

"There's probably clothing for them to wear over their tactical suits in the trucks," Barlow said.

The monitor now switched back and forth between the moving vehicles, and what was happening in the cave. General Sirinov himself drove the front-loader back aboard the Tu-934A. The ramp was raised. The monitor followed Sirinov and two men Castillo guessed were the pilots to the stainless-steel elevator and showed them getting in.

"Nothing much happened after this," García-Romero said. "Those three men—you said you knew one of them?"

"How far is that—*are we*—from the Mex–U.S. border?" Castillo asked, ignoring the question.

"At the closest point, seventy-five, eighty miles," García-Romero said.

"And McAllen-Matamoros, that area? What's that, five hundred miles?"

"Probably," García-Romero said.

"The ninjas came back, right? And the Venezuelan 'businessman'?"

García-Romero nodded. "They returned about four hours after what you just saw."

"So that means they got the barrels across the border near here," Castillo said. "How would they do that, Tío Héctor?"

García-Romero hesitated for a moment, but finally said, "There are people who make a profession of getting people across the border. . . ."

"People *and* drugs, right?"

"Yes, Carlos, sometimes drugs. They call them 'coyotes.'"

"What?" Svetlana asked.

"A coyote is something like a cross between a wolf and a German Shepherd, sweetheart," Castillo said. "With all of the bad, and none of the good, characteristics of both. They attack calves, lambs, dogs, cats, rabbits, and sometimes children. Their numbers are increasing, and there doesn't seem to be much that can be done to control them. In other words, they're sort of a canine drug cartel."

"You really don't like people involved with drugs, do you, baby?" she asked softly.

"Moving right along, Héctor," Castillo said, "would it be reasonable to assume that somewhere near the border, some of these coyotes had been pre-positioned, either by the Venezuelan businessman or the guy from the Russian embassy, to move those two barrels into the United States?"

"*If* they wanted to move those barrels into the United States, that would be the way to do it. Do we know that they wanted to do that? What's in those barrels, anyway?"

"We know they moved those barrels into the States. What we're trying to figure out is how and where. And you don't want to know what's in those barrels, Tío Héctor. Believe me."

"They somehow got one of the barrels to Miami, sweetheart?" Svetlana suggested. "And shipped it from Miami to Colonel Hamilton? And later left the other where your border guards would find it?"

"Yeah. Probably to make us think the first barrel was smuggled into Miami from Cuba."

García-Romero began: "I had no idea anything like this—"

"Let me see if I have this right," Castillo interrupted him. "Borzakovsky came to you . . . Wait. Let me back up. You're in charge of Drug Cartel International, right, Tío Héctor?"

"I can't believe I'm hearing from you what you're suggesting, Carlos," García-Romero said. "I am not in the drug business; this airfield is not a transshipment point for drugs."

"When you accuse Héctor of that, friend Charley," Pevsner said in Russian, "you're accusing me. And that's something I cannot accept, even from you."

"Okay, then, tell me what goes on here," Castillo said.

"Nicolai has already told you," Pevsner said. "There are people who need large amounts of currency shipped from place to place."

"And I'm supposed to believe those large amounts of money are not connected with the drug business? Come on, Alek!"

"You are really trying my patience, friend Charley, but since you are being so intentionally dense, let me spell it out for you—"

"I don't speak Russian," García-Romero interrupted.

Pevsner ignored him, and continued in Russian: "What I do, as you well know, is move things around."

"Like drugs?" Castillo asked sarcastically.

"Not knowingly," Pevsner said. "Not that I think drugs are any more reprehensible a cargo than, say, the shipments of arms I have moved on many occasions and for years for your Central Intelligence Agency, but rather because when, inevitably, one of my shipments of arms, for example, is intercepted by the authorities, all that happens is that I lose the shipment and pay a fine. If the authorities intercept a cargo of drugs, my airplanes are confiscated and the authorities try very hard to make sure everyone goes to jail.

"That said, and again as you very well know, in recent years I have severed my connection with the CIA and, for that matter, with the SVR, when that involves the shipment of arms.

"Just about everything that Nicolai and I now transport around the world is perfectly legal. Moving currency, and the bearers of that currency, from one place to another may not be perfectly legal, but if there is a violation, it is of customs and immigration laws. People caught by the authorities attempting to illegally enter a country are simply returned to where they came from. If customs officers discover they have in their luggage undeclared large amounts of currency, the usual punishment is the seizure of half of it.

"In that connection, an amateur attempt by Hugo Chávez several months ago to send about a million dollars to the president of Argentina—"

"'An amateur attempt'?" Castillo interrupted sarcastically.

"—without it coming to the attention of the authorities failed because the courier used a chartered private jet—a Gulfstream like yours, if memory serves. People using chartered jets attract the attention of the authorities. The Argentine customs people carefully searched the courier's bags as he passed through customs, found the money, refused his offer of a little gift, and confiscated half of the money. The courier had dinner that night with the president. You getting the picture?"

"I really would like to know what you two are saying," García-Romero said.

"If moving money around is so easy, why do they need you to do it?" Castillo asked.

"Discretion, Carlos," Nicolai Tarasov said. "The people we move money for are as much—perhaps more—concerned that no one finds out they are moving money as they are for the money itself. They don't want to be embarrassed as the president of Argentina and Hugo Chávez were when their courier was caught.

"If one of their couriers is caught aboard one of our aircraft—which very rarely happens—we say we didn't know he had the money with him, and the courier tells them he was carrying the money for someone not remotely connected with the people he's actually carrying it for. Half of the money—presuming the customs officials cannot be bribed, and they usually can—is confiscated. The owners of the currency write the loss off as the cost of doing business, and that's the end of it."

"You're telling me the only thing Drug Cartel International is used for is moving money?" Castillo said.

"That's exactly what I'm trying to tell you," Pevsner said. "And that's why I was so surprised when Nicolai said he thought it likely the Tu-934A had come here. I had trouble believing your Uncle Héctor could be that stupid."

Pevsner turned to García-Romero, who of course had recognized his name being said, and switched to Spanish.

"I just told Carlos that I had trouble believing you could be so stupid," he said. "Now, let's turn to that. Start at the beginning, Héctor, and tell us how this fiasco came to happen."

García-Romero looked very uncomfortable.

"Let's hear it, Héctor," Pevsner said coldly.

"Valentin Borzakovsky came to me and said the Russian embassy had a problem," García-Romero began. "He said they had reason to believe the CIA had infiltrated Aeromexpress Cargo . . ."

"What won't those evil Yankees be up to next?" Pevsner asked.

". . . which the Russians use as their air-freight forwarder. Borzakovsky said the Russian embassy really needed to get something from Moscow the Americans couldn't know about," García-Romero finished.

"Do you think those blue beer kegs they unloaded from the Tu-934A might have contained nuclear weapons?" Castillo said jokingly.

But what the hell am I joking about?

They contained Congo-X, which is just about as bad.

"I'm not as naïve as you seem to think, Carlos," García-Romero said. "There were radiation detectors waiting for that shipment."

And if the needles on your radiometers had gone off the scale, and you had said anything, you and everybody who works for you in the cave would be dead and the nukes would be in Mexico.

"Go on, Héctor," Pevsner said.

"He said there would be very little risk. Pavel Koslov of the Russian embassy—who of course has diplomatic immunity—would come here to meet the airplane, immediately load this cargo into Russian embassy trucks, and be gone within minutes."

"How much else do you think your friend Valentin Borzakovsky, this Venezuelan businessman good friend of yours, told Koslov about what goes on here?" Pevsner asked angrily.

García-Romero didn't respond, and instead said, "He offered me one hundred thousand euros for the service."

"You risked everything we have here for a hundred thousand euros?" Pevsner asked incredulously.

"Do you know how much it costs to maintain this facility, Aleksandr?"

"To the penny!" Pevsner snapped. "And the last time I looked, the income made the cost look like a minor operating expense. And you risked losing all that income for a hundred thousand euros? My God, you are a fool!"

"I also thought it might be useful to have the Russian embassy owe us a favor," García-Romero said.

"Did it occur to you, Tío Héctor," Castillo asked, "that once you did this hundred-thousand-euro 'favor' for the Russians that you had jumped into their pocket, and they would be back asking for other 'favors' and this time there would be no euros, just the threat to expose you for what you did?"

"Or that once this happened, we couldn't take the risk of ever using this place again?" Nicolai Tarasov put in before García-Romero could open his mouth.

"Is that all the bad news, Héctor?" Pevsner asked. "Or is there more?"

García-Romero hesitated a long moment before replying.

"There is more," he said. "I don't know whether you think it will be bad news or not."

"Let's have it."

"My men have heard gossip that the coyotes—there were seven or eight of them—were found shot to death near the American border."

"Dead men tell no tales," Castillo said. "You might want to write that down, Alek."

Pevsner's response was not what Castillo—or, for that matter, any of the others—expected.

"Have you any further questions for your Uncle Héctor, friend Charley?" he asked matter-of-factly.

"I've got a couple, including one I expected you to ask," Castillo said.

"Which is?"

"How much does your friend Borzakovsky know about Nicolai and Alek's operations here?"

"Nothing," García-Romero said immediately. "I swear your name didn't come up, Aleksandr."

I don't believe you, Uncle Héctor, and I don't think Pevsner will either.

Did you commit suicide when you made this deal with the Russians?

"Anything else you want to know, Charley?" Pevsner asked.

"How long is it going to take you to put all those surveillance tapes in a box for me?"

"You're going to do what with them?" Pevsner asked.

"Slide them—or copies of them—under the door of that big building in Langley, Virginia."

Pevsner considered that for a long moment, but made no comment.

"And after you've done that, Héctor," Pevsner said, "what you're going to do is shut this place down. I want *all* the surveillance tapes that Charley doesn't take destroyed. I want the system removed. I want everybody who has worked here to find employment as far from here as possible. If this place should suddenly attract the attention of the Mexican government, I want them to find nothing that will tie me—or, for that matter, you—to it in any way."

"You think that maybe we should burn the house down?" García-Romero said sarcastically.

Pevsner considered that a moment, and then said, "You use bottled gas here, right? Bottled gas explodes. Can you handle that, or should I have János show you how that's done?"

"You're serious?"

"Yes, I'm serious. You have a problem with that?"

Careful, Tío Héctor.

The wrong answer will get you in more trouble than you can imagine.

"How much time do I have?" García-Romero asked. "I have several men I trust completely. I could leave them here to arrange the . . . accident."

"While you go where?"

"I was about to say Mexico City, but I think San Antonio would be even better. Better yet, New York."

Pevsner considered that.

"New York would be better," he said. "Twenty-four hours from now, Nicolai will fly over this place. When he looks down, he will expect to see the burned—possibly still burning—ruins of this building."

"That's what he will see," García-Romero said.

Congratulations, Uncle Héctor. You have just said the magic words.

And your bullet-ridden corpse will not be found in the burned ruins of your house in the desert.

[TWO]
Penthouse B
The Grand Cozumel Beach & Golf Resort
Cozumel
Quintana Roo, Mexico
1915 7 February 2007

The fishermen had apparently come home from the sea shortly before the hunters had come home from the hills around Drug Cartel International.

When Castillo and the others walked into the penthouse, the tiled area around the swimming pool was being converted by the resort staff—under the direction of Uncle Remus—into a high-in-the-sky grilled seafood outdoor restaurant. A long table had been set up, and flames were still rising from the just-ignited lava coals in two barbecue grills. An enormous insulated box seemed to be stuffed with king mackerel, and another cooler with bottles of Dos Equis beer.

Max immediately went to sniff at the fish.

Everybody but Colin Leverette and Lester Bradley, who stood at the grills, was sitting around the pool on chaise longues under umbrellas, most of them holding bottles of the Dos Equis.

"I knew Our Noble Leader would return when he smelled food," Uncle Remus said. "And he'd tell us where he's been. Right, Charley?"

"I'll even show you movies of where I've been," Castillo replied, and looked at Lester. "Lester, can we send tapes from surveillance cameras to Casey? Or look at them on the TV? Both?"

Bradley thought about that a moment, nodded, and said, "Yes, sir. That shouldn't be a problem."

"Have at it," Castillo said.

"I'll take over the grill," Svetlana said. "Somehow I suspect cooking is not among Uncle Remus's many skills. And I don't want that fish ruined. I'm hungry."

"You are in the presence, madam, of one of New Orleans's most skilled piscatorial chefs," Uncle Remus said. "Be humble."

"They have *parrillas* in Mother Russia, do they, Sweaty?" Delchamps said as he pushed himself off his chaise lounge.

"We have everything in Mother Russia, Edgar," Svetlana said. "I'm surprised you don't know that."

"I think everybody should have a look at these tapes before we send them to Casey," Castillo said. "Logical conclusion: Let Sweaty get the grills going." He gave in to the temptation, and added innocently, "Aleksandr can help her."

Surprising him, Pevsner went immediately to the grills and politely asked for, and was given, Lester's chef hat. He put it on, then tested the heat coming from the no-longer-flaming lava briquettes by holding his hand, palm down, over them.

"Another seven minutes, I would estimate," he said. "While you're showing the tapes, I will ensure the fish have been properly filleted." And then he smiled at Castillo and added, "Never underestimate people, friend Charley. You might want to write that down."

"Two-Gun, get your laptop," Castillo ordered as Lester hooked up cables from Casey's radio to the television. "I'm going to offer a running commentary as the tapes run, identifying the players, et cetera. We'll then edit the tape and the commentary to make sure the CIA can't identify or locate the airfield or all the players."

"Two questions," Yung replied. "This is going to the CIA? And why shouldn't they locate the airport?"

"Pevsner has a connection with the airport. I don't want them to start linking things."

"Make that three questions," Yung said. "How are you getting it to the CIA? Through Casey?"

"I'd rather slip it under the door, but I haven't figured out how to do that."

"Lester," Edgar Delchamps said, "can you send these tapes to the house in Alexandria?"

"Yes, sir. No problem."

"And can you get me a number in Arlington, Virginia, without it coming to the attention of those nosy people at Fort Meade?"

"According to Dr. Casey, all they will hear at Fort Meade is what sounds like static on the line. And I can make it sound as if the call was made from anywhere."

"Who do you want to receive the tapes, Ace?" Delchamps asked.

"Either the DCI or Frank Lammelle."

"If I have one of the dinosaurs call on Madam Darby and pick up the tape and commentary, and then he slips that under the door addressed to Lammelle, and you also send it to Casey, he will probably send it to the DCI. He's close to those people, right? Then we'd be sure both the DCI and Lammelle got it."

"Then that's what we'll do," Castillo agreed.

"Let's see the tapes, Lester," Delchamps said.

"So our scenario wasn't far off the mark," Edgar Delchamps said, when the tapes had been played. "They did use the Tupolev Tu-934A to move that stuff. The question then is, from where did they move it? From a warehouse full of the stuff in Mother Russia or . . . ?"

"Sweaty says they wouldn't have Congo-X in Russia," Castillo said. "Too dangerous."

"That would tie in with what Tarasov heard happened at that airport—El Obeid—in Sudan," Delchamps said. "Okay, they picked it up in Africa and flew it here. . . . Nonstop?"

"They probably stopped in Cuba," Castillo said. "Probably at Ciego de Ávila. They wouldn't want the Tu-934A to be seen at José Martí."

"And from Ciego de Ávila to this dry-lake airfield?" Alex Darby asked.

Castillo nodded.

"And then where? Back to Cuba?" Darby asked.

"Venezuela," Castillo said. "Tom says the price for getting the Cubans to do more than fuel the Tu-934A would be too high. Chávez, on the other hand, is not half so smart as the Brothers Castro. Sweaty thinks it's probably at La Orchila . . . that island air base."

"What is that, another proof you can't judge a book by its cover?" Delchamps asked.

"What the hell does that mean?" Castillo asked.

"You never heard, Ace, that 'the true test of another's intelligence is how much he—in this case she—agrees with you'? I think your girlfriend's right on the money. Hidden inside that gorgeous body is an unquestionable genius."

"You may get to eat after all," Svetlana called from the grill. "And speaking of that, can we start to cook?"

"Absolutely."

[THREE]
The Lobby Bar
The Alvear Palace Hotel
Avenida Alvear 1891
Buenos Aires, Argentina
1955 7 February 2007

Ambassador Charles M. Montvale had liked the Alvear Plaza Hotel from the moment he walked in the door. He had liked it even better when, following a bellman to a very nice suite, he had walked past the Lobby Bar, an oasis of polished wood and brass, a vast array of liquor bottles, white-jacketed barmen, and a remarkable number of attractive women—at least three of whom were astonishingly beautiful.

"Tell you what, Truman," he said to Ellsworth as their elevator rose silently. "Why don't we have a quick shower and then go down to that bar for a little taste? God knows, it's been a tough day. Say, thirty minutes?"

"Splendid idea," Truman Ellsworth had replied. "I'll see you there in thirty minutes."

Ellsworth's eye had also fallen upon the astonishingly beautiful women in the bar.

Neither had intentions of enticing one of the beautiful women to their suites, there to break the vow both had taken to keep only to the women who had marched down the aisle with them so many years ago.

But it never hurt just to look. Both of them would have agreed if God hadn't wanted men to look at women, He would have made the female of the species flat-chested and given them green teeth and lizardlike skin.

But unexpected things did happen from time to time.

And they were, after all, human.

Ambassador Charles M. Montvale had just finished saying, "It's been an awful day, and I think I'm entitled to another little taste," when I. Ronald Spears appeared at the entrance to the Lobby Bar.

Montvale was not pleased to see him. He had really been looking forward to his second drink. The ceremony that went with the delivering of a Johnnie Walker Black on the rocks in the Lobby Bar of the Alvear was something, he had immediately decided, that the watering holes of the nation's capital and his various clubs would do well to emulate.

First, the bartender laid a tray before his customer. It held a bottle of Johnnie Walker Black Label Scotch whisky; a larger-than-to-be-expected squat glass; a bowl of ice; a silver pitcher of water; silver tongs; and what at first Montvale had thought was a tea strainer, but then he had seen that it had no holes. It was sort of a shot glass with wings.

First the bartender lifted an ice cube—not something spit out of an ice maker, but a *real* ice cube, about an inch square—with his tongs and dropped it into the glass. Then he picked up another and wordlessly asked if his customer wanted a second ice cube. Montvale had stopped this process at three ice cubes, using a gesture he had learned playing blackjack.

The bartender laid the tea strainer/shot glass on the whisky glass. Next, he picked up the bottle of whisky and with great élan filled the shot to overflowing. And then kept pouring. And then he tipped the wings of the shot glass, slowly emptying the contents into the glass over the ice cubes. Finally, with a silver gadget, he stirred the ice cubes gently around in the glass.

Montvale impatiently waved I. Ronald Spears over to the table.

"Mr. Ambassador, there are two telephone calls for you at the embassy."

"Why didn't you transfer them here?" Montvale snapped.

Even as he did so, he knew what the answer was going to be, and was: "Mr. Ambassador, they're on a secure line."

Montvale looked around first for the bartender, to cancel the order for the drink he would now not get to drink, and to sign the bill, and then for the Secret Service agents who were drinking Coke and tonic water elsewhere in the bar.

The communications officer told them he had two calls, one from Supervisory Special Agent McGuire and the other from John Powell, the director of the Central Intelligence Agency.

"Get McGuire on here first," Montvale said as he picked up the secure telephone.

"I have Ambassador Montvale on the line. The line is secure."

"Good evening, sir."

"What did you find out, Tom?"

"None of the people in whom you were interested were in the house in Alexandria, sir, but Mrs. Darby told me she believes Mr. Darby is in Ushuaia."

"Where?"

"I understand it's the southernmost city in Argentina."

"What is she doing, pulling your leg? What the hell is he supposed to be doing there?"

"I understand from her—she seemed rather angry, sir—that he's in the company of a young Argentine woman. You take my meaning, sir?"

"You mean he's down there with some floozy?" Montvale asked incredulously.

"That's what Mrs. Darby implied, sir."

"And you believe her?"

"All I can say, sir, is that's what she told me. She seemed quite upset about it."

"You're keeping that house under surveillance, right, Tom?"

"There will be three agents on it twenty-four/seven, sir."

"Well, keep that up, and keep me informed."

"Yes, sir."

"Thanks, Tom."

"I have Ambassador Montvale on the line, Mr. Powell. The line is secure."

"Hey, Jack, what's up?"

"A good deal. The Russians have been heard from. Sergei Murov—the *rezident*—invited Frank Lammelle over to their dacha to go fishing."

"In the middle of the winter?"

"And when he got there, told them what they want. They will give us all the Congo-X they have. With an implied promise they won't find any more. In exchange, they want the two defectors. And Charley Castillo."

"They say why?"

"Frank had the impression this came right from Putin. Frank said Murov told him, or implied, that not only has Putin's ego been bruised, but some of the people Castillo and his merry band have been whacking around the world were friends—maybe even relatives—of his."

"And you believe this?"

"Frank does. More importantly, President Clendennen does."

"Which means what?"

"That as soon as we find those two Russians Castillo snatched from our station chief in Vienna, we put them on the next Aeroflot to Moscow."

"Did Frank tell Murov we don't have the two Russians?"

"He did. Murov didn't believe him. Anyway, that's moot. My orders are to find the Russians so that we can turn them over."

"Clendennen's going to stand still for that blackmail?"

"I'll say it again, Charles: My orders are to find the Russians so that we can turn them over."

"And Castillo? He's going to turn him over, too?"

"I didn't hear that, because you didn't ask it. But a moment ago, I should have said that my orders are to find the Russians and Lieutenant Colonel Castillo, Retired."

"And do what with Castillo when we find him?"

"The President did not share his thoughts on that with me, Mr. Ambassador."

"Jesus Christ!"

"Yeah. So how you doing? Have you found Castillo?"

"No, but I learned that Alex Darby's in Ushuaia—that's at the southern tip of South America—with some young floozy."

"Darby's doing what?"

"I'm afraid the source is reliable."

"Have you talked to him?"

"I found that out about five minutes ago."

"That might be a good place to stash those Russians."

"That thought occurred to me about ten seconds ago."

"There will be six officers—the most I could scare up on short notice meeting the criteria of reliable and available—on whatever American Airlines flight there is today from Dallas to Buenos Aires, one most likely landing in Argentina in the wee hours of tomorrow morning."

"What the hell is that all about?"

"The President ordered me to send however many men it took to locate and detain the Russians. Shortly, they're on their way there."

"If they should find them, and that's a big if, what are they going to do, kidnap them? The Argentines won't stand for that. No country would."

"This line is terrible. I don't think you heard me when I said, 'The President ordered me to send however many men it took to locate and detain the Russians.'"

"Jesus Christ!"

"Have you found Roscoe J. Danton? More important, have you learned (a) why he's looking for Castillo, and (b) whether he's found him?"

"I'm going to see him tomorrow. After I see the ambassador. I don't know what I'm going to tell him about these people you're sending down here."

"You'll think of something. That's why they pay you the big bucks, Charles."

"Fuck you," Montvale said, and then said, "Break it down."

Truman Ellsworth, Mizz Sylvia Grunblatt, I. Ronald Spears, one of his Secret Service agents, and a middle-aged man he did not recognize were waiting for him in the hall outside the communications cubicle.

"Ambassador Montvale," the man said, "I'm Robert Lowe."

When Montvale didn't immediately reply, Lowe added: "From Mexico City."

And you were ordered down here, what? A week ago?

You should have been here the next day.

Where the hell have you been? In one of those hotels on the white sandy beaches of Cancún or Cozumel, saying a tearful goodbye to your twenty-year-old tootsie?

"I'm really glad to see you, Lowe," Montvale said. "We have a situation here that requires someone of your experience, and I might add, of your reputation."

"I'm here to serve, sir."

"I just got off the horn with the DCI," Montvale said. "He tells me there will be six very good officers of the Clandestine Service on the next American Airlines flight from Dallas to help deal with the problem."

"Which is?"

"I can't get into that here." He turned to Sylvia Grunblatt. "Nothing personal, Mizz Grunblatt, but I'm afraid you don't have the need-to-know."

"Mr. Montvale, in Ambassador Silvio's absence, I am acting for him." She lost her diplomatic cool at that moment, and added: "That makes me, as I'm sure you know, the senior officer of the United States in Argentina."

Jesus, now the goddamned press agent is going to give me trouble?

"What you say may well be true, Mizz Grunblatt, but I have only your word for it. On the other hand, I have been—and Mr. Ellsworth has been—sent down here by the President of the United States personally, and until the President tells me otherwise, I'm not going to breach security. Do we understand one another?"

"I think we'll let Ambassador Silvio decide who's right," Grunblatt said.

"I'm looking forward to that," Montvale said. "What I need from you now, Mizz Grunblatt, is a vehicle to pick up these agency people in the morning."

"Can't help you," she said. "For one thing, I told you there are no free vehicles; the ambassador needed everything in the garage. And, now that I think about it, inasmuch as I presume these six spooks are traveling as tourists, rather than government employees—much less accredited diplomatic personnel—I couldn't order the use of government vehicles if I wanted to."

"I'll look forward to seeing you in the morning when I call on the ambassador, Miss Grunblatt," Montvale said. "Where are you staying, Mr. Lowe?"

Sylvia Grunblatt answered for him: "I'm going to put him in the apartment recently vacated by the Darbys."

"You can move in there tomorrow," Montvale said. "We need to talk. I'll put you up in the Alvear Plaza with us. Let's go, gentlemen."

The manager on duty at the Alvear was the epitome of courtesy and regret, but there wasn't an available room of any type in the house. He could, however, remove the king-size bed in either Mr. Montvale's suite or Mr. Ellworth's, and replace it with two single beds.

"Put them in Mr. Ellsworth's suite," Montvale ordered, and turned to Ellsworth. "It's only for one night, Truman."

An otherwise marvelous dinner in the Alvear Palace's La Bourgogne restaurant was tainted midway by the appearance of the manager on duty. He was profusely sorry to report that the single beds he had planned to put in Mr. Ellsworth's accommodation had already been put into service. He had found another king-size bed, but regrettably, there was not room for it in Mr. Ellsworth's room.

"Would Mr. Montvale possibly consider having it placed in his room?"

"It's only for one night, Charles," Truman Ellsworth said, dripping with compassion.

After dinner, I. Ronald Spears was dismissed with orders to find decent accommodations for the men who would arrive in the morning. He was ordered to meet their plane, install them in wherever he had found for them to stay, and then bring them to the Alvear.

Montvale, Ellsworth, and Lowe then went to the Lobby Bar for an after-dinner drink. It was crowded with people of good cheer, but not one of the patrons of either sex would ever see sixty—or maybe sixty-five—again.

They then all went to Montvale's suite, where, after the hotel staff had very carefully—and thus very slowly—installed the extra king-size bed, Montvale explained the situation to the new CIA station chief, Buenos Aires.

"So what I would suggest you do, Bob, is send two of the guys coming in to Ushuaia, taking Spears with them. Maybe he can learn something from good officers."

"I still have trouble accepting that Alex Darby is catting around down there with a hooker. . . ."

"Maybe she's not a hooker, Bob. It could be a midlife crisis and he's in love. It could also be—unlikely but possible—that he's sitting on these two Russians for Castillo down there. It sounds like something Colonel Castillo would think up. Anyway, I want two good men down there—with I. Ronald Spears—as soon as they can get there. And I want that town really searched. Got it?"

"Yes, sir."

"And the other ones, I think, should nose around the embassy. See if they can get anything from the DEA people, the FBI people, the Secret Service people. Someone has to know something about where to find Castillo and these Russians."

"Yes, sir. As soon as they get here tomorrow, I'll brief them on what we have, and what we want them to do."

Montvale and Lowe went to bed in their adjoining king-size beds shortly thereafter.

Lowe almost immediately went to sleep and began to snore.

X

[ONE]
Penthouse B
The Grand Cozumel Beach & Golf Resort
Cozumel
Quintana Roo, Mexico
2215 7 February 2007

Castillo was standing at the railing of the patio, taking an occasional pull at the neck of a Dos Equis bottle and somewhat inhospitably wishing that the fish-eaters would get the hell out of the penthouse—which would leave him alone with Sweaty—when Edgar Delchamps joined him.

"Got a minute, Ace?" Delchamps asked.

"Always," Castillo said.

Delchamps pointed to a far corner of the patio surrounding the swimming pool. As they started walking toward it, Castillo saw that Alex Darby and Dick Miller were also headed in that direction.

And he knew that he had fucked up somehow and was about to learn how the moment Edgar Delchamps began the chat by saying, "We know that even though you have a lot on your mind, you probably have thought about this . . ."

"But?" Castillo interrupted.

"I recognize that tone of voice, so I'll cut to the chase," Delchamps said. "We just got word from one of the dinosaurs that the tapes and the narrative are in that building at Langley in a position where Frank Lammelle can't help but find them when he goes to work in the morning."

"That was quick!" Castillo said, genuinely surprised.

"Real dinosaurs move much more quickly than the ones you saw in the *Jurassic Park* movies, Ace. You might want to write that down."

"If you say so."

"And when Lammelle and Company finish authenticating the tapes, someone is going to say, 'Hey, you know what? I'll bet this came from Charley Castillo.'"

"What was I supposed to do, not send it?"

"What you were supposed to do—what we were all supposed to do—was fall off the face of the earth and never be seen again."

"Same question: What were we supposed to do once we came up with this? Keep it to ourselves?"

Delchamps didn't respond directly. He looked between Darby and Miller, then back at Castillo, and went on: "And even if Lammelle or one of his guys doesn't attach you to the tapes, Casey is going to send the tapes to the DCI himself, and Casey is going to say something like, 'You can rely on this; I got it from Castillo.' So the President will know you didn't fall off the face of the earth as ordered."

"And you don't think he'll be happy I didn't? According to Casey, they don't have a clue about what's going on with the Congo-X. All I'm guilty of is lending a helping hand."

"You really have no idea how much the agency—everybody in the quote unquote intelligence community—hated the Office of Organizational Analysis, and in particular Lieutenant Colonel C. G. Castillo, do you? And how overcome with bureaucratic joy they were when the President cut your throat and told you to disappear, taking OOA and all its wicked members with you?"

"I did have some small inkling that I wouldn't have won any popularity contests," Castillo said. "Actually, Edgar, I thought about that when I sent the tapes. I would have preferred they would have come from an unknown source. But there were two things wrong with that, starting with I don't think it would have been possible, because of Casey's connection with somebody—probably, but not certainly, the DCI—at the agency. But say I had managed to convincingly send them from Mr. Unknown Source. I don't trust unknown sources, and I don't think Lammelle would have either. So let him know the tapes came from me. I didn't expect a letter from Lammelle—or Jack Powell—like the one Sweaty and Tom got. 'Come home. All is forgiven. We love you.'"

"Let me try this on you: If our late President—who was a really good guy, and for whom you did everything he asked you to, including coming up with the Fish Farm—was willing to cut your throat to cover his ass, what do you think Joshua Ezekiel Clendennen, who is *the* master not only of covering his own ass, but also of throwing people who have done him a service under the bus so he can take the credit, will be willing to do to you?"

"For example?"

"Turning Tom and your girlfriend—and maybe you—over to the Russians, for one thing."

"Where the hell did you get that?"

Delchamps and Darby exchanged glances, then Edgar said, "That's the scenario Alex and I have come up with for what's behind this whole Congo-X operation. If they wanted to hurt us with that stuff, they would have. They haven't hurt us, just let us know they can. Why? They want something. What do they want? They want Tom and Sweaty back. Clendennen gives them to the Russians, they give Clendennen the Congo-X, the problem is done. If he also gives them you, that solves that problem."

Castillo didn't respond for a moment, then looked at Darby.

"That's the way I see it, Charley," Darby said.

"What supports that scenario?"

"Nothing concrete yet, Ace, except the thing that I've developed—that Alex and I have developed—in our long service as spooks: a feeling in the gut that just won't go away."

"You talk to either Tom or Sweaty about this?" Castillo asked softly.

Both Delchamps and Darby shook their heads.

"You've got a solution?" Castillo asked.

"I've got a suggestion that may not be a solution, but it's all I have."

"All *we* have, Charley," Darby said.

Castillo gestured for Delchamps to tell him.

"Disperse," Delchamps said. "Fall off the face of the earth."

Castillo looked thoughtful for a moment, then gestured again for Delchamps to continue.

"If Clendennen isn't already looking for us—even though my gut tells me that he is—he'll really start looking when Lammelle shows that tape to him. They'll probably start in Argentina—"

"We know Roscoe J. Danton is down there looking for you," Darby interjected. "So, they likely do, too."

Delchamps went on: "And when they don't find you—us—down there, they'll look elsewhere, and inevitably find us all gathered here getting sunburned and eating broiled fish in a penthouse."

"I'm sure there's already a satellite picture of the Gulfstream sitting here in somebody's database," Darby interjected again.

"Cut to the chase," Castillo said.

"Darby flies to Washington, where he immediately goes to a bank and asks for a mortgage to buy the house in Alexandria, and then starts looking for a job suitable for his talents with one of those hire-a-spook companies. Blackwater, for example.

"Britton returns to Philadelphia, where Sandra goes back to the classroom, and Jack starts trying to get back in the police department. Peg-Leg goes back to Vegas, where Casey has already given him a job." He looked at Dick Miller, then went on: "Dick, Jake, and Sparkman go to Panama City, Panama, where they immediately put the Gulfstream up for sale, start looking for a better airplane, and go into the private-jets-for-hire business. Two-Gun goes to Montevideo and opens a financial management—read money-laundering—business. Getting the picture?"

Darby added: "The Gulfstream has six—maybe seven—of Casey's latest radios in the baggage compartment. We'd all be in contact."

"What happens to Lester?" Castillo asked.

"He stays here—or around here—with you, Sweaty, Tom, and Uncle Remus. You own a farm here in Old Meh-hee-co, right?"

"And you?"

"I go to Budapest. Where I will find employment with Billy Kocian."

Darby put in: "Everybody could be back here—or be anywhere else—in twenty-four hours, when you decide what we have to do about the Congo-X. And how to keep Sweaty and Tom from being loaded on an Aeroflot flight to Mother Russia."

"And Pevsner?"

"He disappears once again into the wilds of Argentina."

Castillo exhaled audibly.

"Apparently, you have given this some thought."

"There we were, floating around on the ocean, catching our supper and giving this *a lot* of thought," Delchamps said.

When Castillo didn't immediately reply, Delchamps added, "Your call, Ace. But I think we'd all be more efficient if we didn't have members of the Clandestine Service breathing down our necks. Or trying to put handcuffs on us. But if you—"

"Everybody's willing to go along?"

Delchamps nodded.

"They would have joined this little chat," he said, "but Uncle Remus said that you get really antsy when you feel outnumbered."

"When do you plan to leave?" Castillo asked.

"First thing in the morning," Delchamps said.

"I wonder what Pevsner's going to think about this," Castillo said.

"Well, he probably won't like it when he learns he has just sold his new fly-the-high-rollers-around airplane to the LCBF Corporation, but the bottom line there, Ace, is you don't ask your Russian pal anything. You tell him the way it is."

[TWO]
The Oval Office
The White House
1600 Pennsylvania Avenue, N.W.
Washington, D.C.
0915 8 February 2007

"Good morning, Mr. President and Madam Secretary," John Powell, the director of the Central Intelligence Agency, said as he walked into the Oval Office.

"This had better be important, Jack," President Clendennen replied. "I am supposed to take off for Chicago in fifteen minutes, and Natalie has a lunch in New York with a gaggle of UN morons."

"I believe it is important, Mr. President," the DCI replied. "And all I have to do is slip this in the machine . . ."

With a DVD disc in his hand, Powell walked toward a large flat-screen television monitor mounted on a wheeled table.

"Let him do that," Clendennen said, indicating a Secret Service agent. "I know he won't screw up the TV."

"Yes, sir," Powell said, and handed the disc to the Secret Service agent.

"Before it starts to play, Mr. President, I'd like to say, if I may, that we believe this disc to be authentic. That is, the surveillance tapes from which we made this are authentic. And that what you will see when it plays is authentic and has not been altered or changed in any way."

"I'm delighted to hear that, Jack," Clendennen said. "Play your movie."

"What kind of an airplane is that?"

"That's a Tupolev Tu-934A, Mr. President."

"I don't think I've ever seen one before," Natalie Cohen said.

"Few people have. It's a Russian Special Operations aircraft. Magnificent airplane. It's practically invisible to radar, can fly nonstop—with aerial refueling, of course—anywhere in the world at Mach zero point nine and land on a football field. We are offering a hundred twenty-five million for one."

"You better hope Senator Johns doesn't hear about that," the President said. "A hundred twenty-five million! Are the Russians that far ahead of us?"

"In this area, yes, sir. We have nothing like it; the Air Force really wants to take a close look at the Tu-934A. And, in a manner of speaking, sir, the Russians have been ahead of us before. They beat us into space of course, and before that,

Igor Sikorsky—who fled the Communist revolution to come here—is generally recognized as the man who made rotary-wing flight practical."

"And exactly where is *this* example of Russian aeronautical genius landing, Jack?"

"In a dry lake in Mexico, sir. Specifically, Laguna el Guaje, in Coahuila State."

"How do you know that?"

"Our analysts worked with the angle of sun, Mr. President," Powell said. "And with the date and time on the surveillance tapes. At the time shown, the angle of the sun would be like that on the tapes at only Laguna el Guaje."

"I'm impressed, Frank, I really am. What I'm wondering is where you got the tapes."

Powell did not respond directly, and instead said, "The man walking toward the Tupolev, sir, is, with a ninety-nine-point-nine-percent certainty, Pavel Ko-slov, the FSB *rezident* in Mexico City. We computer-compared the image on the surveillance tapes with images in our database."

"I'll be damned."

"Those men, sir, coming down the ramp of the Tupolev are almost certainly Russian Spetsnaz—Russian Special Forces. And that man, sir, is General Yakov Vladimirovich Sirinov. We made that identification ninety-nine-point-nine-percent certain by comparing this image with images of him in our database. Sirinov runs the FSB for Vladimir Putin, Mr. President."

"What are those barrels?" Clendennen asked.

"What we believe, sir, with an eighty to eighty-five degree of certainty, is that those barrels are the ones sent to Colonel Hamilton at Fort Detrick. The scenario is that they were taken across the border near the dry lake; that the first was then moved to Miami, and from there FedExed to Colonel Hamilton, and the second left for the Border Patrol to find near McAllen."

Natalie Cohen said, "If you can compare pictures of people on a computer, Jack, and say they're just about a perfect match, why can't you do the same thing with a couple of what look like blue beer barrels?"

Powell said, "According to Stan Waters—"

"Who?" the President asked.

"J. Stanley Waters, the deputy director for operations, Mr. President. He supervised the analysis of these tapes. He's an old analysis type."

"And what did he tell you?"

"There are more details on a human being that can be compared to another image of that person, Mr. President. An object like these blue 'beer' barrels is more difficult; they look like every other barrel."

"Are these the same barrels? Yes or no?"

"With an eighty to eighty-five percent degree of certainty, Mr. President, we believe they are."

President Clendennen snorted.

"Where did you get these tapes, Jack?" Natalie Cohen asked, and immediately, when she saw the look on his face, regretted having asked. She had guessed the source.

"I think we can safely proceed on the assumption that these are the barrels of Congo-X now at Fort Detrick, Mr. President," Powell said.

"Answer Natalie's question, Jack," the President said.

"They were, in a manner of speaking, slipped under our door, Mr. President, addressed to DDCI Lammelle."

"Tell me what that means," Clendennen said.

"Sir, parties unknown delivered them to my outer office yesterday."

"In other words, you don't know where these came from?"

"No, sir. I don't know where they came from."

"Mr. President, it doesn't matter, does it?" the secretary of State began. "We have them, and they have been determined to be genuine. We now can send Frank Lammelle back to Sergei Murov—"

"Maybe God slipped them under your door, Jack," the President cut her off. "Or little green men from Mars. Or maybe, as incredible as it might sound, Lieutenant Colonel Castillo might even be responsible. Isn't that true?"

"Mr. President, since I don't know where these tapes came from, anything is possible."

"You were both here, I seem to recall, when I made it as plain as I knew how that I didn't want my predecessor's loose cannon, or anyone associated with Colonel Castillo, Retired, connected in any way with our Congo-X problem. Is that right?"

"Yes, sir," Powell said.

"I was here, Mr. President," the secretary of State said.

"Where is Castillo?" the President asked.

"I have no idea, Mr. President," Powell said.

"Nor do I," Cohen said.

"What about Ambassador Montvale, my Director of National Intelligence? Has anyone heard from him?"

"I spoke with the ambassador last night, Mr. President. He's in Buenos Aires. As is Truman Ellsworth. At your orders, sir."

"And has he found Castillo and delivered my orders to him that he is not to get involved in any way with Congo-X?"

"No, sir."

"Did Montvale have anything at all to say?"

"He believes he knows where Mr. Darby is, sir."

"Who is Darby?"

"Until he was recruited for OOA, Mr. President, he was the CIA station chief in Buenos Aires. He retired when OOA was disbanded."

"And he's in Argentina?"

"Ambassador Montvale has information suggesting that Mr. Darby may be in Ushuaia."

"Where the hell is that?"

"It's the southernmost city in South America, sir."

"What's he doing there?" the President asked, and then, before Powell could reply, went on: "Is Usah . . . whatever you said . . . a place where Castillo could hide the defectors?"

"That has occurred to Ambassador Montvale and myself, sir."

"And what have you done about it, either of you?"

"I sent six first-class officers of the Clandestine Service down there, Mr. President, to assist the new station chief. And of course Ambassador Montvale. They should be in Argentina this morning. I'm sure that as soon as they get there, Ambassador Montvale will send at least two of them to Ushuaia."

Clendennen nodded.

"But I must tell you, Mr. President, that Ambassador Montvale told me he has also developed intelligence that suggests that Mr. Darby's presence in Ushuaia has nothing to do with Castillo or the Russians."

"What the hell else would he be doing in some town on the southern tip of South America?"

"He may be there with an Argentine national, a young woman not his wife, if you take my meaning, Mr. President."

"Where the hell did Montvale get that?"

"From Mrs. Darby, sir. She's here in the States."

"I'll be a sonofabitch!"

"May I speak, Mr. President?" the secretary of State said.

The President made an impatient gesture giving her permission to do so.

"Mr. President, I respectfully suggest that this whole business could be put behind us by sending either DCI Powell or—probably preferably—DDCI Lammelle back to Sergei Murov with this tape. And this time, Frank delivers the ultimatum: 'Turn over whatever Congo-X you have, give us a written statement that you neither have control of nor have knowledge of any more of this substance, or we'll call an emergency session of the United Nations and play this tape for the world.'"

The President didn't respond for a moment, then he asked, more or less courteously, "Are you through, Madam Secretary?"

"Yes. For the moment."

"The female is really the deadlier of the species, isn't it?" the President asked rhetorically. "Natalie, do you know what would happen while we're calling the Russian bluff? We'd be right back where we were when my impulsive predecessor sent the bombers to take out the Fish Farm: at the edge of a nuclear exchange."

"With respect, Mr. President, I don't think so," Cohen said.

"What you think doesn't really matter, does it, Natalie? I'm the President."

"With respect, Mr. President, I associate myself with the position of the secretary of State," Powell said.

The President ignored him.

"Now, what's going to happen is that nothing will be done with these tapes until I say so," the President said. "What I intend to do is find those Russians and put them on a plane to Moscow. Once we have done that, we'll evaluate the Russian reaction, and go from there.

"And since the way to find the Russians is to find Colonel Castillo, that is the priority. When I get back from Chicago this afternoon—somewhere around three, I would guess—I want you both back here. Plus the secretary of Defense and the director of the FBI."

"The secretary of Defense is in India, Mr. President," Cohen said.

"I was about to say, Madam Secretary, 'Then his deputy,' but when I think about it, when I think about who that is, I don't want to do that. Have General Naylor here, and if Naylor is in Timbuktu or someplace, get word to him to return immediately. When I walk back in this office this afternoon, I want to see Naylor, or you holding the general's estimated time of arrival in your hand, Madam Secretary.

"This meeting is concluded. Thank you for coming," the President said.

And then he walked out of the Oval Office without shaking hands with either Powell or Cohen.

[THREE]
Aboard Cessna Mustang N0099S
Bahías de Huatulco International Airport
Near Pochutla, Mexico
1015 8 February 2007

"Huatulco, Mustang Double Zero Double Nine Sugar," Castillo called in Spanish. "Will you close out my VFR flight plan from Cancún, please? We just decided to stop for lunch."

"Double Zero Double Nine, are you on the ground?"

"No. I'm on final to a dirt strip next to a marvelous restaurant on Route 200 near Bajos de Chila."

"I know the place. Report when on the ground. Have a nice lunch."

Castillo passed over the coastline and made a slow, sweeping descent over the Pacific Ocean. Although there was a marvelous restaurant near Bajos de Chila, he had no intention of landing on the dirt strip behind it.

When he had dropped almost to the surface of the sea—and had thus, he hoped, dropped off the Huatulco radar—he touched his throat microphone again.

"Huatulco, Double Zero Double Nine on the ground at one seven past the hour."

"Double Zero Double Nine, Huatulco closing you out as of ten-seventeen."

"Thank you."

Two minutes later, having spotted the pier he was looking for, he picked up enough altitude to pass over a small hill on the coastline. At the peak of the climb, he spotted the landing strip he was looking for, dropped the nose, made a straight-in approach, and greased the landing.

Feeling more than a little smug, he pressed the cabin speaker button.

"Welcome to Grapefruit International Airport. Please remain in your seats with your chastity belts fastened until we reach the terminal. We hope you have enjoyed your flight, and the next time you're running from the CIA that you will choose High Roller Airlines again."

"You are insane," his co-pilot said, but she was smiling. Then she gestured, as he turned the Mustang around, out the windows, at rows of grapefruit trees lining the runway as far as the eye could see. "That's all grapefruit?"

"That's all grapefruit."

He taxied about halfway back down the runway, and then turned the nose toward the closed door of a hangar, and then shut the engines down.

"Carlitos," Svetlana said, her voice tinged with concern. When he looked at her, she pointed out the window.

Three very large, very swarthy men, each bearing a shotgun, had come around the side of the hangar and were approaching the airplane.

Castillo waved cheerfully at them, and after a moment, as they recognized him, they smiled and waved back.

"I better get off first," Castillo said. "Otherwise Max will probably get shot by people I've known since I was twelve."

He unstrapped himself quickly, rose from his seat, stepped into the cabin, and began to open the stair door.

"I trust the colonel is aware there are some armed, possibly unfriendly, indigenous personnel out there?" Uncle Remus asked.

The stair door opened and Castillo quickly went down it. Max leapt from the airplane, showed the men his teeth, and headed for the nose wheel.

The larger of the men tossed his shotgun to one of the others, spread his arms, and wrapped them around Castillo.

"Doña Alicia will be so happy, Carlos," he said.

"She's here?"

I should have considered that possibility. But it's too late now.

"Fernando brought her down yesterday. Doña Alicia said it was freezing in San Antonio," he said. And then added quietly: "I don't know about the dog, but I like your lady friend."

"Sweaty, say hello to Pablo," Castillo said. "We grew up together. The others are Manuel and Juan."

When all the introductions had been made, Pablo said, "Carlos, why don't you take one of the Suburbans and go up to the house? Just as soon as we push the plane inside, we'll bring your luggage."

"There's two cardboard boxes in the back," Castillo said, and then indicated with his hands the size. "Bring one of them, please?"

It was a ten-minute drive from the airstrip to the house, down a gravel road that led between the apparently endless grapefruit trees and over two more ridge lines.

No one was on the verandah of the sprawling, red-tile-roofed building to greet them, which Castillo considered surprising.

Castillo got from behind the wheel of the Suburban, waved for the others to follow him, walked across the verandah, pushed open the door, and bellowed, "Abuela, your favorite grandson is here; you can send the fat and ugly one back to the village."

The door to the living room opened, and Randolph Richardson III walked into the foyer and said, "Good afternoon, sir. I'm very glad to see you." Then he spotted Svetlana. "And you, too, ma'am."

Castillo's heart jumped into his throat. He was literally struck dumb and knew that all that would come out of his mouth if he tried to speak would be a croak.

Svetlana walked quickly to the boy.

"Are you kissing old Russian women this week, Randy?"

She went to the boy, put her arms around him, and kissed his cheek. He stiffened and seemed uncomfortable, but didn't try to free himself.

"What?" Svetlana asked. "I kiss you and you don't kiss me?"

After a moment, he raised his head and gave her a quick peck on the cheek. Castillo found his voice.

"What you have to understand, Randy," he said as he walked to the boy, "is that you're surrounded by strange people who hug and kiss each other."

Svetlana freed the boy, who then extended his hand to Castillo.

"Pay attention," Castillo said. "We shake hands with people we don't like. We hug and kiss people we like."

He put his arms around the boy.

"Sometimes, if we're related to them," Castillo said, "we even have to hug and kiss ugly fat people like the one in the door."

Fernando Manuel Lopez was now in the doorway to the foyer. And so was María Lopez, who did not like Carlos Guillermo Castillo very much in the first place, and whose facial expression showed she really disliked his characterization of her husband as fat and ugly.

Castillo kissed Randy's cheek and hugged him. The boy hugged back and then gave him the same sort of peck on the cheek he'd given Svetlana.

Castillo's heart jumped.

Don't blow this by pushing it.

He let the boy go.

"Sorry it didn't work, Fernando," Castillo said.

"What didn't work, Gringo?"

"The plastic surgery. You're even uglier than before."

"Jesus Christ, Gringo!" Fernando said, shaking his head. Then he embraced Castillo.

"Don't blaspheme, Fernando," Doña Alicia Castillo said as she came through the door. "And . . ."

". . . don't call Carlos 'Gringo,'" Fernando and Castillo finished for her in chorus.

The boy laughed.

Castillo embraced his grandmother.

"You could have let us know you were coming," she said, and then she spotted Svetlana and went quickly to her and kissed her.

"I'm so glad to see you, my dear," Doña Alicia said.

Then she moved to Barlow, Uncle Remus, and Lester, and kissed each of them. Every one seemed delighted to see everyone else except Mrs. María Lopez.

And now there was someone else in the foyer.

"How are you, General?" Castillo said as he advanced on Major General Harold F. Wilson, USA (Retired), with his hand extended.

That didn't work, either. General Wilson wrapped his arms around Charley and hugged him.

"Pay attention, Randy," Castillo said.

"I thought I heard a jet flying a little low over here," General Wilson said. "That was you?"

"A Cessna Mustang," Castillo said. "Great little airplane."

"Am I going to get to fly it?" Randy asked. "I flew the Lear here from San Antonio. I mean really flew it. Took it off, navigated cross-country, and landed it."

Castillo knew the boy was telling the truth when he saw the look on María's face. Clearly, she regarded fourteen-year-old boys flying as co-pilot of anything more complicated than a tandem bicycle as one more proof of the insanity of the family into which she had made the mistake of marrying.

"I think we can arrange that," Castillo said. "But only if you promise to forget everything Tío Fernando has taught you about flying."

"Now, you stop, the both of you," Doña Alicia said.

"Speaking of *tíos*," Castillo began.

"Excuse me, dear?" Doña Alicia asked.

"It's very important that Tío Héctor García-Romero does not know that any of us are here, or that we've been in touch in any way."

"What's that all about? He's our lawyer, for God's sake," Fernando said.

"He's also in bed . . ."

Castillo stopped and looked at Randy.

"I know," Randy said. "Little pitchers have big ears. This is where I'm told to go play with my puppy, right?"

"You do have a mouth, don't you?" Castillo asked.

"I wonder where he got that from, *El Señor Boca Grande*?" Fernando said.

"No, Randy," Castillo said. "I'm not going to tell you to go play with your puppy. Where is he, anyway?"

"His father is teaching him how to steal food in the kitchen," Fernando said.

"Well, why not?" Castillo said. "Dogs, like boys, have to grow up sometime. And if you need a teacher, go to an expert."

"Are you talking about your dog or yourself?" Fernando challenged.

"Both," Castillo said, and turned to the boy. "Randy, we both know that you have learned to keep important secrets."

And everybody in this room, from Lester to General Wilson, knows what that secret is.

"I don't think I like where this conversation is going," Fernando interrupted.

"I don't think I do, either," Doña Alicia said.

Castillo ignored both of them. He went on: "So I know, Randy, that if I tell you that this is an important secret—actually secrets, a bunch of them—and if they get out, people can be hurt, or even killed, I know that I can trust you to keep your mouth shut. Okay? If you don't want that responsibility, I'll understand if you want to take Max and his puppy for a walk."

"Jesus Christ, Gringo, he's fourteen years old," Fernando said. "He doesn't need to hear about people getting hurt or killed."

"Carlos, do you know what you're doing?" Doña Alicia asked.

"I'll stay," Randy said. And then added, "Thank you, sir."

"Okay. The family lawyer, Randy, *El Señor* Héctor García-Romero, is up to his ears in the drug business."

"I don't believe that!" María Lopez exploded. "Héctor is Little Fernando's godfather."

"I don't care if you believe it or not, María," Castillo said. "What I'm worried about is your mouth. Will you give me your word to keep it shut?"

"Are you just going to stand there and listen to him talk to me like that?" María demanded of her husband.

Fernando looked at Castillo.

"Gringo, you better be sure you know what you're talking about."

"I do."

"María, honey, if you don't want to hear this, why don't you—"

Castillo cut him off. He said, "María, the best way I know to convince you to keep your mouth shut about Tío Héctor, or anything else you will hear if you decide to stay, is to convince you that if you run your mouth, you'll be putting not only Tío Héctor's life at risk, but your own, and Fernando's and your kids' lives and probably even Abuela's . . ."

She glared at him and then icily demanded, "How could you dare to bring this . . . this *garbage* . . . here?"

"Fair question. First, I own half of this place. Second, I didn't know anyone was here. If I had known, we probably wouldn't be here. But the hand has been dealt, and we have to play it."

"You are sure about Héctor, Carlos?" Doña Alicia asked earnestly.

"Abuela, I'm sorry, but it's true. We were just at a secret airport he operates in the Laguna el Guaje. He doesn't move drugs out of there, just the cash profits from the drug trade. Suitcases full of hundred-dollar bills."

"My God!"

"It's important that Héctor doesn't know we're here. That no one knows we're here. I told Pablo that at the airstrip; he'll deal with it."

"Gringo, what the hell is going on?" Fernando asked.

"You believe him?" María asked her husband incredulously.

"Yeah, sweetheart, I believe him. And you better believe him, too."

"I don't want Héctor to know you know about him," Castillo said. "If he calls here, and I suspect he will, act normally, but tell him you don't know where I am, and that you haven't heard from me."

Doña Alicia nodded.

"Okay," Castillo then said, "what are we doing here? Randy, you were aware that the Army, the armed forces, went to DefConTwo a while back?"

"Just before we bombed some place in Africa?"

Castillo nodded.

"Yeah. Nobody would talk about it, but the G-Three's daughter heard about it, and snooped around. And she has a big mouth."

"What is that, Carlos? DefConTwo?" Doña Alicia asked.

"DefCon stands for Defense Condition. DefConTwo is the next-to-highest degree of readiness to go to war."

"Let me take the briefing, Charley," Uncle Remus said. "You look pretty beat, and we don't want to leave anything out."

Castillo gave him the floor with a wave of his hand.

"The reason the Defense Department went to DefConTwo," Leverette began, "is because the President had learned that the Iranians, the Russians, and some former East Germans were making a biological weapon in the Congo, and he decided that it had to go."

"How did he learn about it?" Randy asked.

Leverette looked at the boy, then at Castillo. "You're right, Charley. He does have a mouth." He looked again at the boy, and said, "You get *one* interruption, Randy. And that was it. Next time, raise your hand."

"Yes, sir."

"Your fa—*Colonel Castillo* was instrumental in getting two senior Russian intelligence officers to defect. They wanted to get out of Russia for a number of reasons, including that they were unhappy about the biological weapons factory in the Congo. As soon as Colonel Castillo got them to Argentina, they told him about it."

Both Leverette and Castillo saw Randy look at Tom Barlow and Svetlana, asking with his eyes if they were the Russians, and then saw Svetlana nod.

"Am I allowed to ask questions, Mr. Leverette?" General Wilson asked.

"Yes, sir. Of course."

"Was that attack based on more than what the defectors told Charley? Or the President? The reason I ask is because there was some talk the President went off half-cocked."

"Sir, it was based on more than what the Russians told us. Colonel Hamilton, from Fort Detrick, went over there himself and brought out samples of the material, and even the cadavers of three people who had died from the effects of the poisonous substance."

"Thank you. I'm really glad to hear that." Then he had a thought and said it aloud: "How the hell did Hamilton get into and then out of the Congo with three bodies?"

"Carefully and surreptitiously, General," Leverette said.

"Tell the general who took Colonel Hamilton into and out of the Congo, Mr. Leverette," Castillo said.

Leverette, clearly uncomfortable, said nothing.

"Why am I not surprised?" General Wilson said.

"That's why they gave him another Distinguished Service Medal when he was retired," Castillo said.

"You were at the retirement parade, Randy," General Wilson said. "You saw both Mr. Leverette and Colonel Castillo being decorated with the DSM."

"Then why did my father say he was kicked out of the Army?"

That pompous asshole and chairwarmer is not your father.

I am.

"He must have been given the wrong information," Castillo said. "It happened so suddenly that it probably looked like we were being thrown out."

"Anyway, we thought the whole thing was over," Leverette went on. "I was in Uruguay, about to go into the cattle business, when the Russian *rezident* in Budapest handed Mr. Kocian a letter. It said that a mistake had been made and that the Russians should come home, all is forgiven."

"You're not going back, are you, Svetlana?" Randy asked nervously.

"No," Svetlana said. "Now shut up and let Uncle Remus finish."

Leverette went on: "The next thing that happened was a barrel of this stuff was delivered to Colonel Hamilton, at Fort Detrick and . . ."

". . . And that brought us, Doña Alicia, to your door," Leverette concluded.

"And what happens now?"

"We eat a lot of grapefruit and maybe do a little fishing while we wait to see what the Powers That Be decide to do with the tapes," Castillo said. "And the one thing we don't do until that happens—for the next four or five days— is talk about this."

"I think we should have an early lunch," Doña Alicia said. "I'll ask them to set up a table on the verandah."

[FOUR]
The Office of the Ambassador of the United States of America
Avenida Colombia 4300
Buenos Aires, Argentina
1315 8 February 2007

Ambassador Juan Manuel Silvio—tall, lithe, fair-skinned, well tailored—stood up behind his desk, smiled, and put his hand out as Ambassador Charles M. Montvale and Truman Ellsworth walked into his office.

"How nice to see you again, Mr. Montvale," Silvio said.

"Ambassador," Montvale said.

"I know you only by reputation, Mr. Ellsworth," Silvio said. "I'm Juan Silvio."

"I've heard about you, too, Mr. Ambassador," Ellsworth said with a smile.

Ellsworth knew much more about Silvio than the scathing description of the diplomat Montvale had given him.

Ellsworth was aware that there was more to his story than the bare, commonly known facts that Silvio's family had escaped from Castro's Cuba on a fishing boat.

He knew that the fishing boat had been a sixty-two-foot Bertram, and that the Silvio family had brought out with them not only the clothing on their backs, but an enormous fish box filled with currency, jewelry, and stock certificates; some of the more valuable antiques from their Havana mansion; and the extra keys to the cars they kept at their Key Biscayne house.

Ellsworth knew Silvio had graduated from his father's alma mater, Spring Hill College, a Jesuit institution in Mobile, Alabama, which had been educating South American aristocrats for two hundred years. And that Silvio had earned a law degree at Harvard, and then a doctorate in political science at the University of Alabama. He had joined the State Department on graduation.

He had done so for much the same reason that Truman Ellsworth had become executive assistant to the director of National Intelligence: not because they needed the job, but because they saw it—the term "noblesse oblige" fit— as their patriotic obligation to serve their country.

Most important, Ellsworth knew that Silvio was not afraid of Montvale.

So far as Ellsworth knew, Silvio had never had to use it, but if push came to shove, he had behind him the enormous political clout of the Cuban-American community in south Florida. The Silvio family had spent a great deal of their money helping fellow Cubans escape from Castro and establish themselves in the United States. This was remembered. And gentlemen always repay their debts.

"May I offer you a cup of coffee?" Ambassador Silvio asked, waving Montvale and Ellsworth into chairs facing his desk.

"No, thank you," Montvale said. "Mr. Ambassador . . ."

"That would be very nice, thank you," Ellsworth said.

". . . I am here at the personal order of President Clendennen," Montvale finished.

"So Ms. Grunblatt told me," Silvio said. "And as soon as we have our coffee, I'll ask how I may be of service. Are you sure you won't . . ."

"I'm sure. Thank you."

"So how may I be of service to you, Mr. Montvale?"

"My orders are to locate both of the Russian defectors and former Lieutenant Colonel Carlos Castillo."

"'Former'? I was under the impression Castillo had been retired. Was that wrong? Did he resign?"

"No. He retired," Montvale said. "Do you know where he is, Mr. Ambassador? Or the Russians?"

"I'm afraid I don't. The last time I saw Colonel Castillo was when you and he were both in this office."

"Do you think if I got Secretary of State Cohen, or the President himself, on the telephone to confirm my mission here, it would improve your memory, Mr. Ambassador?"

Silvio did not rise to the bait.

"Mr. Montvale, when Ms. Grunblatt told me that you had told her that, I telephoned the secretary of State for verification. Secretary Cohen confirmed that you and Mr. Ellsworth are here at the direction of President Clendennen and instructed me to do whatever I can to help you accomplish your mission."

"And I have told you what that mission is."

"And I have told you I have no idea where Colonel Castillo or the Russian defectors might be. But I'll tell you what I can do: Now that everyone's back from the affair in Mar del Plata, and the embassy's vehicles are back in the motor pool, I'll be happy to augment the Suburban in which you must have been really crammed with a vehicle more in keeping with your rank and position. With a driver, of course. For as long as you're here."

"Thank you very much," Montvale said. "Mr. Ambassador, would you be surprised to hear that your former commercial counselor, and my former Buenos Aires station chief, Alexander Darby, is in Ushuaia?"

"Yes, I would. I was led to believe that Mr. Darby had returned to the United States."

"I have been led to believe he's in Ushuaia with a young Argentine woman."

"I find that hard to believe, Mr. Montvale. How good is your source?"

Montvale ignored the question.

"It occurred to me, knowing what little I do about Ushuaia," he said, "that the southernmost city in South America, as remote as it is, would be an ideal place to hide the Russians. What do you think?"

"I think that's absurd," Silvio said.

"You are telling me, and I will tell the President that you have told me, that you think the possibility that Mr. Darby and/or Colonel Castillo are hiding the Russian defectors in Ushuaia is absurd?"

"Yes, I do. Or, rather, yes, Mr. Montvale, that is exactly what I'm telling you."

"I think I'm wasting my time here," Montvale said, and stood up. "Good afternoon, Mr. Ambassador."

"Good afternoon, Mr. Montvale," Ambassador Silvio said, standing up. "On your way out, ask the Marine guard for your car. If you need to contact me, you have my number."

"Oh, I have your number, Mr. Ambassador," Montvale said, and, without shaking hands, marched out of the office.

Silvio and Ellsworth nodded at each other, and then Ellsworth followed Montvale.

Ellsworth thought: *I would bet two cents against a doughnut that nobody— not this fellow Darby, nor Castillo, nor the Russians—is in Ushuaia.*

And I will also bet the same amount that the minute we get into the car, Charles is going to say, "Send the other four Clandestine Service officers down there as quickly as possible. That's where everybody is."

Or words to that effect.

Montvale did.

[FIVE]
Marriott Plaza Hotel
Florida 1005
Buenos Aires, Argentina
1620 8 February 2007

It is said that the bar in the Plaza hasn't changed since General Juan Domingo Perón drank there as a corporal. But this is untrue for several reasons, including the fact that General Perón was never a corporal. It can be more accurately said that the bar has changed very little from the time it opened with the hotel a century ago.

It is a warm and comfortable room, with an L-shaped bar tucked into a corner. There are a half-dozen tables and comfortable leather armchairs.

It is as accurate to say the bar is on the floor below the lobby as it is to say it's on the ground floor. Avenida Florida, level for most of its length, takes a steep dip as it passes the Plaza on its way to Avenida Libertador and the main railroad station.

It is thus possible to turn off Florida and enter the bar almost directly. It is also possible, fifty feet away, to turn off Florida and enter the hotel lobby. If one elects the latter choice, then one must take the stairs or the elevator and go down one floor to get to the bar.

The director of National Intelligence, the Honorable Charles M. Montvale, and his executive assistant, the Honorable Truman Ellsworth, entered the bar by coming down the stairs, shortly after being told in the lobby that Roscoe J. Danton was sitting at the bar alone, second stool from the wall.

This information had come to them from Winston Gump, one of the Clandestine Service officers who had arrived in Buenos Aires that morning. Montvale had drafted Gump to attend him—the phrase he used was "work with"—in the belief that one never knew when one might require the skills of a veteran of the Clandestine Service. For his part, Gump was flattered by having been selected to serve—he thought "serve," not "work with"—the most senior person in the American intelligence community and his executive assistant.

Gump did wonder about Executive Assistant Ellsworth. He didn't look like a male version of a super secretary, nor did he look *that way*, but Gump knew you couldn't always judge a book by its cover, and there were all those stories going around how J. Edgar Hoover and his assistant could hardly wait to get home to put on dresses.

Anything, Gump had learned in his clandestine service, was possible.

"Well, Truman," Montvale said. "Look who's here!"

Ellsworth took the bar stool closest to the wall; Montvale took the one on the other side.

Roscoe J. Danton raised his voice: "Hey, Pedro, look who's here!"

Oh, shit! He's drunk!

On reflection, that might not be entirely a bad thing.

"Friend of yours, Roscoe?" Truman Ellsworth asked as he looked around the bar until he found a man sitting at one of the tables drinking a Coke while trying hard and almost succeeding in pretending he had not heard Danton calling, or seen Danton pointing at Montvale and Ellsworth.

"Not exactly."

"We'll have what our friend is having," Montvale said. "And give him another."

"And maybe one for your not-exactly-a-friend?" Ellsworth asked.

"I'm sure he'd love one, but he's on duty, and from what I've observed, plainclothes officers of the Gendarmería Nacional do not drink while on duty."

"You're suggesting that you're being surveilled by the Argentines?" Montvale asked.

"It was more a statement than a suggestion, Mr. Ambassador," Danton said.

"Either that guy, or one of his cousins, has been with me from the moment I tried to buy a used car."

"You what?"

"A man named Alexander Darby—of whom you may have heard . . . No. Of whom I'm sure you have heard; he was in the Clandestine Service of the CIA, like the guy I suspect you sent in here a couple of minutes ago—was retiring from government service . . ."

"You saw Alex, did you, Roscoe?" Ellsworth asked.

Danton nodded, then went on: ". . . and had put his car up for sale. Clever journalist that I am, I got from the offer of sale his address, which the embassy press officer, *Mizz* Sylvia Grunblatt, wouldn't give me, citing federal rules vis-à-vis privacy."

"So you saw him?" Ellsworth asked.

"Why did you want to see Darby, Roscoe?" Montvale asked.

The conversation was interrupted by the bartender, who delivered three trays with the proper glasses and other accessories for the whisky-pouring, and a whisky bottle.

"You may have cause to regret your impulsive generosity, Mr. Montvale," Danton said. He pointed to the whisky bottle. "That is The Macallan eighteen-year-old Highland single malt Scotch whisky. Were I not on the expense account—or for your generosity—I would shudder to think of the cost."

"My privilege, Roscoe," Montvale said.

"While he's going through that absolutely marvelous pouring routine, Roscoe, you were about to tell us why you wanted to see Alex Darby," Ellsworth said.

"So I was," Danton said. "So I went to his apartment. He and his wife were there—"

"And how is Julia?" Ellsworth asked.

"Well, now that you mention it, she seemed a little pissed with her husband. But I digress. He was there with another CIA dinosaur, a guy named Delchamps. And, and, *and* . . . an Irishman named Duffy, who had with him three guys. Pedro over there was one of them."

Danton waved at Pedro, who did not respond.

"No sooner did I begin to mention that I wanted to ask Darby about a rumor going around—"

"What kind of a rumor?"

"Why do I think you know what kind of rumor?"

"Because, by your own admission, you are a clever journalist," Montvale said. "But tell me anyway."

"Our late, and not too mourned, President had a Special Operations hot-shot working for him. Directly for him. An Army guy, a lieutenant colonel named Castillo. Said Special Operations hotshot . . . I have this from a source I almost believe . . . is said to have snatched two defecting Russians, big ones—from *your* CIA station chief in Vienna, Mr. Ambassador—just as she was about to load them on a CIA airplane and ship them to the States. He and they then disappeared.

"I also have heard a rumor that the Russian defectors told this hotshot that the Russians, the Iranians, and other people had a biological warfare factory in the Congo, and that he told the President, whereupon we went immediately to Def-Con Two, and shortly thereafter a chunk of the Congo was hit by everything in the arsenal of democracy except nukes."

"You told Alex . . . and this Irish fellow, Duffy . . . all that?" Ellsworth asked.

"I didn't get two words beyond mentioning Costello's . . . *Castillo's* . . . name when suddenly I was being asked for my identification and being patted down by Pedro over there."

Danton smiled and waved at Pedro again.

He went on: "Duffy then told me there was a question with my papers, but since I was a friend of Mr. Darby, instead of being hauled off to Gendarmería Nacional headquarters until it could be straightened out, they would allow me to spend the night here in the River Plate Marriott. And they would be happy to drive me there."

"Where do you think Alex is now, Roscoe?"

"Well, he's not in his apartment. The next morning, Duffy showed up here and said that I was free to go. He was sure that I understood the situation and was grateful for my understanding. He also said that if I thought I would need a remise—that's sort of a taxi—to get around Buenos Aires, he knew one he could recommend.

"So, I got in the remise and went back to Darby's apartment. He was gone.

"I still had one card to play. You remember the Secret Service guy on the presidential protection detail who fell off the bumper of the limousine?"

"Tony Santini," Montvale said. "Good man."

"Yes, he is. We have shared a drink or two on occasion. Well, when I knew I was coming down here I remembered that when he got fired from the protection detail, they sent him down here to look for funny money. So, I tried to call him. I got some other Secret Service guy on the phone who told me Tony had retired, but that he thought he was still in Argentina in a country club—that's Argentine for really tightly gated community—outside of town. I remembered the address: the Mayerling Country Club in Pilar. I've got a cousin named Pilar, and Mayerling was the Imperial Austrian hunting lodge where Emperor Franz Josef's son shot his sixteen-year-old girlfriend and then committed suicide.

"So, I got in the remise Duffy suggested, and told the driver to take me out to this place. We go instead to the Gendarmería Nacional headquarters. Out comes Duffy, now in uniform. He's the *generalissimo* or something of the Gendarmería Nacional. Duffy says I really don't want to go to Mayerling. Too dangerous. People started out for Mayerling and were never heard from again. I got the message."

"So, you never got to see Tony," Montvale said. "Pity. I'm sure he would have helped you."

"Yeah, probably."

"Roscoe, we may be in a position to help each other," Montvale said. "Can we go off the record?"

"Yeah, sure. But why bother? You tell me something, I report it, and then you say, 'I never said that,' and Ellsworth says, 'That's right. I was there and the ambassador never said anything like that.'"

"Let me rephrase. What if these rumors you heard were true? What if there was a renegade lieutenant colonel named Castillo who did in fact snatch two senior Russian defectors from the CIA station chief in Vienna? What if he's now trying to sell them to the CIA?"

"No shit?"

"What if the President sent an unnamed but very senior intelligence official—"

"Who used to be a diplomat, Mr. Ambassador?"

"—down here with orders to find Colonel Castillo and these two Russians and then load them onto an airplane and fly them to the States?"

"You're going to pay the ransom, or whatever?"

"That's the point. I'm trusting your discretion on this, Roscoe. I know you're a patriotic American. No. The United States of America will not ransom the Russians. But they will be returned to the States and turned over to the CIA."

"Kidnap them back, you mean?"

"The Russians will be returned to the United States and turned over to the CIA. And Colonel Castillo will be returned to the United States and the United States Army for what is euphemistically known as 'disciplinary action.'"

"Jesus!"

"My search for these people has met with more success than yours, Roscoe," Montvale said.

"You know where they are?"

"I'm in a position to offer you confirmation of those rumors you heard. I'm further in a position to give exclusive rights to—what shall I say?—'the repatriation process' and to the Russians, and to Colonel Castillo."

"If I what?"

"How do I put this? If, splendid journalist that you are, you nevertheless failed to notice any unpleasantness that may occur during the repatriation process, any minor violations of Argentine law—or, for that matter, of American law. Do you take my meaning?"

Roscoe J. Danton thought: *Fuck you, Montvale.*

Once I'm back in the States, I'll write whatever the hell I feel like writing about anything I see.

Roscoe J. Danton said: "Deal. When does this come down?"

"Now. Truman, please call that Air Force colonel and have the plane ready by time we get to the airport."

Truman Ellsworth said, "Yes, sir."

Truman Ellsworth thought: *If I thought there was any chance at all of Castillo, the Russians, or even Alex Darby actually being in Ushuaia, I would at this moment be experiencing shortness of breath, excruciating pain in my chest, and numbness of my left arm and waiting for the ambulance to haul me off to whatever hospital the embassy sends visiting VIPs suffering a heart attack.*

But since I'm sure that all he's going to find down there—at best—is Alex Darby suffering a midlife crisis in the arms of a girl young enough to be his daughter, I'm going to pretend I believe this idiocy.

For one thing, I simply have to see how Charles tries to talk himself out of this fiasco once it comes tumbling down around him. I would never forgive myself if I didn't.

XI

[ONE]
The Oval Office
The White House
1600 Pennsylvania Avenue, N.W.
Washington, D.C.
1405 8 February 2007

Secretary of State Natalie Cohen, Director of the Central Intelligence Agency John Powell, Director of the Federal Bureau of Investigation Mark Schmidt, and General Allan B. Naylor, the commanding general of the United States Central Command, were all in the reception area of the Oval Office when the President of the United States, having returned from his trip to Chicago, entered.

They all rose to their feet when they saw the President. He acknowledged none of them.

Instead, Joshua Ezekiel Clendennen continued walking into his office, sat in the leather chair behind his desk, and issued two orders: "Get me some coffee. And then let them in."

Three minutes later, Cohen, Powell, Schmidt, and Naylor filed into the Oval Office.

"I'm glad you weren't in Timbuktu, General," Clendennen said.

Thinking that the President was joking, Naylor replied in kind: "That's next Thursday, Mr. President."

"You're not going anywhere, General, until this business is finished," the President snapped.

"Yes, sir," General Naylor said.

"Sit down," the President said, gesturing to all of them.

"General, C. Harry Whelan, Jr., and Andy McClarren were talking about you on Wolf News last night. Are you aware of that?"

"Yes, sir."

"Whelan told McClarren that the chief of staff of the Army no longer runs it—he's just in charge of administering it—and that since Central Command controls more troops, more airplanes, more ships, and more military assets in more places all around the world than any other headquarters, then that makes you, as its commanding general, the most important general in the Army. Did you see the program, by any chance?"

"It was brought to my attention, Mr. President."

General Naylor did not think he should get into the details of how the Wolf News program had come to his attention. He had been reading in his living room, and ignoring the television. His wife, Elaine, and their son, Major Allan B. Naylor, Jr., and his family, who had come for supper, were watching the Wolf News program *The Straight Scoop*.

When the Whelan–McClarren exchange concluded, General Naylor's wife and son went to him on their knees, called him "Oh, Great One!" and mimed kissing his West Point ring, then backed out of his presence into the kitchen convulsed with laughter and to the applause of his daughter-in-law and grand-children.

He actually had had to demand to be told what the hell was going on.

What was so funny?

And when he was told, he didn't think it was at all funny.

The chief of staff was going to hear about it, Naylor had said, and he wasn't going to find any humor in it.

And then he'd had an even more disquieting thought. He didn't like C. Harry Whelan, Jr., but it was possible that he was right about this, too. It seemed to be a truism that whoever commanded the most troops was *de facto*, if not *de jure*, the most important general officer.

The President asked, "Would you agree with that assessment, General?"

"Sir, since the chief of staff gives me my orders and writes my efficiency reports—"

"Well, this is one of those rare occasions on which I fully agree with Mr. Whelan," the President said. And then went on: "Does the name 'Sergei Murov' mean anything to you, General?"

"The SVR *rezident* in the Russian embassy, sir?"

The President nodded. "And I believe you know Frank Lammelle, the deputy director of the CIA, pretty well?"

"Yes, sir, I do."

"Mr. Powell, will you please tell General Naylor of the meeting Lammelle had with Murov in the Russian compound on the Eastern Shore?"

"Yes, sir," Powell said, and did so.

When Powell had finished, Naylor said, "Very interesting."

"I have never liked traitors," the President then announced, more than a little piously. "And so I have decided to give the Russians these two. What are their names again, Jack?"

"Colonel Dmitri Berezovsky and Lieutenant Colonel Svetlana Alekseeva, Mr. President," the CIA director furnished.

"Mr. President, do we have them?" Naylor asked. "I was under the impression that—"

"That Lieutenant Colonel C. G. Castillo," the President said, "who snatched them away from our CIA station chief in Vienna, has them?"

"Yes, sir."

"I understand, General, that you are personally acquainted with Lieutenant Colonel Castillo."

"Yes, sir, I am."

During the Cold War, there had been a custom in the regiments of the United States Constabulary in occupied West Germany called the "Dining In." Once a month, the officers of the regiments met for dinner in their regimental officer's club. These were formal affairs, ones presided over by the regimental commander, with seating at the one large table arranged strictly according to rank. Dress uniform was prescribed. Officers' ladies were not invited.

A splendid meal was served, with appropriate wines at each course. After the food had been consumed, and the cigars and cognac distributed, one of the officers—in a rigidly choreographed ritual—rose to his feet, and said, "Gentlemen, I give you the President of the United States."

Whereupon all the other officers rose to their feet and raised their glasses in toast.

The toasting then worked its way down the chain of command until it had reached the regimental commander.

And then the officers got down to some serious informal drinking and socializing, the intention of which was to raise the awareness of officers—particularly officers just reporting for duty—of their role in the Army, the Army of Occupation, the United States Constabulary, and their regiment.

It was at his first Dining In that newly arrived Major Allan B. Naylor, Armor, had first heard about the Gossinger family. The event had been held at the 11th Armored Cavalry Regiment Officer's Club in Bad Hersfeld, which was in Hesse, very close to the border between West Germany and East Germany.

The 11th ACR—"The Blackhorse Regiment"—had the mission of patrolling the border between East and West Germany. Their patrols ran through the Gossinger family's farmlands, which had been cut by the barbed-wire fence and the minefields erected by East Germans at Soviet direction to separate the East and West Germanys. Most of the Gossinger farmlands had wound up in East Germany.

By the time the story of the princess in Castle Gossinger came up, both alcohol and tradition had eased much of the formality of the Dining In. It was now time to tell war stories and other kinds of stories, the idea being more to entertain those who had not heard them than to present an absolutely truthful version of the facts.

For example, the story went that the barbed-wire fence and the minefields had been erected to keep Americans and West Germans from escaping into the Heaven on Earth of the Communist world.

As far as the Gossinger castle was concerned, the good news was that the Gossinger family—the full family name, identifying them as highly ranked in the *Almanach de Gotha*, was "von und zu Gossinger"—had lucked out: After the fence had gone up, their castle was in West Germany.

The bad news was that the Gossinger castle didn't look at all like Neuschwanstein Castle, the one built—damn the expense—by Mad King Ludwig in Bavaria. It instead more resembled a tractor factory.

The good news was that there was a fair princess living in the castle who loved Americans.

The bad news was that her loving of Americans was past tense. She had loved one American. He had ridden up to the castle on his white horse—actually flying a Bell WH-1D "Huey"—dallied awhile, left her in the family way, and disappeared, never to return. Nor to be heard from again.

More bad news was that her daddy—formerly Oberst Hermann Wilhelm von und zu Gossinger, who had been one of the last seriously wounded evacuated before von Paulus had surrendered at Stalingrad—did not like Americans. This was possibly because of the American chopper jockey's relationship with the princess. He had made it clear that any contact with Americans would be rare and brief.

Shortly after the Dining In, Major Naylor had been taken to the castle—formally known as Das Haus im Wald—by the Blackhorse's commander, Colonel Frederick Lustrous, and there introduced to former Oberst Hermann Wilhelm von und zu Gossinger, who received them courteously but rather coldly in his office.

Naylor had obeyed Lustrous's order: "Allan, look closely at the pictures on the shelf behind his desk" as Lustrous explained to Herr von und zu Gossinger that as the Regiment's S-3, Naylor would be dealing with the von und zu Gossingers for the regiment.

Major Naylor was surprised at what he saw on the shelf. There was a photo of General George S. Patton standing with his arm around von und zu Gossinger's shoulder. The third man in the photo Naylor recognized after a moment as Colonel John Waters, Patton's son-in-law, who had been captured in North Africa. Patton and Waters were splendidly turned out, while "Von und Zu"—as Naylor had quickly come to think of the starchy German—was in a tattered suit.

The picture had obviously been taken immediately after the war, probably just after Waters had been freed and just before Patton had died of injuries suffered in a car/truck accident in Heidelberg. And, judging by the way Oberst von und zu Gossinger was dressed, not long at all after he had been released from a POW camp and taken off his uniform for the last time.

But the photograph clearly made the point that Von und Zu had some powerful American friends. Waters was now a general officer.

Naylor got his first look at the princess—Frau Erika von und zu Gossinger—that first visit to the castle, but they were not introduced. She was a slim young woman in a black dress, her blonde hair gathered in a bun at her neck, and had been with her son, a towheaded ten- or eleven-year-old.

At the time, Naylor decided that while the story of the princess getting herself knocked up by some American chopper jockey made a great Dining In story, it was probably pure bullshit.

Over the next two years, he became more sure of that as he developed a personal relationship with the princess. Or, more accurately, as his bride, Elaine, and Erika became friends, as did the boy and Allan Junior, who was a year younger than Karl Wilhelm von und zu Gossinger.

The two women became much closer about a year later, after Von und Zu and his son went off a bridge on the Autobahn near Kassel in their Mercedes at a speed estimated by the authorities at one hundred ninety kilometers per hour (one hundred eighteen miles per hour), which left the princess and her son not only alone in the castle but the sole owners of Gossinger Beteiligungsgesellschaft, G.m.b.H.

By that time Major Naylor had learned the Gossinger assets went far beyond the farmlands now split by the barbed-wire fence and minefields. There were seven newspapers all over Europe, two breweries, a shipyard, and other businesses.

At the funeral of Erika's father and brother, Allan had told Elaine that he thought Erika would now be pushed into marrying Otto Görner, managing director of the Gossinger Beteiligungsgesellschaft, G.m.b.H., empire, who he knew had made his intentions of such known a long time ago, and who had enjoyed the blessing of the late Oberst von und zu Gossinger.

Elaine had told him that Erika had told her she would never marry—Otto or anyone else.

And she hadn't.

Six months after the funeral, Elaine, white-faced, showed up at Naylor's office—something she almost never did—and announced she had to talk to him right then.

"The best of the bad news is that scurrilous story about Karl being the love child of one of our oversexed goddamn chopper jockeys is true," Elaine had reported, and handed him a slip of paper. "That's his name."

On the paper she had written, "WOJG Jorge Castillo, San Antonio, Texas."

"What am I supposed to do with this?" he'd said.

"Find him."

"After all this time? Why?"

"The worst of the really bad news, sweetheart, is that Erika has maybe a month, maybe six weeks, to live. She's kept her pancreatic cancer a secret."

"My God!"

"Very shortly, that Tex-Mex sonofabitch is going to be Karl's only living relative. Find him, Allan."

As any wise major destined for high command would do when faced with a problem that he didn't have a clue how to solve, Naylor turned to the Black-horse's sergeant major. It took the wise old noncom not even thirty minutes to locate Warrant Officer Junior Grade Jorge Alejandro Castillo. He had remembered the name from somewhere, and then he had remembered where.

The sergeant major handed Major Naylor a book entitled *Vietnam War Recipients of the Medal of Honor.*

WOJG Jorge Castillo was in San Antonio, in the Fort Sam Houston National Cemetery. His tombstone bore a finely chiseled representation of the Medal of Honor and dates that indicated he had been nineteen years old at the time of his death.

That presented problems for Naylor and the Army that were difficult to express without sounding like a three-star sonofabitch. But they had to be, as Karl Wilhelm von und zu Gossinger was about to become a very wealthy twelve-year-old. And all of that money was now going to come under the control of some Mexican-Americans in Texas who probably didn't even know he existed.

The Army tries to take care of its own. This is especially true when the person needing help is the only son of a killed-in-action officer whose incredible courage in the face of death earned him the nation's most prestigious medal for valor.

The problem went up the chain of command. Senior officers of the Judge Advocate General's Corps were directed to find ways to save the boy's inheritance from squander by his new family.

Naylor was flown to San Antonio to "reconnoiter the situation" two days after Elaine had walked into his office with the bad news. The commanding general V U.S. Corps telephoned the commanding general of the Fifth United States Army at Fort Sam Houston, and told him Naylor was coming and why.

That officer quickly informed Naylor that the problem was not that the Castillo family was going to squander the inheritance—they owned square blocks of downtown San Antonio, and a great deal else, and didn't need anyone else's money.

Naylor's—and the Army's—problem was going to be to convince them that the boy's mother was not some fraulein of loose morality trying to dump someone else's bastard on them to get her hands into the Castillo cashbox.

Naylor found Doña Alicia Castillo at her office near the Alamo.

When she telephoned her husband, who was in New York City on business, to tell him she had just been told that their only son had left behind a son in Germany, he begged her to take things very slowly, and to do nothing until he could return to Texas and look into it himself.

"He has Jorge's eyes," Doña Alicia had said, and hung up.

Juan Fernando Castillo caught the next flight he could get on to Texas. It took him to Dallas, not San Antonio, but that wasn't going to pose a problem. He had called Lemes Aviation and told them to have the Lear waiting for him in Dallas for the final leg to San Antonio.

When he got to Dallas, however, the Lear wasn't there. When he called Lemes Aviation, he was told that Doña Alicia had taken the jet to New York, so that she and some Army officer could make the five-fifteen Pan American flight to Frankfurt.

Within twenty-four hours of meeting Doña Alicia Castillo, Allan and Elaine Naylor stood in the corridor outside Erika von und zu Gossinger's room in the castle and overheard Doña Alicia say, "I'm Jorge's mother, my dear. I'm here to take care of you and the boy."

Juan Fernando Castillo arrived in Germany ten hours after his wife.

A week later—Erika having decided she didn't want the boy to see her in the final stages of her illness—Naylor and Elaine and Allan Junior had shaken hands and hugged the boy, who now carried an American passport in the name of Carlos Guillermo Castillo and was preparing to board a Pan American 747 airliner bound for New York.

"You don't happen to know where your friend Lieutenant Colonel Castillo is, do you, General?" President Clendennen asked.

"No, sir, I do not."

"Well, I've got a mission for you, General. I want you—as your highest priority—to find Lieutenant Colonel Castillo, wherever he might be, where-upon you will personally hand him orders recalling him from retirement to active duty. You will then personally order him to turn these Russian traitors over to the CIA. And when he has done so, then I want you to place Castillo under arrest, pending investigation of charges that may be laid against him under the Uniform Code of Military Justice. Do you understand these orders?"

Allan Naylor stood stonefaced, and thought: *Goddamn you to hell, Bruce McNab!*

He then said: "May I ask questions, sir?"

The President wiggled his fingers, granting permission.

"Sir, what is my authority to detain or arrest the Russians?"

"That won't pose a problem for you, General. Mr. Lammelle will deal with that."

"Sir, I don't understand."

"From right now—or at least from as soon as Mr. Lammelle can get here from Langley—until this mission has been accomplished, you and Lammelle will be, so to speak, joined at the hip. I wouldn't think, General, of asking you or the Army to do anything that would constitute a violation of any law. Nor would I ask that Mr. Lammelle or the CIA violate any laws. Having said that, we all know that the agency has a certain latitude in the gray areas, and I will personally accept full responsibility for any action that Mr. Lammelle feels he should take to carry out the desires of the commander in chief in this matter. Does that answer your question, General Naylor?"

"Yes, sir."

"How soon can you start on this, General?"

"Sir, I'll have to set up things at MacDill so that I can devote my full time to this. So, as soon as Mr. Lammelle gets here, I'll go there."

"Jack," the President said to the DCI, "Lammelle has a radio in his car, right? Why don't you get on the horn and tell him to meet the general at An-drews? There's no reason he actually has to come here."

"Yes, sir."

"Good hunting, General," the President said. "I don't think I have to tell you to keep me posted, do I?"

"No, sir."

[TWO]
Office of the Commanding General
United States Army Central Command
MacDill Air Force Base
Tampa, Florida
1710 8 February 2007

By the time of the First Desert War, Allan Naylor was a well-respected major general, obviously destined for greater responsibility and the rank that would come with it. He had been selected to be General H. Norman Schwarzkopf's J-3, the Joint Staff's operations officer.

It was the J-3's responsibility to know what assets—usually meaning which units—were available to his general, and lists were prepared and updated daily that showed the names of the units and of their commanding officers.

One day, as they prepared to strike at Iraqi forces, Naylor had noticed on that day's list, under NEWLY ARRIVED IN THEATRE, the 2303rd Civil Government Detachment.

Lieutenant Colonel Bruce J. McNab was listed as the commanding officer.

Naylor felt a little sorry for McNab for several reasons, including that lieutenant colonel was a pretty junior rank for those who had graduated from the Point, and that command of a civil government detachment was not a highway to promotion. But Naylor also had decided that the lowly status was almost certainly Scotty McNab's own fault. He had always been a troublemaker. And Naylor had heard somewhere and some time ago that McNab had gone into Special Forces—another dead end, usually, for those seeking high rank—and this meant that McNab had somehow screwed up that career, too, the proof being that he now held only the rank of a light bird and was commanding a civil government detachment.

Two days later, the list, under CHANGES, noted: "Change McNab, Bruce J. LTC Inf 2303 CivGovDet to COL, no change in duties."

Naylor had thought that McNab had been lucky the Desert War had come along. Now he would be able to retire as a full bird colonel.

And then the shooting war began, and Major General Naylor gave no further thought to Colonel McNab.

Two days after that, Naylor learned from the public relations officer that in the very opening hours of the active war, the co-pilot of one of the Apache attack helicopters sent in to destroy Iraqi radar and other facilities had performed these duties with extraordinary skill and valor.

The Apache had been struck by Iraqi fire, which wounded both the pilot and co-pilot, blinding the former. A lesser man than the co-pilot would have landed the Apache and waited for help. This one, in the belief the pilot would die unless he got prompt medical attention, flew the battered, smoking, shuddering Apache more than a hundred miles back across the desert to friendly lines, ignoring the wounds he had himself received, and the enormous risk to his own life.

"The G-One, General," the public relations officer said to Naylor, "has approved the Impact Award of the Distinguished Flying Cross for this officer. Can General Schwarzkopf find time to make the presentation personally?"

"Why is that important?"

"The public relations aspect of this, General Naylor, is enormous. Once we release this story—especially with General Schwarzkopf personally making the award—it will be on the front page of every newspaper in America."

"Why enormous?"

"The co-pilot is a twenty-one-year-old second lieutenant, General. He just got out of West Point. And there's more, General, much more!"

The first thing General Naylor thought was: *Then Charley Castillo probably knows him. He also just got out of the Point.*

That was immediately followed by: *What the hell is a twenty-one-year-old second lieutenant months out of Hudson High doing flying an Apache over here?*

"What more?" Naylor had asked.

"This kid's father won the Medal of Honor in Vietnam, General, flying a Huey helicopter."

"Colonel, you don't win the Medal of Honor. You *receive*, are *a recipient* of, the Medal of Honor," Naylor corrected him in a Pavlovian reaction, and then said, "Let me see that thing."

The name of the officer who had performed so heroically was Second Lieutenant Carlos G. Castillo.

"Where is this officer?" he asked softly.

"In your outer office, sir."

"Get him in here," Naylor ordered.

The hand with which Lieutenant Castillo saluted General Naylor was wrapped in a bloody bandage. Much of his forehead and right cheek carried smaller bandages.

"Good afternoon, sir. Allan said if I had a chance, to pass on his regards."

"Right about now, you were supposed to be starting flight school, basic flight school. How is it you're here, and flying an Apache?"

"Well, when I got to Rucker, it came out that I had a little over three hundred hours in the civilian version of the Huey, so they sent me right to Apache school. And here I am."

Naylor had thought: *And damn lucky to be alive.*

Questions of personal valor aside, standing before me is a young officer who is blissfully unaware that he has been a pawn in what is obviously a cynical scheme on the part of some senior aviation officers who wanted to garner publicity for Army Aviation—"Son of Vietnam Army Pilot Hero Flies in Iraq"—and turned a blind eye to his lack of experience, and the very good chance that he would be killed.

Goddamn them!

They probably would've liked it better if he had been killed. It would have made a better story for the newspapers: "Son of Hero Pilot Dies Like His Father: In Combat, at the Controls!"

Sonsofbitches!

Ten minutes later, General H. Norman Schwarzkopf agreed with Major General Naylor's assessment of the situation.

"What do you want to do with him, Allan? Send him back to Fort Rucker?"

"That would imply he's done something wrong, sir."

"Then find some nice, safe flying assignment for him," Schwarzkopf said. "Anything else?"

"No, sir. Thank you, sir."

That then posed the problem of where to find a nice, safe flying assignment for Second Lieutenant Castillo out of the reach of glory-seeking Army Aviators.

"McNab."

"Allan Naylor, Scotty. How are you?"

"Very well, thank you. How may I serve the general?"

"Tell me, Scotty, are there any Hueys on your T O and E?"

"Somebody told me you're the J-Three. Aren't you supposed to know?"

We may be classmates, but I'm a major general, and you're a just-promoted colonel. A touch more respect on your part would be in order.

"Answer the question, please."

Scotty McNab affected an officious tone, and said, "Rotary-wing aircraft are essential to the mission of the 2303rd Civil Government Detachment, sir. Actually, sir, we couldn't fulfill the many missions assigned to us in the area of civil government without them. Yes, sir, I have a couple of Hueys."

"Colonel, a simple 'Yes, sir' or 'No, sir' would have sufficed," Naylor snapped.

"Yes, sir."

By then Naylor had been half-convinced that McNab's disrespectful attitude was induced by alcohol. He had an urge to simply hang up on him, but that would not have solved the problem of finding Second Lieutenant Castillo a nice, safe flying assignment.

"I'm about to send you a Huey pilot, Colonel. A Huey *co-pilot*."

"What did he do wrong?"

"Excuse me?"

"What did this guy do to get banished to civil government?"

"As a matter of fact, Colonel, this officer was decorated not more than an hour ago by General Schwarzkopf with the Distinguished Flying Cross," Naylor said sharply. He heard his tone, got control of himself, and went on: "The thing is, Scotty, this officer is very young, has been through a harrowing experience, has been wounded, and what I was thinking . . ."

"Got the picture. Send him down. Glad to have him."

"Thanks, Scotty."

"Think 'Civil Government,' General. That's what we're really all about."

Not long after the shooting war had ended, Schwarzkopf's aide-de-camp arrived in Naylor's office, and announced: "General Schwarzkopf asks you to be in his office at 1500, when he will decorate Colonel McNab, General. You're friends, right?"

"Colonel McNab is to be decorated? With what? For what?"

"With the Distinguished Service Cross, General. And afterward, the President's going to call to offer his congratulations on his promotion. The Senate just confirmed his star."

"Jack, are we talking about Colonel McNab of Civil Government?"

"Well, sir, that's what they called it. But that's not what it really was."

"Excuse me? If it wasn't Civil Government, what was it?"

"Sir, maybe you better ask General Schwarzkopf about that."

At 1445, General Naylor went into General Norman Schwarzkopf's office and confessed that he was more than a little confused about Colonel McNab's 2303rd Civil Government Detachment and what he had been told was to happen at 1500.

"You weren't on the need-to-know list, Allan," Stormin' Norman said. "I told McNab I thought you should be, but he said if he ever needed anything from you, he'd tell you what he was up to. And it was his call. My orders were to support him, but he didn't answer to me. He took his orders from the CIA."

"Sir, what was he up to?"

"He ran Special Operations for the campaign. And did one hell of a job. They grabbed two intact Scud missiles and a half-dozen Russian officers—including two generals—who were showing the Iraqis how to work them. Embarrassed the hell out of the Russians. There was a lot more, but you don't have the need-to-know. I'm sure you understand."

Naylor understood, but that was not the same as saying he liked being kept in the dark.

At 1500, Colonel Bruce J. McNab, followed by Second Lieutenant Castillo, marched into General Schwarzkopf's office, came to attention, and saluted. Allan Naylor could not believe his eyes.

Colonel McNab was a small, muscular, ruddy-faced man with a flowing red mustache. He wore aviator sunglasses, a mostly unbuttoned khaki bush jacket with its sleeves rolled up, khaki shorts, knee-length brown socks, and hunting boots. On his head was an Arabian headdress, circled with two gold cords, which Naylor had recently learned indicated the wearer was an Arabian nobleman. An Uzi submachine gun hung by a strap from his shoulder.

Castillo was similarly dressed, except he had no gold cords on his headdress, and he had a Colt CAR-15 submachine gun slung from his shoulder.

"What the hell are you two dressed up for, Scotty?" General Schwarzkopf asked.

"Sir, I researched what Lawrence of Arabia actually wore during his campaigns in the desert—and it was not flowing robes—and adopted it for me and my aide-to-be."

"It's a good thing the press isn't here," Schwarzkopf said. "They'd have a field day with you two."

Schwarzkopf offered his hand to Castillo.

"Good to see you again, Lieutenant," he said.

"Thank you, sir."

"And speaking of Lieutenant Castillo," McNab said, and handed Schwarz-kopf two oblong blue medal boxes. "These are for him. I'm sure he'd rather get them from you, sir."

"What are they?"

"The Silver Star for the business with the Russian generals. And the Purple Heart, second and third awards."

"I sent him to you, Scotty," Naylor heard himself say, "to get him out of the line of fire."

"Didn't work out that way, General," McNab said. "Charley's a warrior."

"I have General McNab for you, sir," Command Sergeant Major Wes Suggins, the senior noncommissioned officer of the United States Central Command, announced to General Naylor from the office door.

Naylor gave him a thumbs-up gesture and snatched the secure telephone from his desk.

"Good evening, sir," Lieutenant General Bruce J. McNab, commanding general of the Special Operations Command at Fort Bragg, North Carolina, said cheerfully. "And how are things on beautiful Tampa Bay?"

"General, I want you in my office at oh-seven-thirty tomorrow," Naylor said.

"Perhaps, if I may make the suggestion, sir, your quarters would be a better place to meet, sir," McNab said. "I suspect we are going to say unkind things to one another, and that sometimes adversely affects the morale of your gnomes."

"Oh-seven-thirty, General," Naylor said, coldly furious. "My office, and leave your wiseass mouth at Bragg."

"I hear and obey, my general," McNab said cheerfully.

Naylor slammed the secure telephone into its cradle.

The damned call didn't take thirty seconds and he made me lose my temper! Referring to my staff as my "gnomes"! Goddamn him!

Allan B. Naylor had never liked Bruce J. McNab during their four years at the United States Military Academy at West Point. He had come to dislike him intensely in later years, and now he could not think of an officer he had ever despised more.

[THREE]
Morton's Steakhouse
1050 Connecticut Avenue, N.W.
Washington, D.C.
1930 8 February 2007

Sergei Murov sat at the bar of the restaurant, drinking twelve-year-old Chivas Regal while he watched in the mirror behind the row of bottles the head-waiter stand at the entrance. Murov was waiting for the syndicated columnist C. Harry Whelan, Jr., to show up.

Murov knew that the headwaiter—and other restaurant staff—were aware of who the freely spending cultural attaché of the embassy of the Russian Federation was. And he was equally certain—Washington being the small town that it really was, where everybody knew each other's business—that they had at least heard and probably believed that he was the head Russian spy.

Murov wanted the word to get out around town that he had had a private dinner in Morton's with Whelan. The FBI would be helpful in this regard. The usual quartet of FBI special agents had been waiting outside the embassy with two cars and had followed him here.

He knew how they worked. The cars were now parked on opposite sides of Connecticut Avenue so that they could easily follow him no matter which direction he took when he left the restaurant. One special agent had followed him into the restaurant and was now sitting at the end of the bar. The second agent-on-foot was now standing in the alley outside the kitchen against the possibility that the wily Russian spy might try to elude surveillance by sneaking out of Morton's through the kitchen.

One of the FBI men had almost certainly already radioed the information to whoever was supervising his surveillance that he was in Morton's, and just as soon as C. Harry Whelan arrived and joined him, that information, too, would be passed on.

That information, however, would not be shared with anyone—at least immediately—outside the J. Edgar Hoover Building. But the information would get around where Murov wanted it to go via the headwaiter, who would be on the receiving end of at least one "Flying C-Note"—he loved that phrase—for making discreet telephone calls to various print and television journalists telling them that C. Harry Whelan, Jr., had just walked into Morton's and was breaking bread with Sergei Murov behind a screen erected at Murov's request.

"Good evening, Mr. Whelan," the headwaiter said when the journalist walked through the door. "Nice to see you again. Your regular table?"

"I think I'll have a little taste first, thank you," Whelan said, gesturing toward the bar. "Oh, look who's there!"

Sergei Murov had gotten off his bar stool and was smiling at Whelan. Whelan walked to him and they shook hands.

Whelan, too, knew that a substantial percentage of the headwaiter's income came to him off the books and thus tax-free in the form of Flying C-Notes given him as an expression of gratitude by various print journalists and television producers for keeping them up to date on where C. Harry Whelan and others of Inside-the-Beltway prominence were, had been, or were going to be, and who they were talking to.

Whelan was usually delighted with the system, and especially so today when he knew the word would spread that he had had dinner with Murov. Murov met with only the more important journalists, and actually very few of those.

Whelan had no idea what Murov wanted from him, and would have been very surprised if he got anything at all useful from the Russian. But the word would spread. Among those it would annoy to learn that he was bending elbows with the Russian spymaster was Andy McClarren, anchor of Wolf News's most popular program. Whelan recently had come to think that Straight Scoop McClarren was getting more than a little too big for his kilt.

This was by no means the first, or even the tenth, time that he'd met Murov at Morton's. He knew what was going to happen: There would be some very good whisky at the bar, and then, when they had moved to a table, some really first-class wine, and one of Morton's nearly legendary steaks.

People often quoted Whelan's evaluation of Morton's Steakhouse: "The food is so good in Morton's that it's almost worth about half what they charge for it."

And afterward, Murov would not only insist on paying the check, in cash, but also would leave the actual bill lying on the table, from where he knew Harry would discreetly—and thinking Murov didn't notice—slip it in his pocket.

Murov had diplomatic privilege, which would allow him to turn the bill over to the IRS for a refund of the tax. He had decided, the first time he'd seen Whelan grab the bill, that the Russian Federation could easily afford forfeiting the returned taxes if that meant a very important—and thus potentially very useful—journalist would come to the conclusion that he was putting something over not only on the IRS but also on the *rezident* of the Russian embassy. It is always better if one's adversary thinks he is far more clever than oneself.

"How are you, Sergei?" Whelan greeted Murov.

"What a pleasant surprise!" Murov said. "Have you time for a drink, Harry?"

"I could be talked into that, I think," Whelan said, and slipped onto a bar stool.

He ordered a Famous Grouse twelve-year-old malt Scotch whisky with two ice cubes and half as much water as whisky.

As the bartender was making the drink, Murov said, "I saw you on Wolf News, Harry. '*Straight Scoop* something'?"

"You and four million other people," Whelan said somewhat smugly.

"I thought your '*arf-arf*' business was hilarious, but I wondered what it did to your relationship with President Clendennen."

"It went from just-about-as-bad-as-it-can-get to worse."

"What was that all about, anyway, at Fort Detrick?"

"I don't know, Sergei. I think you know what really goes on out there."

"I haven't a clue."

"The hell you don't. Okay, they have a biological weapons laboratory out there. That's probably classified Top Secret, but it's really about as much of a secret as McClarren's wig."

"Really? That red hair isn't his?"

"That's why they always shoot him up," Whelan said, demonstrating with his hands a low camera angle pointing upward. "If they shoot him down, or even straight on, you can see the cheesecloth or whatever it is under the hair."

"You really are a fountain of information, Harry," Murov said.

Whelan thought: *Actually, of disinformation.*

As far as I know, all that red hair comes out of Ol' Andy's scalp.

But the bartender heard what I just said, and before the night is over, it will be all over Morton's.

And before the week is out, Jay Leno will have made a joke about Old Baldy and His Red Rug.

Whelan said, "So, what happened at Fort Detrick was that they had an accident. Somebody dropped a bottle or somebody forgot to close a door. They're prepared for something like that. The emergency procedures were put into play. Since the world didn't come to an end, we know that the emergency procedures worked. But in the meantime, Homeland Security, the Defense Department, every other agency determined to prove it's on the job protecting the people, rushed up there, and the Wolf News photographers in the helicopter got those marvelous shots of everybody getting in everybody's way. Chasing their tails. *Arf-arf.*"

Twenty minutes and two drinks later, Murov called for the bartender, told him he was ready for his table, and asked for the bill. When it was presented, Murov laid three twenty-dollar bills on the bar, and told the bartender to keep the change. The headwaiter appeared, bearing menus and trailed by the sommelier bearing the wine list.

C. Harry Whelan, Jr., slipped the bar bill into his pocket and followed everybody to a table set against a wall behind a folding screen.

Ten minutes after that, a waiter had delivered a dozen oysters on the half-shell and the sommelier had opened and poured from a bottle of Egri Bikavér, which Murov told Whelan he had learned to appreciate as a young officer stationed in Budapest.

"'Bull's blood,' they call it," Murov said. "The Hungarians have been making wine for a thousand years."

"What were you doing in Budapest?" Whelan asked. "As a young officer?"

"I was in tanks," Murov said.

Bullshit. You were in the KGB, or the OGPU, or whatever they called the Soviet secret intelligence service in those days.

You are a charming sonofabitch, Sergei, but you didn't get to be the Washington rezident *because you're a nice guy.*

You're dangerous.

What the hell do you want from me?

They tapped the rims of their glasses together.

"I'm going to tell you a story, Harry," Murov said, "one that would go over very well if you went on *The Straight Scoop* tonight with it—"

Well, here it comes!

Whelan interrupted: "Sergei, my experience has been that if someone tries to feed you a story . . ."

Murov went on: "—but I think when you hear the whole story, you will decide to wait a little before coming out with it." Murov paused, then added: "And if you decide to break the story immediately, I will of course deny it. And since it touches on the incredible, I really think people would believe my denial."

"Why are you being so good to me, Sergei?"

"Because it is in my interests to do so. And because, frankly, you are the most important journalist to whom I have access."

Whelan thought: *That makes sense.*

Murov reached for, and then placed on the table, a very elegant dark red leather attaché case. When Whelan saw it, he thought of the wine—bull's blood.

Murov took two sheets of paper from the attaché case, laid them on the table, closed the attaché case, returned it to the floor, and then handed Whelan the two sheets of paper.

"What am I looking at? It's in Russian."

"Underneath is the translation. What you're looking at is a letter from Colonel Vladlen Solomatin."

Whelan read the translation, and then looked at Murov, his eyebrows raised in question.

"When you have your own translation of the Russian made, Harry," Murov said, "I think you'll find that one's quite accurate. I know that because I did it myself."

"I confess I don't understand what this is all about," Whelan said.

"Those warmongers who scurrilously accuse me of being a member of the SVR rather than the innocent diplomat that I am would also allege that my superior in the SVR is Vladlen Solomatin. The second directorate of the SVR is in charge of SVR agents around the world, exercising that authority through the senior SVR officer in each country, commonly called the *resident*. Are you hearing all this for the first time, Harry?"

"Absolutely. This is all news to me."

"I'm not surprised. Anyway, so I'm told, most of these *resident*s know each other. We . . . excuse me . . . *they* went to school together, served together, et cetera. You understand?"

"Sort of an old boy's club, right?"

"Precisely," Murov said. "Not very often, but once in a great while, people who are not in the SVR form close friendships with people who are. In our embassies—as, I am sure, in yours—cultural attachés know who the *resident/* CIA station chief is even if that is supposed to be a secret. Am I right?"

"Probably. Are you going to tell me who the SVR *resident* in your embassy here is, Sergei?"

"No. But I know who he is, even though I am not supposed to."

"And I'm sure that secret is safe with you," Whelan said as he reached for the bottle of Egri Bikavér. "Vladimir Putin may sleep soundly tonight."

Whelan saw in Murov's eyes something that told him Murov did not like the sarcasm or—maybe particularly—the reference to Putin.

Good!

"Colonel Dmitri Berezovsky and I are friends from childhood," Murov said. "And we went to Saint Petersburg University together."

"And Berezovsky is . . . ?"

"The former commercial attaché of our embassy in Berlin."

"Read *rezident?*"

Whelan had asked the question to annoy Murov and was genuinely surprised when Murov replied: "All right, the former *rezident* in Berlin. And I was therefore genuinely surprised when word came that he and his sister, who was the *rezident* in Copenhagen, had deserted their posts shortly before they were to be arrested on charges of embezzlement."

"This letter," Whelan said, tapping the document with his fingers, "says they didn't do it. 'Come home. All is forgiven.'"

"They didn't do it. Svetlana's husband was trying to pay her back for leaving him. In the SVR, husbands are expected to control their wives; if they can't, it puts their character into question."

"Are you pulling my leg, Sergei?"

"Not in the slightest. Svetlana—"

"You keep using her first name. You know her, too, huh?"

"Very well. As I was saying, Svetlana not only moved out of their apartment, but had begun divorce proceedings against Colonel Alekseev. Having one's wife—particularly a wife who is a co-worker, so to speak—find one wanting in the marital situation is very damaging to an officer's career. Evgeny's father was a general—"

"Evgeny's the husband?"

Murov nodded and said, "Colonel Evgeny Evgenyvich Alekseev. And Evgeny wanted to be a general, too. And I would suppose there was a human element in here as well."

"Human element?"

"Aside from everything else, his losing Svetlana. She's a strikingly beautiful woman. Charming, elegant. Evgeny was crazy about her. Jealous."

"Does the term 'soap opera' mean anything to you, Sergei?"

"I know what a soap opera is, of course."

"This sounds like a soap opera. A bad one."

Murov sucked in his breath audibly. And then he was spared having to reply immediately by the waiter.

"Excuse me," the waiter interrupted. "Are you ready to order, gentlemen?"

He was pushing a cart loaded with steaks, chops, lobster, and other items from which one could select one's steak, chop, lobster, or other item.

Whelan seriously doubted one actually got what one selected. For one thing, all the cuts were lying on a bed of ice, and were therefore presumably below room temperature, and you weren't supposed to grill steaks unless they were at room temperature. For another, it was reasonable to assume the diner would pick the best chunk of meat. If this then went to the grill, another good-looking steak would have to be added to the cart.

It would therefore be easier to let the customer *think* he was selecting his entrée, and actually serve him with something from the kitchen, and he was sure they did just that.

"Filet mignon, pink in the middle, with Wine Merchant's sauce, asparagus, and a small salad, please," Whelan ordered without looking at the selection on the cart.

"Twice, except because of the big portions I'll have mushrooms instead of asparagus," Murov said, then looked at Whelan, and said, "We can rob from one another's side dish," then turned back to the waiter, and added, "And bring another bottle of the Egri Bikavér."

The waiter repeated the order and then left.

"You will recall I used the phrase 'touches on the incredible,'" Murov said, "when we began."

"That was an understatement, but go on," Whelan said. "What happened?"

"Well, all of this apparently pushed him over the edge. He decided to pun-ish her. Or maybe he did what he did consciously, thinking that losing a wife who was a thief would be less damaging to his career than a wife who had kicked him out of the marital bed. So he started to set up her and her brother on false embezzlement charges."

"Sounds like he's a really nice guy," Whelan said.

Murov exhaled audibly again.

"One does not get to be the Berlin *rezident* of the SVR without a very well-developed sense of how to cover one's back," Murov said.

"I suppose that would also apply to the Washington *rezident* of the SVR."

Murov ignored the comment. He went on: "Dmitri learned what was going on . . ."

"Why didn't he go to his boss and say, 'Hey, boss. My sister's husband is trying to set me up. Here's the proof.'"

"Because his boss was his cousin, Colonel V. N. Solomatin. I'm sure Vladlen would have believed him, but Solomatin's superior was—is—General Yakov Sirinov, who runs the SVR for Putin. And Sirinov was unlikely to believe either

Vladlen or Dmitri for several reasons, high among them that he believed Dmitri was a personal threat to his own career. The gossip at the time Sirinov was given his position was that it would have gone to Dmitri if Dmitri and Putin had not been at odds. And also of course because Vladlen and Dmitri were cousins."

The odds are a hundred to one that I am being fed an incredible line of bullshit. But, my God, what a plethora of details! Murov should have been a novelist. Either that, or he's telling me the truth.

Careful, Harry! Not for publication, but you're really out of your league when dealing with the Washington rezident *of the SVR.*

"So Dmitri did what any man in his position would do."

"The SVR Washington *rezident,* for example?"

Murov looked at him, shook his head, smiled, and said, "No. What the Washington *rezident* would have done in similar circumstances would have been to call Frank Lammelle, and say something like, 'Frank, my friend, when I come out of Morton's tonight, have a car waiting for me. This spy's coming in from the cold.'

"Dmitri didn't have that option. He was in Berlin. His sister was in Copenhagen. And they were being watched by other SVR officers. They couldn't just get on a plane and come here. But what they could do, and did, was contact the CIA station chief in Vienna and tell her that they were willing to defect, and thought the best time and way to do that was to slip away from the festivities at the Kunsthistorisches Museum."

"I don't understand," Whelan confessed. "What festivities? Where?"

"There was going to be a gathering in Vienna of *rezident*s and other SVR officers. As a gesture of international friendship, the Hermitage Museum in Saint Petersburg sent Bartolomeo Rastrelli's wax statue of Russian tsar Peter the First on a tour of the better European museums. First stop was Vienna's Kunsthistorisches Museum."

"Okay."

"The CIA station chief set things up. The CIA sent a plane to Vienna with the plan that, as soon as Dmitri and Svetlana got into it, it would take off, and eight hours later Dmitri and Svetlana would be in one of those safe houses the agency maintains not far from our dacha on the Eastern Shore here.

"So far as General Sirinov was concerned, the business at the Kunsthistorisches Museum was going to provide him with two things. First, an opportunity to get all his people together without attracting too much attention. Second, when everybody was gathered, and people asked the whereabouts of Colonel Dmitri Berezovsky and Lieutenant Colonel Svetlana Alekseeva, Sirinov was going to tell them they were under arrest for embezzling funds of the Russian Federation, and then put them on an Aeroflot aircraft to Moscow."

"Sirinov . . . is that his name?"

Murov nodded.

"He knew these two were going to defect?"

Murov nodded.

"And here is where the plot thickens," Murov said. "There were CIA agents waiting in Vienna's Westbahnhof for Dmitri and his sister. And there were representatives of the SVR waiting for them. And they never showed up."

"What happened to them?"

"It took General Sirinov several days to find out. There were two problems. First, the officer responsible for meeting them at the railway station, the Vienna *rezident*, Lieutenant Colonel Kiril Demidov, was found the next morning sitting in a taxicab outside the American embassy with the calling card of Miss Eleanor Dillworth, the CIA station chief, on his chest. Poor Kiril had been garroted to death."

"Jesus Christ!" Whelan exclaimed.

"And then, the second problem was that General Sirinov was naturally distracted by world events. You will recall that your President somehow got the idea that the Iranians were operating a biological warfare laboratory in the Congo and rather than bring his suspicions to the United Nations, as he was clearly obligated to do, instead launched a unilateral attack and brought the world dangerously close to a nuclear exchange."

Do I let him get away with that?

What good would arguing with him do?

"Are you going to tell me what happened to Colonel Whatsisname and his sister?"

"That is the real question," Murov said. "Eventually, General Sirinov learned that within hours of their scheduled arrival in Vienna, they were flown out of Schwechat on Lieutenant Colonel Carlos G. Castillo's Gulfstream airplane. That was the last time anyone has seen them."

"How did Castillo get involved?"

Murov shrugged.

"General Sirinov's intention had been to present the arrest of Dmitri and Svetlana to Putin as a *fait accompli*. Now he had to report that not only were they not under arrest, but no one had any idea where they might be, although of course the CIA was presumed to be somehow involved.

"Putin—who, as I said, has known Dmitri and Svetlana for years—thought there was something fishy about the embezzlement charges and ordered Sirinov to have another look. Sirinov discovered Evgeny's little scheme. Putin was furious, both personally and professionally."

"What does that mean?" Whelan asked.

"In addition to his personal feelings about the injustice done to Colonel Berezovsky and Lieutenant Colonel Alekseeva, Putin knew that SVR officers all over the world were thinking, *That could happen to me.*"

"Including you, Sergei?"

"Well, since I'm not an SVR officer, no. But to answer what I think you're asking, 'Was the Washington *rezident* thinking that what happened to two fine SVR officers like Berezovsky and Alekseeva could happen to him?' I happen to know he was. And Putin, knowing this, ordered that things be made right. If he could get through to Berezovsky and Alekseeva and get them to come home, and they were promoted . . . If the injustice done to them . . ."

"I get the point," Whelan said.

Why am I starting to believe him?

"So Putin went to Vladlen Solomatin and told him what he wanted to do. And that letter was written. The problem then became how to get the letter to Berezovsky and his sister. The decision was made—by Putin personally—to go right to the top. So the Washington *rezident* invited Frank Lammelle to our dacha on the Eastern Shore—you know where I mean?"

Whelan nodded.

"And explained the situation, gave him the letter from Solomatin, and asked that he deliver it, and made it clear that his cooperation in the matter would not be forgotten.

"Lammelle, however, said he was sorry, but he didn't think he could help, as much as he would like to. Then he related an incredible story. Castillo had had no authority to take Berezovsky and Alekseeva from Vienna. Castillo had never been in the CIA, but had been in charge of a private CIA—called the Office of Organizational Analysis, OOA—that your late President had been running. OOA was disbanded, and its members been ordered to disappear *the day before* you bombed the Congo. Lammelle said he had no idea where Castillo or Berezovsky and Alekseeva could be."

"You're right. That's incredible," Whelan said.

"What's really incredible, Harry, is that the *rezident* believed Lammelle. They had over the years developed a relationship. In other words, they might say 'No comment' to one another, but they would not lie to one another. Over time, that has worked to their mutual advantage."

Murov topped off their wineglasses.

"That's why I asked you to dinner, Harry," Murov said. "To propose something I think will be mutually advantageous."

Whelan said, "'And what would that be?' Harry Whelan, suspicious journalist, asked, as he put one hand on his wallet and the other on his crotch."

Murov chuckled.

"Your wallet, maybe, Harry. But I am really not interested in your crotch. Would you like me to go on, or should we just forget we ever had this conversation?"

"I'm all ears."

"Putin wants this problem resolved. There is great pressure on the *rezident* to solve it. He came to me and said he thought the greatest obstacle to solving it is President Clendennen . . ."

"Clendennen? He's the obstacle? How's that?"

"The *rezident* thinks the President just wants the problem to go away, and he thinks the President believes the best way to do that is to do nothing. His predecessor never told him a thing about the OOA. He has no idea what it is, or was. He's never heard of Lieutenant Colonel Castillo, and therefore knows nothing of Castillo taking two Russian defectors away from the CIA, and if he did, he has no idea why, or what Castillo has done with the defectors. Getting the idea?"

"Yeah," Whelan said. "So, what am I supposed to do about it?"

"Start looking for Castillo and the OOA . . . at the White House. Ask Clendennen to tell you about *his* secret private CIA, and the man who runs it for him. When he tells you he knows nothing about it, ask him why you can't find Castillo. Tell him you suspect he's hiding Castillo, and that unless you can talk to Castillo and get a denial from him, that's the story you're going to write: *'President Denies Knowledge of Secret Special Operations Organization.'*"

"And he says, 'Go ahead, write it. I don't know what you're talking about.' Then what?"

"Then you tell him that after you write it, and he denies it, you're going to write another story: *'Former CIA Station Chief Confirms That Rogue Special Operator Stole Russian Defectors from CIA.'* And that the only way you're not going to write the story is if Castillo tells you it's not true."

"And who is this former CIA station chief? And why would he tell me this?"

"It's a she. Her name is Eleanor Dillworth. The day after Kiril Demidov was found in the taxicab outside the American embassy with Dillworth's calling card on his chest, she was fired. She feels she has been treated unfairly."

"Why should I believe her?"

"Roscoe J. Danton does. She went to him with this story. He's now in Buenos Aires looking for Castillo."

"How do you know that?"

"The *resident* there told me. He's actually very good at what he does."

He wouldn't tell me that if it wasn't true.

It's too easy to check out.

"Just for the sake of argument, Sergei: Say I believe you. Say I do all this—I'd start by talking to this Dillworth woman—what's in it for me?"

"Well, Harry, it would be a hell of a story. Especially once we get Colonel Berezovsky and his sister out in the open, if they told their story to you, and only to you. And of course I would be very grateful to you. And so would the *resident*. That might be very useful in the future, wouldn't you agree?"

"I can see that," Whelan said. "But I can't help but wonder why you're being so good to me."

"Because you are not only a very nice fellow, Harry, but the most important journalist I know."

"Oh, bullshit!" Whelan said modestly.

But I probably am *the most important journalist you know.*

Murov took his cell phone from the breast pocket of his suit, opened it, punched buttons, and then put it on the table.

"What's this?" Whelan asked.

"It's what they call a cell phone, Harry."

Whelan took a closer look, and then picked it up.

The telephone was ready to call a party identified as DILLWORTH, E.

"You said you'd want to start by talking to Miss Dillworth," Murov said.

If I push the CALL *button, I'll probably wind up talking to some female Russian spy.*

But what good would that do him?

He pushed the CALL button.

A female voice answered on the third buzz.

"Miss Eleanor Dillworth, please."

"May I ask who's calling?"

"My name is C. Harry Whelan."

"What can I do for you, Mr. Whelan?"

"Do you know who I am, Miss Dillworth?"

"If this is the talking head I see on Wolf News, yes, I do."

"Miss Dillworth, I'm running down a story that a rogue special operator named Castillo stole two Russian defectors from you. Would you care to comment?"

"Where did you hear that?"

"I'd rather not say just now, Miss Dillworth, but if this story is true . . ."

"It's true."

"I'd like to talk to you about it at some length."

"Okay. When and where?"

I have had too much of the Egri Bikavér.

"It's too late tonight. But what about first thing in the morning? Would it be convenient for you to meet me at the Old Ebbitt Grill? Do you know it?"

"What time?"

"Half past eight?"

"See you there, Mr. Whelan."

"How will I recognize you?"

"I'll recognize you. Half past eight."

She hung up.

Whelan closed the cell phone and handed it back to Murov. Murov returned it to his jacket pocket and then put out his hand.

"I presume we have a deal, Harry?" he asked.

Whelan took the hand.

Forty-five minutes later, Sergei Murov laid three one-hundred-dollar bills on the waiter's leather check folder and told him to keep the change.

"Mind if I look at that?" Whelan asked, and picked up the bill.

"They don't give that Egri Bikavér away, do they?" he asked.

"They don't give anything at all away," Murov said.

Whelan slipped the check in his pocket, and followed Murov out of the restaurant.

XII

The driveway of Quarters One was empty as the Chrysler Town & Country minivan that General Allan B. Naylor, Sr., had chosen over a staff car for his official vehicle pulled into it. The vehicle had of course come with a driver, and Naylor was traveling with his senior aide-de-camp, Colonel J. D. Brewer.

"I wonder where the hell she is," Naylor said, making obvious reference to his wife.

"Does she know you're here?" Brewer replied.

"Who knows?" Naylor said as he opened his door. "Can I interest you in a drink? I hate to drink alone."

"Allan's here," Colonel Brewer said, pointing back to the street at a Chevrolet Suburban.

"Offer's still good," Naylor said.

"Offer is accepted."

"You can take off, Tommy," Naylor said to the driver. "I'll see that Colonel Brewer gets home. Don't be late in the morning."

"No, sir. I won't be. Good night, sir. Good night, Colonel."

The two got out of the van and walked up the driveway and entered the house by the kitchen door.

Major Allan B. Naylor, Jr., in khaki trousers and a flowered Hawaiian shirt, was sitting at the kitchen table holding a bottle of Heineken beer.

"Well, if it isn't the *commanding* officer of Headquarters and Headquarters Company," Brewer said.

"With all possible respect, Colonel, sir, go fuck yourself," Allan Junior said.

When Allan Junior had been released from the hospital, mostly recovered from mortar shell wounds suffered in Afghanistan, he had been placed on limited duty and assigned "temporarily" as executive officer of Headquarters and

Headquarters Company, Central Command. It was a housekeeping job and he hated it.

Armor Branch Officer Assignment had asked him where he would like to be assigned when he was taken off the "limited duty" roster. He had requested, he'd said, "any of the following": the 11th Armored Cavalry at Fort Irwin, California, where The Blackhorse now served as "the enemy" in training maneuvers; Fort Knox, Kentucky, the Cavalry/Armor Center; or Fort Hood, Texas, which always had at least one armored division.

When his orders had come, ten days ago, they had named him commanding officer of Headquarters and Headquarters Company, Central Command, and informed him it was at least a two-year assignment.

Brewer was not really offended by Allan Junior's comment. For one thing, he had known the young officer since he was a kid in Germany; he thought of him as almost family. And he really felt sorry for him.

"If you don't watch your mouth, Major, you're liable to find yourself an aide-de-camp. Trust me, that's a much worse assignment."

"Well, Jack, you can go to hell, too," General Naylor said, and then asked, "Allan, where's your mother?"

"She and my wife and my sister and *all* your grandchildren are in Orlando, at Disney World. I am under maternal orders to look after you."

General Allan B. Naylor, Sr., USA, Commanding General, United States Central Command, had four aides-de-camp—a colonel, two lieutenant colonels, and a captain.

They were his personal staff, as opposed to his command staff at Central Command. The latter was headed by General Albert McFadden, USAF, the deputy commander. Under General McFadden were nine general officers— four Army, three Air Force, and two Marine Corps—plus four Navy flag officers—one vice admiral, two rear admirals (upper half), and one rear admiral (lower half), plus enough full colonels, someone had figured out, to fully staff a reinforced infantry platoon if the fortunes of war should make that necessary.

Approximately one-third of these generals, admirals, and colonels was female. All of General Naylor's personal staff were male.

Despite what Senator Homer Johns frequently said—and apparently believed—General Naylor's personal staff did not spend, *at God only knows what cost to the poor taxpayer*, their time catering to the general's personal needs, polishing his insignia, mixing his drinks, shining his shoes, carrying his luggage, peeling his grapes, and myriad other acts, making him feel like the commander of a Praetorian Guard enjoying the especial favor of Emperor Caligula.

Colonel J. D. Brewer, whose lapels had carried the crossed sabers of Cavalry before he exchanged them for the insignia of an aide-de-camp, was in overall charge. One of the lieutenant colonels dealt with General Naylor's relationship with Central Command. The other dealt with General Naylor's relationship with Washington—the Pentagon, the chief of staff, Congress, and most importantly, the White House.

The captain was in charge of getting the general—which meant not only Naylor, but those officers he needed to have at his side, plus the important paperwork he had to have in his briefcase—from where he was to where he had to be. This involved scheduling the Gulfstream, arranging ground transportation and quarters, and ensuring that Naylor never lost communication with either MacDill or Washington.

Jack Brewer and his boss went back together a long time. Brewer had been a second lieutenant in The Blackhorse on the East German–West German border when Naylor had been there as a major. Later, Brewer, as a major, had been the executive officer of a tank battalion in the First Desert War. He had been a promotable light colonel during the Second Desert War, and now he was waiting, more or less patiently, to hear that his name had been sent to Capitol Hill for confirmation by the Senate of his promotion to brigadier general.

It was said, with a great deal of accuracy, that Brewer's rapid rise through the ranks had been the result of the efficiency reports that Naylor had written on him over the years.

"Following your mother's orders," General Naylor said, "you can start looking out for your old man by getting that bottle of Macallan from the bar and fixing Jack and me a drink."

"The Macallan?" Allan Junior asked. "What are we celebrating?"

"Actually, what we're marking is almost the exact opposite of a celebration," Naylor said.

The telephone rang as Allan Junior was walking out of the kitchen to get the single malt. He snatched its handset off the wall.

"Quarters One, Major Naylor, sir."

He listened, then put his hand over the microphone, and turned to his father.

"It's Charley," he said to his father, referring to Captain Charles D. Seward III, his father's junior aide. "He says that Mr. Lammelle is having dinner with

Mr. Festerman and will spend the night with him, rather than in the VIP Quarters. He wants to know what you want him to do."

Bruce L. Festerman was the liaison officer of the Central Intelligence Agency to the United States Central Command.

Naylor walked to his son and took the telephone receiver from him.

"Charley," he ordered, "ask Mr. Lammelle if it would be convenient for him to have you pick him up at half past eight in the morning. If so, drive him slowly to the office. I want to be through with General McNab before he gets there. If that doesn't work, call me back."

When Naylor had returned the telephone to its cradle, Allan Junior said: "The deputy director of the CIA and Scotty McNab. What the hell's going on?"

Colonel Brewer had wanted to ask the same questions, first when Lammelle had been waiting for him and General Naylor at Andrews Air Force Base in Washington, and later at MacDill, when General Naylor had walked into his office and, even before he sat down, had told Sergeant Major Wes Suggins to get General McNab on the horn.

But he hadn't asked. He knew Naylor would tell him what he thought he should know when he thought he needed to know it.

Brewer's natural curiosity—both personal and professional—was not to be satisfied now, either.

"I thought you were fetching the bottle of Macallan," General Naylor said.

"Yes, sir," Allan Junior said. "Coming right up, sir."

The younger Naylor returned with two bottles of Scotch whisky—the single malt Macallan and a bottle of blended Johnnie Walker Red Label. General Naylor's father had taught him—and he had taught his son—that one never took two drinks of really superb Scotch in a row. One drank and savored the superb whisky. A second drink of the superb would be a waste, however, as the alcohol had deadened the tongue to the point where it could not taste the difference between a superb Scotch and an ordinary one—or even a bad one.

General Naylor drank his Macallan without saying a word. When that was gone, he poured a double of the Johnnie Walker, added a couple of ice cubes to his glass, moved the cubes around with his index finger, and then looked up.

"Did either of you see that actor—the guy who usually has a big black mustache—in the movie where he played Eisenhower just before D-Day?"

"Tom Selleck," Brewer said. "*Countdown to D-Day.*"

"Something like that," Naylor said. "Allan?"

"Yeah, I saw it. Good movie."

"Very accurate," Naylor said. "Down to his chain-smoking those Chesterfields. My uncle Tony, who was at SHAEF, said Eisenhower's fingers were stained yellow from the cigarettes."

He took another swallow of his drink, and his son and aide waited for him to go on.

"There was a segment where one of his officers, a two-star, let his mouth run in a restaurant. Do you remember that?"

His son and his aide nodded.

"That was also quite accurately shown in the movie. Uncle Tony knew all the players. The officer was in his cups, in a restaurant, and came close to divulging when the cross-channel invasion would take place. He was overheard, and someone reported him."

"Eisenhower should have had the sonofabitch shot," Allan Junior said. "Instead, they knocked rings and he walked. He didn't even get thrown out of the Army."

"Did you read that line in the Bible that says something about 'Judge not, lest ye be judged'?" General Naylor said. "He was Ike's roommate at the Point."

"What are you saying, Dad? That if that general had gotten his commission from ROTC and/or wasn't Ike's classmate, that would have been different?"

"Would you so callously order your roommate at West Point shot under similar circumstances?"

Allan Junior raised his eyebrows, then said, "I thought about that when I saw the movie. I don't know whether I'd have either one of them shot, but I damn sure wouldn't let either one of them walk. When that two-star put men's lives at risk letting his mouth run away with him, he forfeited his right to be an officer."

"He was reduced to colonel and sent home," General Naylor said.

"And the men whose lives he put at risk were sent to the landing beaches of Normandy. This Long Gray Line we march in, Dad, isn't perfect, and I don't think we should pretend it is."

Allan Junior turned to Colonel Brewer and started to say something.

"Stop right there, Allan," Brewer cut him off. "I'm not going to get in the middle of this."

"I am now facing a somewhat similar, personally distasteful situation," General Naylor said, "involving an officer who also marches in the Long Gray Line, and of whom I'm personally very fond."

His senior aide-de-camp and his son looked at him, waiting for him to continue.

"If I have to say this, this is highly classified, and to go no further," General Naylor said. "Classification, Top Secret, Presidential."

"Which explains why Mr. Lammelle is here?" Brewer asked.

Naylor nodded.

"President Clendennen this afternoon ordered me to locate Lieutenant Colonel C. G. Castillo, Retired, wherever he might be, and to place him under arrest pending investigation of charges which may be laid against him under the Uniform Code of Military Justice."

"What charges?" Allen Junior demanded.

"Mr. Lammelle was similarly ordered by the President this afternoon to accompany me wherever this mission might take us. If, when we find Colonel Castillo, he has two Russian defectors with him, as he most probably does, Lammelle is to take them into custody. It is President Clendennen's intention to return them to the Russians."

"What are the charges someone's laying against Charley?" Allen Junior demanded.

His father did not reply directly. He instead said, "Jack is thoroughly conversant with all the details of our strike on the Congo. How much do you know, Allan?"

"Not very much beyond the Russians and the Iranians were operating a biological weapons lab, and the previous POTUS decided that taking it out made more sense than taking the problem to the UN. If that's correct, then I say, hooray for him."

"What was being made in that laboratory was a substance now known as Congo-X. It is highly dangerous to an almost unimaginable degree. Our leading expert on that sort of thing, a colonel at our biological warfare operation at Fort Detrick, told the previous POTUS—to borrow your nomenclature— that any accident at the Congo laboratory would be infinitely more catastrophic than the nuclear meltdown at Chernobyl was. It is not hard to extrapolate from that what damage would result should this substance be used as a weapon against us.

"It can be fairly said that the previous POTUS took action not a minute too soon."

"Then thank God he had the balls to do it," Allan Junior said.

General Naylor nodded, sipped his Scotch, then said, "Unfortunately, the raid—as massive as it was—apparently did not destroy all the Congo-X. Two quantities of it—packed in what look like blue rubber beer barrels—have turned up. One was sent to Fort Detrick by FedEx from a nonexistent laboratory in Miami. A second was found on our side of the Mexican–U.S. border where the Border Patrol could not miss it. Colonel Hamilton, the expert at Fort Detrick, has confirmed both barrels contained Congo-X.

"The next development was when the Russian *rezident* in their Washington embassy had Lammelle to their compound—they call it their dacha—in Maryland. There he as much admitted that they had sent the Congo-X to Fort Detrick. He then strongly implied that Prime Minister Putin is personally determined to have the two Russians returned to Russia. Putin also, it was implied, holds Castillo personally responsible for the deaths of several SVR officers in various places around the world. He wants Colonel Castillo, too.

"If this is done, the Russians will turn over to us all stocks of Congo-X in their control and offer assurances that no more of it will ever turn up."

"Dad, Clendennen's not actually thinking of caving in, is he? He can't possibly believe the Russians—Putin, specifically—will live up to their promises."

"The President has decided the most prudent course for him to follow is to turn the defectors over to the Russians. He said several times he's always held traitors in the utmost contempt."

"And Charley? Is he going to turn Charley over, too?" Allan Junior asked incredulously.

"I can't believe that he would do so," General Naylor said.

"Did you ask him?"

"No, I didn't ask him. He's the President of the United States."

"So what are you going to do?"

"Follow my orders."

"What are the charges they're bringing against Charley?" Allen Junior asked.

"I don't know."

"But you're going to arrest him anyway?"

"I don't like the tone of your voice."

"And I don't like what I'm hearing here."

"That's not really germane, is it?"

"What I'm hearing is bullshit," Allan Junior pursued.

"That's quite enough, Allan."

"Starting with that Top Secret Presidential classification," Allan Junior went on. "Information is classified to keep it from our enemies. The Russians know all about this. This is classified to keep it off Wolf News, so that Clendennen can cover his political ass."

"I said, enough!"

"Tell me this, Dad: What has Charley done wrong? Exactly what article of the Uniform Code of Military Justice has he violated?"

"Willful disobedience of a lawful order."

"What order was that?'

"When he flew the defectors out of Vienna to Argentina—without any authority to do so—Ambassador Montvale came to me and suggested the best way to deal with the problem was for me to send an officer from Special Operations Command—Charley was then assigned to Special Operations Command and thus subject to its orders—down there and order him to turn the Russians over to the CIA officers Montvale would have with him. I did so. I sent a colonel from Special Operations with Ambassador Montvale. He ordered Charley to turn the Russians over to Montvale. Charley refused to do so."

"Charley was then working for the President," Allan Junior said. "He was not subordinate to Special Operations Command. Your colonel had no authority to order him to do anything."

"Okay, that's it, Allan. I am not going to debate this with you."

Allan Junior stood up, and said, "Good evening, Colonel Brewer. It's always a pleasure to see you, sir."

He walked to the door.

"Where do you think you're going?" General Naylor challenged.

"I'm going to see if I can find Charley, and if I can, I'm going to warn him about what you're trying to do to him."

"Major, you have been advised that what you heard here tonight is classified Top Secret Presidential," General Naylor said, coldly angry.

"So court-martial me. Let's see how Wolf News plays that story."

He walked out of the kitchen and slammed the door closed after him.

After a long moment, General Naylor said, "I don't think he knows where Castillo is any more than we do."

"I hope he doesn't. In his frame of mind, if he finds him, he will tell him."

"Suggestions solicited."

"I think you ought to keep him on a short leash until this is over."

"Particularly since I know the lieutenant colonel promotion board is sitting."

"Has sat. And selected Allan from below the zone. I suspected that was why he was here when we got here; he wanted to tell you."

"Get him back here, Jack," Naylor ordered.

Brewer took a cell phone from his pocket and pushed an auto-dial button.

"Major Naylor," he said twenty seconds later. "This is Colonel Brewer. General Naylor's compliments. It is the general's desire that you attend him immediately. Acknowledge."

He pushed the OFF button.

"Major Naylor is on his way, sir."

"Don't you mean 'Lieutenant Colonel (Designate),' Jack?"

Lieutenant Colonel (Designate) Allan Naylor, Jr., returned to the kitchen of Quarters One two minutes later.

He walked to where his father was sitting, came to attention, saluted, and recited, "Major Naylor reporting to the Commanding General as ordered."

General Naylor glanced at Colonel Brewer, then met his son's eyes.

"Major," he said, "you are attached to my personal staff for an indefinite period. You are not to communicate with Lieutenant Colonel Castillo or anyone connected in any way to him in any way under any circumstances. Neither will you communicate in any way under any circumstances with any sort of media. That is a direct order. Indicate that you understand and intend to comply with that order by saying 'Yes, sir.'"

"Yes, sir."

"You will proceed to your quarters and will remain there until you receive further orders from either myself or Colonel Brewer. You will pack sufficient uniforms and civilian clothing to last for a period of seven days. You will go into no further detail when discussing this with your wife or anyone else than that you will be accompanying me on official business. The foregoing has been a direct order. Indicate that you understand and intend to comply with that order by saying 'Yes, sir.'"

"Yes, sir."

"You are dismissed."

"Yes, sir."

Major Naylor saluted his father, and when it was returned, did an about-face, and marched out of the kitchen.

When General Naylor heard the sound of Allan Junior's Suburban starting, he held up his glass in a toast, and said, "Congratulations on your promotion, son. You've made me very proud of you."

[TWO]
7200 West Boulevard Drive
Alexandria, Virginia
0705 9 February 2007

The convoy of four blackened-window Secret Service GMC Yukons turned off West Boulevard Drive and drove—not without difficulty; four inches of snow had fallen during the night—up the steep drive to the house.

Four men in business suits quickly got out of the first vehicle in line and moved as swiftly as they could through the fresh snow and the drifts of previous snowfalls to the sides and rear of the house.

Three men—Supervisory Special Agent Thomas McGuire, Special Agent Joshua Foster, and Mason Andrews, the assistant secretary of the Department of Homeland Security—got out of the second Yukon and made their way—again not without difficulty; the snow-covered walk was steep—to the front door. McGuire pushed the button for the doorbell. Chimes could be heard.

They waited a full minute. Nothing happened.

McGuire pushed the doorbell again, and again there was no response from within the house.

McGuire took a cell phone from his pocket and punched an auto-dial number.

"With whom am I speaking, please?" he asked a moment later. Then he said, "Mrs. Darby, this is Supervisory Special Agent McGuire of the United States Secret Service. We are at your front door. Will you please open it to us?"

He put the telephone back in his pocket and announced, "She said she'll open the door as quickly as she can."

"She damned well better," Mason Andrews said, brushing snow from his bald spot.

The door opened. Mrs. Julia Darby stood there in her bathrobe. Another woman, also in her bathrobe, stood beside her. To their side stood a man of obvious Asian extraction. The unknown woman in the bathrobe held a cell phone to her face and there was a flash.

Mason Andrews thought: *I'll be goddamned! She just took our picture.*

"Hello, Tom," Mrs. Darby said. "I'm afraid you're wasting your time. We gave at the office."

Andrews stared at her. *What did she say?*

"Mrs. Darby," McGuire said, holding out his credentials for her to see, "this is Secret Service Agent Foster, and this is Mr. Mason Andrews, the assistant secretary of Homeland Security."

"Hello, I'm Julia Darby."

"May we come in?" Mason Andrews asked.

"I don't think so," the Asian man said. "The introduction of Mr. McGuire's credentials implies this is somehow official business of the Secret Service. The Third Circuit Court of Appeals has held that granting law enforcement officials access to a residence constitutes a waiver by the home owner of his or her rights against unlawful search and seizure. We do not wish to waive those rights."

Mason Andrews thought: *Who the fuck is this guy?*

He demanded: "Who are you?"

"My name is David W. Yung, Jr. I am Mrs. Darby's attorney."

"And you're refusing to let us in?"

"That is correct," Two-Gun Yung said. "Unless you have a search warrant, I am on behalf of my client denying you access to these premises."

"We're the Secret Service!" Special Agent Foster announced.

"So Mr. McGuire has said," Two-Gun said. "We are now going to close the door, as all the cold is getting in the house."

"We'll be back with a search warrant!" Assistant Secretary Andrews announced as the door closed in his face.

"I don't believe that!" Assistant Secretary Andrews said in the front seat of the Yukon. He mopped at the melting snow on his bald spot with a handkerchief. "Absolutely incredible! We should have just pushed that little Jap out of the way and grabbed Darby."

"Unfortunately, Mr. Secretary, the lawyer was right. Without a search warrant, we have no right to enter those premises," McGuire said.

"Well, we'll get a goddamned search warrant! Where does one get a goddamned search warrant at . . ." He looked at his watch. "Quarter after seven in the morning?"

"That may be difficult, Mr. Secretary," McGuire said. "In order to get a search warrant, you have to convince a judge that you have good and sufficient reason to believe that illegal activity is taking place on a certain premises, or that a fugitive is evading due process of law—in other words, arrest—on said premises."

"Goddamn it, we know that Darby is in there! We know he entered the country in Miami and flew here, and your own goddamned agents reported they saw him entering that house. What else do we need, for Christ's sake?"

"Sir, we have no reason to believe that any activity violating federal law is taking place in the house. And Mr. Darby is not a fugitive; no warrants have been issued for his arrest on any charge."

"You're telling me there's not a goddamned thing we can do? I don't believe this."

"Sir, what I hoped would happen when we came here was that Mrs. Darby, or perhaps Mr. Darby himself—we've been friends for years—would invite us into the house and we could discuss the location of Colonel Castillo amicably. If you want to, I can have another shot at that."

"Jesus Christ!"

"Other than that, sir, I don't know what else to tell you."

"Just stand there in the door, please, Mr. Secretary," Two-Gun Yung said ten minutes later.

There were now two photographers inside the house, the woman who had used the photographing capability of her cellular telephone earlier, and a man now holding what looked like a professional-grade video camera.

Andrews stood in the door.

"Ready, Harold?" Two-Gun asked.

"Lights, action, camera!" Harold replied, intentionally botching the sequence.

"Mr. Secretary, please identify yourself and give us the date and time."

Andrews complied.

"Now, repeat after me, please: 'I make the following statement voluntarily and without mental reservation of any kind.'"

Andrews did so.

"I acknowledge that I have informed Mrs. Julia Darby that by allowing me and Mr. McGuire of the Secret Service into her home, a compassionate gesture to get us out of the cold and snow, she in no way gives up her rights against unlawful search and seizure as provided by the U.S. Constitution—"

"Go slowly," Andrews interrupted. "I can't remember all that."

"We'll try it again. 'I acknowledge that I . . .'"

"'. . . and further that anything said in conversation by anyone here today will not be used in any court of law for any purpose,'" Two-Gun finally concluded.

With some obvious effort, Andrews repeated that.

"Is that it, Counselor?" Mrs. Darby then asked.

"It will be as soon as Harold sends a copy of that digital recording to that great file room in the sky," Two-Gun replied.

"Consider it done," Harold replied.

"Why don't we all go in the living room and have a cup of coffee while Dianne makes breakfast?" Julia Darby suggested.

"Hello, Tom," Alex Darby said, putting out his hand. "Long time no see."

"How are you, Alex?" McGuire replied. "Alex, this is my boss, Assistant Secretary of Homeland Security Mason Andrews."

"How do you do?" Darby said.

"You're a hard man to find, Mr. Darby."

"I guess that would depend on who's looking for me," Darby said.

"A lot of people are looking for you, including Ambassador Montvale."

"Whatever would make Ambassador Montvale look for me?"

"The President of the United States sent him to find you, Mr. Darby. Right now, he's in Ushuaia."

"Whatever for? I mean, why is he looking for me in Ushuaia, of all places?"

"Oh, Tom," Julia Darby said. "I was kidding you about that."

"Kidding him about what?" Darby asked his wife.

"I told him you were probably down there with your girlfriend," Julia said. "I never for a moment thought he would take me seriously. Especially the girlfriend part."

Darby looked at McGuire. "Yeah, I'm a little long in the tooth for that sort of thing, Tom."

Mason Andrews said, "There is reason to believe that you know where Colonel Dmitri Berezovsky, Lieutenant Colonel Svetlana Alekseeva, and Lieutenant Colonel Carlos G. Castillo are."

"As I think you know, Mr. Andrews," Darby replied, "Colonel Castillo was ordered by the President—the late President, not Mr. Clendennen—to fall off the face of the earth and never be seen again. I believe that Colonel Castillo is obeying those orders."

"You're telling me you don't know where he is—where the Russians are?"

"I didn't say that. What I said was that I believe Colonel Castillo has obeyed the order from the President to disappear."

"Then you do know where he is? Where the Russian defectors are?"

"I didn't say that, either."

"Are you aware that it's a felony, Mr. Darby, to lie to, or mislead, a federal officer?"

"Mr. Andrews, a point of order," Two-Gun said. "One, right now, you're not a federal officer, but rather simply someone whom Mrs. Darby has compassionately allowed to warm himself in her house. Two, if Mr. Darby were ever to be interviewed by any federal officer, he would, on advice of counsel, refuse to an-swer any questions put to him that either might tend to incriminate him, or cause him to violate any of the several oaths he took as an officer of the Clandes-tine Service of the CIA to never divulge in his lifetime anything he learned in the performance of those duties."

Mason Andrews looked between Two-Gun and the Darbys, then an-nounced, "I can see that I'm wasting my time here. Let's go, McGuire."

"But you haven't had any breakfast," Julia Darby said. "Dianne's making a Spanish omelet."

"And breakfast is the most important meal of the day," Two-Gun offered. "Haven't you heard that, Mr. Secretary?"

Andrews glared at him but didn't respond.

"And one more thing, Mr. Andrews," Two-Gun said. "Those Secret Service agents of yours who have been watching the house?"

"What about them?"

"The right of a governmental agency to surveille does not carry with it any right to trespass. The next time I see one of them on this property, I'm going to call the Alexandria police and charge them with trespass. And if they are indeed Secret Service agents, since you and I have had this little chat, that would con-stitute trespass after warning, which is a felony."

Andrews, his face white, marched toward the front door, calling over his shoulder, "Goddamn it, McGuire, I said let's go."

In the Yukon, Andrews slammed the door shut and turned to McGuire.

"As of this minute, McGuire, you're placed on administrative leave. It is my intention to have you separated from the Secret Service and I think you know why."

"I haven't a clue, Mr. Secretary."

"Goddamn it! Whose side are you on, anyway? You enjoyed watching those bastards humiliate me."

"Mr. Secretary, I took an oath to defend the Constitution against all ene-mies foreign and domestic. I have done so to the best of my ability."

"Sending the director of National Intelligence on a wild-goose chase to Ushuaia is your idea of defending the Constitution? Jesus H. Christ!"

"I told Ambassador Montvale that Mrs. Darby said Mr. Darby might be there. That's all."

"You'd better be prepared to tell a grand jury that Mrs. Darby did just that. Lying to or making a misrepresentation to a federal officer is a felony. Your pal is going to jail, McGuire, and if I can figure out some way to get you before a grand jury for lying to Ambassador Montvale, I will."

"Oh, come on, Andrews. You know Montvale almost as well as I do. Can you really imagine the Great Charles M. getting up in a courtroom and testifying under oath that one of his underlings sent him on a wild-goose chase anywhere? Much less all the way to the bottom of the world? And that doesn't even touch on the question of who he was looking for and why."

Secretary Andrews considered that for thirty seconds.

"Get out of the car, you sonofabitch! Walk back to Washington!"

McGuire got out of the Yukon.

But instead of walking back to Washington, he went to the door of the house, rang the bell, and when the lady of the house answered, asked if there was any Spanish omelet left to feed someone who had just lost his job.

[THREE]
Office of the Commanding General
United States Army Central Command
MacDill Air Force Base
Tampa, Florida
0730 9 February 2007

"General, General McNab is here," Colonel J. D. Brewer announced at Naylor's office door.

"Ask the general to come in, please," Naylor said.

McNab marched into the office, stopped six feet from Naylor's desk, raised his right hand to his temple, and said, "Good morning, General. Thank you for receiving me."

McNab was wearing what was officially the Army Service Uniform but was commonly referred to as "dress blues." The breast of his tunic was heavy with ribbons and devices showing his military qualifications, including a Combat Infantry Badge topped with circled stars indicating that it was the sixth award; a Master Parachutist's wings; seven other parachute wings from various foreign armies; and the Navy SEAL qualification badge, commonly called "The Budweiser." The three silver stars of a lieutenant general gleamed on his epaulets.

Naylor was wearing a camouflage-patterned sandy-colored baggy uniform called Desert Battle Dress Uniform. On it was sewn the insignia of Central Command, the legend US ARMY, a name tag reading NAYLOR, and, attached with

Velcro to the button line of his jacket, a strip with four embroidered black (called "subdued") stars, the insignia of his rank.

Naylor took his time before returning the salute, and after McNab had dropped his hand, took his time again before saying, "You may stand at ease, General. Please take a seat."

"Thank you, sir," McNab said as he settled into one of the two leather armchairs before the desk. "I trust the general is well?"

"Just so we understand one another, General, there was an implication you made just now that you were invited here. You were ordered here. There is a difference I think you should keep in mind."

"Yes, sir. Permission to speak, General?"

"Permission granted."

"Sir, the general errs. Sir, the general does not have the authority to issue orders to me."

Naylor blurted, "That's what you think, McNab!"

"It's what the chief of staff thinks, General. I telephoned him yesterday following your telephone call. I thought perhaps my status—or your status—had changed and I hadn't been notified. The chief of staff said there was no change in your status or mine. We are both commanders of units directly subordinate to Headquarters, U.S. Army. The only officer who can give orders to either of us is the chief of staff."

"You called the chief of staff?" Naylor asked incredulously.

"Yes, sir. And the chief suggested that a way out of this little dilemma would be for me to make a courtesy call on you. Which is what I'm doing now, General."

Naylor thought: *You sonofabitch!*

McNab went on: "I got a look at the lieutenant colonel's promotion list on the way down here, General. And saw that Allan has been selected, below the zone. May I offer my congratulations?"

"Thank you."

"How may I assist the general, now that I'm here?"

"Prefacing this by stating I am acting at the direct order of the President, you can tell me where I can find Lieutenant Colonel Carlos G. Castillo."

"The chief of staff didn't mention that you were working for the President, General. Perhaps he had reasons he did not elect to share with me."

"Are you questioning my word, General?"

"No, sir. If the general tells me the general is working at the direct order of the President, I will of course take the general's word."

"Where can I find Castillo, General?"

"I have no idea, General."

"You have no idea?"

"Are you questioning my word, General?"

"No."

"Good."

"What can you tell me, General, about Castillo?" Naylor asked.

"You mean about how the President wants to make a human sacrifice of him to the Russians?"

"What did you say?"

"When I came here, I held the naïve hope that you were going to close the door, and then say, 'You may find this hard to believe, but the President wants to turn our Charley over to Putin, and what are we going to do about it?' How foolish of me."

"You don't know that President Clendennen intends to do that," Naylor said.

"Do you *know* he doesn't? Or didn't he tell you that Murov told Frank Lammelle that Putin wants the Russians *and Charley*?"

"How do you know about that?"

McNab met Naylor's eyes, and said, "You don't really expect me to answer that, do you, Allan?" After a long moment, he added, "Yeah, now that I think about it, I think you do."

"What I *do* know, General—"

"Haven't we played your silly little game long enough, Allan?"

"What silly game is that, General?"

"You sitting there in that ridiculous desert costume—as if you expect the Castros or Hugo Chávez to start dropping parachutists on Tampa Bay in the next ten minutes—pretending to be a soldier when all you are is a uniformed flunky carrying out the orders—which you damned well know are illegal—of a political hack who would turn his mother over to Putin if he thought it would get him reelected."

"You are speaking, General, of the President, the commander in chief."

"Did you get it all, or should I say it again?"

"What I should do is place you under arrest!"

"How did you get to be a four-star general—never mind, I know—without learning you never should issue an order—or carry one out—without considering what the secondary effects will be?"

"Stand up and come to attention, General!" Naylor ordered.

McNab crossed his legs, shook his head, and chuckled.

"Goddamn you!" Naylor flared. "I said, come to attention!"

"For example, Allan," McNab said calmly as he took a cigar case from an inside pocket, "one of the thoughts that occurred to me when I heard what the bastard was up to was to take him out. I thought that through and realized that would cause more damage to the country than it would do good. Since we presently don't have a Vice President, the order of succession would put the Speaker of the House in the Oval Office, and from what I've seen, he's as much an idiot as Clendennen is.

"Anyway, I took an oath to defend the Constitution, and unfortunately there's nothing in that that says you can shoot the President, even if the bastard deserves it, as this one clearly does."

"McNab, you're out of your mind!"

"I also considered taking this story to that red-headed guy on Wolf News. What's his name? Oh, yeah . . ."

He paused as he bit the end off a long, thin, black cigar and then carefully lit it.

"You can't smoke in here," Naylor said. "You can't smoke in any government building."

Naylor stared at McNab and thought: *He's sitting here calmly discussing the pros and cons of assassinating the President of the United States, and I'm scolding him for smoking?*

What the hell is the matter with me?

What I should do is push the button for the sergeant major, and when he and Jack Brewer come in, say, "I have placed General McNab under arrest. Please escort the general to the visiting senior officers' quarters and hold him there."

And then what do I do?

Call the chief of staff and tell him?

Tell him what?

McNab has friends. Somebody who was there in the Oval Office when the President gave me this mission not only told him exactly what was said, but lost no time in telling him.

Is there a plot against the President? Is that what this is all about?

That's a credible possibility.

McNab is entirely capable of being involved in something like a coup d'état.

So do I go to the chief of staff with that? Or the President?

With what? All I have is suspicions.

What I have to do is find out as much as I can from the sonofabitch!

McNab blew a smoke ring.

"I always have trouble with names," McNab said. "Okay! I got it! His name is Andy McClarren and the show is called *The Straight Scoop*. Are you familiar with it?"

Naylor thought: *I'm not going to let him drag me into a discussion.*

When it became evident that Naylor wasn't going to reply, McNab went on: "You really should watch it, Allan. They say it's the most watched show on television. You might learn something from it.

"Anyway, as soon as I thought that through, I realized that when the dust had settled, all that that would accomplish would be Congress considering impeaching the sonofabitch, and that would tell the world what an idiot we have in the White House, which wouldn't do the country any good, and even if the impeachment went through, which would take a lot of time, all we'd be doing is replacing one idiot with another.

"So I decided to put Andy McClarren on the back burner. I may have to go that route, but I'd rather not."

"So, then what are your intentions, General?"

And I will be very surprised if you don't tell me them in sufficient detail to hang yourself, you egotistical maniac!

"Well, the first thing, obviously, is to find Charley and see what he wants to do."

"To see what *he* wants to do?" Naylor blurted incredulously.

"By now, I'm sure, Charley knows people are looking for him and his girl-friend—"

"His *girlfriend*?"

"Her name is Svetlana. They call her 'Sweaty.' Real beauty. Dark red hair, built like a brick . . . outdoor sanitary facility."

"You've lost me, McNab. What does this woman have to do with any of this?"

"She's one of the defectors Putin wants back. She was a light colonel in the SVR. The other one—he was a full bird—is her brother."

"And Castillo is . . . emotionally involved with her?"

"Think Romeo and Juliet, Allan."

"Has he lost his mind?"

"His heart, certainly. His mind, I don't think so. If Charley doesn't want to be found, finding him is going to be difficult. And if you think he's going to pop to attention, salute, and load himself and his girlfriend and her brother on an airplane en route to Moscow, think again."

"He's a retired officer. Subject to recall."

"He's also Karl Wilhelm von und zu Gossinger, a German national, who owns a bunch of newspapers. I wonder if our commander in chief had that in mind when he told you to go fetch him. What is it the politicians say? 'Never get in an argument with somebody who buys ink by the barrel.'

"Let's say that Charley and the Russians are in Germany. In his house in Fulda, eating knockwurst and drinking beer, not a care in the world, as Charley/Karl is a German citizen, and the Russians have been granted political asylum by the German Republic in exchange for their cooperation in certain intelligence matters."

"Is that what he's done?" Naylor asked.

"I don't know. I'm sure he's considered it. But I hope he doesn't have to. That would really piss Putin off, and there would be bodies all over the place as Putin's SVR assassins tried to whack Charley's girlfriend and her brother for traitorously spilling the beans about the SVR to the Krauts, and Charley's pals took them out. Several of Charley's pals, as I'm sure you heard, are very good at taking out officers of the SVR."

"And you don't think Putin knows these Russians told us about the bio-warfare laboratory in the Congo?" Naylor exploded. "Don't you think Putin considers that a traitorous act?"

McNab took a moment to form his reply, then said, "One: President Putin stood in the well of the UN, you will recall, and told the whole world the Russians knew nothing, absolutely nothing, about the so-called Fish Farm. Two: As the CIA has never had the Russians under their benevolent control, the Russians have not spilled the beans about the Fish Farm to us, either. How could they? The Russians knew absolutely nothing about it."

"They know the Russians told us. That's why they want them back."

"That's why they want Charley, too. That's what this whole thing is all about. That's why I want to ask Charley what he wants to do about all this. Maybe he's got some ideas. He's always been very resourceful, Allan, you know that."

"What makes you think you can find him?"

"That will take me a couple of days. First, I have to find someone who knows and who trusts me. I can think of several people who are in that category."

Naylor thought: *What I should do now, McNab, is tell the President that you know how to get in contact with Castillo and have the President order you to find him.*

Naylor said: "General, since you tell me that you believe you know how to locate Colonel Castillo and the Russian defectors, I feel duty-bound to inform the President of that fact."

"If you did that, Allan, this whole sordid story would be on *The Straight Scoop* with—what's his name again?—with Andy McClarren tonight."

"You could be held incommunicado—"

"That would last only until Andy McClarren, or C. Harry Whelan, Jr., heard about it. And they would."

"—and ordered not to discuss this with the press or anyone else. You are not immune to the provisions of the Uniform Code of Military Justice, General, and it would behoove you to keep that in mind."

"We took an oath—the day we threw our hats in the air so long ago—to obey the lawful orders of officers appointed over us. I can't understand how you think an order making a human sacrifice of a fellow officer can possibly be considered legal."

"Perhaps a general court-martial would determine that."

McNab stood up. He said, "Well, it's been a pleasure talking to you, General. We'll have to do this more often."

"I didn't give you permission to leave, General."

McNab ignored him. He said, "What I'm going to do is go find Charley and see what he wants to do. You do what you want, Allan. But if you're smart you'll mark time until I get back to you. Which reminds me: I'm going to leave a GS-Fifteen civilian with you. His name is Vic D'Allessando, and before he was a GS-Fifteen, he was a CWO-Five, and before that, he was a sergeant major. Some people think he's associated with Gray Fox, but I can't comment on that, as—as I'm sure you know—everything connected with Gray Fox is classified.

"Vic has a radio which will allow him to stay in touch with me no matter where I am. I will keep him posted on how I'm doing in finding Charley, and he will tell you. Vic will also keep me posted on your location, and if you leave MacDill, or Lammelle does, before I tell you that you can, Plan A—that's telling Andy McClarren—will kick in. I don't think you want that to happen."

"You think you can sit in my office and tell me what to do? Goddamn you, McNab!"

"Of course not. But what I can do is tell you what's going to happen if you elect to do certain things. And in *that* regard, if Vic D'Allessando suddenly becomes not available to me or other people on that net, Plan A—McClarren— will automatically kick in."

McNab put on his green beret, popped to attention, and saluted.

He did not wait for Naylor to return it, but immediately did an about-face movement, and marched out of his office.

Naylor knew that Franklin Lammelle, the deputy director of the CIA, was in his outer office when he heard McNab say, "Well, hello, Frank. Whatever brings you to beautiful Tampa Bay?"

The automatic door closer shut off any reply Lammelle might have made.

The door opened thirty seconds later, and Colonel Jack Brewer put his head in.

"General, Mr. Lammelle is here."

"Ask him to come in, please," Naylor said.

"And Major Naylor and a man from Global Communications, who says he has an appointment."

"Ask them to wait, but you come in, please, Colonel."

Naylor got up from behind his desk and met Lammelle as he came through the door.

"Good morning, General," Lammelle said. "Can I ask what Scotty McNab was doing here? Is he going to be working with us, I hope, on this?"

"Actually, Mr. Lammelle, I've just about decided I made a terrible mistake vis-à-vis General McNab."

"Excuse me?"

"What I am now convinced I should have done was place him under arrest."

"Excuse me?"

"Let me tell you what just happened, and then you tell me what you think I should have done—should do—about it."

Five minutes later, Frank Lammelle said, "General, I'm in no position to comment upon, much less judge, your differences with General McNab vis-à-vis insubordination, that sort of thing, but—and you may not like hearing this— it looks to me that instead of being a problem, McNab may be the answer to ours."

"I don't see that," Naylor said.

"Our problem is that we have been charged with locating Colonel Castillo, and through him, to take control of the two Russians. And we don't know where any of them are."

"A subparagraph of 'facts bearing on the problem' there, it seems to me," Naylor said, "would be 'how to transport the Russian defectors and/or Castillo from where we find them to where they have to go.' Or words to that effect. And where do they go, to add that factor?"

"Castillo," Lammelle replied, "is going to have to be transported to either Washington, or, perhaps, some military base in the United States. The Russians only have to be transported someplace where they can be turned over to the SVR. I think that will probably mean that we'll have to transport them to some place served by Aeroflot. We turn them over at the airport to officers of the SVR, who will then repatriate them."

Naylor glanced at Colonel Jack Brewer, then looked at Lammelle, and said, "And how are we going to do that? Am I supposed to take soldiers with me? Soldiers for that sort of thing come from Special Operations, the Delta Force, or Gray Fox. Which of course are commanded by General McNab."

"General, since eight o'clock this morning, a Gulfstream V has been sitting at Saint Petersburg–Clearwater International. It is registered to a CIA asset—a chicken-packing company in Des Moines, Iowa. I was amazed to learn how much chicken the United States exports.

"Anyway, the plane will attract no undue attention. The crew are CIA. The aircraft is equipped with the very latest—and I mean the very latest—avionics that the AFC Corporation has for sale. All sorts of bells and whistles. Communication with that airplane and Langley is available wherever that airplane is—on the ground or in the air, anywhere in the world. That airplane is going to follow you and me no matter where General McNab leads us. There are four Clandestine Service officers aboard. Once we lay eyes on Colonel Castillo and the Russians, transporting them wherever they have to go will pose no problems at all."

"What if they resist?" Colonel Brewer asked.

"The officers are equipped with the very latest nonlethal weaponry—and the other kind as well, of course. What the nonlethal weaponry provides, in a pistol about the size of a Glock, are six darts with a range of about fifty feet. Anyone struck with one of these darts will lose consciousness in fifteen seconds or less. They will regain consciousness without intervention in about two hours. They can be brought back immediately by injection."

"Fascinating," General Naylor said. "Then, if I understand you, Mr. Lammelle, it is your recommendation that we sit tight and do nothing while we wait for General McNab to find Castillo and the Russians?"

"That is my recommendation, General."

Naylor looked at his aide-de-camp, and said, "You see anything wrong with that, Jack?"

Colonel Jack Brewer said, "No, sir. It makes a lot of sense to me."

"And what about the man McNab left here?" Naylor asked.

"He's very good," Lammelle said. "I've known Vic D'Allessando for a long time. He's been around Delta Force and Gray Fox for years."

"Which tends to suggest that his greatest loyalty may be to General McNab," General Naylor said.

"Well, I suggest we treat him with respect and as a member of the team," Lammelle said. He stopped and opened his briefcase. "And if he shows any suggestion of being about to interfere with our mission, General . . ." He paused and took from the briefcase what looked like a Glock semiautomatic pistol with a grossly swollen slide. He aimed it at a leather couch and pulled the trigger. There was an almost inaudible *psssst* sound. ". . . in fifteen seconds or less, General, your couch will be sound asleep."

"I will be damned," Naylor said, and went to the couch, found the dart, and pulled it free. He held it up for a better look, and then held it against his pinkie finger. It was about as long, and perhaps half as thick.

"Amazing," General Naylor said, then looked at Brewer. "Can you think of anything else, Jack?"

"Yes, sir," Brewer said. "Lieutenant Colonel (Designate) Naylor."

"What about him?" Lammelle asked.

Naylor told him.

"Just to be sure, General," Lammelle then said, "I suggest you maintain the current close personal supervision. I'm frankly uncomfortable, taking into consideration what you've told me, with the thought of leaving him here when we go off wherever we're going. There's no telling . . ."

"I agree. Where we go, Allan Junior goes," General Naylor said.

"May I see that dart, General?" Colonel Brewer asked.

Naylor handed it to him.

XIII

[ONE]
The President's Study
The White House
1600 Pennsylvania Avenue, N.W.
Washington, D.C.
0929 9 February 2007

Assistant Secretary of Homeland Security Mason Andrews was more than a little nervous when he entered the President's study with Frederick P. Palmer, the United States attorney general.

He was fully aware that he was the *assistant* secretary of Homeland Security and that *the* secretary should be dealing with the President on this matter. Andrews had the previous evening telephoned *the* secretary, who was in Chicago, brought her up to speed, and asked her for direction. She had agreed with him that it was a very delicate area, and that proceeding carefully was obviously necessary. She said she'd like to sleep on the problem, and that he should call her back in the morning, say at about nine, before his nine-thirty appointment with the President.

When he had done so, he had been informed that the secretary was not available at the moment; something—not specified, but important—had come up and the secretary simply was not available.

Mr. Andrews then had had an unkind thought.

That bitch is covering her fat ass by staying out of the line of fire.

Again.

But, fully aware that one does not make an appointment on an urgent matter with the President of the United States and then break it, he was in the outer office at nine-twenty with the very-reluctant-to-be-there attorney general. It had been necessary to tell the attorney general that if the AG couldn't find time in his schedule for the meeting, he would tell the President just that.

"All right, Andrews," President Clendennen greeted them. "Make it quick."

"Mr. Darby has been located, Mr. President," Andrews announced.

"Ambassador Montvale was told to keep me posted. Why am I hearing this from you?"

"Sir, I don't believe Ambassador Montvale knows about this."

"I'm confused. I don't like to be confused. Why don't you start at the god-damn beginning, Andrews? Maybe that way . . ."

"Yes, Mr. President. Sir, at half past four yesterday, Immigration, in response to the LDND order, notified the Secret Service that Mr. Darby had entered the United States—"

"In response to the what?" the President interrupted.

"The LDND order. That means 'locate, do not detain.'"

"And that means?"

"When the subject of an LDND order is located by any agency, that agency notifies the agency that issued the order—in this case, the Secret Service— where and under what circumstances the subject was located. In this case, as I said, Immigration yesterday afternoon notified the Secret Service that Alexander Darby had arrived in Miami on a flight from Panama."

"Cut to the chase, Andrews. And what did Darby have to say about Castillo and the Russians?"

"Nothing, sir."

"He was arrested, right? He's in custody?"

"No, sir."

"You're telling me the Immigration people had this guy, and then he got away? My God!"

"Sir, there never has been a *warrant* out on Mr. Darby—just the LDND order."

"What's the point in locating somebody and then not arresting him?"

"Sir, even if there is an arrest warrant," the attorney general explained, "and in this case no warrant has been issued, it's sometimes useful to see where the subject goes, and to whom he talks."

"Well, where did Darby go, and who did he talk to?"

"He flew here, sir, into Reagan National," Andrews said. "By that time, the Secret Service was on him, and they followed him to a residence at 7200 West Boulevard Drive in Alexandria. That site, sir, was already under Secret Service surveillance. It has been since the LDND order was issued. It is owned by Colonel Castillo."

"Don't tell me Castillo has been there, right under the nose of the Secret Service, all the time?"

"No, sir. We don't believe that he is."

"So, when you finally found out where this Darby character is, and who he was talking to, what did he say when you asked him where Castillo and the Russians are?"

"What happened at that point," Andrews began, "was that Supervisory Special Agent McGuire—"

"I know Tom," the President interrupted. "Good man, if it's the same guy. Used to be on the presidential protection detail, right?"

"Yes, sir. That's the man. Sir, McGuire notified me about Darby's location, and first thing this morning, a minute or two after seven, I was at the door—"

"He notified you last night! Why didn't you go over there last night?" the President demanded.

"It was after midnight, Mr. President."

"So what?"

"Perhaps you're right, Mr. President. I deferred to Mr. McGuire's judgment. Now I realize that was probably a mistake, too."

"Okay, so there you were—was McGuire with you . . . ?"

"Yes, sir."

". . . at the door of this house at seven in the morning. Then what happened?"

"At first, Mr. President, they wouldn't even let us in. They had a lawyer, a Japanese gentleman, who said his name was Yung—"

"Sir," the attorney general interjected, "I think there is a very good chance that this lawyer is a former FBI special agent named David W. Yung, Jr., who is also under a LDND order. And he's of Chinese, not Japanese, ancestry—"

"Why are we looking for this ex–FBI agent-slash-lawyer of some kind of *Oriental* ancestry?" the President interrupted. "And what's that got to do with anything?"

"He was one of Castillo's men in OOA, Mr. President," the attorney general said.

"So, what happened at the door?" the President asked.

"We identified ourselves, and asked if we could come in. Yung said not without a search warrant. He also said that if they did let us in, it would constitute a waiver of the owner's rights against unlawful search, and they weren't going to do that."

"It has to be Yung," the attorney general thought aloud. "An FBI agent, lawyer or not, would know about that decision of the Third Circuit Court of Appeals."

"So you didn't get in. Then what?" the President said.

"We got in, sir," Andrews said. "After I promised that I understood we were being admitted only as a compassionate gesture on the part of Mrs. Darby to get us out of the snow and the cold, and that she had not waived any of her rights vis-à-vis unlawful search and seizure. And they filmed us acknowledging that, sir."

"They *filmed* you?" the President asked incredulously.

"Yes, sir. There was another man there with what looked to me like a professional movie camera."

"And *then*? Jesus Christ, cut to the goddamned chase!"

"Mr. Darby was in the kitchen, sir," Andrews said.

"And did you ask him if he knew where Colonel Castillo and the two Russians are, and if you did, what did he say?"

"He was evasive, sir. And the lawyer said that if Mr. Darby found himself being interrogated by a federal officer, he would advise him, as his lawyer, not to answer any questions the answers to which might tend to either incriminate him, or cause him to violate the CIA secrecy laws which forbid him to ever disclose anything he learned while he was an officer of the Clandestine Service."

"Mr. President, I'm afraid we're not going to learn much from Mr. Darby," the attorney general said.

"I was beginning to suspect that," the President said, thickly sarcastic.

"There is one thing we can do, Mr. President," Andrews said.

"What's that?"

"We can squeeze Mrs. Darby. When she told McGuire her husband was in Ushuaia with his girlfriend, information on which Ambassador Montvale based his decision to go to Ushuaia, she had invited McGuire into her home. She had waived her rights when she did so. Giving false information to a federal officer is a felony."

The President considered that a long moment.

Then he picked up his telephone and said, "Come in here."

A secretary and a Secret Service agent appeared almost immediately.

"Are we in touch with Ambassador Montvale?"

"Yes, sir," the Secret Service agent said. "He's in Ushuaia, Argentina. There's a communications radio in his Gulfstream III."

"Send the ambassador a message, please," the President said. "'Mr. Darby is in Alexandria, Virginia. You can come home now, repeat, now.'"

"Yes, sir," the secretary said. "Is that all of it, Mr. President?"

"That's all of it. Get that right out, please."

"Yes, Mr. President," the Secret Service agent said.

When they had left, closing the door behind them, the President turned to Mason Andrews.

"You heard that, Andrews?"

"Yes, sir."

"If you think, when the ambassador gets back here, that Wolf News is going to take a picture of him in a courtroom, with his hand on a Bible, swearing before God and the world that he—*my* director of National Intelligence—went halfway around the world on *my orders* as commander in chief on the word of a housewife having her little joke at our expense, you're even more incredibly stupid than you showed you were this morning, Andrews."

"Now get the fuck out of the goddamned Oval Office and never come back!"

[TWO]
1155 9 February 2007

Word had quickly spread among the inner circle of White House functionaries that President Clendennen's current rage was one that would go down in history. So it was with a certain trepidation that White House Press Secretary John David "Jack" Parker stood at the door of the President's study and waited for permission to enter.

It was almost a minute in coming, but finally President Clendennen signaled with his fingers for Parker to enter.

"And what bad news are you bringing, Porky?" Clendennen asked.

"I'm afraid it's not good news, Mr. President."

"Why doesn't that surprise me?" Clendennen asked rhetorically. "Are you aware of what happened in here this morning?"

"No, sir. I understand the attorney general and Assistant Secretary Andrews asked for an appointment, but—"

"You know where Ambassador Montvale is?"

"In Argentina."

"The stupid sonofabitch! Director of National Intelligence, my ass. His title should be Director of National Stupidity. He'd damned well better be on his way back here."

"I'm afraid, Mr. President, that I don't understand."

The President related what had transpired earlier in his office, ending his narration with a question: "How would you describe, Porky, Ambassador Stupid standing up in court, with Wolf News filming him, and swearing on a Bible that he went to some goddamn place I can't pronounce in Argentina on my orders looking for a man who was just across the Potomac in Alexandria?"

Parker took a deep breath before replying.

"Sir, I would describe that as a public relations disaster."

"You're goddamn right it would be. But what could be worse than that?"

"Excuse me, sir?"

"How about some press sonofabitch—C. Harry Whelan, Jr., for example—asking Ambassador Stupid why he was looking for this Darby guy in the first place. That would be worse, Porky. And Ambassador Stupid would be stupid enough to tell him."

"Speaking of Mr. Whelan, sir . . ."

"Dare I hope he's been run over by a truck?"

"Mr. Whelan came to see me just now, sir."

"Close your mouth and put your hand on your wallet, Porky. I'm afraid to ask why."

"Sir, Mr. Whelan said he was about to publish this, and wanted to give us a chance to correct any errors he might have made before he did."

Parker handed the President a sheet of paper.

Clendennen snatched it, and read:

BY C. HARRY WHELAN, JR.
COPYRIGHT 2007
WORLDWIDE RIGHTS RESERVED

SLUG: WHITE HOUSE LAUNCHED STRIKE ON IRANIAN BIOLOGICAL
WARFARE FACTORY IN CONGO BASED ON INFORMATION FROM
RUSSIAN DEFECTORS IN HANDS OF SECRET, POSSIBLY ILLEGAL,
"PRIVATE CIA" CONTROLLED BY PRESIDENT

WASHINGTON—(INSERT DATE) THIS REPORTER HAS LEARNED THAT
THE STRIKE ON THE ALLEGED IRANIAN BIOLOGICAL WARFARE
LABORATORY IN THE CONGO WAS BASED SOLELY ON INFORMATION
GATHERED BY A SUPER-SECRET INTELLIGENCE AGENCY
REPORTING DIRECTLY TO THE PRESIDENT.

THE ORGANIZATION, HIDDEN INSIDE THE DEPARTMENT OF
HOMELAND SECURITY AND CALLED THE OFFICE OF
ORGANIZATIONAL ANALYSIS, WAS HEADED BY A LEGENDARY
ARMY SPECIAL FORCES OFFICER, LIEUTENANT COLONEL C. G.
CASTILLO, AND STAFFED WITH PERSONNEL, SOME DESCRIBED
BY INTELLIGENCE INSIDERS AS "UNSAVORY," FROM THE CIA,
THE FBI, AND THE ARMED FORCES.

THE ORGANIZATION APPARENTLY OPERATED WITHOUT
CONGRESSIONAL OVERSIGHT, DID NOT ANSWER TO THE DIRECTOR
OF NATIONAL INTELLIGENCE, NOR MAINTAIN LIAISON WITH
OTHER INTELLIGENCE AGENCIES, AND WAS APPARENTLY FUNDED
BY THE PRESIDENT'S "CONFIDENTIAL FUNDS."

WHEN IT APPEARED TO THE OOA THAT THE CIA WAS ABOUT TO
BUNGLE THEIR ATTEMPT TO CAUSE THE DEFECTION OF TWO VERY
SENIOR RUSSIAN SVR OFFICERS IN AUSTRIA, THE OOA
SNATCHED THE RUSSIANS FROM THE CIA IN VIENNA AND TOOK
THEM TO AN UNDISCLOSED LOCATION OUTSIDE THE UNITED
STATES.

PRESIDENT CLENDENNEN——
BREAK MORE TO FOLLOW

"Sonofabitch!" the President said. He'd said it twice while reading the story, and a third time now that he'd finished.

Jack Parker announced: "He says, Mr. President, that he will give us seventy-two hours to respond."

"Sonofabitch!" the President said again. "Porky, the way this goddamn thing is written, it sounds as if I'm responsible. It doesn't even mention my predecessor, goddamn him to hell."

Parker, who wondered if the President was calling the wrath of the Almighty upon the head of his predecessor, or on that of Mr. Whelan, did not reply.

The President said nothing for sixty seconds, during which time the contortions of his face and the somewhat angry tapping of his fingers on his desk suggested he was deep in thought.

"Deny it, Porky," he said finally. "Tell the sonofabitch to publish anything he wants. We'll just deny everything. I didn't know a goddamn thing about the OOA or Castillo until Ambassador Stupid walked into the Oval Office the day after my predecessor, that sonofabitch, dropped dead. Just deny any knowledge. What's he going to do, ask Castillo, for Christ's sake?"

"Mr. President, I don't think that will work," Parker said.

"Why not?"

Parker handed him another sheet of paper.

"Mr. Whelan said he thought you might . . . What he said, sir, was that our trying to stonewall wouldn't bother him at all; that it was always a better story when you can prove the White House lied. He said it was only because of his admiration for you that he was giving you the chance to see what he's going to write, so it wouldn't come as a sucker punch. And so far as asking Colonel Castillo is concerned, Mr. Whelan says the only way to keep him from publishing would be for Colonel Castillo, personally, to convince him he had his facts wrong. I had the impression, sir, that he thinks we have Colonel Castillo and are hiding him someplace where the press can't get to him."

As Clendennen looked at the sheet, Parker added, "Then he gave me that, which he says he will publish if we deny any of the facts in the first story."

"Sonofabitch!" Clendennen said again as he read:

```
BY C. HARRY WHELAN, JR.
COPYRIGHT 2007
WORLDWIDE RIGHTS RESERVED


SLUG: FORMER CIA STATION CHIEF IN VIENNA CONFIRMS
"PRESIDENTIAL CIA" STOLE TWO VIP RUSSIAN DEFECTORS FROM
HER; SAYS IT COST HER HER JOB


WASHINGTON—(INSERT DATE) ELEANOR DILLWORTH, A
TWENTY-NINE-YEAR VETERAN OF THE CIA'S CLANDESTINE
SERVICE, HAS TOLD THIS REPORTER THAT THE OFFICE OF
ORGANIZATIONAL ANALYSIS — THE SUPER-SECRET, POSSIBLY
ILLEGAL INTELLIGENCE ORGANIZATION OPERATING OUT OF THE
WHITE HOUSE AND ANSWERING ONLY TO THE PRESIDENT — DID IN
FACT MAKE OFF WITH TWO VERY SENIOR RUSSIAN INTELLIGENCE
OFFICERS AND TOOK THEM TO AN UNKNOWN DESTINATION "HOURS
BEFORE" THEY WERE TO BOARD A CIA AIRCRAFT SENT TO
VIENNA, AUSTRIA, TO FLY THEM TO THE UNITED STATES.


DILLWORTH TOLD THIS REPORTER——
BREAK MORE TO FOLLOW
```

"Can't we shut this Dillworth broad up?" the President asked. "Why is she determined to embarrass my administration?"

"Sir, I believe she thinks she was unfairly treated after Castillo stole the Russians from under her nose. She was relieved of her duties in Vienna and brought back to Langley."

"Jesus Christ, didn't it occur to her that if she allowed Castillo to steal the Russians from her that that's proof she wasn't doing her fucking job?"

The President reached for the red telephone on his desk.

"Get me Jack Powell," he ordered, then slammed the handset back in the cradle.

The protocol dealing with telephone calls between the President and those on the priority list—of whom John Powell, the director of the Central Intelligence Agency, was one—required the person called to "be available"—in other words, be on the line—within sixty seconds.

Thirty-two seconds after the President had slammed the handset into its cradle, a blue light-emitting diode on the cradle began to flash.

The President grabbed the handset and began the conversation by asking, "Why the hell did you fire this Dillworth woman?"

Then he pushed the LOUDSPEAKER button on the cradle, so that Parker could hear the conversation.

"You're speaking of Eleanor Dillworth, Mr. President?" the DCI asked.

"The one with twenty-nine years in the Clandestine Service. Used to be our head spy in Vienna. That one."

"She wasn't fired, Mr. President."

"That's not what she told C. Harry Whelan, Jr. She also told him that our friend Castillo stole the Russians from under her nose. Unless I can somehow talk him out of it, Whelan's going to publish that in I don't know how goddamn many hundred newspapers and chat about it on Wolf News. That's going to make her and the CIA look pretty foolish, wouldn't you say?"

"Mr. President, Miss Dillworth has not been fired. What happened was that it was decided—after they found the dead Russian in a taxicab outside our embassy . . ."

"And when the CIA looks pretty foolish, this administration looks pretty foolish, wouldn't you say?"

". . . the decision was made to get Miss Dillworth out of Vienna to avoid undue press attention there."

"The last I heard, Austrians can't vote in our elections. Who the hell cares about Viennese newspapers?"

"Perhaps that decision was ill-advised, Mr. President."

"Who made it? Ambassador Stupid? You've heard about that? Ambassador Stupid is in that town with the funny name at the bottom of Argentina looking for this guy Darby, who is in Alexandria."

"Yes, Mr. President, that has been brought to my attention."

"I asked you who made the decision to fire this female."

"I did, Mr. President. At the time—"

"At the time, it was a stupid decision. Well, how are we going to shut this woman up?"

"Mr. President, I just don't see how that's possible."

"So, what do we do?"

"Mr. President, there is some good news. Actually, I was just about to call you when you called me."

"Let's have the good news. God knows we need some."

"I just got off the phone with Frank Lammelle, sir. He said that General Naylor has sent General McNab to find Castillo."

"Where did he send him? Nome, Alaska? I don't think we've looked there yet. Or in Timbuktu."

"I believe General McNab went to South America, sir."

"Haven't we already looked there?"

"Sir, Colonel Castillo spent most of his career working for General McNab. They have a close personal relationship. It's possible that Castillo would turn over the Russians to McNab."

"That raises a presumption and a question: We're presuming that McNab can find Castillo. And if he does, what if Castillo tells him to go fuck himself? He already told Ambassador Stupid and the colonel Naylor sent down there with him to do that."

"As far as presuming that General McNab can find Castillo, sir, I think we can safely do that. People with knowledge of Castillo's location who would not tell anyone else would tell General McNab. Because of their close relationship."

"I wonder."

"And after General McNab locates Castillo, there is a Plan B in case Castillo remains intractable."

"Which is?"

"Lammelle and I feel, Mr. President, that once Castillo knows he has been found, he would agree to a face-to-face meeting with McNab and Lammelle. To see if some accommodation could be reached. He knows he can't remain on the run forever."

"What do you think he wants that we're prepared to give him?"

"That doesn't matter, sir. What we're trying to do is arrange the meeting. General Naylor, General McNab, meeting at a place of Castillo's choice, a place he will feel is safe."

"And what will that accomplish?"

"The place will not be as safe as Castillo thinks."

"How are you going to arrange that?"

"At this moment, there is an agency airplane—a Gulfstream V—sitting at Saint Petersburg–Clearwater International. On it are four officers of the Clandestine Service. When the meeting is set up and Lammelle and Naylor go to meet him, the airplane will follow them. Anywhere in the world."

"That sounds too simple," Clendennen said after a moment. "It presumes that Castillo won't suspect the CIA would try something like that. And from what I've seen of the sonofabitch, whenever he gets in a battle of wits with the CIA, you lose."

"What we think will happen is this, Mr. President. We believe Castillo will announce that he will be at a certain location. Probably in Argentina. He will not be there. His people will be. They will search General Naylor and Mr. Lammelle. In Mr. Lammelle's briefcase, skillfully concealed, they will find the very latest version of an AFC Corporation GPS transmitter. It permits the tracking of a target within six feet anywhere in the world. They will naturally confiscate it before Lammelle and the general are permitted to get back on the airplane to go to where Castillo will actually meet them."

"Leaving the four spooks on your airplane where?"

"Prepared to follow Lammelle and Naylor to wherever the chase leads them. There is a second GPS transmitter concealed in the heel of Lammelle's shoe. And when he actually sees Castillo and hopefully the Russians, he will stamp his foot three times in rapid succession, which will cause the transmitter to send a signal that will mean, 'We've found him. Come and get him.'"

"That sounds like something you saw in a bad spy movie," the President said. "And what happens then? Castillo says, 'Okay. You got us,' and he and the Russians get on the airplane? Bullshit."

"The Clandestine Service officers are armed with a weapon that fires a dart that causes the target, within fifteen seconds, to fall into a harmless sleep lasting between two and three hours."

"And then they are taken where?"

"To the nearest airport served by Aeroflot, Mr. President. All that has to be done is for us to tell Mr. Sergei Murov where they are. He will arrange for the repatriation of the Russians."

"And the 'expatriation' of Castillo," the President said. "Does that bother you, Jack?"

"I've given that some thought, Mr. President. Frankly, I don't like it. But if Colonel Castillo is the price the Russians want for their Congo-X, I don't see where you have much of a choice. I have even come to think that Castillo would understand why you were forced to that conclusion."

"Well, Jack, you know what Harry Truman said: 'The buck stops here.' I have to do what I think is best for the country."

"Yes, sir."

"I have serious doubts about this plan of yours, Jack. But right now I don't see we have much choice but to go forward with it. When does Lammelle say we'll hear something from General McNab?"

"He didn't, sir. I would guess within seventy-two hours, one way or the other."

"Ambassador Stupid will be back from Argentina a lot sooner than seventy-two hours. Maybe he'll have some ideas, as unlikely as that sounds."

"Yes, sir."

"Not to go any further, Jack, but as soon as I can figure out how to get rid of him quietly, Montvale's going to have to go. That job will be open. You get Castillo and the Russians on that Aeroflot airplane and it's yours."

"I'm sure that was another very difficult decision for you to make, Mr. President. And I would be honored to take over, if you decide that's what should be done."

"Let me know of any developments, Jack. *Any.*"

And then the President hung up.

[THREE]
Level Four BioLab Two
U.S. Army Medical Research Institute
Fort Detrick, Maryland
1510 9 February 2007

The senior scientific officer of the U.S. Army Medical Research Institute—Colonel J. Porter Hamilton (B.S., USMA, '84; M.D., Harvard Medical School, '89; Ph.D., Molecular Physics, MIT, '90; Ph.D., Biological Chemistry, Oxford, '91)—and his principal assistant—Master Sergeant Kevin Dennis, USA (Certificate of High School Equivalency for Veterans, Our Lady of Mount Carmel High School, Baltimore, Maryland, '98)—were both attired in the very latest Level Four chemical/biological hazardous material protective gear.

It was constructed of a multilayer silver-colored fabric completely enclosing their bodies. The helmet of the garment had a large glass plate so they could see pretty well, and was equipped with a communications system that when activated provided automatic video and audio recording of whatever they said and whatever they were looking at. It also provided access to both the BioLab Two and Fort Detrick switchboards and—a modification personally installed by Colonel Hamilton, assisted by Master Sergeant Dennis—encrypted communication with an underground laboratory at the AFC Corporation in Las Vegas, Nevada. Finally, there was provision for Colonel Hamilton and Master Sergeant Dennis to communicate with each other privately; no one could hear what they were saying and it was not recorded.

Each suit was connected by two twelve-inch-diameter telescoping hoses on their backs to equipment which provided purified air under pressure to the suits, and also purified the "used" air when it flowed out of the suits.

Colonel Hamilton had more than once commented that when he looked at Kevin Dennis "suited up," he thought he looked as if they were in a science fiction movie and would not have been at all surprised if Bruce Willis joined them to help in the slaying of an extraterrestrial monster.

There was all sorts of equipment in the laboratory, including an electron microscope which displayed what it was examining on as many as five fifty-four-inch monitors.

Colonel Hamilton placed the communication function of the helmet on INTER ONLY, and then asked, vis-à-vis what was on the left of the five monitors, "Opinion, Kevin?"

"Colonel, that shit's as dead as a doornail."

"Let us not leap, Kevin, to any conclusions that, if erroneous, might quite literally prove disastrous."

"Okay, but that shit's as dead as a doornail."

"What are we looking at?"

Master Sergeant Dennis consulted a clipboard that was attached, through the suit, to the six-inch stump that was all that remained of his right arm.

"Batch two one seven decimal five."

"And what have we done to this?" Colonel Hamilton inquired.

"The same thing we've done to two one seven decimals one through four."

"Which is?"

"Fifteen minutes of the helium at minus two-seventy Celsius."

Minus two hundred seventy degrees Celsius is minus four hundred fifty-two degrees Fahrenheit. To find a lower temperature, it is necessary to go into deep space.

"Present temperature of substance?"

"Plus twenty-one decimal one one one one Celsius, or plus seventy Fahrenheit."

"And it has been at this temperature for how long a period of time?"

"Twenty-four hours, sixteen minutes."

"What was the length of thawing time?"

"Exposed to plus twenty-one decimal one one one one Celsius, it was brought up from minus two hundred seventy Celsius in eight hours and twelve minutes."

"With what indications of chemical or biological activity during any part of the thawing process?"

"None, nada, zip."

"Sergeant Dennis, I am forced to concur. That shit *is* as dead as a doornail."

"And so's all of batch two one seven. You give Congo-X fifteen minutes of the helium at minus two hundred seventy Celsius, and it's dead."

"It would appear so."

"Who are you going to tell, Colonel?"

"I have been considering that question, as a matter of fact. Why are you asking?"

"I don't like what Aloysius told us they're trying to do to Colonel Castillo."

"Frankly, neither do I. But we are soldiers, Kevin. Sworn to obey the orders of officers appointed over us."

"But what I've been wondering, Colonel, is what happens if we tell the CIA and somehow it gets out. Either we tell the Russians, 'Fuck you, we learned how to kill this shit' or they find out on their own?"

"Frankly, Kevin, I don't understand the question."

"Two things we don't know. One, how much Congo-X the Russians have."

"True."

"And, two, we don't know if they know how to kill it. But let's say they do know that helium at near absolute zero kills it. You know how much we had to pay for the last helium we bought?"

"I entrust the details of logistics to my trusted principal assistant," Hamilton said.

"A little over fifteen bucks a liter. You know how many liters it took to kill batch two-seventeen?"

"I don't think, Kevin, that cost is of much consequence in the current situation."

"Eleven liters to freeze about a half a kilo. Call it a hundred and sixty bucks. And that was freezing decimal two kilos at a time. I haven't a clue how much helium it would take to freeze just one beer keg full of Congo-X. But a bunch."

"I am not following your line of thought, Kevin."

"I had to go to four different lab supply places to get the last shipment. Not one of them could ship us one hundred liters, which is what I was trying to buy. There's not much of a demand for it out there, so there's not a lot of it around. And we don't have the capability of making large amounts of it, or of transporting it once it's been liquefied.

"The Russians know this. If they hear we know how to kill Congo-X, they're liable to use it on us—whether or not the President gives them Castillo and the Russians—before we can make enough helium to protect ourselves."

"We don't know how much Congo-X they have," Hamilton said.

"We have to find out, Colonel, and I'd rather have Castillo try to find out than the CIA."

"But is that decision ours to make, Kevin?"

"Well, it's not mine, Colonel, and I'm glad I'm not in your shoes."

Colonel Hamilton tapped his silver-gloved fingertips together for perhaps thirty seconds.

"Kevin, there is a military axiom that the worst action to take is none at all. If you don't try to control a situation, your enemy certainly will."

"That's a little over my head, Colonel."

"Switch your commo to the Casey network," Colonel Hamilton ordered.

[FOUR]

"So what's new by you, Jack?" Aloysius Francis Casey (Ph.D., MIT) asked ten seconds later of Colonel J. Porter Hamilton (Ph.D., MIT), addressing him by his very rarely used intimate nickname.

The Massachusetts Institute of Technology had brought together Casey and Hamilton, although they had not known each other at the school, or even been there at the same time. They had met at a seminar for geopolitical interdependence conducted by that institution, for distinguished alumni, by invitation only.

Both had accepted the invitation because it had sounded interesting. And both had fled after the second hour, and met in a Harvard Square bar, by chance selecting adjacent bar stools.

Dr. Casey had begun the conversation—and their friendship—by asking two questions: "You were in there, right?" and then, after Dr. Hamilton (in mufti) nodded: "You think that moron actually believed that bullshit he was spouting?"

Dr. Hamilton had been wondering the same thing, and said so: "I have been wondering just that."

"Aloysius Casey," Casey had said, putting out his hand.

"My name is Hamilton," Dr. Hamilton replied, and then, having made the split-second decision that if Casey were one of the distinguished alumni, he would have said, "I'm Dr. Casey" and not wanting to hurt the feelings of the maintenance worker/ticket taker/security officer or whatever he was by referring to himself with that honorific, finished, "Jack Hamilton."

He hadn't used "Jack" in many years. He still had many painful memories of his plebe year at West Point during which he had been dubbed "Jack Hammer" by upperclassmen. If he was a bona fide Jack Hammer, the upperclassmen had told him, he would do fifty push-ups in half the time this fifty had taken him. This was usually followed by, "Try it again, Jack Hammer."

"Hey," Casey had said, grabbing the bartender's arm, "give my pal Jack another of what he's having and I'll have another boilermaker."

When the drinks were served, Casey touched glasses and offered a toast, "May the winds of fortune sail you. May you sail a gentle sea. May it always be the other guy who says, 'This drink's on me.'"

"In that case, I insist," Hamilton had said.

"You can get the next one, Jack," Casey had replied.

Three drinks later, Jack asked Aloysius what his role in the seminar for geopolitical interdependence had been.

"Well, I went there, of course. And every once in a while, I slip them a few bucks—you know, payback for what I got—and that gets me on the invitation list, and every once in a while I'm dumb enough to accept. What about you, Jack, what do you do?"

"I'm a soldier."

"No shit? Me, too. Or I was. I was a commo sergeant on a Special Forces A-team. What branch?"

"Originally infantry. Now medical corps."

"No shit? I'm impressed. What do you do?"

"I'm involved in biological research. What about you?"

"I try to move data around. I make stuff that does."

At that point, Colonel Hamilton experienced an epiphany.

"The AFC Corporation. You're *that* Aloysius Francis Casey."

"Guilty."

"My lab is full of your equipment."

"How's it doing?"

"I couldn't function without it," Colonel Hamilton said. "I can't tell you how pleased I am we've met."

A week later, Colonel Hamilton had visited the AFC Laboratories in Las Vegas. In the course of explaining how he used AFC data equipment in his Fort Detrick laboratory, and what kind of capabilities in that area he would like to have if that was possible, he of course had to get into some of the specifics of the work of his laboratory.

Three weeks after that, while in Las Vegas to view the prototypes of the equipment Casey was developing for him, Hamilton was introduced to some of Casey's Las Vegas friends. He quickly came to think of them as "those people in Las Vegas." And then, gradually, he came to understand that he had become one of them.

"Aloysius, I don't want those people to hear this conversation."

"Ouch! You know the rules, Jack. What one knows, everybody knows. That's the way it works."

"Then I can't talk to you. Goodbye, Aloysius. And tell those people goodbye, too. Hamilton out."

Colonel Hamilton then signaled to Sergeant Dennis that they were leaving the sealed laboratory. The process took ten minutes, and included both chemical and purified water showers and then fresh clothing.

When they came through the final airtight door, four people were waiting for them—two women and two men, all cleared for Top Secret BioLab.

Hamilton knew that at least one of them, possibly two, were reporting to the CIA. And he strongly suspected that one of them was reporting to the Russians, either through an intermediary or directly to the Russian *rezident*. And he thought it entirely likely that one or more of them was on the payroll of those people in Las Vegas.

He was greatly frustrated that neither he nor Kevin Dennis—although they had set many traps—had been able to positively identify even one of them.

So they lived with the problem, following the adage that a devil one knows is better than a devil one does not.

"There have been some indications that we are making some progress," Colonel Hamilton announced to them. "And some disturbing signs that we are yet again on a path leading nowhere. We won't know more until tomorrow morning. Make sure everything is secure, and then you may leave. Please be on time in the morning; we have a busy schedule tomorrow."

When they had gone, Kevin Dennis asked, "What is Aloysius going to do, Colonel?"

"I really don't know, Kevin, but I can't take the risk that what I want to say to him will go any further than him."

"You think he will call back?"

Hamilton shrugged.

"I don't know," Hamilton said. "I'm taking some small solace from the motto of those two brilliant young men who started Yahoo: 'You Always Have

Other Options.' But between you and me, I have no idea what other options there might be."

Thirty seconds later, both Hamilton's and Dennis's CaseyBerrys vibrated.

It was Casey.

"I see that you're both on," his voice announced as it returned from a twenty-four-thousand-mile trip into space.

"Well, Aloysius," Hamilton said, "how nice to hear from you. Say hello to Aloysius, Kevin."

"Hello, Aloysius," Dennis said.

"Jack," Casey said, "do I have to say I wouldn't do this for anybody but you?"

"How about Castillo? Would you cut some of those people out of the loop if it would keep him from being thrown to the Russians?"

"I called back, didn't I?"

"And not only are those people not going to hear this conversation, but I have your word that you won't tell them anything about it?"

"You have my word, Jack, but I'm damned uncomfortable with this. I don't like lying to those people." He paused, then added, "And in my book not telling somebody something is the same thing as lying."

"What I'm afraid of is that one—or more—of them has either concluded, or will conclude, that if Castillo and the Russians are the price for the Russian stock of Congo-X, the President was right to agree to pay it."

"In other words, you don't trust them. Jesus Christ, Jack, you know who they are!"

"Their most endearing quality to me is their ruthlessness," Hamilton said. "I daresay they wouldn't be as rich as they are without that characteristic. But I have noticed a tendency on the part of wealthy ruthless people to regard people on their payroll as expendable."

"What the hell is that supposed to mean?"

"I think Colonel Castillo made a mistake in taking that money from those people when he began this project. What was it, two hundred thousand dollars?"

"That's all he asked for. They'd have given him whatever he asked for. A couple of million, if that's what he wanted."

"If he took only two dollars, people like those people would still have felt, 'He took the money, he's ours. We can do with him what we decide is in the best interests of the country.'"

After a moment's hesitation, Casey said, "I'm one of those people, Jack. And so are you."

"You and I are functionaries, Aloysius. Useful, but not, so to speak, anointed, as they are, by the Almighty. Have those people asked you what you think of the President's willingness to sell Castillo and the Russian spooks—without whom that laboratory in the Congo would still be manufacturing this obscene substance—to the Russians?"

"They didn't have to ask me. They know how I would feel about that."

"They haven't asked me either, Aloysius, what I think about it. Nor have they solicited my suggestions vis-à-vis what should be done about it by 'we people.' Which is what triggered my line of thought in this area. Have you considered the possibility that those people simply don't care what we think, Aloysius?"

There was a thirty-second silence which seemed much longer.

"Jesus Christ, Jack," Casey said finally, "you're right. I'm ashamed to admit that I never questioned anything those people did, or asked me to do. Well, fuck them!"

"It's not black-and-white, Aloysius. Those people do more good than harm. But when the harm they're capable of might be directed at people like Castillo and the Russians, I can't go along."

"Didn't you hear me say 'Fuck them'?"

"Don't say that to those people. Let them think they are still on Mount Olympus graciously protecting people like you and me—and of course the United States—from our ignorance."

"Okay."

"Do those people know where Castillo is?"

"Yeah. Of course. They have his position indicator on their laptops. So do you. He's at his grandmother's place in Mexico." Casey paused, then added, "Shit! You think maybe somebody already told the CIA?!"

"I have to think that's possible. Can you devise a spurious position indicator for him?"

"Where do you want him to start moving to in twenty seconds, Jack?"

"Doesn't he have family in Germany? Do you know where?"

"Yeah. Outside Frankfurt. But what about Budapest?"

"What's in Budapest?"

"A guy on Charley's net. He's sort of like an uncle to him. Billy Kocian?"

"I don't know the name."

"Good guy. Trust me."

"Budapest sounds fine."

"I can call Billy and tell him what's happening. And . . . what I could do, Jack, is put Charley's position indicator on one of those boats that sails up and down the Danube between Vienna and Budapest. That would drive those people bonkers wondering what the hell he's up to."

"A splendid idea!"

"Anything else I can do for you?"

"Aloysius, do you—or your people—ever work with extremely low temperatures, using gases in the minus two-hundred-degrees Celsius area?"

"All the time. The colder you get something, the faster everything electrical moves. Twice a week, I say, 'Eureka! This will work!' and then everything that cold turns brittle and shatters when somebody in Los Angeles or Chicago burps, and we're back to Step Fucking One."

"Helium?"

"Of course. It's a little pricey, but you can go down to about minus two-seventy Celsius with helium."

"You've got a pretty good source of supply for helium?"

"Yeah. Several of them. Where are you going with this, Jack?"

"You could order, say, a thousand liters, two thousand, even more, of helium without attracting much attention?"

"Why would I want to do that?"

"Because we may need at least that much to kill Congo-X."

"Helium kills Congo-X?"

"Fifteen minutes in a helium bath at minus two-seventy Celsius kills it."

"So it can be killed! I was really getting worried about that."

"You were not alone," Hamilton said. "We don't know how much the Russians have. I suspect that if the President doesn't give them Castillo and the Russians very soon, they will deliver more of it to encourage him to do so. My concern is that there will be an accident when they do so. I—"

"I get the picture," Casey interrupted. "I'll load what helium I have here . . . maybe three hundred liters, maybe a little more . . . on my Gulfstream. As soon as we know where the Russians have sent the new Congo-X, the helium will be there in no more than three hours. And I'll lay my hands on as much more as I can get as soon as I can."

"Aloysius, we can't let those people learn any of this."

"I'm not as dumb as I look and sometimes act, Jack. I already figured that out."

"Good man!"

"As soon as we hang up here, I'll get through to Charley, and tell him both what's going on and to get the hell off Grandma's place as soon as he can."

"Splendid!"

[FIVE]
Apartment 606
The Watergate Apartments
2639 I Street, N.W.
Washington, D.C.
0755 10 February 2007

When Roscoe J. Danton finally found the ringing house telephone in the living room and picked it up, he was not in a very gracious mood.

Mr. Danton had returned to Washington four hours before after a fifteen-hour flight from Ushuaia, Patagonia, Argentina, whence he had traveled—on what, he had concluded, was a wild-goose chase that belonged in *The Guinness Book of World Records*—with Ambassador Charles M. Montvale and Montvale's executive assistant—The Honorable Truman Ellsworth—and four CIA spooks to locate Alexander Darby, who allegedly could point him to Lieutenant Colonel C. G. Castillo.

The Gulfstream III twin-engine jet aircraft had been noisy and crowded. What food there had been was damned near inedible. The toilet had stopped up. And because there had been no functioning socket into which to plug his laptop, once its battery had gone dead, he couldn't do any work.

Mentally, he had composed a blistering piece that would subject Montvale and Ellsworth to the scorn of the world. But even as he'd done that, he knew he would never write it. He not only felt sorry for them, but had come to like them.

He also had spent a good deal of time trying to come up with a version of what had happened to tell Christopher J. Waldron, the managing editor of the *Times-Post*, something that would not result in Waldron concluding that Roscoe J. Danton had either been drunk or was a moron or both.

He had gotten to bed a few minutes before four.

And now the fucking house phone goes off!

In the five years I've lived in the Watergate, I haven't talked on the goddamn thing five times!

"What?" he snarled into the instrument.

"Mr. Danton, this is Gerry in the garage."

"And how may I be of assistance, Gerry?"

"There's something wrong with your car, Mr. Danton. The alarm keeps going off."

"That happens, Gerry"—*As you should know, you fucking cretin. You work in the garage*—"when someone bumps into it. It'll stop blowing the horn and flashing the headlights in three minutes."

"Yeah, I know, but yours keeps going off. This is the fifth time it's gone off. You're going to have to do something."

"What would you suggest?"

"Well, you could disconnect the battery. That'd shut the alarm system off."

"Gerry, if you could do that for me, I'd be happy to make it worth your while. How does ten dollars sound?"

"Sounds fine to me, Mr. Danton, but your car is locked and I have to get under the hood to disconnect the battery. You can't open the hood from outside."

In the background Danton could then hear the sound of a horn going *bleep-bleep-bleep.*

"There it goes again," Gerry said unnecessarily.

Roscoe Danton sighed audibly.

"I'll be right down," he said.

Which means I'll have to get dressed. I can't go down there in my underwear.

There were three men watching the blinking headlights on Roscoe's car. One of them had sort of a uniform on, and was presumably Gerry. The other two were wearing suits.

Which means they probably live here, which means I will shortly get one of those fucking letters from the tenants' association demanding to know how I dare disturb the peace and tranquillity of the Watergate Apartments, blowing my horn in this outrageous way.

As he approached his car, the lights stopped blinking and the horn stopped bleating.

"Why hello, Roscoe," one of the men in suits said. "Nice to see you again. But we are going to have to stop meeting this way. People will talk."

I am actually losing my mind. I'm hallucinating.

How could Alexander Darby possibly be standing next to my car in the Watergate garage?

"My name is Yung, Mr. Danton," the other man in a suit said, putting out his hand. "I'm glad to meet you. Alex has told me a good deal about you."

Alex Darby said, "Gerry, we can take it from here. Thanks very much for your help."

"Anytime," Gerry said, and took the extended twenty-dollar bill and walked toward his booth near the entrance.

"Got your passport with you, Roscoe?" Darby asked.

In a Pavlovian reflex, Danton patted his suit jacket pocket, and immediately regretted it.

"Good," Yung said. "If you want to talk to Colonel Castillo, you're going to need it."

"Who are you?"

"My name is David W. Yung. I'm Colonel Castillo's attorney."

"Did you find Ushuaia interesting, Roscoe?" Darby asked.

"How do you know about that?"

"Well, as the saying goes, 'You can take the man out of the agency, but you can't take the agency out of the man.'"

Yung put in: "What we're going to do, Roscoe—you don't mind if I call you Roscoe, do you?"

"Yeah, I think I do."

"If you're going to be difficult, Roscoe, not a problem," Yung said. "We'll just leave and go find C. Harry Whelan, Jr. We know he also wants to meet Colonel Castillo. We'd rather have you, but only if you want to go along. We're not going to drug you, or anything like that, and take you against your will."

"Take me where?"

"I'll tell you what we have in mind if you let me call you Roscoe. If you do, in turn you may call me Two-Gun."

I'm smiling. I have every right to be royally pissed.

And maybe I should even be frightened—was there an implied threat in that "We're not going to drug you"?

But what I'm doing is smiling.

"Two-Gun"? They call him "Two-Gun"?

"You may call me Roscoe, Two-Gun."

"Thank you. Now, Roscoe, presuming you are willing, you are going to drive you and me to BWI. You have a first-class ticket on the Aero-Mexico ten-forty-five flight to Mexico City. Once I see your plane take off, I will drive your car back here and turn it over to Gerry's capable hands. You will be met at the airport in Mexico City and taken to meet Colonel Castillo."

"And the Russians?"

"Actually, one of the Russians has expressed an interest in meeting you, Roscoe."

"Where is Castillo, Two-Gun?"

"You will learn that later."

"And if I say no?"

"Then we shall regretfully have to stuff you in the trunk of your car. And by the time Gerry hears your piteous cries for help—and finally figures out where they're coming from—Alex and I will have folded our tent and disappeared."

Goddamn it! I'm smiling again.

"Okay. Give me ten minutes to throw some things in a bag and grab my laptop."

"No. If we're going, it has to be right now."

"Why?"

"There's about one chance in ten that Alex and I were not as successful as we believe we were in eluding the Secret Service guys surveilling our house, which raises the possibility that there may be some of them outside."

"What makes you think they won't see, follow, stop, whatever, us when you and I leave?"

"Because just before we leave, Alex is going to leave the garage as if Satan himself is in hot pursuit. If there are no Secret Service agents waiting for him outside, fine. If there are, Alex will lead them on a tour of the scenic spots of our nation's capital while you and I make our leisurely way to Baltimore-Washington International."

"And Harry Whelan won't be involved, right?"

"I was afraid you would ask that."

"Meaning he will be?"

"Meaning he will be offered the same opportunity."

"Can I cut his throat?"

"When you come back, you can do anything you want to."

"I haven't a clue why I'm going along with this," Roscoe J. Danton said as he put the key in the car door.

XIV

J. Stanley Waters, the CIA's deputy director for operations, stood looking over the shoulder of DCI John Powell at the screen of a laptop computer. The screen showed an arrow positioned over a map of Budapest, Hungary. A box beside the arrow held the legend HOTEL GELLÉRT, SZENT GELLÉRT TÉR 1 and the local date and time.

"There is our friend Castillo right now," the DCI said.

"What's he doing in the Hotel Gellért in Budapest?" Waters asked.

"Does it matter? Just as long as the case officers know where to find him when they get there."

"It would have been easier, and maybe quicker, to send the plane from Tampa. We know the guys on the plane are good, know the score, and if we had sent it over there the moment we saw he was headed for Europe, they would be there, or almost there, now."

"So you've been saying, five or six times," the DCI said.

"I stand chastised."

"And well you should," the DCI said, only half-jokingly.

When enough time for that to have sunk in had passed, the DCI went on: "And what you can do with this software, Stan—that Casey is really a fucking genius—is program a time lapse into it. Like this."

He tapped a few keys. The map changed and now showed a map covering the world from near Acapulco to Budapest.

"This arrow is when Castillo started to move from Grandma's house," the DCI said. "That was at sixteen-thirty Acapulco time yesterday. I'll set this thing to show us where he was by the hour."

He tapped keys.

"There it is . . ."

A series of arrows appeared on a line from Acapulco to Budapest.

"Unfortunately, there was a cloud cover, so we couldn't get a very good picture of what's moving. But enough to categorize it as a small jet. One hour later . . ."

He used his finger as a pointer.

". . . it was almost halfway to Cancún, and two hours later, it was almost in Cancún, telling us it was making about three hundred thirty knots, which suggests that he's flying the family Lear, which makes sense, as we know the Gulfstream III is in Panama City, Panama.

"An hour after that, having taken on fuel in Cancún, he was about two hundred miles on his way to Panama City. . . . Watch the arrow jump, Stan. Another hour, another three hundred forty nautical miles, and then another, et cetera, until he reaches Panama City, Panama.

"And there Castillo sat for almost three hours until he boarded Varig Flight 2030 for Madrid."

"Jack, for Christ's sake, you're like a kid with your goddamn computer!"

"Indulge me," the DCI said. "And there he is in Madrid."

"Goddamn it, Jack!"

"And finally, courtesy of Lufthansa, there he is in Budapest."

"What do you think he did with his airplane in Panama City?"

"No telling. We should know by the morning when we get the satellite imagery. It could be sitting on the tarmac there, or that Air Force guy, Torine, could have flown it somewhere. I never understood how that worked. Torine was a pretty senior full colonel, and our boy a very junior lieutenant colonel. So how come Torine works for Castillo?"

"I have no idea. What are you going to do with Lammelle?"

"What do you mean, do with him?"

"You are going to tell him that Castillo is in Budapest?"

"I could tell Frank, but he would have to tell General Naylor, and General Naylor would naturally want to know how Lammelle, or the CIA, knows where Castillo is. The truthful answer to that would be that, courtesy of Aloysius Francis Casey, those people in Las Vegas are tracking Colonel Castillo through a GPS transmitter in his laptop. And we don't want to reveal that, do we?"

"So Frank just sits at MacDill?"

"Unless McNab thinks he has found Castillo, and they all rush off to the wrong place to put them in the bag. You wouldn't believe, Stan, how low our director of National Intelligence has sunk in the President's esteem as a result of his wild-goose chase in Argentina. It would be unfortunate if Lammelle came to be known as a Wild-Goose Chaser in the mold of Ambassador Montvale, but that's the way the ball just might bounce. If that should happen, of course, it would tend to eliminate Frank as a replacement for me when Clendennen gives Montvale the boot and I become the DNI. I would recommend you to replace me if it were not for your unfortunate tendency to mock my interest in Casey's electronic toys."

"I can reform, Jack."

"You had fucking well better, Stan."

[TWO]
Office of the Commanding General
United States Army Central Command
MacDill Air Force Base
Tampa, Florida
1605 10 February 2007

"Vic needs a minute, General," Command Sergeant Major Wes Suggins said from McNab's door.

Naylor did not like the rapport that had developed almost immediately between his sergeant major and D'Allessando, but he both understood it—*Sergeants major are in fact the backbone of the Army and that's especially true with men like these two, who function at the highest levels of the service*—and he knew that he couldn't warn Suggins against D'Allessando, who was in fact at this moment not a trusted member of the team but the enemy.

He motioned for Suggins to admit D'Allessando, and called, "Come on in, Vic."

"Afternoon, General," D'Allessando said. "Call for you."

He handed Naylor what looked like a BlackBerry but was in fact a CaseyBerry. Naylor took it.

"General Naylor."

"General McNab, General. And how are things on beautiful Tampa Bay this afternoon?"

The sonofabitch has this thing on LOUDSPEAKER.

And I will be damned if I will give him the satisfaction of knowing I don't know how to turn it off.

"I've been wondering when we were going to hear from you, General," Naylor said.

"I can understand that, General."

"I'm a little surprised you didn't call on a secure line."

"This is about as secure a line as you can get, actually."

"Have you found what you're looking for?"

"I'm always looking for peace, love, and affluence, but I suspect you're asking, 'Did you find Charley?'"

D'Allessando chuckled.

Don't let either of these bastards make you lose your temper!

"And did you?"

"I managed to have a chat with him."

"And? Where is he?"

"He didn't say. But he's agreeable to talk with you, if you like, as an old friend."

"Right now, General, we're not old friends, but a general officer and a lieutenant colonel."

"Oh, I guess I misspoke. Or at least should have made this clear. I spoke with a German national by the name of Karl Wilhelm von und zu Gossinger. During the course of our conversation, he said he was surprised that I didn't know that Lieutenant Colonel Castillo, Retired, having been ordered by the President of the United States to disappear and never be heard from again, was in compliance with his orders."

"General, the President of the United States has ordered me to order Colonel Castillo—"

"General, how can you order someone to do anything who has disappeared and will never be heard from again?"

D'Allessando chuckled again and smiled at Naylor.

"Something amuses you, D'Allessando?" Naylor snapped.

"Looks like you have a problem, General," D'Allessando said.

"Get the hell out of my office!"

"Yes, sir," D'Allessando said, and put out his hand. "May I have my Casey-Berry, please?"

You sonofabitch, that's going to cost you!

"What Herr von und zu Gossinger said he is willing to do, General," McNab went on, "is meet you in Cancún tomorrow morning."

"Cancún, Mexico?" Naylor asked incredulously.

"That's the one. And he wants you to fly there commercially. There's an Aeromexico flight out of Lauderdale tonight at seventeen-thirty; it'll put you in there a little after oh-one-thirty. They call it the Drug Dealer's Red-Eye. He says it probably would attract less attention if you didn't wear your uniform . . ."

Sonofabitch!!!

". . . and he hopes you and your party will be his guests at El Dorado Royale in Cancún. People from El Dorado Royale—it's a five-star hotel—will meet your flight. How many will there be in your party, General?"

"That would presume I'm going along with this, wouldn't it?"

"Excuse me, General?"

"Myself, Mr. Lammelle, Major Brewer, and, I presume, Mr. D'Allessando. And my son."

"Oh, Allan's coming? Good. I'm sure Herr von und zu Gossinger will be glad to see him. And it'll be educational for him, won't it?"

"Is that about it?"

"General, I think I should tell you that I don't think Char . . . *Herr von und zu Gossinger* is going to be in Cancún. I don't think he entirely trusts Frank Lammelle. But it's the first step. And we are playing by his rules, aren't we?"

"For the moment," Naylor said.

"Your tickets will be waiting for you at the airport. First class, of course. There's nothing cheap about our . . . Herr von und zu Gossinger, is there? Nice to talk to you, General."

There was a muted click and General Naylor realized that General McNab was no longer on the line.

[THREE]
Office of the Director
The Central Intelligence Agency
Langley, Virginia
1625 10 February 2007

"What are you going to do, Frank? Send the Gulfstream down to Cancún ahead of you?" Jack Powell asked.

"No. I think what I'll do is move it to the Lauderdale airport now, and then have it follow the Aeromexico flight once they're sure we're actually on it. Castillo may be up to something clever, like actually being in Disney World, or someplace, and this whole Mexican thing may be a diversion."

"Well, wherever you go, the people in the Gulfstream will know. Keep me posted, Frank."

The director of the Central Intelligence Agency hung up.

"Have a nice wild-goose chase, Frank," he said aloud, although there was no one to hear him.

Then he said, slowly, savoring each syllable, "John J. Powell, the director of National Intelligence."

He thought it had a certain ring to it, a certain *je ne sais quoi.*

[FOUR]
Room B-120
El Dorado Royale Spa Resort
Kilometer Forty-five, Carretera Cancún-Tulum
Riviera Maya
Quintana Roo, Mexico
0230 11 February 2007

Vic D'Allessando had almost wished, as he crawled across the floor of Frank Lammelle's room toward the bed, that the sonofabitch would wake up. He would have loved an excuse to pop the bastard with one of the darts in the Glock-like air pistol he held in his hand.

But luck—at least, that kind of luck—had not been with him.

Frank Lammelle hadn't stirred as D'Allessando first pried the heels off Lammelle's shoes, removed the GPS transmitter from the right heel, and then replaced both. Not even when D'Allessando had grunted with the effort.

Neither had he stirred when D'Allessando went into Lammelle's briefcase, found Lammelle's Glock-like dart gun, removed the gas cylinder from the stock, and replaced it with a gas cylinder he had exhausted earlier shooting darts at the pineapple atop the tray of fruit that the El Dorado management had sent to his room as a welcoming gift.

Once he was back in his room, one floor up and directly above B-120—it might have been necessary, had Lammelle fastened the mechanical door lock, to gain entrance to his room by climbing down from the balcony—Vic checked his watch. The entire operation had taken twelve minutes, thirty seconds.

"Here," D'Allessando said in Russian, handing the GPS transmitter to a tall blond man in a nautical uniform. "Tell me, Captain, on the *Queen of the Caribbean*, are there lifeboats on an upper deck exposed to the sky?"

"Lifeboats, no," the blond man said. "Life rafts, yes."

"Then please put it someplace on one of the life rafts where it will not be seen, not get wet, and is in the best position to send a clear signal."

"I know just the place."

"And what time do you sail?"

"At half past eight."

"Marvelous! *Bon voyage!*"

"And when we get to Málaga, what do I do with the GPS transmitter?"

"I expect the battery will go dead before you're halfway across the Atlantic. Just put that gadget in a life raft, check it a couple of times a day, and after a week, toss it over the side."

[FIVE]
En route to Cancún International Airport
Cancún
Quintana Roo, Mexico
0915 11 February 2007

They were traveling in the same kind of minibus sent the night before to bring them from Cancún International Airport to El Dorado Royale Resort. It was manufactured in Mexico on a Mercedes-Benz chassis, and could hold fourteen passengers and their luggage in air-conditioned comfort.

This morning it held General Naylor, Colonel Brewer, Lieutenant Colonel (Designate) Naylor, Mr. Lammelle, Mr. D'Allessando, and two rather massive white-jacketed members of the El Dorado Royale's staff, one driving the bus and the other sitting in a jump seat beside him to handle the luggage and an enormous insulated container that held their lunches.

"Where are we going?" Frank Lammelle suddenly demanded to know. He was sitting alone on the row of seats at the back of the bus.

"We're off to see the Wizard, Frank," Vic D'Allessando said. "I told you where we're going: Where Charley told me to take you."

"Not good enough, D'Allessando. I want to know where."

"Pull to the side of the road, please," Vic called in Russian.

The bus pulled off to the side and stopped.

"That was Russian!" Lammelle challenged.

"God! You could tell?"

"What the hell is going on here?" Lammelle demanded. "I want you to tell me where we're going!"

"Or what? You'll stamp your foot?"

Lammelle's face showed that he understood, but he said nothing.

"Wouldn't do you any good, anyway, Frank," D'Allessando said. "Charley's not anywhere close."

"I know that. Castillo's in Budapest."

"Your computer tell you that, Frank?"

"You know fucking well it did. So what's going on here?"

"Allan—*Allan Junior*—did you ever see Ol' Frank's computer? He thinks—he's wrong, but that's what he thinks—it shows where Charley is. Why don't you let Allan Junior see your computer, Frank?"

"Fuck you, D'Allessando," Lammelle said.

"That's not nice!"

"Get out of the aisle, you sonofabitch. I'm getting off the bus."

"Sorry. Not permitted. When you go off to see the Wizard, you've got to go all the way."

Lammelle came out with his Glock-like air pistol, aimed it at D'Allessando, and squeezed the trigger. Nothing happened. He squeezed the trigger again.

"Funny thing about air pistols, Frank," D'Allessando said. "They don't work without air."

And then he took his Glock-like air pistol from under his pillowing Mexican resort shirt, aimed at Lammelle, and squeezed the trigger. There was a *psssst* sound.

"Shit!" Lammelle said, looking down at the dart in his chest.

"Allan Junior," D'Allessando said, "why don't you help Ol' Frank sit down before he falls down? And on your way back, bring his computer."

"What the hell is that you shot him with?" Allan Junior asked, as he moved down the aisle.

"I guess I'm not the only one your father didn't tell about Lammelle's CIA wonder gun," D'Allessando said. "Which raises the question, What do I do with General Naylor and his faithful sidekick, Colonel Brewer?"

Everyone watched as Lammelle went limp and as Allan Junior lowered him onto the row of seats. Then Allan Junior came down the aisle carrying a laptop.

D'Allessando called out in Russian.

The minibus began to move.

"General," D'Allessando said, "Charley said I was to treat you with as much respect as possible under the circumstances. Are you going to try anything brave and noble? Or . . . are you willing to give me your parole, sir?"

"That's a seldom-used term, isn't it?" General Naylor said. "The last time I think an officer gave his parole was when Colonel Waters—General Patton's son-in-law—gave his to his German captors, who then took him to the Katyn Forest and showed him the graves of the thousands of Polish officers the Russians had murdered."

"With all respect, General, thanks for the history lesson, but that doesn't answer my question."

"It seemed germane here. One of the German officers to whom Colonel

Waters gave his parole was Oberst Hermann von und zu Gossinger, Colonel Castillo's grandfather. Yes, Mr. D'Allessando. If you give me your word that we are en route to see Colonel Castillo, I will offer my parole. And if memory serves, the Code of Honor says that my parole includes that of my immediate subordinates, which would mean you also have the parole of Colonel Brewer and my son, Major Naylor."

"Isn't that Lieutenant Colonel (Designate) Naylor, General?" D'Allessando asked.

"Yes, it is."

"Thank you, sir," D'Allessando said. "Okay, we're headed for the business side of Cancún International. An airplane will be waiting for us. What I would like to suggest to anyone watching is that one of our number has been at the sauce and needs help to board the airplane. Now, will your parole permit you to help me do that?"

"I'll carry the sonofabitch aboard myself," Allan Junior said.

[SIX]
Laguna el Guaje
Coahuila, Mexico
1105 11 February 2007

Looking with frank fascination out the window of the Cessna Mustang as it was towed under what looked like an enormous tarpaulin, General Allan Naylor saw a number of very interesting things.

There were four aircraft already in the cave/hangar/whatever it was: One of them he recognized as what he thought of as "Doña Alicia's Lear." There were two Gulfstreams, a III and a V. He presumed the III was Castillo's airplane, the one in which he and Dick Miller and the others had flown away from their retirement parade at Fort Rucker. He had no idea who the Gulfstream V belonged to.

And there was a Black Hawk helicopter, with its insignia and a legend painted on the fuselage identifying it as belonging to the Mexican Policía Federal Preventiva. Naylor knew the U.S. government had "sold" a dozen of them to Mexico to assist in the war against drugs. He had smarted at the time—and smarted again now—at the price the Mexicans had paid for them, which came to about a tenth of what the Army had paid for them. And he naturally wondered what a Policía Federal helicopter was doing here.

But what he found most fascinating was Lieutenant Colonel C. G. Castillo, who was standing with another man, a woman, and Castillo's dog, Max, watching the aircraft come into the cave. The humans were dressed identically in yellow polo shirts and khaki trousers.

Now that I think about it, just about everybody in the cave is wearing yellow polo shirts and khaki trousers. Is there something significant in that?

The woman—who was wearing an enormous gaudily decorated sombrero that looked like it belonged on the head of a trumpet player in a mariachi band—was leaning her shoulder against Castillo's and holding his hand.

And the other guy—he looks like her, and they're brother and sister—has to be Berezovsky.

What I am looking at is former Colonel Dmitri Berezovsky of the SVR, the Russian Service for the Protection of the Constitutional System; and former Lieutenant Colonel Svetlana Alekseeva, also of the Sluzhba Vneshney Razvedki.

McNab was right—she is built like a brick . . . outdoor sanitary facility.

"Hey, Dick," Lieutenant Colonel (Designate) Naylor called to the Mustang pilot, Major H. Richard Miller, Jr. (U.S. Army, Retired), whom he had known since his plebe year at the U.S. Military Academy. "Is that Charley's Russian spy holding his hand?"

"That's her. We call her 'Sweaty.' She calls him 'my Carlos.'"

"Nice," Lieutenant Colonel (Designate) Naylor said. "Very nice. Maybe thirteen on a scale of one to ten."

"She's okay, Allan," Miller said. "But don't let her looks dazzle you. Sweaty's one tough little cookie."

"Here comes General McNab," Colonel Brewer said.

General McNab, when he climbed aboard the Mustang, was also wearing a yellow polo shirt and khaki trousers.

"General Naylor, welcome to Drug Cartel International Airfield," McNab said, and then, raising his voice, asked, "Everything under control, Vic?"

"I had to—hold that. *With great pleasure*, I darted Lammelle. He's about to come out of it. Got a place to put him on ice?"

"Just the place. I'll put him in with Roscoe J. Danton. Then when Frank wakes up, he'll have someone to talk to."

Naylor thought: *Roscoe J. Danton? Is he talking about the reporter from the Times-Post?*

I will be damned if I'll give him the satisfaction of asking.

McNab backed down the stair doors and said something in Russian. A moment later two burly blond men came onto the airplane.

"Over there," D'Allessando said in Russian. "Be careful, he's dangerous."

Forty-five seconds later, the deputy director of the Central Intelligence Agency was off the airplane and, slung in a fireman's carry over the shoulder of one of the burly men, was being carried toward a stainless-steel elevator door set in the rock wall.

McNab appeared again at the stair door opening.

"General," D'Allessando said, "General Naylor has given me his parole, which also covers Colonel Brewer and Lieutenant Colonel (Designate) Naylor."

"Wonderful! If we had to chain him, it would have been hard to get him down the stairs. Anytime it's convenient, General, you may disembark."

Castillo and the Russians were at the foot of the stair door when Naylor came down it. He noticed that Charley and the woman were still—or again—holding hands.

Castillo waited until Colonel Brewer, Allan Junior, and Vic D'Allessando had come down the stairs.

"At the risk of being rude, and with great respect, General Naylor, if you have something to say to me, let's get it out of the way," Castillo said.

"Colonel, I have been ordered by the President of the United States to place you under arrest. Mr. Lammelle was ordered by the President to take possession of the two Russian defectors you are believed to hold. You will, therefore, consider yourself under arrest, and when Mr. Lammelle is capable of receiving them, you will turn them over to him."

"Sir, again with great respect, that's just not going to happen. Will you explain to me, please, what your understanding of the parole you have given Mr. D'Allessando is?"

"Colonel, as I understand the Code of Honor, I have waived my right to attempt to escape or take any hostile action against my captors until after I inform you that I am withdrawing my parole. My parole covers both Colonel Brewer, whom I don't believe you know, and Lieutenant Colonel (Designate) Naylor."

"Thank you, sir. Gentlemen, may I present Dmitri Berezovsky, formerly colonel of the SVR, and Lieutenant Colonel Svetlana Alekseeva, also formerly of the SVR. They are here of their own volition, not as my prisoners. Having said that, I am responsible for their being here, and consider them to be under my protection."

"I see the way you're hanging onto her, Charley," Allan Junior said. "I wondered what that was all about."

General McNab laughed. General Naylor glared at him.

"This is very difficult for my Carlos," Sweaty flared. "You will not mock him!"

"Colonel Sweaty, I wouldn't think of it!" Allan Junior said.

"Only my friends can call me Sweaty," she replied evenly.

"Right now, Colonel Sweaty, getting to be your friend is right at the top of my list of things to do. Let me begin by saying I love your sombrero and that adorable puppy."

Berezovsky, having wordlessly shaken hands with General Naylor and Colonel Brewer, now offered his hand to Allan Junior.

"Be careful, Colonel," Berezovsky said. "Her bite is twice as bad as her bark."

"I'm not a lieutenant colonel yet. Just picked to be one. I'm glad to meet you."

"If our official business is over for the moment, General Naylor?" Castillo said.

"I have nothing further to say to you officially, Colonel."

"In that case, Uncle Allan, I'm damned glad to see you, even in these circumstances."

"Me, too, Charley," Naylor said, and after an awkward fifteen seconds, they embraced.

"Lunch is being prepared," Sweaty said. "The beef, compared to Argentina, is unbelievably bad."

"Do we have to do anything for Lammelle, Vic?" Castillo asked.

"Castration with a dull knife might be a good idea, but if you're asking because of the dart, no." He looked at his watch. "He should be coming out of it in the next ten minutes or so. I'd love to be there when he wakes up and finds those two Russians sitting on him. He'll think he's been shipped off to Moscow. What are they, Charley? Spetsnaz?"

"Ex."

"Where'd you get them?"

"We borrowed them from Sweaty's and Dmitri's cousin. He flew a dozen up yesterday from Argentina after Sweaty had another good idea."

"Which was?"

"I'll tell you when we're upstairs," Castillo said, and gestured toward the elevator. Then he added, "Thank God you can't trust lawyers—maybe especially Mexican lawyers. Isn't there a politically incorrect joke about that?"

"Meaning what?"

"Cutting a long story short, this place was supposed to have been burned to the ground after they exploded all the butane. But the Mexican lawyer who was supposed to do that—was trusted to do that—didn't."

"Aleksandr will kill him," Sweaty said.

"Pay attention, Allan," Castillo said. "That was not a figure of speech."

General Naylor thought: *And that comment was not Charley being cute.*

[SEVEN]

Castillo led the group into a dining room and waved them into chairs around an enormous table. Naylor saw there was already one man sitting at the table—*I wonder who that guy is?*—and two burly, fair-skinned men armed with Uzi submachine guns, one sitting by each of the room's two doors.

And I don't think Charley's pulling our leg about the Spetsnaz, either.

They look like Russians and they look like special operators.

Proof of that came immediately when Sweaty said something to them in Russian, to which one of them responded as an enlisted man does to an officer.

Castillo added something—gave an order—in Russian and the other Russian popped to attention and said something that was obviously, "Yes, sir."

Both of them left the dining room.

"Sweaty ordered one of them to get us some coffee," Castillo explained, "and I told the other one to fetch Mr. Danton."

"May I ask questions?" General Naylor said.

"Yes, sir. Of course," Castillo replied.

"Danton is the reporter?"

"Yes, sir. That was Sweaty's idea. I'll get into that in a minute."

"And General McNab? Has he also given you his parole?"

"Charley never asked me for it, General," McNab answered for him.

Thirty seconds later, one of the Russians led Roscoe J. Danton into the room.

"Please have a seat, Mr. Danton," Castillo said. "I presume you know everybody?"

"I don't know who these gentlemen are," Danton said, indicating Colonel Brewer, Allan Junior, Vic D'Allessando, and Aloysius Francis Casey.

"My name is Casey," Aloysius said.

"Colonel Brewer is my senior aide-de-camp," General Naylor said. "And that's my son, Lieutenant Colonel (Designate) Allan Naylor, Junior."

"I try very hard to keep my name out of the newspapers, Mr. Danton," D'Allessando said. "Think of me as a friend of Charley's. You can call me Vic."

"And was that Frank Lammelle they just carried into my cell?"

"Yes, it was," Castillo said. "And I'm crushed that you think of that lovely room with an *en suite* bath and such a lovely view as a cell."

"If there's a guy with a submachine gun at the door keeping you inside," Danton said, "that's a cell."

"Point taken," Castillo said. "I think I should begin this by telling you, Mr.

Danton, that General Naylor, Colonel Brewer, and Lieutenant Colonel (Designate) Naylor are not here voluntarily. They have given me their parole."

"What the hell does that mean?"

"It means that under the Code of Honor, they will—"

"What 'Code of Honor'?" Danton interrupted.

"I don't really know. I think of it as the Code of Honor," Castillo said, and looked at General Naylor. "Is there a more formal name, sir?"

"I don't really know," Naylor said. "What it means, Mr. Danton, is that I—personally and on behalf of my staff—have given Colonel Castillo our parole, which means that we will neither attempt escape nor undertake any hostile action without first notifying him that we have withdrawn our parole."

"You're serious, aren't you?" Danton asked, and when Naylor nodded, said, "You take that Code of Honor business seriously? Incredible!"

"I don't think that's the only thing you're going to hear, or see, in the next couple of days that you may find incredible," Castillo said.

Two Russians appeared with a huge thermos of coffee and a tray with cups, cream, and sugar.

Castillo waited until the fuss caused by that dissipated and then rapped his spoon against the thermos. Everybody looked at him.

"Here we go," he said. "While I am a graduate of the U.S. Army Command and General Staff School—where one learns how to write a staff study—I have to confess that when it was time for me to actually go to Fort Leavenworth, either they really couldn't find room for me, or an unnamed senior officer decided I could make a greater contribution to the Army by running his errands. So he pulled some strings, the result of which was that I took the course by correspondence—in addition to my other duties—rather than in the academic setting of Leavenworth."

General Naylor realized he was smiling, and when he looked, he saw General McNab—the unnamed senior officer—was, too.

"The result of that was I cannot come up with as good a staff study as most people can. But as General McNab has told me so many times over the years, you gotta go with what you got.

"Statement of the Problem: The Russians and the Iranians, probably with a lot of help from former East Germans and maybe the Czechs and even the Japanese, none of whom find anything wrong with using biological weapons on soldiers and civilians, came up with a substance we now call Congo-X, because it was manufactured in a laboratory in the Congo.

"Our own expert in this area, Colonel J. Porter Hamilton, cutting to the chase, describes Congo-X as 'an abomination before God.'

"Surprising me not a hell of a lot, Congo-X slipped through the cracks at Langley. It was the stated opinion of the CIA that what was going on in the Congo was a fish farm.

"We learned what was really going on there through dumb luck—"

"Colonel," Roscoe J. Danton interrupted, "if I take notes, will I be wasting my time?"

"I think taking notes is a good idea."

"I'll need my laptop."

Castillo said something in Russian, and then, "Your laptop's on the way. Now, where was I?"

"Something about dumb luck," Danton said.

"Oh, yeah. What I should have said was 'stupidity and incompetence.' I've got to go off at a tangent here. I'm sure that everybody here will be surprised when I tell you that there are some Russians who have moral qualms about biological warfare because of their deep religious convictions. And even more surprised that some of these good Russians get to rise high in the ranks of the Sluzhba Vneshney Razvedki, which in English is the Service for the Protection of the Constitutional System.

"And I'm sure that you will be shocked to hear that the SVR is just as bad as our beloved CIA when it comes to bureaucratic infighting and empire-building. The head villain here is Vladimir Putin, who—despite what title he's running under—actually runs the SVR, which among other things ran the 'Fish Farm' in the Congo.

"In an attempt to restore the SVR to the sort of glory their predecessor secret police organization had before the Soviet Union imploded, Putin decided that a number of people—Russians, Germans, Austrians, Argentines, and Americans, the latter including your lecturer here today—had to be whacked or eliminated.

"He succeeded in whacking the German, a journalist who was asking too many questions about German involvement in supplying the Fish Farm, and the Austrians, who had been deep-cover CIA assets successfully engaged over the years in getting Russians and other Eastern Bloc people to switch sides.

"The attempted assassination of the Argentine failed, but Putin still had high hopes of taking me out when I went to the German's funeral. The murdered German worked for the *Tages Zeitung* newspaper chain, which, as most of you know, I own—"

"You *own* the *Tages Zeitung* chain?" Danton asked incredulously.

Castillo nodded. "Incredible, right? Stick around. It gets better. Anyway, they knew I would go to the funeral. So Putin sent a team of assassins—former

members of the Hungarian Államvédelmi Hatóság—to Germany, with orders
to report to Colonel Berezovsky, the SVR *rezident* in Berlin. Berezovsky would
tell them when and where to whack me when I showed up at the funeral."

Danton pointed to Berezovsky and asked with his eyebrows: *Him?*

Castillo nodded.

"It was to be Colonel Berezovsky's final assignment. When he was finished
whacking me and went—with his sister, Lieutenant Colonel Svetlana Alekseeva,
the SVR *rezident* in Copenhagen—to an SVR meeting in Vienna, they were
going to be charged with embezzlement and flown off to Moscow. Berezovsky
was a threat to Putin's control of the SVR, and had to go. And so did his sister.

"The mistake Putin made—the stupidity he demonstrated—was to underestimate Colonel Berezovsky. Berezovsky knew all about Putin's plans for him
and Sweaty—"

Danton pointed at Svetlana and asked, "'Sweaty'?"

"Only to her friends," Castillo said. "Anyway, Berezovsky had gotten in
touch with the CIA station chief in Vienna, Miss Eleanor Dillworth, and told
her he and his sister were willing to defect.

"Miss Dillworth lost no time in telling Jack Powell, and Jack Powell lost no
time in telling our late President of the genius of his Vienna station chief, im-
plying that Miss Dillworth had brilliantly entrapped Dmitri and Sweaty when,
in fact, they had walked in her door.

"Colonel Berezovsky was not very impressed with Miss Dillworth. He was
in fact very nervous about what was going to happen in Vienna. He thought she
was entirely capable of throwing him and Sweaty under the bus if anything—
any little thing—went wrong.

"And then Dmitri saw in the *Frankfurter Rundschau* a picture of me getting
off my Gulfstream on the way to the funeral. He knew that Karl Wilhelm von
und zu Gossinger was also a lieutenant colonel in the U.S. Army with alleged
intelligence and Special Operations connections. And who had his own airplane.

"Brilliant fellow that my future brother-in-law is, he reasoned—"

"Did you say 'future brother-in-law'?" Danton asked incredulously.

General Naylor thought: *That's exactly what he said. My God!*

"I thought everybody knew," Castillo said. "Love is where you find it, Mr.
Danton."

"Jesus Christ!"

"My fiancée is offended when someone takes the Lord's name in vain, Mr.
Danton."

"Sorry."

"As I was saying . . . Dmitri, clever fellow that he is, reasoned that if he called off the Államvédelmi Hatóság and I was not whacked, maybe I would show my gratitude to him by flying him and Sweaty out of Europe. Which is what happened."

"Is it?" General Naylor asked. "Is that what actually happened, Charley?"

"Yes, sir."

"I never understood why you would steal the defectors from the CIA," Naylor admitted.

"I didn't know about Miss Dillworth until later, General. What Dmitri told me at the time was that the SVR was going to be waiting for him and Svetlana in the Sudbahnhof in Vienna."

"So you flew them to Argentina? Why Argentina?"

"They have family there, sir," Castillo said.

"Well, why didn't you turn them over to the CIA in Argentina?" Naylor asked.

"Well, just about as soon as we got to Vienna, sir, Dmitri, as an expression of his gratitude, told me about the Fish Farm in the Congo. When Ambassador Montvale came down there, I tried to tell him about the Fish Farm, but he gave me the CIA answer: It was nothing but a fish farm."

"You still should have turned these people over to the CIA."

"Two reasons I didn't, sir. The first being that I believed Dmitri about the Fish Farm, and knew that if I turned them over to the CIA, they would not believe him, and that would be the end of it. I knew I had to follow that path."

"And the second reason?"

Castillo exhaled audibly.

"Maybe I . . . no . . . *certainly* I should have given this as my first reason, sir: By the time Montvale showed up in Buenos Aires, certain things had happened between Svetlana and me. I knew there was no way I was ever going to turn her or her brother over to the CIA, the Argentine SIDE, the Rotary Club of East Orange, New Jersey, or anyone else."

Naylor shook his head, but said nothing.

"In the end," Castillo went on, "that turned out, for several reasons, to be the right decision. I decided that my duty required I take action on my own. And that turned out to be the right decision, too. And is why I decided to take action on my own in that situation."

"What action was that, Colonel?" Danton asked.

"The question obviously was: 'What's really going on in the Congo?' There was only one way to find out. I arranged to send people in there to find out."

"On your own authority," General Naylor said. "You had no right to do that, and you knew it."

"I saw it as my duty to do just that," Castillo said.

"What exactly did you do?" Danton asked.

"I sent Colonel J. Porter Hamilton, the man who runs our bio-warfare laboratory at Fort Detrick, to the Congo with a team of special operators. He found out it was even worse than we suspected, told—more importantly, convinced—our late President of this, and the President ordered it destroyed."

"And what happened to you for doing what you did without authorization?"

"Well, for a couple of minutes the President wanted to make me director of National Intelligence . . . I'm kidding. What the President did was tell me to take everybody in OOA to the end of the earth, fall off, and never be seen again. And I've tried—we've all tried—to do just that."

"And?" Danton pursued.

"The curtain went up on Act Two. Two barrels of Congo-X appeared, one FedExed from Miami to Colonel Hamilton at Fort Detrick, the second left for the Border Patrol to find on the Texas–Mexico border."

"Where did it come from?"

"Almost certainly from the Congo. We know that a Russian Special Operations airplane—a Tupolev Tu-934A—landed at El Obeid Airport, in North Kurdufan, Sudan—which is within driving range of the Fish Farm—and took off shortly afterward, leaving seventeen bodies behind.

"We suspect it flew first to Cuba for refueling, and then it flew here, where two barrels of Congo-X were given to the Mexico City *rezident* of the SVR, who then drove off with them, presumably to get them across the border into the United States."

"How do you know that?" General Naylor challenged.

"We have it all on surveillance tape, sir. I'll show the tapes to you, if you'd like. There's a very clear picture of General Yakov Sirinov, who is apparently in charge of the operation. The Tupolev Tu-934A then left here, and is presently on the ground at La Orchila airfield. That's on an island off the coast of Venezuela."

"How could you possibly know that?" General Naylor demanded.

"I'd show you the satellite imagery, sir, but if I did, you'd know where I got them."

"I don't think I'd have to look very far, would I, General McNab?" Naylor asked unpleasantly.

Castillo said, "You have my word that I did not get them from General McNab. And, sir, with respect, your parole does not give you the right to question me, or anyone else. Please keep that in mind."

He let that sink in, and then went on: "Now, for Facts Bearing on the

Problem, Scene Two. The Russian *rezident* in Washington, Sergei Murov, had Frank Lammelle—speaking of whom, Vic: Should we have someone take a look at him?"

"He has two of your Spetsnaz watching him, Charley. I think they'll be able to tell if the SOB croaks."

Castillo nodded, then went on: "The Russians had Lammelle over to their dacha on Maryland's Eastern Shore, where Murov, the *rezident*, admitted they sent the Congo-X to Colonel Hamilton, and then offered to turn over all Congo-X in their control and give us their assurance that no more will ever turn up. All they want in return is Dmitri, Sweaty, and me.

"The President thinks the price is fair. He sent General Naylor to arrest me, and Frank Lammelle to arrest Sweaty and Dmitri. . . ."

"Is that true, General Naylor?" Danton asked.

"Any conversations I may or may not have had with the President, Mr. Danton," Naylor said, "are both privileged and classified."

"It's true," General McNab said.

"How do you know?" Danton asked.

"Because that's what General Naylor told me," McNab said. "Under the Code of Honor, people—especially general officers—don't tell fibs to each other. They may try to make human sacrifices of fellow officers, but telling fibs is a no-no. Telling a fib will get you kicked right off that Long Gray Line."

"Colonel Brewer, please be prepared to report that exchange in detail," Naylor said.

"Jesus Christ, Allan!" McNab said. Then, "Sorry, Sweaty, that just slipped out."

"The question is moot," Castillo said. "Colonel Berezovsky and Lieutenant Colonel Alekseeva are not going to be involuntarily repatriated. And I ain't goin' nowhere I don't want to go, neither."

"So what are you going to do, Charley?" Allan Junior asked.

"It took me a lot longer than it should have for me to figure this out, Allan, but what I'm going to do is something they told me on that fabled plain over-looking the Hudson when I was eighteen. When, if I made it through Hudson High and became an officer, my first duty would be to take care of my people.

"I forgot that over the years. The truth of the matter was that falling off the face of the earth didn't bother me much. There I was, with Sweaty, on the fin-est trout-fishing river in the world. The President of the United States had re-lieved me of my responsibilities.

"Then Dmitri and Sweaty's cousin, Colonel V. N. Solomatin, who runs the Second Directorate of the SVR with Putin looking over his shoulder, wrote a letter to Dmitri and Sweaty, telling them to come home, all is forgiven.

"Since he didn't know where they were, he had the *resident* in Budapest give the letter to a friend of mine there who he thought knew how to get in touch with me. He was right. Several hours later, Sweaty and I were reading it in Patagonia.

"What was significant about the letter was not that Putin thought anybody would believe that all was forgiven, but that he wasn't going to stop until Sweaty and Dmitri paid for their sins. That letter was intended to give Clendennen an out: He wasn't forcing Sweaty and Dmitri to go back to Russia. 'Knowing that all was forgiven—here's the letter to prove that—they went back willingly.'

"Then the Congo-X appeared in Fort Detrick. Just about as soon as that happened, some people who knew the OOA—"

"The what?" Roscoe Danton interrupted.

"The Office of Organizational Analysis, the President's—"

"Okay. Now I'm with you," Danton said.

"Okay. Some people—"

"What people?" Danton interrupted again.

"I'm not going to tell you that now; I may never tell you. I haven't figured out what to do about them yet."

"Let me deal with the bastards, Charley," Aloysius said.

"I'd love to, Aloysius, but I want to be invisible when this is all over, and that would be hard to do if all those people suddenly committed suicide by jumping off the roller coaster on top of that tower in Las Vegas. People would wonder why they did that."

Casey chuckled.

"That's not exactly what I had in mind, but close," he said.

"You realize, Colonel," Danton said, "that all you're doing is whetting my appetite. Presuming that I come out of this alive, I'm going to find out who these people are. So, why don't you tell me now?"

Castillo considered that.

"Tell him, Carlos," Sweaty said.

"You think that's smart?"

"I think you have to tell Mr. Danton everything," she said. "Or eliminate him. He either trusts you—us—completely, or he's too dangerous to us to stay alive . . ."

"Was that a threat?" Danton challenged, and thought: *No, it was a statement of fact. And the frightening thing about that is I think he's going to listen to her.*

Sweaty ignored him. She went on: ". . . and now is when you have to make that decision."

Danton thought: *I realize this is overdramatic, but the cold truth is that if these people think I'm a danger to them, they're entirely capable of taking me out in the desert, shooting me, and leaving me for the buzzards.*

Why the fuck did I ever agree to come here?

"Dmitri?" Castillo asked.

"I think she's right again," Berezovsky said, after a moment's consideration of the question.

"My consiglieri having spoken, Mr. Danton . . ." Castillo said, and paused.

Roscoe Danton wondered: *Consiglieri?*

Where the hell did he get that? From The Godfather?

Castillo met Danton's eyes, then went on: "There is a group of men in Las Vegas who have both enormous wealth and influence, the latter reaching all over, and, in at least two cases I'm sure of, into the Oval Office. Not to the President, but to several members of his cabinet. They're all patriots, and they use their wealth and influence from time to time to fund intelligence activities for which funds are not available.

"When *those people* learned that OOA had been disbanded, they thought they could hire it as sort of a mercenary Special Operations organization."

"*Those people* have names?" Danton asked.

"Giving them to you would be a breach of trust," Castillo said. "We never agreed to this proposal when it was made, but neither, apparently, did we say 'Hell, no' with sufficient emphasis.

"It was from those people that we first learned of the Congo-X at Fort Detrick. They got in touch and wanted us to look into it. I was going to do that anyway, as it obviously was likely to have something to do with Dmitri and Sweaty as well as the threat it posed to the country.

"I made the mistake of taking two hundred thousand dollars in expense money, following my rule of whenever possible you should spend other people's money rather than your own, and this, I am afraid, allowed them to think the mercenaries were on their payroll."

"What was wrong with that?" Danton asked.

"Well, for one thing, we're not for hire. But what happened, I have come to believe, is that when they learned that President Clendennen had decided to swap Dmitri, Sweaty, and me in exchange for the Congo-X that the Russians have, they decided that made sense, and that since I was a mercenary, I was expendable."

"They told you this?" Danton asked.

"No. But I'm not taking any of their calls," Castillo said. "Or letting them know where I am."

"They think Charley's on a riverboat between Budapest and Vienna," Aloysius said. "And that I'm in Tokyo."

"I don't understand that," Danton said.

"You're not supposed to," Sweaty said. "Go on, Carlitos."

"What are you going to do?" Danton said.

"Well, there is some good news. We've learned how to kill Congo-X," Castillo said. "Right now, nobody knows that but us—"

"You know something that important and you're not going to tell the President?" General Naylor blurted.

"If we told him, sir, there are several probabilities I'm not willing to accept. One would be that he would want to know how we came to know this before he did; that would place Colonel Hamilton in an awkward position."

"Goddamn it, Charley!" Naylor exploded. "Hamilton is a serving officer. He is duty-bound."

"Sir, with respect. You are violating your parole. I have told you that you are not permitted to question me. But I'll answer that. Inasmuch as Colonel Hamilton marches beside us in the Long Gray Line, I'm sure he considered the Code of Honor before deciding that to keep this information to ourselves for the time being was necessary. He realized that if President Clendennen knew that we can now neutralize Congo-X, the Russians would learn that in short order. Right now, we don't want to give them that."

There was silence for a moment.

Then Danton asked, "So, what are you going to do, Colonel?"

"Depending on how much Congo-X the Russians have, that reduces the threat to the United States just about completely, or doesn't reduce it much at all," Castillo went on.

"The odds are that the Congo-X that General Sirinov flew out of Africa is all of it. Dmitri says that the Russians knew how awful this stuff is. Burned once, no pun intended, by Chernobyl, they didn't want to run the risk of having any of this stuff inside Russia.

"If he's wrong, and the Russians have warehouses full of Congo-X, or have the means inside Russia, or in Iran, or someplace else, to make more of it, then the United States is in deep trouble.

"So what we have to do is find out how much Congo-X they have. I don't think Putin would answer that truthfully. So we have to ask the only other man who might, General Yakov Sirinov."

"How the hell are you going to do that? And what makes you think he'll tell you the truth?" Danton asked.

"We're going to raid the Venezuelan airfield, La Orchila, grab the general, load him on his Tupolev Tu-934A, fly him here, and ask him."

"You're going to invade Venezuela?"

"We're going to launch a raid on a Venezuelan airfield, not invade. When you invade, you try to stay. With a little luck, we should be in and out in no more than fifteen minutes, twenty tops."

Danton repeated, "'Load him on his Tupolev'?"

Castillo nodded. "The CIA has a standing offer of one hundred twenty-five million dollars for a Tu-934A. We're going to get them one; we need the money."

"To answer your other question, Mr. Danton," Sweaty said, "once we get General Sirinov here, I'll be asking the questions. He will tell us the truth."

"And now you'll have to excuse me for a few minutes," Castillo said. "I have to go buy another Black Hawk. While I'm gone, we'll show you the surveillance tapes."

"'Buy another Black Hawk?'" Danton parroted.

"That's right," Castillo said. "You don't know how that works, do you?"

"Uh-uh."

"Well, the U.S. Army buys them from Sikorsky. They run right around six million dollars. Then the State Department sells them to the Mexican government—to be used in their unrelenting war against the drug cartels—for about one-tenth of that, say, six hundred thousand.

"The next thing that happens is that—in the aforementioned unrelenting war run by the Policía Federal Preventiva against the drug cartels—the helicopter is reported to have been shot down, or that it crashed in flames.

"Next, a Policía Federal Preventiva palm is crossed with a little money—say, a million or so—and the Black Hawk rises phoenix-like from the ashes. The drug cartels find them very useful to move drugs around. That tends to raise the price. The one downstairs cost us one point two million, and I have been warned that the bidding today will start at a million three."

"Incredible!" Danton said.

"Enjoy the movies, Mr. Danton," Castillo said. "I'll be back as soon as I can."

[EIGHT]
The Office of the Director of National Intelligence
Eisenhower Executive Office Building
17th Street and Pennsylvania Avenue, N.W.
Washington, D.C.
1210 11 February 2007

"Mr. McGuire is here to see you, Mr. Ambassador," Montvale's secretary announced.

"Ask him to come in, please," Montvale said, and, as Truman Ellsworth watched from a leather armchair, then rose from behind his desk and walked toward the door, meeting McGuire as he entered the office.

"Hello, Tom," Montvale said. "What can I do for you?"

McGuire hesitated, and then said, "I suppose you've heard I don't work here no more."

Montvale nodded. "Mason Andrews lost very little time in telling me; he was here two minutes after Truman and I got here this morning."

"How are you, Tom?" Ellsworth said.

He got out of his armchair, went to McGuire, and gave him his hand.

McGuire hesitated again.

"I decided I couldn't just fold my tent, Mr. Ambassador, without facing you and telling you I was sorry . . ."

"You're not going to be prosecuted, Tom, if that's what's worrying you. To do that, Andrews would need me to testify and I made sure he understands that's just not going to happen."

McGuire finished, ". . . but when I walked in here just now, I realized I couldn't do that. When Mrs. Darby told me Alex Darby was down there in . . ."

"Ushuaia," Ellsworth furnished.

". . . with some floozy, I knew that wasn't so. And when I told you, I told myself that you were too smart to swallow that whole. But what I came to tell you, Mr. Ambassador, is that I hoped you would."

"I appreciate your honesty, Tom. Are you going to tell me why?"

"I just had enough of the whole scenario, Mr. Ambassador. I think what the President's trying to do to Charley Castillo is rotten. I didn't want to be part of it. I hope they never find him."

"Prefacing this by saying that I'm about to join you in the army of the unemployed . . ."

"Excuse me?"

"You've been around the White House for a long time, Tom. What inferences would you draw if I told you that that red telephone no longer directly connects the director of National Intelligence to the President?"

He gave McGuire time to consider that, then went on: "And when the director of National Intelligence—to whom the President is now referring to as the 'director of National Stupidity'—attempts to telephone the President using the White House switchboard, the President's secretary answers and tells me the President is busy and will get back to me. Or words to that effect."

"He's going to throw you under the bus, too?" McGuire asked.

"That is the inference I have drawn. Does that sound reasonable to you?"

"Then I am sorry, Mr. Ambassador. I didn't think what I did would cost you your job."

"What you did, Tom, probably contributed to that, but I don't think it was the only thing that made President Clendennen decide he could do without my services. He really isn't quite as stupid as he appears. I think it is entirely likely that he has known for some time what I think of him. He would like nothing better than to have Roscoe J. Danton write a column detailing how his director of National Stupidity went on a wild-goose chase to Ushuaia, but he can't do that because Roscoe would be sure to ask him why he sent Truman and me to Argentina in the first place, and he can't be sure how far he can push my reluctance to embarrass the Office of the President—for that matter, Clendennen himself—before it is overwhelmed by my contempt.

"Inasmuch as he knows that I won't oblige him by resigning, what he's doing is looking for a way to fire me in conditions that won't reflect adversely on him."

"Is Danton going to write about . . . you going to Ushuaia?"

"I don't know. I'm having trouble getting in touch with him. Just before you came in, Truman and I decided that we will take our lunch at the Old Ebbitt Grill. Not only are we fairly sure that the Executive Dining Room will no longer welcome us, but we suspect we can find Mr. Danton at one of his favorite watering holes, the Old Ebbitt.

"We'll have to walk. Truman and I no longer have access to the White House fleet of Yukons."

"My God!"

"If you don't mind the walk, Truman and I would be delighted if you were to join us."

"You don't have to do that, Mr. Ambassador."

"I want to do it," Montvale said. "Please join us."

XV

"Sorry to have taken so long," Castillo said when he walked into the dining room trailed by Max. "Unexpected problems at the used helicopter lot."

"But you got another Black Hawk?" Sweaty asked.

"I got another one. But the price went up to one point four million, and I suspect it's not going to be as nice as the one downstairs."

"Colonel, can I ask where you're getting all that money?" Roscoe Danton said.

"The LCBF Corporation actually purchased the Black Hawks, and is loaning them to us," Castillo answered.

"That's 'those people' in Las Vegas?" Danton asked.

"Oh, no," Castillo said. "The LCBF Corporation has absolutely nothing to do with those people in Las Vegas."

"Then what the hell is it?"

"I'd really like to tell you, Roscoe," Castillo said solemnly. "I really would. But if I did, I'd have to kill you."

That earned a chuckle from not only the Special Operations people around the table—there was one more of them now, CWO5 Colin Leverette (Retired) having come in while they were watching the surveillance camera tapes—but also from Lieutenant Colonel (Designate) Allan Naylor, Jr.

General Naylor, however, who had heard the comment often, was not amused.

He thought: *These Special Operations types, from Charley's teenaged ex-Marine "bodyguard" Lester Bradley up to Lieutenant General Bruce McNab, have an almost perverse sense of humor. They're different. They have no respect for anything or anyone but each other.*

And then he thought: *Why do I suspect that things did not go well when Charley was off buying another Black Hawk?*

And I think he was telling the truth about that, too. We give the Mexicans multimillion-dollar helicopters, which then promptly wind up in the hands of the drug cartels.

Castillo said, "Well, now that you've seen the movie starring General Yakov Sirinov and his Dancing SVR Ninjas . . ."

There he goes again! Why does he feel compelled to make a joke even of that?

". . . I think we should move to the war room, where I will attempt to explain our plan."

"Am I permitted to make a comment?" the elder Naylor asked.

"Yes, sir. Of course."

"That tape should be in the hands of the President. He could have the secretary of State demand an emergency session of the UN Security Council. . . ."

"Not until we know how much Congo-X the Russians have," Castillo said very seriously, and then his voice became mocking: "And now, lady, Max, and gentlemen, if you'll be good enough to follow me to the war room?"

He bowed deeply, holding one arm across his middle and pointing the other toward the door.

Naylor thought: *I'd like to throw something at him.*

He glanced at McNab, who was smiling.

What's he smiling at? Charley playing the clown?

Or me?

The war room had been a recreation/exercise room. There was a Ping-Pong table, a pocket billiards table, and half a dozen exercise machines of assorted functioning.

The exercise machines had been moved into a corner of the room. The billiards and Ping-Pong tables were covered with maps. Lester Bradley was at a table on which sat a Casey communicator and several printers. There were armchairs, most of them in a semicircle facing large maps taped to a wall. Another armchair was alone against the side of the wall. And again, there were two burly, fair-skinned, Uzi-armed men sitting by the doors to the room.

"Colonel Castillo, I think we should discuss my understanding of my parole."

"With respect, sir, will you hold that until I ask the deputy director of the Central Intelligence Agency if it's convenient for him to join us?" Castillo replied, and then issued an order in Russian.

Thirty seconds later, Frank Lammelle was ushered into the room by two burly Russians. He was wearing a shirt and trousers. He was barefoot. His wrists were encircled with plastic handcuffs. The handcuffs were held against his waist by another plastic handcuff attached to his belt.

"Good afternoon, Frank," Castillo said.

"You're going to jail for this, Castillo."

Castillo issued another order in Russian. One of the ex-Spetsnaz operators left the room and returned a moment later with a folding metal chair. Castillo showed him where he wanted it, and then, not gently, guided Lammelle into it.

"Lester, go sit in the armchair. Take Mr. Lammelle's air pistol with you."

Bradley complied.

"Frank," Castillo then said, "you pose a problem for me. General McNab, General Naylor, and General Naylor's staff are also here involuntarily. But they have given me their parole under the Code of Honor. I'm fairly sure you've heard of it. I'm also absolutely sure—you being the DDCI—that you wouldn't consider yourself bound by it. So I will not accept your parole.

"Which means you will sit there in handcuffs. If you even look like you're thinking of getting out of the chair without my express permission, Lester will dart you. I should tell you that he's not only a former Marine gunnery sergeant but also a crack shot. He was a designated marksman on the March to Baghdad. He will also dart you if you speak without my permission. You understand?"

"You heard what I said about you going to jail for this, you sonofabitch!"

"You are entitled to one emotional outburst before Lester darts you. You just used it. Lester, put a dart in the back of his neck the next time he says anything."

"Aye, aye, sir."

"And, Frank, the next time you use language that offends my fiancée, I will let Max bite you. Show the man your teeth, Max," Castillo said, then spoke a few words in Hungarian while pointing at Lammelle.

Max, growling deep in his throat, walked to Lammelle and showed him his teeth. Lammelle squirmed on the folding chair.

All the special operators in the room, plus Lieutenant Colonel (Designate) Naylor, chuckled.

General Naylor thought: *There's that perverted sense of humor again!*

And Allan thinks that threatening to sic that enormous dog on Lammelle is perfectly acceptable conduct!

"Oh, that's right," Castillo said. "You haven't met my fiancée, have you, Frank? Sweetheart, say hello to Frank Lammelle. He used to be a friend of mine. Frank, the lady is former Lieutenant Colonel Svetlana Alekseeva of the SVR. And sitting next to her is her brother, former Colonel Dmitri Berezovsky of the SVR. I know you've been anxious to meet them."

There was a moment's silence.

"Lester, if Frank doesn't say 'Pleased to meet you' or 'How do you do?' in the next three seconds, dart him."

Lammelle very hastily said, "Pleased to meet you."

The special operators and Allan Junior now laughed.

"Colonel, regarding the Code of Honor," General Naylor said.

Goddamn it, I'm smiling! What the hell is happening to me?

"Yes, sir?"

"I don't know what your intentions are here, but I think I should tell you that when I am no longer constrained by my parole, I will feel free to relate to the proper authorities anything I see or hear here."

"Yes, sir. That's understood. It's not a problem, sir, as you remain here—in other words, not in a position to tell anyone anything—until this operation concludes."

Castillo looked around the room.

"I think I should make it clear before I start that—as much as I know I could have used his wise counsel—I did not ask General McNab for any assistance in coming up with this plan. The Code of Honor would have precluded him giving me any assistance."

"You're wrong about that, Charley," McNab said.

Naylor glared at him.

"On the other hand," Castillo, ignoring the comment, went on, "I have been privileged over the years to watch General McNab plan and execute maybe two dozen operations such as this one. What I'm doing now is praying that enough of his expertise has rubbed off on me so that this one will work."

He looked at Svetlana.

"And I meant that, Sweaty, about praying. That wasn't a figure of speech."

"I know, my Carlitos," Svetlana said.

"Okay, here we go," Castillo said. "Statement of the Problem: We have to interrogate General Yakov Sirinov to determine how much Congo-X the Russians have. To do this, we have to bring the general, plus whatever Congo-X he has in his possession, here.

"We know from satellite imagery that General Sirinov went from here to the airfield on La Orchila, the island off the coast of Venezuela. The latest satellite imagery we have, as of oh-six-hundred today, no longer shows the Tu-934A aircraft, but does show half a dozen of the Spetsnaz operators near what appears to be one of those canvas-and-poles, throw-it-up-overnight hangars. It is therefore reasonable to presume the Tu-934A is in the hangar; it is unlikely that Sirinov would leave the Spetsnaz in Venezuela. . . ."

"Colonel," Roscoe Danton said, "you never said where are you getting the satellite imagery . . ."

Castillo nodded. "That's another of those questions, Roscoe, that I'd like to answer, but . . ."

"I know," Danton said. "You'd have to kill me if you did."

"Right," Castillo said. "Now, as far as personnel go, we're going to use as few Americans as possible. Colonel Berezovsky said that we stand a good chance, if we have the element of surprise on our side and use our ex-Spetsnaz people, to confuse Sirinov's Spetsnaz to the point where their efficiency will be substantially reduced."

"Explain that to me, Charley," General McNab said softly.

"Dmitri and our Spetsnaz get off the plane, the chopper, whatever we wind up using. Dmitri points to the nearest of Sirinov's Spetsnaz and says, 'I am Colonel Berezovsky. Take me to General Sirinov.' Dmitri thinks, and Sweaty thinks, and I agree, there's a good chance we can get away with that. If we do, we stick a pistol up Sirinov's nose. . . ."

"And if you don't?" McNab asked.

"Then we can probably disarm Sirinov's Spetsnaz. Or, if necessary, take them out."

"You don't want to start by taking them out?" McNab said.

"We're trying to avoid taking anybody out," Castillo said.

Berezovsky put in: "I think going in there with guns blazing would be counterproductive, General. And possibly disastrous. We don't know what would happen if one of those rubber barrels was subjected to machine-gun fire. We don't want little pieces of Congo-X scattered all over that airfield."

"Good point," McNab said. "What did you say, Charley, about 'whatever we wind up using'? That sounds like you're not planning to use the Black Hawks."

"We may not be able to use them," Castillo said. "The closest staging point we can use is Cozumel. And that island is thirteen hundred nautical miles, give or take, from La Orchila. The ferry range of a Black Hawk is in the book at twelve hundred. We might be able to stretch that to thirteen hundred—we probably could; Dick and I have a lot of time in Black Hawks watching the fuel exhaustion warning light blinking at us—but that would put us in La Orchila with dry tanks."

"Auxiliary fuel cells?" General Naylor asked.

"I don't know where I can get any, sir," Castillo said. "And even with fuel cells, we'd have to top off the Black Hawks, and the fuel cells, at La Orchila.

That would take twenty minutes at least. I don't want to be on the ground more than fifteen minutes. And that's presuming we would be able to refuel at La Orchila."

"So what is your alternate plan?" McNab said.

"Overload the Gulfstream III—I can get a lot of people in there; maybe fifteen—to go in under the radar at first light and hope Dmitri's 'Take me to General Sirinov' order dazzles Sirinov's Spetsnaz. Then we load him and what Congo-X he has on his Tu-934A and come back here."

"What would happen to your Gulfstream?" Naylor asked.

"Sir, maybe there would be fuel there, and time to refuel. Unlikely, but possible. If not, Sparkman leaves with what fuel remains and heads for Barranquilla, Colombia. And we get on the Tu-934A and come here."

"Charley," McNab asked softly, "what would your wish list be for this operation?"

"General, we've given that very subject a lot of thought," Castillo said. "If I had my druthers, I'd commandeer four UH-60Ms from the One-Sixtieth Special Operations fleet. Two to use and two for redundancy. All with stub wings and external tanks. They would be armed with GAU-19 fifty-caliber Gatling guns and AGM-114 Hellfire laser-guided missiles to take out the commo building."

He paused, and then went on, "And since I have been a very good boy, I would like Santa to also bring me a Red Ryder BB gun and an anatomically correct Barbie doll."

McNab, D'Allessando, and Allan Junior laughed.

"Well, you asked me," Castillo said. "And, oh, I forgot: An aircraft carrier—preferably the USS *Ronald Reagan*—sitting somewhere out there on the blue Caribbean so that I and my stalwart band could have a last meal on the Navy before we sallied forth to battle the forces of evil."

This got the expected laughter.

"But since I don't believe in Santa Claus, I guess we'll have to go with my tired old Gulfstream III. Among other things, I suspect we're running out of time."

"How much time do you think you have?" General Naylor asked.

"Seventy-two hours tops, sir. If I had to bet, I'd wager that in forty-eight hours the Tu-934A will be on its way somewhere."

"Somewhere?"

"Sir, I have no idea where it will go. Maybe Cuba. I just don't know."

General Naylor then suddenly said, "Colonel Castillo, I herewith inform you I am withdrawing my parole."

"Oh, for Christ's sake, Allan!" General McNab said disgustedly. "Now what?"

"Yes, sir, General Naylor," Castillo said evenly. "I regret to tell you, sir, that I am placing you under arrest."

"Colonel Castillo, are you still determined to proceed on an operation that not only is unauthorized but in my professional opinion is suicidal?"

"Sir, I see going ahead with this as my duty. I beg you, sir, please don't get in my way."

General Naylor nodded, then said, "Colonel Brewer, make note of the time."

"Yes, sir. It's fourteen twenty-eight, sir."

General Naylor went on: "Make note of this, please, Colonel Brewer. Write it down. Quote. Having at fourteen twenty-seven withdrawn my parole, at fourteen twenty-eight, in the realization that I was not going to be able to deter Lieutenant Colonel Castillo from proceeding on an unauthorized operation involving Congo-X in Venezuela, I came to the conclusion that my duty lay in increasing his chances of success, as the failure of his operation would cause more damage to the United States than its success."

"Sir, I don't understand," Castillo said.

"Get me on a secure line to my headquarters at MacDill and it will be made clear to you, Colonel."

The two looked into each other's eyes for a long minute.

"Do what he says, Carlos," Svetlana said softly.

Castillo turned to Lester Bradley, and ordered: "Give the air pistol to Uncle Remus, Lester, and get a secure line to MacDill."

"Aye, aye, sir. Where will the general be calling from?"

"Mexico City," Naylor said. "I wish to speak with my deputy, General Albert McFadden, USAF."

Lester looked at Castillo for permission, and when Castillo nodded, said, "Aye, aye, sir."

"And put it on the loudspeaker," Naylor said.

"Office of the Deputy Commander, Central Command. Sergeant Major Ashley speaking, sir."

"This line is secure," Lester announced. "General Naylor calling for General McFadden."

"One moment, please."

"Hello, boss. Where the hell are you?"

"Mexico City, Albert. And you know why I'm here."

"Yes, sir. I do."

Naylor moved to the map on the wall.

"What's the Navy got, capable of refueling four UH-60Ms, in the area of eighteen degrees north latitude, eighty-five degrees west longitude? I need it there no later than tomorrow."

"What the hell is going on, Allan?"

"Don't ask questions, please. Answer mine, but don't ask any. And this conversation goes no further than your ears. Understand?"

"Yes, sir. Just a moment, General."

"I can have the USS *Bataan* at that point by sixteen-hundred hours, sir."

"Tell me about the *Bataan*."

"It's a *Wasp*-class amphibious assault ship," General McFadden said.

"I know the class. That'll do fine. Make sure it's on station as of oh-eight-hundred tomorrow. Alert them, Top Secret, to be prepared to receive and fuel four UH-60Ms."

"Yes, sir. Sir, I'm guessing this is a black operation?"

"About as black as it can get. Hold one, Albert," General Naylor said, and turned to McNab.

"General McNab, I presume the four UH-60Ms will be coming from Fort Campbell?"

"Yes, sir," McNab said, and joined Naylor at the map.

"Where's the best jumping-off place for them to fly out to the *Bataan*, would you say?"

"Sir, can we use the Navy base at Key West?" McNab asked.

"General, I'm the commander in chief of Central Command. Of course we can use NAS Key West. Albert?"

"Yes, sir?"

"Tell Boca Chica airfield to be prepared to receive the Black Hawks, and order them to keep their mouths shut about it."

"Yes, sir."

"I'll get back to you, Albert. General McNab needs the phone."

"Sir, how do I get in touch with you?"

"You don't. I'll check in with you periodically. Naylor out."

"Lester," McNab then said. "Get me the One-Sixtieth Special Operations Aviation Regiment at Fort Campbell, Kentucky. Make it look like I'm calling from Washington."

"Yes, sir."

General Naylor looked around the room. "Why do I feel I'm basking in the approval of a number of people who five minutes ago thought I was a chicken-shit sonofabitch?"

"Dad," Lieutenant Colonel (Designate) Allan Naylor, Jr., said, "why don't we all try to forget what you were five minutes ago?"

[TWO]
The President's Study
The White House
1600 Pennsylvania Avenue, N.W.
Washington, D.C.
0905 12 February 2007

"Good morning, Mr. President," John Powell, the director of the Central Intelligence Agency, said as he walked into the room.

"You're here to tell me that the Russians and Castillo are now en route to Moscow, right?"

"No, sir, I regret that I am not. But there have been some interesting developments, Mr. President, that suggest we're a good deal closer to that solution of the problem than we were at this time yesterday."

"Let's hear them. Before a National Park Service policeman finds another beer barrel of that stuff at Nine Hundred Ohio Drive, Southwest."

"Mr. President, Nine Hundred Ohio Drive?"

"The Lincoln Memorial, Jack. You don't know where it is?"

The President looked very pleased with himself.

"Jack," he went on, "we promised that Russian sonofabitch . . . what's his name, the *rezident*?"

"Murov, sir. Sergei Murov."

"We promised *Murov* his two traitors and Castillo several days ago. If I were this guy, I would be wondering why that hasn't happened, and if I were this guy, I think I would be tempted to leave another barrel of this stuff somewhere—say, at Nine Hundred Ohio Drive, Southwest—as a little reminder. You heard what that Fort Detrick scientist . . . what's his name, the black guy . . . ?"

"Colonel Hamilton, sir. Colonel J. Porter Hamilton."

". . . had to say about how dangerous this stuff is."

"Yes, sir, I did."

"I don't want any more barrels of Congo-X popping up anywhere. You understand?"

"Yes, sir. Of course."

"Now, with that in mind, tell me about the interesting developments."

"Sir, General Naylor has been heard from."

"Where is he?"

"Sir, according to Bruce Festerman—"

"Who the hell is he?"

"Festerman is the CIA liaison officer with Central Command at MacDill, Mr. President. We've been on the phone a half-dozen times since yesterday afternoon."

"And?"

"General Naylor called General McFadden, his deputy, from Mexico City and ordered that a ship, the USS *Bataan*, which is a *Wasp*-class amphibious assault ship, be moved to a location in the Caribbean and be prepared to receive and refuel four Black Hawk helicopters. He also ordered the Navy base at Key West to do the same thing; in other words, be prepared to receive and refuel four UH-60s. It seems clear, sir, that the helicopters will be flown from Key West to the *Bataan*."

"Why?"

"I don't know, sir. What I suspect is that General Naylor has learned where Castillo and/or the Russians are, somewhere in Mexico, and is going to go get them."

"And what does Lammelle think?"

"Sir, that's a development I don't quite understand."

"What development don't you understand?"

"Sir, the GPS transmitter in Lammelle's shoe places him aboard the *Queen of the Caribbean,* a cruise ship, which is now in the Caribbean bound for Málaga. There has been nothing from him."

"And the GPS transmitter in Castillo's laptop places him aboard a river steamer on the Danube between Budapest and Vienna, right?"

"Yes, sir."

"And now you're telling me General Naylor thinks he's found Castillo in Mexico?"

"I am making that inference, sir. I can't imagine why else General Naylor has—"

"Well," the President interrupted, "one possibility is that Lammelle has suddenly decided he needs a vacation, and taking a cruise is the way to do that. But, sitting around here, Jack, with nothing to occupy my mind, I have been thinking of all the bad spy movies I've seen over the years to see if anything in them might be useful."

"Sir?"

"For example, do you think it's possible that somebody shot Lammelle with that whiz-bang dart gun of his and then loaded him onto the cruise ship?"

"Why would anyone want to do that, sir? You're suggesting that Castillo—"

"I'm suggesting General Naylor might have done it. Or more likely, now that I think about it, General McNab."

"Why would they want to do that, sir?"

"To keep him from fucking up what they're doing to put Castillo and the traitors in the bag."

"I don't think that's likely, Mr. President."

"Tell me about Castillo on the river steamer. You sent people over there, right?"

"Yes, sir."

"And what have they found out?"

"The ship is called *Stadt Wien*," Powell said. "It plies the Danube back and forth between Budapest and Vienna."

"I already know that. The question is, is Castillo—and maybe the Russians—on it or not?"

"We've learned that Castillo never made a reservation on it."

"That wasn't the question."

"We don't know, Mr. President."

"Did it occur to your people to go aboard the damned ship and look for him?"

"They couldn't get a ticket, Mr. President. And without a ticket you can't get on the *Stadt Wien*. Apparently, sir, you have to make reservations at least two weeks in advance." Powell hesitated and then went on: "What the *Stadt Wien* is, Mr. President, is somewhere the Viennese and the Budapesters take their romantic interests for an overnight trip. Not always their wives, if you take my meaning. It's very popular."

"Jesus Christ, Jack! Castillo hasn't been over there two weeks. How the hell could he have made a reservation on this Hungarian *Love Boat*?"

"Mr. President, all I can tell you is that's where Casey's GPS locator shows he is."

"Presumably fucking the woman traitor as they cruise up and down the Danube? Jack, listen closely: I don't think Castillo is anywhere near Europe. I think Naylor and McNab have found him in Mexico. And presuming neither the CIA nor Ambassador Stupid get involved and fuck things up for them—the more I think about it, Naylor or McNab *did* shoot Lammelle with that dart gun and load him on that cruise ship to get rid of him—"

President Clendennen interrupted himself, took a deep breath, and then went on: "Jack, what I want you to do is get in touch with all your Clandestine Service officers who are running around chasing their tails looking for Castillo and the Russians and get them back to Langley. And then lock them in. Naylor is going to bag Castillo if you don't get in the way. You understand me?"

"Yes, Mr. President."

"The next time you walk in that door, Jack, I want you to tell me that you've just learned from General Naylor that he's dealt with the problem. And I don't want to see you until you can do that."

[THREE]
Cozumel International Airport
Isla Cozumel
Quintana Roo, Mexico
1010 12 February 2007

Dick Miller and Dick Sparkman had flown the Policía Federal Preventiva UH-60 from Drug Cartel International to Cozumel. They had carried with them all but two of the ex-Spetsnaz special operators and all the weapons and other equipment that would be needed.

Both pilots had been more than a little pissed—and vocally so—with their assigned tasks in the operation. Miller had wanted to fly with Castillo in the UH-60 in the assault, and Sparkman had simply presumed until the last minute that he would be Jake Torine's co-pilot when the Tu-934A was flown out of La Orchila.

Uncle Remus Leverette had similarly taken for granted that he would be in on the assault and was more than displeased with his assigned role: He was now to "hold the fort" at Laguna el Guaje. It was more than a figure of speech. There was a small but real chance that some members of the drug cartel—either not having heard, or not caring that Drug Cartel International was closed—would drop in.

If this should happen, Uncle Remus would politely suggest to them that they come back another day—say, in a week—and if that didn't work, he would take the appropriate measures. The drug runners would, if possible, be disarmed, placed in plastic handcuffs, and confined.

If the disarmament option didn't work, they would be eliminated.

To assist him in this task, in addition to the two ex-Spetsnaz operators, Uncle Remus had Mr. Vic D'Allessando, former Gunnery Sergeant Lester Bradley, and Lieutenant "Peg-Leg" Lorimer (Retired). Former Special Forces

Sergeant Aloysius F. Casey and Generals Naylor and McNab were to be the reserve force.

General McNab had voiced no objection to this, but everyone knew if there was shooting, McNab would be in the middle of it.

Lieutenant Colonel (Designate) Naylor—having been told that he would be useless on the actual assault due to the fact that he (a) was a tank driver, (b) had no Special Operations training, and (c) spoke no Russian—first pleaded to be taken along. Then, when his pleas fell on deaf ears, he said very unkind things to Colonel Castillo.

Colonel Castillo forgave the outburst, kissed him on the forehead, and charged him with sitting—literally, if that became necessary—on the deputy director of the CIA, Mr. Lammelle.

All of those remaining at Drug Cartel International had come to see—if very reluctantly—that there was no valid argument against Castillo's logic in making the assignments. The more the operation was polished, the more it became apparent how much success would depend upon Dmitri Berezovsky's ability to dazzle—or at least substantially confuse—General Sirinov's Spetsnaz until they had a pistol up the general's nose.

Castillo didn't plan to open his mouth, but if he had to, his Russian was so fluent that people thought he came from Saint Petersburg. None of those being left to hold the fort spoke the language so well. And although Uncle Remus's Russian was nearly as good as Castillo's, there were very few Russians as black as God had made Uncle Remus.

Colonel Jake Torine's Russian was very limited, but he could read the lettering they would find on the instrument panel of the Tu-934A. Navigation of the airplane would be by the Casey GPS system installed on their laptops.

Max, as he was wont to do, suspected his master intended to leave him behind. So, when Castillo, Sweaty, Dmitri, and Roscoe J. Danton got into the Cessna Mustang for the flight to Cozumel, they found Max already lying in the aisle looking at Castillo with melancholy eyes that melted his master's heart.

What the hell! When we leave Cozumel, I'll chain him to the seat. Sparkman will be flying this back. He and Sweaty can deal with him; he likes them.

That did not come to pass.

When the Policía Federal Preventiva UH-60 had been refueled at Cozumel, and after Castillo had spent an hour explaining the cockpit specifically and the aircraft generally to Colonel Torine, he had climbed out to see how the loading of the Spetsnaz was going.

He found that everybody had changed into their combat uniforms, which were in fact commercially available summer-weight camouflage-pattern hunting jackets and trousers. They and the khaki trousers/yellow polo shirts every-one wore at Laguna el Guaje had been purchased at three Walmarts in Mexico City, Distrito Federal, by Peg-Leg Lorimer, who had charged them to his LCBF Corporation American Express card.

Peg-Leg reported, on his return from his shopping trip, that his purchases had just about wiped out the stocks in all three Walmart stores.

"When that information is sent by the Walmart computers to Walmart headquarters in Bentonville, Arkansas," Peg-Leg said, "the company will rush to replace the deleted stocks. This in turn will result in a gross overstock of khaki trousers, yellow polo shirts, and summer-weight camouflage-pattern hunting clothes in Mexico City. Walmart executives will be baffled.

"But I strongly suspect that Ol' Jack Walton," Peg-Leg concluded, "will be smiling down at us from that Great Watering Hole in the Sky, pleased that we outfitted this operation from his daddy's store."

John Walton—son of the founder of Walmart, and at his death the eleventh-richest man in the world—had earlier in his life been awarded the nation's third highest award for valor, the Silver Star, while a Special Forces sergeant in Vietnam.

Among those donning their Walmart combat uniforms was former Lieutenant Colonel Svetlana Alekseeva of the SVR, who was rolling up the sleeves of hers when Castillo came around the nose of the Black Hawk. Max was lying on the floor of the Black Hawk's cabin, watching with his head between his legs.

"What the hell do you think you're doing?" Castillo demanded.

"Carlos, I don't like it when you use that tone to me."

"You and Max are going back to the lake on the Mustang!"

She pointed at the runway. Castillo looked. The Mustang was beginning its takeoff roll.

"Well, Svet, you got that past me. But now you can wait here. You're not going."

"Of course I'm going. Wherever did you get this idea I wasn't?"

"Honey, for Christ's sake, we don't know what's going to happen at La Orchila. People are likely to get hurt."

"Did you ever think, Generalissimo Carlitos," she snapped, "you poor man's von Clausewitz, what would happen if one of Sirinov's Spetsnaz takes Dmitri out the moment we land? When you speak Russian, you sound like a Saint Petersburg poet." She wet her finger and ran it over her eyebrow, the gesture's meaning unmistakable. "You'd make the Spetsnaz giggle. I was a podpolkovnik of the SVR and I sound like one. I know how to deal with Spetsnaz and I'm going!"

After a moment's reflection, Castillo asked, "And Max? You want to take him too, I suppose, Podpolkovnik Alekseeva?"

"Absolutely! You get Max to show his teeth to Yakov Sirinov the way you did to Lammelle and he'll wet his pants. I may not even have to hurt him."

Castillo considered that a moment, and then asked, "Have you got a weapon?"

"Of course I've got a weapon," she snapped, still angry. "I've always got a weapon. You should know that. You've been looking up my dress from the day we met."

Castillo had an immediate, very clear mental image of that day.

Svetlana's skirt had risen high as she nimbly jumped from the tracks of Vienna's Sudbahnhof onto the platform, revealing that she was wearing red lace underpants with a small pistol—he later learned it was a Colt 1908 Pocket Model .32 ACP—holstered on her inner thigh just under them.

Roscoe J. Danton walked up.

"Not to worry, Charley," he said. "I understand Colonel Alekseeva was speaking off the record."

"Roscoe, sometimes he makes me very, very angry," Sweaty said.

Jake Torine walked up.

"I didn't hear that either," Torine said, and then went on: "It's about time for us to get going, Charley."

[FOUR]
The USS *Bataan* (LHD 5)
North Latitude 14.89, West Longitude 77.86
The Caribbean Sea
1255 12 February 2007

Almost as soon as he spotted the *Bataan*, Castillo saw that four black 160th SOAR UH-60M helicopters were already sitting on her deck, their rotors folded.

"I think I should tell you, First Officer, that the *Bataan* has a very impressive array of weaponry—including four forty-millimeter Gatling guns—with which to discourage strange and possibly hostile aircraft from approaching."

Torine gave him the finger and activated his microphone.

"*Bataan*, this is Keystone Kop."

"Keystone Kop, *Bataan*, be advised we have you in sight. Go ahead."

Castillo said, "What he meant to say, First Officer, was 'gun-sights.'"

"Well, *Bataan*," Torine spoke into the microphone, "if you have us in sight, then I guess I don't have to tell you I estimate we are at one thousand feet about two klicks off your stern. Request permission to land."

"Keystone Kop, are you carrier-qualified?"

Torine looked at Castillo.

"Lie, Jake. We don't have enough fuel to go back to Cozumel."

"Affirmative, we are carrier-qualified."

"Keystone Kop, be advised that *Bataan* is headed into the wind. The wind down the deck is at twenty knots. Acknowledge."

"*Bataan*, Keystone Kop understands wind down the deck is at twenty, and *Bataan* is headed into the wind."

"Keystone Kop, you are cleared to land. Be advised a rescue helicopter is to port."

"I think he knows we were lying," Torine said. "You really have never done this before?"

"Only as a passenger," Castillo said. "And what I think the pilot told me that day was that if the wind across the deck is at, say, twenty knots, and you're indicating twenty knots, that means you're in a hover over the deck, which, relatively speaking, has an air speed of zero."

As Castillo very carefully lowered the Black Hawk onto the deck—*I am really in a ground effect hover, even if I'm indicating that I'm making twenty knots. How can that be?*—he found it easier to look at the "ground," which was to say the deck, of the USS *Bataan* out the left window of the cockpit rather than the deck forward of the helo. That way he could tell, relatively speaking, if the *Bataan*'s island was moving—in which case he was in trouble—or not.

And when he did, he saw that he knew several of the 160th's Night Stalker pilots. They were standing, arms folded, waiting for him to crash, on the deck next to the superstructure that was the island.

One of them—a tall, graying, hawk-featured man wearing, like the others, the black flight suits favored by the 160th—he knew well. And he knew that hanging from the zipper of Arthur Kingsolving's black flight suit was the "subdued" insignia of his rank. Castillo couldn't see it, but knew it was the black eagle of a full colonel.

The Black Hawk touched down.

"You can exhale now, Jake," Castillo said as he reached for the rotor brake control. "We're on the ground. More or less."

"Art Kingsolving's here."

"I noticed. I hope you are going to tell me you outrank him."

"No, I don't. But your question is moot. Active duty officers always outrank retired old farts."

"I don't know about you, but I think of myself as a prematurely retired young fart," Castillo said.

"And there is a welcoming delegation," Torine said.

"Why don't you go deal with them while I finish shutting this thing down?"

The Navy delegation consisted of the officer of the deck, a chief petty officer, and two petty officers, one of them the master-at-arms and the other a medic.

They quite naturally had decided that the senior person aboard the helicopter with Mexican police markings would be riding with his staff in the passenger compartment, and lined up accordingly.

The first person—more accurately, the first living thing—to exit the helicopter was an enormous black dog, closely followed by a redheaded woman in battle dress who was screaming angrily at the dog in what sounded like Russian. Close on her heels came a man holding a camera who began to snap pictures of the Navy delegation, the helicopters on the deck, and the dog, who was now wetting down the front right wheel of the helicopter.

The co-pilot's door opened and, for a moment, decorum returned as Colonel Jake Torine, USAF (Retired), came out, popped to rigid attention, faced aft, and crisply saluted the national ensign.

Then he did a crisp left-face movement, raised his hand to his temple, and holding the salute, politely announced, "I request permission to come aboard, sir, in compliance with orders."

"Very well," the officer of the deck said, returning the salute. Then he said, "Sir, the captain's compliments. The captain requests the senior officer and such members of his staff as he may wish attend him . . ."

At that point, protocol broke down.

The Army pilots who had been standing next to the island came trotting across the deck, including the one that the officer of the deck knew to be a full colonel.

"I'll be a sonofabitch if Charley didn't steal another one," one of the Night Stalkers shouted.

"This time from the Mexican cops," another of them clarified.

"Zip your lips," Colonel Kingsolving snapped. He then turned to the officer of the deck. "Mister, I need a word with Colonel Castillo before he attends the captain on the bridge."

"Colonel, when the captain requests—"

"This time he's just going to have to wait," Kingsolving said, and then turned to Castillo, who, having exited the helicopter, was now exchanging hugs, pats on the back, and vulgar comments with the pilots.

"Colonel Castillo," Colonel Kingsolving called sternly. "I need a word with you right now."

Castillo freed himself, marched up to Kingsolving, came to attention, and saluted.

"Follow me, Colonel," Kingsolving ordered, and marched down the deck until they were alone.

"Face away from the island," Kingsolving ordered.

Castillo turned his back to the ship's superstructure.

"All McNab told me," Kingsolving said, "was to send the Black Hawks out here via Key West. 'The op commander will meet your senior pilot on the *Bataan*.' Your name wasn't mentioned."

"You didn't hear I was retired?"

"Yeah, and when we have time, I want to ask you about that."

"'Senior pilot'?" Castillo asked.

"I'm not supposed to be here, Charley. The first time I talked to him, McNab told me I was not to go. And then he called me back and said if I was thinking of having a case of selective deafness, the brigadier's selection board is sitting right now, and if this op gets out—even if it goes as planned—I can forget a star."

"You're here," Castillo said. "You don't want to be a general?"

"Two reasons, Charley. I'm one of those old-time soldiers who doesn't send his people anywhere he won't go himself."

"McNab was right. Even if I can carry this off, I think there's going to be serious political implications."

"Because you stole that helicopter from the Mexicans?"

"Because, for example, the last time I saw Frank Lammelle earlier today, he was wearing plastic handcuffs and Vic D'Allessando was sitting on him."

"Ouch! Charley, how long is this operation of yours going to take?"

"With a little bit of luck, we should be back on the *Bataan* by oh-eight-thirty tomorrow."

"Back from where? Where you're going to do what? Just the highlights."

Castillo told him.

"Now I'm really glad I came," Kingsolving said. "I told you there were two reasons I suffered temporary deafness. The captain of the *Bataan*, Tom Lowe, is a really good guy. I've done a couple of operations with him. Obviously, the more he knows about this one, the better all around. The problem with that is I don't want him standing at attention before a white-suit board of inquiry trying to explain why he knowingly participated in an obviously illegal operation."

"How do you want me to handle that?"

"There is a way, but I suspect that as a fellow marcher in that Long Gray Line, it will really bother you. The Code of Honor, don't you know?"

"Try me. I lie, cheat, and steal all the time, and spend a lot of time hanging out with others that do."

"Would you be willing to swear on a stack of Bibles that the only thing you told Lowe was where you wanted him to have the *Bataan* and when, and aside from assuring him that it was a duly authorized, wholly legal operation, didn't tell him anything else?"

"Absolutely."

"Thank you, Charley."

"For what? You're the guy who just watched his star disappear down the toilet."

"One more question. Who the hell is the redhead?"

"Would you believe, my fiancée?"

"No."

"How about she's an SVR lieutenant colonel?"

"I thought female SVR lieutenant colonels weighed two hundred pounds and had stainless-steel front teeth. Come on, we've got to see the captain."

"Can I bring my dog?"

"Request permission to come onto the bridge with a party of officers," Kingsolving said from the door to the bridge.

"You and your party of officers have the freedom of the bridge, Colonel Kingsolving," Captain Thomas J. Lowe, USN, said. He was a man in his late thirties, tall and deeply tanned.

Castillo marched up to him, stood tall, and announced, his voice raised, "Captain, I am Lieutenant Colonel C. G. Castillo. I regret that the nature of the mission I have been ordered to carry out by the United States Central Command is such that I can tell you very little except where we wish you to place your vessel and when."

"Welcome aboard the *Bataan*, Colonel."

"Captain, may I introduce my officers?"

"Certainly. But may I suggest that we deal with first things first? Where do you want the *Bataan*, and when?"

"If you have a chart, sir?"

"Right this way, Colonel," Captain Lowe said, and led Castillo into the chart room.

"Colonel, this is my navigator, Mr. Dinston."

Mr. Dinston was a lieutenant junior grade who looked like he was nineteen. The two shook hands.

"Show Mr. Dinston where you want us to go, Colonel," Captain Lowe said.

Castillo bent over the chart table, found La Orchila island, and then put his finger on the map.

"Fifty miles east of that island," he said. "I want to be there at oh-three-thirty tomorrow."

"What's on that island?" Mr. Dinston asked.

"I'm sorry, but you don't have the need to know," Castillo said.

"Yes, sir. Sorry, sir."

"Don't feel bad, Jerry," Captain Lowe said. "Neither do I."

He met Castillo's eyes as he spoke.

"Plot the course, Jerry," Captain Lowe ordered, "and bring it to the wardroom."

"Aye, aye, sir."

"Before we get started," Castillo said, when everyone was in the wardroom and the door had been closed, "Captain Lowe was never in this room nor anywhere else when any aspect of this operation except where we're asking him to place his ship was discussed. Everybody got that?"

There came a murmur of "Yes, sir."

"Would you like to say anything, Captain, before we get started?"

"Housekeeping," Captain Lowe said. "Could I get my chief in here and get the cabin assignments out of the way?"

"Captain, you don't have to ask me permission to do anything," Castillo said. "This is your ship."

"I know," Captain Lowe said. "I'm being nice. Colonel Kingsolving told me he thinks that most of you will shortly be in jail."

The chief looked as if he had been in the Navy for longer than anybody in the room was old. And he got right to the point: "How many oh-sixes we got? Raise your hands, please."

Kingsolving and Torine raised their hands.

"Dmitri," Castillo said, "raise your hand." Then he explained: "Colonel Berezovsky is a Russian, chief. They don't do ranks by numbers."

"Not a problem," the chief said. "There are three staterooms for visiting oh-sixes. You'll find the keys in the doors. We also got three staterooms, two officers per, for oh-fives and oh-fours. How many oh-fives?"

Castillo raised his hand. "Two, chief," he said and pointed at Svetlana.

"You're an oh-five?" the chief, dubious, asked her.

Svetlana looked at Castillo for guidance. He nodded, and Captain Lowe, seeing this, said, "Colonel, anything you can tell me, you can tell the chief."

"I am a former podpolkovnik of the Sluzhba Vneshney Razvedki, Chief Petty Officer," Sweaty said just a little arrogantly.

"Yes, ma'am," the chief said. "Okay, so we put you, ma'am, in one of the oh-five staterooms, and Colonel Castillo in the other, leaving one. How many oh-fours we got?"

"Excuse me, Chief Petty Officer," former Podpolkovnik Alekseeva of the Sluzhba Vneshney Razvedki said. "Put Lieutenant Colonel Castillo in one of those oh-five staterooms with me."

"Excuse me?"

"You seem surprised," Sweaty said. "Don't officers of the U.S. Navy sleep with women?"

"Sometimes, Colonel, some of us do," Captain Lowe said grinning broadly. "You heard the colonel, chief. Get on with it."

The chief recovered quickly, and the remaining accommodations were parceled out among the other officers. There was one captain; the rest of the 160th's pilots were warrant officers.

The chief left, closing the wardroom door behind him.

Castillo laid his laptop computer on the table and opened it.

"Overview," he said. "The target is on the airfield on the Venezuelan island of La Orchila. The target—*targets*, plural—are a Russian general named Yakov Sirinov, whom we are going to snatch; the Tu-934A aircraft, which he flew onto La Orchila; and the cargo that that bird carried."

He looked down at the computer, saw that it was on, and tapped several keys.

"These are the latest satellite images of the target," he went on, then leaned over for a closer look, and added, "as of forty-five minutes ago."

"You have imagery like that on your laptop?" Captain Lowe asked.

"Yes, sir."

Lowe bent over the laptop.

"How could a poor sailor get a laptop like that?" Lowe asked.

"Well, I could give you this one," Castillo said, affecting a serious tone, "but then I would have to kill you."

With one exception, the others in the room laughed. It was an old joke, but it was theirs.

The exception was former Podpolkovnik Svetlana Alekseeva of the Sluzhba Vneshney Razvedki.

"Captain," she flared, "you will have to excuse Colonel Castillo. He never grew emotionally after he entered puberty. Whenever there is serious business at hand, he makes sophomoric jokes."

"What is this, dissension in the ranks?" Castillo asked. "Or the beginning of a lover's quarrel?"

Sweaty let loose a thirty-second torrent of angry words in Russian.

Dmitri Berezovsky laughed, then said, "Captain, gentlemen, permit me to offer an explanation. In our family, my mother used to say that what my sister needed more than anything was a strong man who would take her down a peg or two on a regular basis. She has finally found such a man, and doesn't like it."

This produced from Sweaty another torrent of vulgar and obscene Russian language.

"If our mother ever heard her speak like that," Berezovsky went on, "which on occasion she did, our mother would wash her mouth out with laundry soap."

This was too much for the men in the room who had been studiously ignoring the exchange. Most of them chuckled, and several laughed.

Sweaty, red-faced, opened her mouth to deliver another comment.

"Colonel," Castillo said very softly. "Zip your lip. One more word and you're out of here and off the operation."

Carlito and Sweaty locked eyes for a very long moment.

And then wordlessly she sat down.

Castillo turned to the laptop.

"If you'll gather around here, please," he said, "you'll see that while the Tu-934A is not visible, there are Spetsnaz guarding this canvas temporary hangar, which makes it fairly certain that the Tu-934A is inside.

"Now, this is what we're going to do. Please hold comments until I've finished.

"I want to arrive at first light . . ."

Some five minutes later, when Castillo had finished, he said, "Okay, comments, please. But I'm not going to start with the juniors, the way a good commander is supposed to. We're starting at the top. Captain Lowe, your thoughts, please."

Lowe took a full thirty seconds to consider his response.

"There's a maybe ten-minute period, during which we will be recovering the UH-60s, that worries me. We'll be headed, slowly, into the wind. If Venezuelan Air Force or Navy aircraft find us with our hand still in the cookie jar, so to speak . . . But there's nothing we can do about that. And insofar as being attacked *after* we recover the choppers, that would be an *unprovoked* attack on a U.S. Navy vessel in international waters, which is an act of war. I don't think they would do that. And of course we're able to defend ourselves pretty well."

"Thank you, sir. Colonel Kingsolving?"

"Charley, the only question in my mind concerns the UH-60 you stole from the Mexican cops. What are you going to do about that? Torch it?"

"Well, sir, first, I didn't steal it. I bought it."

"You bought it? You going to tell me about that?"

Castillo told him.

"Unbelievable!" Kingsolving said. "But back to my question: What are you going to do with it, torch it?"

"I'll tell you what I'd like to do with it," Castillo said. "I'd like to fly it back out to the *Bataan*. And then the first time the *Bataan* goes to its homeport . . . Where is that, Captain Lowe?"

"Norfolk. And as soon as we finish this operation—this is day fifty-six of a sixty-day deployment—we'll be headed there 'at fastest speed consistent with available fuel.'"

"Then the first thing Captain Lowe does when he docks the *Bataan* at Norfolk will be to lower the Mexican UH-60 onto the wharf while the Mexican ambassador and the State Department idiots who sold it for a tenth of its value to the Mexicans watch. They then—did I mention that our own Roscoe J. Danton will be there, as will the ever-vigilant cameras of Wolf News?—they will attempt to explain how that particular UH-60, after having died a hero's death in Mexico's unrelenting war against the drug cartels, was resurrected."

"That'd work, Charley," Danton said. "And I'm so personally pissed as a taxpayer about that bullshit that I will even arrange for C. Harry Whelan, that sonofabitch, to be there with me."

"Then why not do it?" Kingsolving asked.

"One small problem, sir. Who would fly it out to the *Bataan*? Jake and I'll be flying the Tu-934A back to the land of the free and home of the brave with only a fuel stop at Drug Cartel International."

"I'll fly it," Kingsolving said.

"Sir, I have painful memories of standing tall before you while you lectured at length on the inadvisability of flying UH-60 aircraft without a co-pilot. I seem to remember you telling me with some emphasis that anyone who did so was an idiot."

"Charley, if I went in with you on the Mexican UH-60, and then flew it back out here, that means we would have to land only one of the 160th choppers in there to take your Spetsnaz back to the *Bataan*. That would reduce the danger that one of my guys would dump one of ours at La Orchila, causing God only knows what consequential collateral political damage."

"You don't see any risk like when your guys take out the commo building?"

"As I understand your plan, Colonel, the idea is for my guys to hit the commo building in the dark, so they will never learn what happened to them, or who did it."

Castillo was silent for a moment.

Next came dissension in the ranks of the 160th Special Operations Aviation Regiment pilots.

Four of the Night Stalkers, just about simultaneously, spoke without permission. They all said about the same thing: "Colonel, let me fly that fucking Mexican chopper."

To which Colonel Kingsolving replied, "Zip your lips, or nobody gets to go."

There was another period of silence.

"Vis-à-vis my counseling you on the inadvisability of flying UH-60 aircraft without a co-pilot, Colonel," Kingsolving said, "I meant every word of it. But there is an old military axiom that I'm really surprised you did not learn at our beloved alma mater. To wit: When you are the senior officer, you are, in certain circumstances, permitted to say, 'Do as I say, not as I do.'"

"I'm going to fly that Mexican UH-60 back and forth to the island of La Orchila, Charley. Period."

"There goes your star, you realize."

"That thought did run through my mind, frankly. But what the hell. If they made me a general, they'd say I was too valuable to fly myself anywhere, with or without a co-pilot. And I don't want to fly a desk in the Pentagon."

Then he looked at Captain Lowe.

"I think we're through here, Captain. Is the Navy planning on feeding us lunch?"

[FIVE]
The USS *Bataan* (LHD 5)
The Caribbean Sea
2055 12 February 2007

Former Podpolkovnik Svetlana Alekseeva was not in sight when Lieutenant Colonel C. G. Castillo entered the stateroom.

He was not really surprised. She had not spoken a word to him at lunch, then had spent the entire afternoon with the Spetsnaz somewhere below deck, presumably checking their equipment and seeing to it they understood their roles in the operation.

They had had a conversation of sorts at dinner.

"May I please have the butter?" she had asked him.

"Of course," he had said. "My pleasure."

"Thank you," she had said, ending their conversation.

Now, alone in the stateroom, Castillo decided that she had run down the old chief and told him she had changed her mind about sharing his quarters. Earlier, Captain Lowe had shown him the *Bataan*'s sick bay—actually a small, fully equipped hospital—and while doing so, Castillo had noticed there were sleeping quarters for nurses.

She's probably in one of those.

He took off his Walmart battle dress, and lay down on the lower of the two bunks the room offered.

I'll take a shower at 0230, he decided, *not now.*

Taking one then will wake me up.

He closed his eyes.

"If you think we're going to make love without you taking a shower, think again," former Podpolkovnik Svetlana Alekseeva announced not sixty seconds later.

He opened his eyes. She was standing beside the bunk bed wearing a thin cotton bathrobe.

"Am I permitted to say I'm a little surprised?" Charley asked, after having regained his breath perhaps ten minutes later.

"In eight hours, the Venezuelans may have the both of us stretched out on a wooden table, the way your Green Berets stretched out Che Guevara," Svetlana said. "I did not want to spend all eternity knowing that I had had the chance to spend my last hours making love with you, and threw it away."

"Good thinking," he said.

"Right now, I don't like you very much—how dare you talk to me the way you did?—but I love you."

He had a wildly tangential thought. "Where's Max?"

She pointed.

Max was lying with his head between his paws on the stateroom's small desk, nearly covering it, and looking at them.

"How long's he been there?" Charley asked.

"He was sleeping under the bunk. But you were making so much noise, I guess you woke him up."

XVI

[ONE]
The USS _Bataan_ (LHD 5)
North Latitude 12.73, West Longitude 66.18
The Caribbean Sea
0355 13 February 2007

"I have a confession to make, sir," Castillo said as a man wearing a soft leather helmet and goggles and holding illuminated wands crossed on his chest approached the UH-60 with Policía Federal Preventiva markings. The Black Hawk helicopter was sitting, with rotors turning, at the extreme aft portion of the _Bataan's_ flight deck.

"This is not the place, my son. But make sure you see me before you take communion," Colonel Kingsolving said, playing along.

"I think you better follow me through, sir," Castillo went on, his tone serious.

"Something wrong, Charley?" Kingsolving asked, now with concern in his voice.

"I think you better follow me through, sir," Castillo repeated. "Or take it."

"Too late to take it," Kingsolving said. "There's the 'go' signal. If you don't want to abort, I'll follow you through."

"Here we go," Castillo said.

He lifted off, hovered for a moment, and then reduced forward speed from twenty knots to ten. The deck moved out from under the aircraft at a speed of ten knots, and a moment later, he was looking at the stern of the *Bataan*.

The UH-60 dipped its nose toward the sea, picked up speed, and then began a steep climbing turn to the right into the dark sky.

"You all right? You want me to take it, Charley?"

"I've got it. I'm all right now," Castillo said.

Out his window he could see one of the 160th's Black Hawks being quickly pushed to the aft of the flight deck.

"Interesting departure," Kingsolving said. "Where'd you learn how to do that, at Pensacola?"

"What I was going to confess, sir, was that I don't have very much experience in night-launching a UH-60 from a carrier."

"Oh, shit!" Kingsolving said, after considering that for a moment. "Please don't tell me that was your first."

"Yes, sir. I won't tell you that."

"I had a look at your flight records, Charley, while they were trying to make up their minds whether to give you The Medal or court-martial you the last time you manifested suicidal behavior involving a UH-60. You remember that? When you went after Dick Miller?"

"If I thought that going after Dick was suicidal, I wouldn't have done it."

"You were the only aviator in Afghanistan who didn't. I was astonished to see that as long as you've been flying, you've never dinged a bird—getting shot down not counting. Never. Not any kind of a bird. Do you have an explanation for that?"

"Clean living and a pure heart?"

"You don't think what you did just now was suicidal?"

"Straight answer?"

"Please."

"No, I didn't. You following me through on the controls took care of the safety factor, and now I know how to launch at night in a UH-60 from a carrier. You never know when that might come in handy."

Kingsolving didn't reply.

"Kidnapper One and Two, Keystone Kop," Castillo said to his microphone. "I'm going to circle the ship at two thousand feet. Join up on me five hundred feet behind."

[TWO]
La Orchila Island
Bolivarian Republic of Venezuela
0502 13 February 2007

It was just getting light as the three UH-60s approached the island.

Castillo estimated he would be on the ground in three minutes, give or take.

One of the 160th's Black Hawks following him would laser-target the commo building and report when it had done so, but would not fire until Castillo gave the order.

The other would hover over the airfield to the left of the hangar. It would be prepared to clear the tarmac in front of the hangar with its GAU-19 .50 caliber Gatling guns if the Spetsnaz guarding them offered significant resistance.

Castillo had spent a good thirty minutes trying to impress on its pilots that a disaster beyond comprehension would occur if the fire from their weapons struck—which would virtually atomize—the blue barrels they had come to seize. He thought he had succeeded—the chief warrant officers flying the gunship were both veteran special operators, not excitable young men, and both wore the wings of Master Army Aviators.

"I wonder what General Buckner—or his father—would think of this?" Colonel Kingsolving said.

"Of what?" Castillo asked.

"Our assault on the Bolivarian Republic of Venezuela. 'Bolivarian' makes reference of course to General Simón Bolívar, the great Liberator."

"What the hell are you talking about?"

"General Simon Bolivar Buckner, Senior, West Point Class of '44—Class of *1844*—was a Confederate general. He was forced to surrender Fort Donelson, Kentucky, to his classmate, General Ulysses Grant. Buckner gave Grant his parole, and was later exchanged. I thought about that when you told me about General Naylor giving you his parole."

"Thanks for sharing that with me, Colonel."

"His son," Kingsolving went on, "General Simon Bolivar Buckner, Junior, Hudson High Class of '08, was the most senior officer killed in combat in the Pacific during World War Two. He was commanding the Tenth Army on Okinawa when struck by Japanese artillery."

Over their headsets suddenly came: *"Keystone Kop, Kidnapper One. I have my laser on the target, acknowledge."*

"Kidnapper One, Keystone Kop acknowledges you have target acquisition," Castillo answered.

"They are both, I believe, buried at West Point," Kingsolving went on.

"Well, maybe they'll bury us there."

"Keystone Kop, Kidnapper Two has a visual on armed and moving possible belligerents."

"Kidnapper Two, Keystone Kop acknowledges you have visual on possible belligerents. Hold fire until I clear. Acknowledge."

"Kidnapper Two acknowledges hold fire."

Kingsolving said, "I'd rather thought you'd prefer interment beside your father in the National Cemetery in San Antonio."

"If those Spetsnaz waving those Kalashnikovs at us start shooting them, we're both probably going to be buried right here," Castillo said, and then, remembering what Sweaty had said the night before, added: "After we're displayed on a table, like Hugo Chávez's hero, Che Guevara."

He waited another two seconds, then said, "Kidnapper One, engage, engage."

He then switched to the intercom to alert Berezovsky and his four ex-Spetsnaz waiting in the back of the UH-60 with Mexican federal police markings.

"Dmitri, we'll be on the ground in three seconds. *Ve con Dios.*"

He heard what he had said, and thought: *I'll be goddamned—I meant that! Go with God, Dmitri!*

Jesus H. Christ! Are Sweaty and her brother turning me into a believer?

He saw the exhaust flare from the first Hellfire missile race through the air, and then from another, and then from a third.

There's not going to be much left of that communications building.

Castillo then touched down, and immediately unfastened his seat/shoulder harness.

"Try not to get shot moving over here to the pilot seat," he said, and then he was out the Black Hawk's door.

He reached back in and grabbed his Uzi, then went quickly around the nose of the helicopter, passing Kingsolving as he did.

Castillo found that there was a sort of a standoff on the tarmac.

Dmitri Berezovsky—with his four ex-Spetsnaz standing behind him, more or less holding their weapons at port arms—was facing a half-dozen men wearing the striped shirts of the Spetsnaz armed with a variety of weapons.

"I asked, who's in charge?" Berezovsky said more than a little arrogantly.

And then there was a female voice.

"Lower that (expletive deleted) muzzle, you (expletive deleted) moron!"

former SVR Podpolkovnik Svetlana Alekseeva shouted. "What the (expletive deleted) is wrong with you, raising a weapon to Polkovnik Berezovsky? Are you as (expletive deleted) stupid as you look?"

The muzzle was lowered.

One of the Spetsnaz stepped forward, saluted, and said, "Major Koussevitzky, sir."

"Stefan," Berezovsky said. "I didn't recognize you."

"Good to see you again, Polkovnik. May I ask what . . ."

"We are here to arrest General Sirinov," Berezovsky said. "Where is he?"

"In the hangar, sir."

"I regret that the circumstances require that I take your arms," Berezovsky said. "Lower them to the ground."

"You are here to arrest the general, Polkovnik?" Koussevitzky asked softly.

"I regret that is necessary, but I'm sure you know why."

Koussevitzky considered that a full twenty seconds before he unstrapped his pistol belt and let it fall to the ground, then put his Kalashnikov automatic rifle on the tarmac.

"You heard Polkovnik Berezovsky," he said to his men. "Lower your weapons to the ground."

Berezovsky waited until the order had been complied with, and then spoke to one of the ex-Spetsnaz standing behind him.

"Have those weapons put aboard the helicopter," he ordered, and then turned to Koussevitzky.

"Take me to the general, Stefan," Berezovsky ordered. Then he pointed to Sweaty, to one of his ex-Spetsnaz, and to Lieutenant Colonel C. G. Castillo, USA (Retired), and said, "You, come with me."

Castillo said, "Yes, sir" in Russian, hoping he didn't sound like a Saint Petersburg poet of indeterminate sexual orientation.

The Tu-934A was inside the canvas-walled and -roofed temporary hangar. So were four very small travel trailers being used as makeshift barracks. As they walked toward the trailers, General Sirinov came out of one of them. He was dressed but he needed a shave.

I guess we woke the sonofabitch up.

"General, consider yourself under arrest," Berezovsky announced.

"I don't know what you think you're doing, Berezovsky," Sirinov said.

He seemed to be unfazed by what was happening.

"Please turn around and put your hands behind you," Berezovsky said as he took a plastic handcuff from a pocket.

"I will not."

Sweaty, holding Max on his leash beside her, walked up to him. While doing so, she took her Colt .32 ACP model 1908 from her pocket.

"And the beautiful Svetlana," Sirinov said. "Wherever did you get that absurd uniform? And that dog?"

"Turn around, Yakov, and put your hands behind you," Sweaty ordered.

"Or what? You'll shoot me with your toy pistol?"

Sweaty aimed her toy pistol quickly, and shot General Sirinov in the right foot.

He looked at his bleeding foot, then screamed with the pain and fell to the ground, looking up at her in enraged disbelief.

"Roll onto your stomach, Yakov, or I'll put the next round into your other foot," Sweaty said.

Max growled.

General Sirinov rolled onto his stomach.

Berezovsky knelt beside him and applied the plastic handcuffs.

Sirinov was moaning in pain.

"If you don't give me any more trouble, when we're on the plane I'll give you some morphine," Sweaty said.

"Where are the pilots of the airplane?" Berezovsky asked Koussevitzky.

Koussevitzky pointed to one of the trailers.

"Get them out here," Berezovsky ordered. Then he pointed at Castillo, and ordered, "Get our pilot in here."

Castillo said, "Yes, sir" in Russian, and hoped his conscious attempt to sound like a basso profundo had been at least partially successful.

He went onto the tarmac, saw Jake Torine, and waved him over. He saw that Sirinov's Spetsnaz were now all sitting on the tarmac. They had plastic handcuffs around both their wrists and their ankles.

They don't look worried.

They look terrified.

And so did the Tu-934A pilots when they walked up to Berezovsky.

Castillo went to them, and ordered, "Show the colonel and me around the airplane. If you do anything suspicious, Podpolkovnik Alekseeva will shoot you in the foot."

"You're going to fly the Tu-934A?" one of them blurted.

"That's the idea," Castillo said. "Start by opening the ramp door."

When the ramp came down, Castillo could see there were three blue barrels firmly strapped to the floor, plus a tracked forklift inside.

"Up the ramp," he ordered.

When they were in the cockpit, Castillo asked, "Where are the rest of the blue rubber barrels?"

He believed the pilots when they assured him, with almighty God as their witness, that there were no more blue rubber barrels anywhere.

It was a very brief cockpit tour, just long enough for the Tu-934A pilots to show Torine and Castillo the engine start procedures and to tell them the best rotation speed during takeoff.

General Sirinov, still moaning with pain, was carried aboard and attached with plastic handcuffs to the strapping holding the blue plastic barrels in place.

Torine stayed in the cockpit while Castillo led the pilots and Sweaty off the airplane. He saw that Berezovsky and Koussevitzky were in a far corner of the hangar. He and Sweaty walked to them.

"I have offered to take Stefan with us," Berezovsky said. "Understandably, he is concerned with what Putin would do to the family of a traitor. There are six unmarried Spetsnaz who should come with us. Stefan suggests we make it appear they are coming involuntarily."

"Major," Castillo asked, "what makes you think Putin won't—"

"It would help if Podpolkovnik Alekseeva found it necessary to shoot me," Koussevitzky said.

"Well, I suppose . . ." Castillo said.

There was the pop of her toy pistol and Koussevitzky fell to the ground, bleeding from a wound to his right upper leg.

"We'll try to get you and your family out, Stefan," Sweaty said. "Really try."

"May God protect you and yours, Svetlana," Koussevitzky said.

"And yours," Sweaty said.

Berezovsky knelt beside him and put him in plastic handcuffs.

"How do we get the hangar doors open?" Castillo asked.

"You have to push," Koussevitzky furnished. "They're like curtains."

"What happens if we start engines in here?"

"You'd burn the hangar down."

"Good idea. Get everybody out of here," Berezovsky ordered. "And then get the Spetsnaz we're taking with us firmly tied up and ready to get on the UH-60."

"Get aboard, Sweaty," Castillo ordered.

"I'll get aboard when you do," she replied.

There was no time to argue with her.

Castillo went outside the hangar, and made hand signals toward the sky to order the Night Stalker Black Hawk code-named Kidnapper Two to land.

"Push the hangar doors open," Podpolkovnik Alekseeva ordered in a Russian command voice that would have passed muster at Fort Bragg. "And then help Polkovnik Berezovsky clear the hangar."

As soon as the doors had been pushed aside, Castillo heard the whine of a Tu-934A engine being started. And he saw Kidnapper Two, cargo doors slid open, coming down the runway almost on the ground. It touched down.

Two of Berezovsky's ex-Spetsnaz carried Major Koussevitzky out of the hangar and lowered him to the ground twenty meters from it. Then they ran back into the hangar as he heard the whine of the second Tu-934A engine being started.

The ex-Spetsnaz came back out of the hangar, leading the Tu-934A's pilots, their hands in plastic handcuffs. They deposited them next to Major Koussevitzky. One of them then ran back into the hangar. The other ran across the tarmac to where a half-dozen Spetsnaz in handcuffs were sitting.

Roscoe J. Danton appeared, furiously capturing everything for posterity—after of course it was published in *The Washington Times-Post*—on his camera.

Two of the ex-Spetsnaz pulled one of the handcuffed Spetsnaz to his feet and loaded him—not very gently: "threw him aboard" would be a more accurate description—onto the Policía Federal Preventiva UH-60, and then threw two more of the Spetsnaz aboard.

Roscoe J. Danton captured this, too, with his camera.

One of the ex-Spetsnaz looked at Castillo and Svetlana.

"He wants to know if he should load the others aboard," Sweaty said.

Castillo pointed across the tarmac and ordered: "Put those three on the helo coming in, and then get on yourself."

Castillo then ran twenty yards—with Max bounding happily after him—so that Colonel Kingsolving could see him clearly from the cockpit of the Policía Federal Preventiva UH-60. Then he made hand signals telling Kingsolving to take off.

The helicopter immediately broke ground, lowered its nose, and moved away, gaining speed.

Kidnapper Two stopped, still not touching the ground, where an ex-Spetsnaz stood waiting with the remaining Spetsnaz men bound with plastic handcuffs. Roscoe J. Danton's camera was at the ready to capture what happened next: As soon as the first of the handcuffed Spetsnaz had been assisted aboard, a black-suited special operator jumped out of the Black Hawk and helped the Spetsnaz throw the other two aboard.

The ex-Spetsnaz looked again at Castillo for guidance.

"Get aboard," Castillo shouted, and then signaled to the pilot to take off.

As it did, Roscoe J. Danton made a photographic record.

There was a change in the pitch of the Tu-934A engines and Castillo turned to see that it was moving slowly out of the hangar. Castillo took one last look around, ran to Roscoe J. Danton, and tried to lead him to the ramp of the Tu-934A.

Mr. Danton was not sure he wished to go at this time. He resisted. Castillo grabbed the strap of Roscoe's camera, jerked hard on it, breaking it, and then, when Roscoe started to protest, grabbed the camera itself, ran to the open ramp of the Tu-934A, and threw the camera aboard. Roscoe then jumped onto the airplane to retrieve his camera.

While he was so engaged, Castillo grabbed Sweaty's arm and led her to the ramp of the Tu-934A. She leapt nimbly onto it.

So did Max, after considering for ten seconds the wisdom of doing so. In that time, the airplane moved away, rolling faster.

For a very terrifying moment, Castillo was afraid he wouldn't be so nimble as the love of his life and his dog. He ran after the plane and made a running dive onto the ramp, landing on his stomach.

Max got to him first and licked his face as he was trying to get up. Mr. Danton recorded for posterity Max licking his master's face as he lay on the ramp. Then Sweaty pulled Castillo to his feet, and he moved as fast as he could toward the cockpit. Max chased after him.

When Castillo got to the cockpit, he saw that Torine had lined up the airplane on the runway. He dropped into the right seat and quickly clamped on a headset.

"Closing the ramp," Torine's voice came matter-of-factly over the earphones. "Throttles to takeoff power."

The Tu-934A began to move.

"Call out airspeed for me, First Officer, if you'd be so kind," Torine said.

Castillo found the airspeed indicator in the split second when the needle jumped off the peg and pointed to forty. The landing gear began rumbling.

That's kilometers. The pilots told us rotation speed was one-fifty.

That's not quite a hundred knots.

You can rotate this great big sonofabitch at a hundred knots?

Is that what you call misinformation?

Was that Russian pilot lying to us?

"Seventy," Castillo called out. "That's klicks, Jake.

"Ninety . . .

"One-ten . . .

"One-thirty . . .

"One-fifty."

"Rotating," Torine said calmly.

A moment later, the rumble of the landing gear died.

"One-ninety . . .

"Two-ten."

"Get the gear up, First Officer. It's that lever with the wheel on top."

Castillo found the lever and moved it.

"Gear coming up . . .

"Gear up.

"Jesus! Two-eighty."

"Now let's see how it climbs," Torine said, as if to himself.

Castillo felt himself being pressed hard against the cushions of his seat.

Torine said, "No wonder the agency is willing to pay all that money—what was it, one hundred twenty-five million?—for one of these. This is one hell of an airplane, First Officer."

Castillo had a very clear mental image of Sweaty—and maybe everybody else in the fuselage—all in a pile of broken bones against the closed ramp.

The pressure on his back against his seat suddenly stopped. Jake had leveled off.

"Put your goddamn harness on," Torine ordered.

As soon as he saw that Castillo had done so, Jake dove for the surface of the water.

Castillo now had a very clear image of everybody sliding forward in the fuselage to end in a pile of broken bones against the cockpit door.

Torine read his mind.

"Now take the harness off, First Officer," he ordered, "and go back and see how our passengers are enjoying the flight."

Castillo found all the passengers except two were in their seats. Dmitri Berezovsky was standing beside one of the blue plastic beer barrels, examining it thoughtfully. Sweaty was on her knees beside General Yakov Sirinov, in the process of administering to him what Castillo presumed was the morphine she had promised.

Castillo went back to the cockpit and strapped himself in.

The airspeed and altimeter dials indicated that they were flying at eight hundred and forty kilometers per hour—or about five hundred knots—at a hundred meters—or five hundred feet—above the Caribbean Sea.

Fuel consumption at that speed and altitude would be horrendous, and there was of course the danger that they would go into the drink.

But, on the other hand, they didn't have that far to go, and at five hundred feet they wouldn't be a blip on anybody's radar screen.

"You want to take it, Charley, while I get my laptop?"

"I'll get your laptop. You drive," Castillo replied.

[THREE]
Laguna el Guaje
Coahuila, Mexico
0940 13 February 2007

Jake Torine carefully nosed the Tu-934A into the cave, and turned to Charley Castillo.

"I would tell you to shut it down, First Officer, but I'm afraid you'd break something."

"After that hard landing, I expect a lot of it would break easily," Castillo replied.

"That was a greaser and you know it. And did you notice the thrust reversers?"

Castillo had had another vision of everybody in the fuselage slamming into the cockpit wall when he'd activated the thrust reverser controls. The Tu-934A had slowed as if it had caught the cable on the deck of an aircraft carrier.

"I noticed," he said.

"The agency will be getting a hell of a bargain when the LCBF Corporation sells this to them for a hundred and twenty-five million," Torine said. "Have you considered asking for more?"

"Don't be greedy, Jake," Castillo said. "Where's the ramp lever?"

General Allan Naylor, Lieutenant General Bruce J. McNab, Lieutenant Colonel (Designate) Allan Naylor, Jr., Uncle Remus Leverette, Vic D'Allessando, Lester Bradley, Frank Lammelle (now wearing shoes and socks, and no plastic hand-cuffs), Aloysius F. Casey, and a burly man in a business suit were all standing at the foot of the ramp.

Max raced down the ramp, barked hello, and headed for the landing gear.

Salutes were exchanged, as a Pavlovian reaction. Even the burly man in the business suit saluted. With his left hand.

What the hell is that? Who's that guy? Castillo wondered.

He asked, "So, what's happened?"

There had been radio silence during the flight from the island. That had been Castillo's decision. Once everybody was airborne, they were on their own. They could neither help—nor be helped by—anyone else. That being the case, there was nothing to talk about.

"What else has happened? About what?" General McNab asked innocently, and then took pity on him. "All aircraft having been recovered—including one Mexican UH-60 flown by an officer whose ass I will have just as soon as I can get my hands on him—the USS *Bataan* is proceeding at best speed consistent with available fuel to Norfolk."

Castillo smiled. "Then it looks like we got away with it."

"God answered our prayers," Sweaty said.

"You have the Congo-X?" General Naylor asked.

"Yes, sir. And General Sirinov."

"You got away with Phase One, Colonel," General Naylor said. "The military part. Phase Two, the political part, now begins. I suspect that will be more difficult, and our chances of success less in Phase Two."

Castillo looked at Lammelle.

"Hey, Frank, I see they turned you loose. More or less. How the hell are you? And what do you think of this airplane the agency is about to buy?"

"Leave him alone, Charley," McNab said.

"Congratulations, Charley," Lammelle said. "That was—"

"What did you do, Frank, change sides?" Castillo said. "The last I heard, you were going to shoot me with your air pistol and load me on an Aeroflot flight to Moscow."

"I told you to leave him alone, Charley!" McNab said firmly.

"Yes, sir."

"Dennis!" General Naylor said.

The man in the business suit took a step forward, came to attention, and barked, "Sir!"

"Colonel, this is Master Sergeant Dennis. He is Colonel Hamilton's principal assistant. He will tell you what he wants done with the Congo-X."

Castillo took a closer look at Master Sergeant Dennis.

No wonder he salutes with his left hand—he doesn't have a right arm.

"What do you need, Sergeant?" Castillo asked.

"Sir, Colonel Hamilton sends his best regards."

"Thank you."

"Sir, where is the Congo-X?"

Castillo gestured up the ramp. "In there. Behind that front-loader, or forklift, whatever it is. There are three barrels of it."

"Is there any more of it, Colonel?" General Naylor asked. "Were you able to determine that?"

"According to General Sirinov, sir, that's all of it. I believe him."

"He's telling the truth," Sweaty said.

General Naylor looked at her. "How do you know that?"

"Because he knows that if I find out he's lying," Sweaty said, "he will die a very slow and painful death. This time with no morphine."

"This time?" General Naylor asked.

"Colonel Alekseeva shot General Sirinov in the foot," Castillo said. "And later took pity on him and gave him a shot of morphine."

"She was aiming for his foot, right?" McNab asked. "I mean, that wasn't a near miss or anything like that?"

"No, sir. She was aiming for his foot."

"I knew she was my kind of girl," McNab said.

Naylor glared at him.

"Where is General Sirinov?" Naylor asked.

"Plastic-cuffed to the first barrel behind the cockpit," Castillo said.

"Allan, get in there, free the general, and see what attention he needs," Naylor said.

"You can go get him," Sweaty said. "But do not take off his cuffs. And take someone . . . No. I will go with you. He is a very dangerous man."

"You want me to go get him, Charley?" Uncle Remus asked.

"No," Castillo said. "Go see if you can operate that forklift, or whatever it is. Sweaty, take Lester with you. Tell General Sirinov that Lester's the fellow who took out Lieutenant Colonel Yevgeny Komogorov, and he would like nothing more than putting a bullet in his eye."

Two minutes later, General Sirinov, obviously in pain, limped down the ramp, supported by Allan Junior and trailed by Lester Bradley, who held a 1911A1 Colt .45 pistol at his side, and by Sweaty.

"Okay, Frank," General McNab said.

Lammelle walked to Sirinov.

"General," he said in Russian, "my name is Lammelle. Does that mean anything to you?"

"I know who you are, Mr. Lammelle," Sirinov said in English.

"Are you going to answer my questions, General? Or should I—for the time being—simply have you confined?"

Castillo wondered: *How did Lammelle get in the act?*

What the hell's going on with him?

"Under the circumstances, Mr. Lammelle, answering whatever questions you have for me seems to be the obvious best option of those pointed out to me by our mutual friend Svetlana."

"Can you make it to the elevator?" Lammelle asked, pointing to it.

Sirinov nodded.

"Do you want to go with them, Colonel?" Castillo asked Sweaty.

"Of course," she said.

"Stick with them, Lester," Castillo ordered.

"Yes, sir."

There came the sound of a diesel engine starting, and a moment later Uncle Remus drove the forklift down the ramp.

"With your permission, Colonel?" Master Sergeant Dennis said, and when Castillo nodded, walked up the ramp into the Tu-934A.

[FOUR]

With great skill—and very carefully—Uncle Remus lowered one of the blue beer barrels onto a layer of insulated blankets in the bottom of a pit dug in the floor of the cave.

When Master Sergeant Dennis unfastened the web straps around the barrel and gave Uncle Remus the "up" signal, Uncle Remus raised the arms of the forklift, and then backed away from the pit.

Then he stood up and took a bow.

"What would we do without you?" Castillo asked.

"I shudder at the thought," Uncle Remus said, and then turned to Master Sergeant Dennis. "What do you want me to do, Sergeant? Get another barrel, or help you load the helium on top of this one?"

Dennis thought it over before replying.

"It would be better if we got all the barrels in the ground first," he said. "And then put the helium packages, the bags, on top. If one of the bags got ripped, and the helium contacted the arms of the forklift, they would shatter. Helium makes a witch's teat look like the sun."

"You got it, Sarge," Uncle Remus said, and steered the forklift back to the ramp of the Tu-934A.

[FIVE]

"What we did in the lab, Colonel," Master Sergeant Dennis explained in the dining room of the house, after taking a swallow from a bottle of Dos Equis beer, "that killed that shit, was to expose it to the helium—at minus two-seventy Celsius for fifteen minutes."

"And that killed it?" Castillo asked.

"Dead as a fucking doornail, Colonel," Dennis confirmed, then drained his bottle. "Do you suppose I could have another one of these?"

"Give the nice man another beer, Uncle Remus," Castillo ordered.

"And then we let it thaw," Dennis went on. "It took eight hours and twelve minutes at seventy degrees Fahrenheit."

"And it was then really dead?" Castillo said.

"Dead fucking dead," Dennis confirmed. "But what we don't know, Colonel, is how cold the helium we used just now was. It was way the fuck down there, but it may not have been all the way down to minus two-seventy Celsius. So what Colonel Hamilton told me to do was give it a thirty-minute bath. We did that. And more. The helium is still on the barrels."

"Makes sense. What are you going to do about thawing it?"

"We also don't know about the thawing. If we took the helium off now, it's seventy-four Fahrenheit in the cave—probably seventy-six or -seven by now—so it would thaw faster. But it might not be all the way dead, if you take my meaning, when it's thawed faster."

Castillo had a sinking feeling in his stomach.

"So, then what do we do?"

"It's ninety-two Fahrenheit in the sun outside," Dennis said. "Or was, just before you landed. It's probably a little hotter now."

"What are you suggesting—that we thaw it in the sun?" Castillo asked, confused. "Wouldn't that increase the risk that it wouldn't be 'all the way dead'?"

"It may be dead now, and we're just wasting time thawing it."

"What are you suggesting, Sergeant Dennis?" Castillo demanded.

Dennis looked very uncomfortable.

Castillo had an epiphany, and softly asked, "What does Colonel Hamilton think will happen if Congo-X is thawed rapidly?"

Dennis didn't immediately reply.

"Goddamn it, Sergeant! What did Colonel Hamilton say?"

"He said that when magicians freeze goldfish with dry ice and then bring them back to life, they can do that because they were never completely dead.

He said that he thinks when you get something down to minus two-seventy Celsius, it's completely dead, and you couldn't bring it back even by thawing it in a microwave."

"Did he tell you not to tell me this?"

Dennis nodded.

"Did he say why?"

"He said if you heard he said it, you would treat it like he was talking in a cathedral—I don't know what the hell he meant by that—and base your decisions on that."

"Speaking '*ex cathedra*,' Sergeant?"

"Right."

"If we put one of those kegs in the sun for as long as it takes to thaw it, could you determine if the Congo-X was dead here?"

"I've got stuff with me that'll let me test it so I'll know with ninety-percent certainty whether or not that shit is still alive or not. To be absolutely sure, we'd have to test it in the lab at Fort Detrick."

"How did you get here, Sergeant?"

"Mr. Casey picked me up in his airplane at Baltimore/Washington. Nice airplane!"

"And Colonel Hamilton didn't come. Why?"

"We don't trust the people in the lab. They would tell somebody—probably those fuckers in Las Vegas—that he was gone. So I went to the PX, called the lab, and asked for the day off. Then I got on the bus and went out to Baltimore/Washington."

"If we put one of those beer kegs in the sun, how long would it take to thaw?" Castillo asked. "Let me put that another way: How long would we have to leave one of those kegs in the sun before loading it on Mr. Casey's G-Five to fly it to Fort Detrick, so that it would be thawed, or damned near thawed, when it got there?"

"I been thinking about that, Colonel. It's about seventy Fahrenheit in the airplane. I suppose you could up that some, if you wanted to?"

"Probably to eighty, maybe a little higher," Castillo said.

"We'd have to leave the keg in the sun for two hours fifteen. Better yet two hours thirty. I think it would be pretty well thawed by the time we got it into the lab."

Castillo looked at Leverette, and said, "Uncle Remus, will you please help Sergeant Dennis move one of those beer barrels into the sun—somewhere no one will see it? And then you two sit on it." He heard what he had said, and added, "Correction. You don't have to actually sit on it, but I want eyes on it all the time."

"You know what you're doing, Charley?"

"Hoping that I'm right, that Colonel Hamilton is right, and that Master Sergeant Dennis is right. Is that enough for you?"

"I always like you better when you admit you don't really know what the fuck you're doing," Uncle Remus said. "Let's go, Dennis."

[SIX]

"The freezing process, I gather, is over, or nearly so?" General Naylor asked when Castillo walked into the war room.

"Sir, with respect, I have no intention of discussing anything about this operation in the presence of Mr. Lammelle."

General McNab's bushy eyebrows went up. "You never learned in Sunday school what Saint Luke said, Charley? '*There* is *more joy in heaven over one sinner who repents . . .*' Et cetera?"

"I don't believe this!" Castillo said. "The sonofabitch wanted to load Sweaty, Dmitri, and me on an Aeroflot—"

Dmitri Berezovsky laughed.

Castillo looked at him in disbelief.

"Actually, General," Roscoe J. Danton—whose smile showed he was enjoying the situation—said, "I believe what Saint Luke actually said was, '*There is joy in the presence of the angels of God over one sinner who repents.*'"

"I think I like that better," McNab said. "I never thought of it before, but I could get used to thinking of myself as an 'angel of God.'"

Berezovsky laughed again.

"How dare any of you think of yourselves as angels of God!" Sweaty flared.

"But, I'll concede, it's a stretch," McNab said.

"I used to wonder where Carlitos learned his blasphemous irreverence and childish sense of humor. Now it's perfectly clear. I hope God will forgive you, General McNab. I won't."

"Right now," Castillo said, "if Sweaty tries to turn the both of you heathens into sopranos, I'd be inclined to help her. Now, who turned Frank loose, and why, and what the hell is he doing in here?"

"Frank is now on our side," McNab said. "Get used to it."

"Let me try to explain this in heathen terms," Allan Naylor, Jr., said. "One heathen to another. Like another acquaintance of ours, whose name Satan himself could not tear from my lips, Brother Frank saw the error of his ways, 'fessed up, and is now allied with the forces of goodness and purity."

"And you believe him?" Castillo asked incredulously. "All of you believe it? And you expect me to believe it?"

"It's true, Charley," Lammelle said.

"Charley, Frank obeyed an order without thinking it through," General Naylor said. "That's easy to do. You're supposed to follow orders. What's hard is admitting that you know the order is wrong, and then doing something to make it right. In Frank's case, that was doubly difficult for him. Not only did it constitute disobeying the President, but he knew he could have just kept his mouth shut and done nothing. He knew us all well enough to know we weren't going to harm him . . ."

"Harming him did run through my mind. Vic D'Allessando said we should castrate him with a dull knife."

He looked at D'Allessando.

"I'm with McNab, Charley," D'Allessando said. "Sorry."

Castillo said nothing.

". . . but instead, he is putting his career on the line," General Naylor finished.

Castillo thought: *That shoe fits your foot, too, doesn't it?*

"Is that what happened to you, Uncle Allan?" he asked softly.

Naylor met his eyes, but said nothing.

Colonel Jack Brewer broke the silence.

"The general's question, Colonel Castillo," he said, "was whether the freezing process has been satisfactorily completed."

Castillo hesitated.

"Well, has it?" Sweaty demanded.

Castillo looked at her for a long moment, then at Lammelle, and then back at Sweaty.

What choice do I have?

"The answer to that is we don't really know," he said. "What Master Sergeant Dennis told me . . ."

"So, what do you want to do?" General Naylor asked, when Castillo had related what had happened just before he'd come to the war room.

"In two hours, I want to put Sergeant Dennis and the beer keg that's thawing in the sun in Aloysius's G-Five and fly it to Fort Detrick. We have to know if the helium has really killed it and the only way to do that is in Colonel Hamilton's lab."

"Fly it to Baltimore/Washington, right?" Lammelle asked.

Eyes jumped to Castillo to see how he was going to react to Lammelle having asked a question.

Castillo nodded.

"In for a penny, in for a pound, Charley," Lammelle said. "If I went with it, I could have an agency vehicle . . . It'll fit in a Yukon, right?"

Castillo nodded again, but didn't speak.

". . . meet the airplane and personally make sure it gets to Fort Detrick. The only one who could interfere with that, or ask me questions I don't want to answer, would be Jack Powell, and I don't think Jack would actually go out to the airport even if he heard I was coming. Worst scenario there, I think, would be Powell sending Stan Waters—"

"Who?"

"J. Stanley Waters, deputy director for operations. Who wants my job, and therefore does everything Jack tells him to. I trust him a little less than you trust me."

"Okay. We get the stuff to the lab at Detrick. Sergeant Dennis tells me Hamilton can find out in half an hour whether the Congo-X is really dead. And what would you do after you dropped off the Congo-X? Wait for Hamilton to run his tests?"

"That would be information I'd like to have."

"And with which you could head straight for the White House, right?"

"Yeah, Charley, if I were so inclined, I could head straight for the White House. But what I plan to do is head straight for Langley to see what I can learn there."

"And if Jack Powell does go out to the airport? Or sends your buddy Waters?"

"Can I have my dart gun back?"

After a perceptible pause, during which he wondered again, *What choice do I have?* Castillo said, "You know what they say, Frank: 'In for a penny, in for a pound.' Lester, give Mr. Lammelle his dart gun."

"There will be room for me on that plane, right?" Roscoe J. Danton said. And then he quickly added: "Colonel, I've got pictures of that stuff on the Tu-934A on the island. And what you and Uncle Remus and the Sergeant did to it here. I'd like to follow it all the way to the lab at Fort Detrick."

Castillo didn't immediately reply.

"And before I go, I'd like to get pictures of you and Jake getting on that airplane," Roscoe went on.

"Which raises the question, Charley," McNab said, "of flying that airplane across the border and to Washington without getting it shot down."

"What General McNab and I talked about, Colonel," Naylor said, "and what we recommend, is that he and I go on the Russian aircraft to Washington. I can call MacDill, inform them that we're coming, and get us an Air Force escort."

"Which means the White House will know," Castillo thought aloud.

"But not the circumstances," McNab said.

"And I'll have time to get from Baltimore/Washington so that I can get pictures of the Tu-934A landing at Andrews," Roscoe J. Danton said.

"And that raises the question of Roscoe J. Danton," Castillo said. "What captions will he put under all those pictures he's been taking?"

"Frankly, Colonel, I don't know," Danton replied. "But I'm sort of like Frank. I've learned to tell the difference between the good guys and the bad guys."

"I see we're back to a choice between trusting Roscoe and killing him," Castillo said.

"You may think that's funny," Sweaty snapped, "but I don't."

"And that unsolicited and unwelcome opinion raises yet another question," Castillo said. "What do I do with Big Mouth here and her big brother?"

Sweaty said unkind things to him in Russian.

Castillo went on: "I think the best thing to do is have Miller and Sparkman take them—and the Spetsnaz that Cousin Aleksandr was so kind to loan us, plus whichever of Sirinov's Spetsnaz want to go to Argentina—to Cozumel to meet the Peruaire freighter."

"You're out of your mind!" Sweaty said in English.

"I think not, Charley," Dmitri Berezovsky said.

"You mean you don't think I'm out of my mind, or you don't want to go to Argentina?"

"I can't wait to get back to Argentina. You remember that my wife and daughter are there? But before this is over, we will certainly be talking with the Washington *resident*, Sergei Murov, and perhaps even dealing with Vladimir Vladimirovich Putin himself. Svetlana and I know them both well. I think you need our counsel."

"What kind of passports do you have?" Lammelle asked.

"You mean besides our Russian Federation diplomatic passports?"

"Right."

"Argentine and Uruguayan."

"Are they in your names?"

Berezovsky shook his head.

"How much inspection will they stand?"

"My cousin assures me they were issued by the respective foreign ministries," Berezovsky said.

"And would your cousin know?"

"I think he would."

"Who is your cousin?"

"If he tells you, Frank, I'd have to kill you," Castillo said.

"His name is Aleksandr Pevsner," Sweaty said. "And if your knowing that in any way ever endangers him or his family, I *will* kill you."

"On a threat credibility scale of one to ten, I think I'd rate that as a ten," Lammelle said. And then added, "Well, knowing that name explains a lot of things I didn't really understand. Pevsner is really your cousin?"

"Our mothers are sisters," Berezovsky said.

"Charley, if they're determined to go . . ." Lammelle began.

"We are," Berezovsky said.

". . . and I agree they could be very useful," Lammelle went on. "Hide them in plain sight."

"Where?" Castillo asked.

"The Monica Lewinsky Motel," Lammelle said.

"The what?" Sweaty asked.

"If a President of the United States can hide his girlfriend there, it should be good enough for mine," Castillo said. "How do you plan to get them there?"

"I wouldn't want Senator Johns to hear about this, but I have a limo, armored, with radios, et cetera, and driven by agency officers," Lammelle said.

"You want to fly them to Baltimore/Washington on Casey's airplane?" Castillo asked.

Lammelle nodded.

"And General Sirinov?"

"On the Tu-934A. If Roscoe can get Wolf News out there to cover its arrival—"

"He would be on TV and Murov would see that," Castillo interrupted, "but what do we do with him afterward?"

"I think General Sirinov would be comfortable in the Monica Lewinsky Motel," Lammelle said. "And he'd be available if we need him, and we probably will."

"Have you got enough people—people you can trust—to handle all this?"

"Yes, I do," Lammelle said. "Your call, Charley."

"What other options do I have?"

"Not many—none—that I can think of," Lammelle said.

Castillo counted something on his fingers, then announced, "There's room for Lester on the Tu-934A. So he goes, too, to sit on General Sirinov. Miller and Sparkman take the Spetsnaz to Cozumel as soon as they can—in the next thirty minutes—in our G-Three, then come back here and pick up Uncle Remus and Peg-Leg—and anybody I've forgotten. By then Uncle Remus and Peg-Leg will have Drug Cartel International all cleaned up. And then they go to Baltimore/Washington."

He paused for a good thirty seconds, and then asked, "Any comments?"

"I want to know about this motel," Sweaty said.

"You'll like it, sweetheart," Castillo said. "Inside plumbing and all the other conveniences one would expect in a Motel-8. Any other comments?"

There were none.

"Okay, then that's it. That's what we'll do."

[SEVEN]
Office of the Director
The Central Intelligence Agency
Langley, Virginia
1305 12 February 2007

"Keep me advised, Bruce," DCI John Powell said. "We absolutely can't afford to have this get away from us."

He took the telephone handset from his ear, very slowly replaced it in the base, then met the eyes of J. Stanley Waters, the DDCI for operations.

"Festerman says that Naylor called Central Command and ordered that a flight of F-16s meet him over the Gulf of Mexico prepared to escort his plane into U.S. airspace and then to Andrews."

"Where in the Gulf of Mexico? When?"

"Right in the goddamn middle of it. And right now."

"Where did he call from?"

"Mexico City," Powell said. "But I'm not sure I believe that. What I'm beginning to suspect is that Casey's communications is not quite as miraculous as advertised. Or that Casey is fucking with us."

"Why would he do that?"

"Maybe because he likes McNab more than he likes me."

"Do we know what kind of an airplane Naylor has?"

"No. And that bothers me, too. All Naylor told MacDill is the call sign. He told MacDill 'Big Boy' will be at thirty thousand feet moving at five hundred knots."

"That doesn't sound as if that's Naylor's Gulfstream."

"No, it doesn't. Which may be because Naylor's Gulfstream is on the tarmac at MacDill."

"I forgot that," Waters said.

"Yeah," Powell said.

"You think he has Castillo? Or the Russians? Or both?"

"Well, he could be smuggling drugs. But I'd say it's likely that he has either or both, wouldn't you?"

"Looks that way. What are you going to do?"

Powell picked up his telephone.

"This is DCI Powell. Get onto whoever would know and get me a track on all aircraft operating over the middle of the Gulf of Mexico, or headed toward the middle, at thirty thousand feet and five hundred knots. The one I'm looking for will probably not—repeat, not—have a transponder. Got it?"

He hung up.

"Are you going to tell the President, John?"

"No. I thought this would be our little secret."

He picked up a red telephone and punched one of the buttons on it.

"Jack Powell, Mr. President. I have just learned that General Naylor has ordered that a flight of F-16s . . .

"Mr. President, I assure you that I'm doing all that's humanly possible to add to what I know, what I just told you . . .

"Yes, sir, Mr. President, I'll leave here immediately . . .

"Yes, sir, Mr. President, I fully understand that I am to take no action of any kind in this matter without your prior permission."

[EIGHT]
The Mayflower Hotel
1127 Connecticut Avenue, N.W.
Washington, D.C.
1745 13 February 2007

The manager on duty, who wore a frock coat with a tiny rose pinned to the lapel, intercepted the party before they were more than one hundred yards into the lobby.

"Mr. Barlow?"

"I am Thomas Barlow," Berezovsky said.

"My name is Winfield Broom, Mr. Barlow, I am the manager on duty. Welcome to the Mayflower."

"Thank you," Berezovsky said.

"From time to time, little mistakes are made, but sometimes—as now—they have a pleasant result."

"I don't think I understand."

"Well, when Mr. Darby called to make your reservations, we were of course happy to accommodate him and you. But then Mr. Darby called back a few minutes later and asked if Mr. von und zu Gossinger still kept an apartment here. I told him he did, although we haven't seen him for some time. And then thirty minutes after that, Mr. von und zu Gossinger himself called. He said he was skiing in Gstaad, but that he would be very pleased if you would stay in his apartment while you're here."

"That's very kind of Mr. von und zu Gossinger," Barlow said.

"Right this way, please," Mr. Broom said, gesturing toward the elevator bank.

"This is really very nice," Svetlana said five minutes later. "Not at all what comes to mind when you hear 'motel.'"

"I'm glad you think so," Mr. Broom said. "Now, the sauna is separate . . ."

"Why does Mr. von und zu Gossinger call this hotel the 'Monica Lewinsky Motel'?" Svetlana asked.

"I'm sure I have no idea, madam," Mr. Broom said, just a little huffily. "Now, if you'll please come this way?"

[NINE]
Old Ebbitt Grill
675 15th Street, N.W.
Washington, D.C.
1750 13 February 2007

"Truman, I told you that if we just waited, Roscoe would inevitably show up," Ambassador Charles M. Montvale said to Mr. Truman Ellsworth looking over his shoulder to the end of the massive bar. "Hello, Roscoe!"

"Your office said I could find you here," Danton said, taking a seat next to them at the bar.

"Waiting for my master's call, Roscoe. The odds are strongly against it ever coming."

"I'll have one of those," Danton said to the bartender. "And if these two are not already over their limit, give them another."

"What happened to you after we came back?" Ellsworth asked.

"I thought you would never ask," Danton said, and told them . . .

"And Castillo's on the airplane with Naylor?" Ellsworth said when he finished.

"Naylor, McNab, and General Yakov Sirinov."

"That, I am having a hard time believing," Montvale said.

"What if I told you the airplane is a Tu-934A?"

"Even harder to believe."

"Charles, I think Roscoe is serious," Ellsworth said.

Montvale looked at Danton, who nodded.

"The plane should land at Andrews about nine o'clock," he said.

"And the Russians?"

"Maybe I'll tell you later. What I need right now is a way to get onto Andrews."

"I think we could arrange that," Ellsworth said. "And I submit, Charles, that we are indebted to Roscoe."

"I'd like to see this myself," Montvale said.

"And I would like somehow to get in touch with C. Harry Whelan, that sonofabitch, and get him and Wolf News out there," Danton said.

"That also I can handle," Ellsworth said. "He's been driving us crazy wanting to talk to us. The ambassador has qualms—which I frankly don't share— about embarrassing the President."

"The *Office* of the President," Montvale corrected him. "I would happily embarrass Clendennen but I can't figure out how to separate in the mind of the people the asshole from the office he holds."

The obscenity and a general slurring of speech confirmed to Danton that the ambassador and Ellsworth had been at the bar for some time.

Danton looked at Ellsworth with a raised eyebrow.

"The ambassador is no longer on the red phone circuit," Ellsworth said. "The President won't even return the ambassador's calls. And we no longer have access to the White House Yukon fleet."

"That sonofabitch!" Danton said.

"He has also taken to referring to me as 'Ambassador Stupid,'" Montvale said. "The director of National Stupidity."

Ellsworth said, "You wouldn't look stupid, Charles, if you were at Andrews when Castillo and Company arrive."

"True."

"I've got some caveats," Danton said. "I don't want to get into the Congo-X business until Lammelle has a chance to deal with Murov, the *rezident*."

"My, people have been baring their hearts to you, haven't they, Roscoe?" Montvale asked.

"What I'd really like to do is have Sirinov on Wolf News, being carried off the Tu-934A."

"Carried off? He has been injured?"

"Sweaty shot him in the foot," Danton said.

"'Sweaty'?"

"Former Podpolkovnik Svetlana Alekseeva of the SVR," Danton said.

"And where did this altercation occur?"

"I can't tell you that. Not now."

"I don't want to be responsible in any way for any Congo-X being released anywhere," Montvale said.

"That's not a problem. We know how to kill it. We've killed all the Russians have. Hamilton's got some in his lab, but the Russians are out of ammo."

"How do you know that?" Montvale asked softly.

His speech, Danton noticed, was no longer slurred.

"Frank Lammelle told me thirty-five minutes ago. He was then at Fort Detrick."

Montvale considered that a moment, and then said, "Truman, be so good as to call Mr. Whelan. Tell him I will agree to be interviewed tonight, providing that it is on my terms, and that he and a camera crew are outside in thirty minutes."

"My pleasure," Ellsworth said.

"If he agrees, I will spend that thirty minutes getting those terms from Roscoe and drinking black coffee. I understand that the only thing that black coffee does to a drunk is make him a bright-eyed drunk, but perhaps C. Harry Whelan, who is not too bright, will not notice.

"If Whelan agrees to come, call the limousine service and have a car outside in thirty minutes."

"Yes, Mr. Ambassador," Truman Ellsworth said as he took his cell phone from his pocket.

[TEN]
The President's Study
The White House
1600 Pennsylvania Avenue, N.W.
Washington, D.C.
2055 13 February 2007

DCI Jack Powell put his hand over the telephone microphone.

"Mr. President, that airplane is on final approach to Andrews."

"Have they got cameras out there? I want to see it," the President said.

"Wolf News does, Mr. President," presidential spokesman Jack Parker said, and, when the President turned, pointed to one of the televisions mounted on the wall.

The monitor showed a flashing banner—WOLF NEWS BREAKING NEWS ANDREWS AIR FORCE BASE WASHINGTON DC—and an image of the Tu-934A making its approach.

"Turn the fucking sound up, Porky! I'm not psychic!"

The stirring strands of the "William Tell Overture" filled the President's study.

"Shit," the President said, then asked, "What kind of an airplane is that?"

"I believe that's a Tupolev Tu-934A, Mr. President," Powell said.

"Where the hell did Naylor get that?" the President asked rhetorically.

Wolf News cameras followed the airplane as it touched down, and until its landing roll took it far down the runway.

Then C. Harry Whelan and Roscoe J. Danton appeared on the screen.

"Good evening. This is C. Harry Whelan. What we all have just seen is the landing of a super-secret Russian airplane, the Tupolev Tu-934A. And standing with me is my good friend, the distinguished, prize-winning journalist Roscoe J. Danton of *The Washington Times-Post*, who knows the details of this incredible intelligence accomplishment."

"What the hell is he talking about?" the President asked.

"Thank you, Harry," Danton said, patting Whelan's back almost affectionately. "The CIA has had a long-standing offer of one hundred and twenty-five million dollars to anyone who could bring them one of these airplanes. That prize—I see the deputy director of the CIA, Franklin Lammelle, standing over there beside our director of National Intelligence, Ambassador Charles M.

Montvale, both of them wearing big smiles; they were the brains behind this incredible operation—"

"*What the hell is Lammelle doing out there with Ambassador Stupid?*" the President asked. "*I thought he was with Naylor, getting Castillo and those Russian traitors.*"

"*I don't know, Mr. President,*" DCI Powell said.

"—has apparently just been claimed by two recently retired American officers, Colonel Jacob Torine, U.S. Air Force, and Lieutenant Colonel Carlos Castillo, U.S. Army."

"*Oh, for Christ's sake!*" the President said.

"Where did they get it, Roscoe?" Whelan asked.

"From an island off an unnamed South American country."

"How do you know that, Roscoe?"

"I'm proud to say I was with them, Harry."

"But you won't identify that country?"

"I don't think I'd better at this time, Harry."

"But you are telling the millions of Wolf News watchers that these two former officers—"

"*Retired* officers, Harry."

"All right, Roscoe, old buddy, 'retired' officers. These two *retired* officers invaded an unnamed South American country—"

"'Invaded,' Harry, implies boots on the ground. We were on the ground twelve minutes and twenty-two seconds. You really can't call that an invasion, can you?"

"—and stole this super-secret Russian airplane—"

"I think that they like to think they 'took possession of it,' Harry."

"And now the CIA is going to pay them one hundred and twenty-five million dollars?"

"That's what Franklin Lammelle told me earlier today."

"We've heard that General Allan Naylor is aboard that airplane. True?"

"As soon as they reached American soil, they turned it over to the military. I don't really know what happened after that, but I can guess."

"Please guess, Roscoe, for the millions of Wolf News viewers around the globe watching this exclusively on Wolf News."

"I would guess that General Naylor decided the Tu-934A belonged in Washington, and that since Colonel Torine and Colonel Castillo were the only ones who knew how to fly it . . ."

"Well, that makes sense," Whelan said. "Oh, look, here it comes! Get a shot of that!"

The monitor showed the Tu-934A taxiing to where Whelan and Danton were standing. Then the aircraft turned around, the engines died, and the ramp started to slowly open.

A siren was heard, and then an ambulance appeared on the screen.

"An ambulance!" C. Harry Whelan said. "Looks like someone on the T-O—whatever you said . . ."

"*Tu*-934A, Harry. Yes, I would say that the appearance of an ambulance would suggest there's someone in need of medical attention."

Two men in white coats got out of the ambulance and ran up the ramp. Moments later, they came out carrying an unconscious man on a stretcher. Lester Bradley walked beside them.

"Who's that, Roscoe?" Whelan asked.

"I have no idea," Danton said. "I don't speak Russian and he doesn't speak English."

"*Who the fuck was that on the stretcher?*" the President of the United States inquired.

"*The guy on the stretcher, Mr. President, was General Yakov Sirinov,*" DCI Powell said.

"What happened to him, Roscoe?"

"Another Russian shot him. I don't think he's seriously wounded."

The stretcher was loaded into the ambulance.

Colonel Torine and Lieutenant Colonel Castillo appeared in the door, acknowledged the applause of the Air Force personnel, and then trotted down the ramp, with Max beside them. They got into the ambulance, which immediately drove off.

Generals Naylor and McNab appeared in the ramp door, walked down it, and got into a staff car.

"I want those two bastards here in thirty minutes," the President ordered. "I want—"

"Mr. President," Porky Parker said. "May I respectfully suggest that we have to carefully consider the ramifications of this?"

President Clendennen glared at him. "The next time those two sonsof-bitches go to Fort Leavenworth, they'll be in handcuffs on their way to the Army prison. . . ."

"Porky's right, Mr. President," DCI Powell said. "If we've invaded some South American country—"

"*If*? *If*? You just heard Roscoe J. Danton tell the whole goddamned world we did! Putin was probably watching us carry that general we kidnapped off that fucking airplane we stole."

"Or is watching it being replayed for him as we speak," Parker said. "I'm told the Ministry of Information tapes Wolf News and then distributes the significant stories around the Kremlin."

"That's true, Mr. President," DCI Powell said. "I really think we should get the secretary of State's input on this, so we can decide how to react."

"Well, get her here. In thirty minutes."

"Secretary Cohen is in New York, at the UN, Mr. President," Porky Parker said. "At a reception for President Chávez of Venezuela."

"And if you plan to arrest General Naylor, Mr. President," DCI Powell said, "I think we ought to hear what the attorney general has to say. And/or the secretary of Defense."

"Maybe we should all give this some thought, Mr. President, overnight," Porky Parker said. "Collect all the facts, and then, say, at ten tomorrow morning . . ."

"We really don't want to act precipitously in the heat of the moment," DCI Powell said.

The President looked between them for a good thirty seconds before saying, "Okay, ten tomorrow morning. Just make sure they're all here."

He then walked out of the presidential study, slamming the door behind him.

A moment later there was the sound of a vase falling to the floor.

Or perhaps of one being thrown against a wall.

[ELEVEN]
The Mayflower Hotel
1127 Connecticut Avenue, N.W.
Washington, D.C.
0925 14 February 2007

There is another, more elegant, name for it, in keeping with the elegance of the Mayflower itself, but most people think of it simply as "The Lobby Bar."

It's on the left of the hotel, and has windows opening on the Desales Street sidewalk. It offers morning coffee and a simple but of course elegant breakfast menu.

There were perhaps twenty people in it when Sergei Murov walked in.

"Over here, Sergei," Frank Lammelle called.

He was standing beside one of the tables near the window. There were three men and a woman sitting at the table.

"Thank you for coming, Sergei," Lammelle said as Murov approached the table. "I know it was more than a little inconvenient for you."

"Anything for you, Frank," Murov said.

"I don't think you know this fellow, but I understand you've been anxious to meet him. Charley, say hello to Sergei."

"How do you do, Colonel Castillo?" Murov said in English as he sat down.

"Frank's been telling me a lot about you, Sergei," Castillo said in Russian. "But not that you look like cousins."

"My Carlitos sounds as if he's a Saint Petersburger, wouldn't you agree, Sergei?" Sweaty asked.

She put her hand out. Murov rose, bowed, took her hand, kissed it, and then sat down.

"Svetlana, you are even more lovely than I remembered," Murov said.

"And of course you and Dmitri are old friends, right?" Lammelle said.

"We have known each other for a very long time," Murov said. "But perhaps 'acquaintances' would be the more accurate term."

"Charley's right," Berezovsky said. "You and Frank do look like cousins."

A waiter appeared with a silver coffee service on a tray and poured a cup for Murov.

"Lovely place, the Lobby Bar, isn't it, Sergei?" Lammelle asked.

"I come here often," Murov said.

"So I expect you'll miss it?"

"Excuse me?"

"As soon as he gets to his office, your ambassador will be getting a call from Secretary of State Cohen. She will suggest to him that it would be best if you voluntarily gave up your post here and returned to Moscow. Today. If that is not acceptable, you will be declared *persona non grata*. In that case, you would have seventy-two hours to leave the country, but you will be leaving, Sergei."

"Is that why you asked me to come here, Frank, to tell me that?"

"No. Actually, it was to ask a favor of you. I want you to take something to Moscow for me when you go, and see, personally, that it gets into the hands of Mr. Putin."

"What would that be?"

"It looks like a blue rubber beer keg," Castillo said. "I happened to come across it on a little island off the coast of Venezuela."

"Not to worry, Sergei," Sweaty said. "It's quite dead. It would be nice if you dropped it on Yakov Vladimirovich's foot, but I don't want to kill you or him. Or anyone else that way."

Murov lost his diplomatic composure.

"It's dead?"

"As a doornail," Castillo said.

"And that's why I'd like you to take it to Mr. Putin, so he can see that for himself. And the sooner the better, of course," Lammelle said. "Today. Rather than insisting on the seventy-two hours to which you are entitled before being expelled."

"If you look out the window, Sergei, you will see that the beer barrel is being loaded into your Mercedes SUV right now," Castillo said.

Murov looked.

"There's just a little more, Sergei. I'm sure you have by now seen the Wolf News report . . ."

"You can't miss it. It's been on since last night."

"Then you probably noticed that nothing was said about Congo-X."

Murov nodded.

"Not a word about General Sirinov jumping Spetsnaz into the Congo, to see if we'd missed any Congo-X when we took out the Fish Farm," Lammelle said. "Not a word about him personally flying into El Obeid Airport in North Kurdufan, Sudan, on a Tu-934A when they did find some that we missed. Not a word about the seventeen bodies he left at the airfield when he took off for what we now call 'Drug Cartel International Airport' in Mexico. Not a word about him watching as Pavel Koslov, the Mexico City *resident*, loaded the two beer kegs you sent to Fort Detrick into a Mexican embassy Suburban for later movement across the border. Not a word about his then flying to La Orchila Island in Venezuela with what was left of the Congo-X."

"We have movies of most of this, Sergei," Castillo said.

"And General Sirinov has decided it's safer for him to be here, talking to Frank, than it would be for him in Moscow, trying to explain his failure to Vladimir Vladimirovich," Berezovsky said.

"And are you also talking to Frank, Dmitri?" Murov asked.

"I could tell you no, but you wouldn't believe me."

"We can keep it that way, Sergei," Lammelle said. "If Vladimir Vladimirovich agrees that getting into the question of Congo-X would not be good for either Russia or the United States."

"'Keep it that way'?"

"Well, your Ministry of Information could deny the whole thing. They could say it wasn't a brilliant intelligence operation, that they had sold the Tu-934A to . . . what's the name of that corporation, Charley?"

"LCBF. The LCBF Corporation," Castillo furnished.

"Who then turned a quick profit by selling it to the CIA."

"No one would believe that," Murov said.

"There are always some people who will believe anything," Sweaty said. "Including that Vladimir Vladimirovich is a fool."

"I don't quite understand, my dear Svetlana."

"Sorry, Frank," Svetlana said. "I know how much you and Sergei love to show each other how brilliant and civilized you are, but I've had enough of it."

"Which means?" Murov asked.

"You tell Vladimir Vladimirovich that I said that if so much as a thimbleful of Congo-X turns up anywhere, or if I even suspect he's trying to hurt any member of my family—and that includes my Carlitos, of course—I will make sure that every member of the SVR learns in detail how reckless and incompetent he is.

"And if he thinks this is an idle bluff, tell him to watch what happens if Koussevitzky's wife Olga—he's a Spetsnaz major; I shot him in the leg and left him on that island—and the entire Koussevitzky family are not in Budapest within seventy-two hours of your arrival in Moscow. I'll have two out of three SVR officers giggling behind Vladimir Vladimirovich's back, whispering that what he did when he was head of the KGB in Saint Petersburg was close his door and write poetry."

She wet her index finger with her tongue and ran it over her eyebrow.

"Dmitri," Lammelle said. "You're right. Her bite is worse than her bark."

"In other words, what you're proposing is an armistice," Murov said.

"On one hand," Castillo said, "I don't believe in the tooth fairy. Putin's going to have a hard time swallowing what we've done to him. He may not be able to. On the other hand, there's been an armistice in Korea for fifty years, during which fewer people on both sides have been killed than would have died if the war was still on. I'll take my chances with that. You tell Putin what Svetlana said."

Murov looked at Castillo and then at Svetlana. He stood.

"It's been very interesting seeing you again," he said. He offered his hand to Lammelle and Berezovsky. "And to meet you, Colonel," he said, offering his hand to Castillo. He then waited for Svetlana to put out her hand, which took a good fifteen seconds. He bowed and kissed it. "And it has been a joy to spend a few minutes—however stressful—in the company of the most beautiful daughter of the Motherland I have ever known. But now I must leave. I have a plane to catch."

He walked out of the Lobby Bar. Castillo, Lammelle, Berezovsky, and Svetlana looked out the window, and in a moment Murov appeared. He walked to the Mercedes SUV—the driver of which had taken advantage of the diplomatic privilege of parking wherever the hell the impulse strikes, and it was now block-ing the curbside lane of Desales Street—jerked open the rear window to the cargo area, looked inside, and then slammed the window closed. He got in the passenger seat, slammed the door, and then the Mercedes drove off.

Castillo looked at Svetlana.

She said, "You heard what he said about the 'most beautiful daughter of the Motherland'?"

"What I want to know is what all you Russians have against Saint Peters-burg poets."

Lammelle stood, and said, "And now you'll have to excuse me, I have an appointment at the White House."

[TWELVE]
The Situation Room
The White House
1600 Pennsylvania Avenue, N.W.
Washington, D.C.
1005 14 February 2007

"I'm so glad you could join us, Mr. Lammelle," the President said sarcastically.

"Sir, it's a longer walk here from the Monica Lewinsky Motel than I remem-bered. My apologies for being late."

"No problem, if you remembered to bring your resignation with you."

"I'll give it verbally and leave right now, if that is your desire, Mr. President."

Lammelle looked around the room. It was nowhere near close to capacity. The secretaries of State and Defense were seated at the large table, as were the director of Central Intelligence, the attorney general, the director of the FBI, the director of National Intelligence and his executive assistant, and Generals Naylor and McNab. Plus, of course, the presidential spokesman, Mr. Jack Parker.

"You'll leave when I tell you that you can. Take a seat, Lammelle."

Lammelle sat down. Secretary of State Natalie Cohen stood up, leaned across the desk, and laid an envelope before him.

"What's this?" the President demanded.

"My resignation, Mr. President," she said.

"I haven't asked for it."

"Yes, I know," she said, and sat down.

General Naylor stood up, leaned across the table, and laid an envelope on the table.

"That's my resignation, sir," he said.

The President looked at General McNab.

"Well?"

"Well, what, Mr. President?"

"Aren't you going to offer your resignation?"

"No, sir."

"You didn't think I was going to let you get away with what you did, did you?"

"I don't know what you mean, Mr. President."

"You know goddamn well what I mean!" Clendennen flared. "You've been in this up to that goddamned mustache of yours! Placing the entire country in danger!"

"Sir, I don't understand."

"Maybe after the goddamn Russians open barrels of Congo-X all over the country, you will."

"Sir, that's just not going to happen. The Russians don't have barrels of Congo-X."

"Excuse me, General," Frank Lammelle said. "The Russians do have one barrel of Congo-X. It's dead, but I suppose you could still call it Congo-X. Or maybe I should have said, the Russians have one barrel of Dead Congo-X. I gave it to Mr. Murov, who is going to take it to Moscow later today to show it to Mr. Putin."

"You're telling me there is no longer a Congo-X threat?" Clendennen asked, incredulous.

"With the exception of a couple of quarts of live Congo-X in Colonel Hamilton's laboratory at Fort Detrick," General Naylor said, "there is no Congo-X anywhere in the world. Colonel Castillo seized all that the Russians had when he staged the raid on La Orchila Island in Venezuela. Colonel Hamilton will continue to experiment with it to see if he can find a better way to kill it."

"Why wasn't I told of this?" Clendennen demanded angrily.

"Because no one who knew you trusted you, Mr. President. You had proven you susceptible to Russian blackmail," Natalie Cohen said. "I saw it as my sworn duty under the Constitution to thwart your announced intentions and did so."

"And now, Madam Secretary, you have resigned," the President said. "What are your intentions now? Are you going to write a book? Go on Wolf News?"

"Frankly, sir, I haven't made up my mind. But I must tell you, sir, that I do not share Ambassador Montvale's qualms about embarrassing you personally, or the Office of the President."

"Madam Secretary," presidential spokesman Jack Parker said. "Have you—"

"Butt out, Porky," the President snapped. "You're supposed to be a god-damned fly on the wall, and that's all."

"No, sir. That's not true. I took the same oath Secretary Cohen did. May I continue, sir? Or would you like my resignation right now?"

After a moment, the President said, "Go on, goddamn it."

"Madam Secretary, have you considered the public relations aspects of what will happen when word gets out that you have resigned, that General Naylor has resigned, and as I strongly suspect he will, Ambassador Montvale has also resigned?"

"Yes, I have," she said. "What are you suggesting, that I not resign? Sorry, Jack, I just don't have the desire to deal anymore with the President."

"Ambassador Montvale, are you going to resign?" Parker asked.

"Yes. And I'm aware of the collateral damage all of this might cause the country. But I can no longer in good faith serve a man who tried to do what the President would have done had not Colonel Castillo—and others—stood up to him."

"I'm going to put my two cents in here," the attorney general said. "I'm a lawyer. We're trained to compromise. You want it all at once, or in pieces?"

"Go slowly, please," Montvale said dryly. "I'm known as Ambassador Stupid, you know."

"My take on this whole thing is that it's an intelligence failure, Mr. Ambassador," the attorney general said. "I think that Jack Powell—the CIA—never really met its responsibilities. If they hadn't insisted that laboratory in the Congo was a fish farm, and if that woman—the Vienna station chief—hadn't scared those two Russians off with her incompetence, we would have learned about it from them. Instead, we had this Keystone Kop business—and it would be funny, if the circumstances were not so terrifying—of everybody chasing Colonel Castillo—unsuccessfully chasing him—all over the world while he did the Venezuelan operation—in essence the CIA's work—for them—"

He stopped in midsentence and caught his breath.

"And since I know you well enough, Mr. Ambassador, to refuse to believe that had you known about this—had Jack Powell promptly told you what you were entitled to know—you would have taken the appropriate action, and none of us would be sitting at this table this morning."

"Now, wait a minute!" Powell protested.

"So Powell has to go," the attorney general went on, "to be replaced by Lammelle, who instead of assisting in the President's plan to arrest Castillo and swap him to the Russians—and the illegality of that boggles the mind—worked with General Naylor and Castillo and solved the problem of Congo-X."

"I can't take credit for that—" Lammelle began.

"Shut up, Frank. I'm not finished. If I had to search the world for the two people who most detest Joshua Ezekiel Clendennen and at the same time have an unparalleled knowledge of what he should be doing, I'd come back with Natalie Cohen and Charles M. Montvale.

"So . . . Natalie withdraws her resignation, and the President announces he has chosen Charles M. Montvale as his Vice President."

"That's insane!" the President of the United States said.

"Mr. President, if it goes the other way, if Secretary Cohen and General Naylor resign," Porky Parker said, "and I do and Mr. Lammelle does, and it comes out—and it will—that you were willing to cave in to the Russians, the Congress will be drawing up articles of impeachment within seventy-two hours."

"And we all remember the last time that happened," the attorney general said. "It was a disaster for the country."

"Yes, it was," President Clendennen said. "And with that in mind, for the good of the country, for the good of the Office of the President, I am inclined to accept Ambassador Montvale's offer—"

"You miserable goddamned shameless hypocritical sonofabitch!" Natalie Cohen exploded.

It was the first time anyone in the room had ever heard her use anything stronger than "darn."

Her face flushed.

"Excuse me," she said, and then looked at Montvale. "Mr. Ambassador, this may be one of those situations where if we don't stand up to what we know are our obligations, and leave, those who take our offices may be worse for the country. . . ."

"You think I should take it, Natalie?" Montvale asked.

She nodded. "I think you should take it, and if you do, I'll stay."

"Do it, Charles, please," Truman Ellsworth said.

"I'll take your offer of the vice presidency, Mr. President, on the following conditions: First, that you decline Secretary Cohen's resignation."

"Agreed, of course, for the reasons—"

"Second, that you decline General Naylor's resignation."

"I never asked for it in the first place."

"Third, that you send Truman Ellsworth's name to the Senate for confirmation to replace me as director of National Intelligence."

"Of course. I have always held Mr. Ellsworth in the highest poss—"

"Fourth, that Mr. Parker make the announcement that I am your choice to be Vice President of the United States within the next three or four minutes, before you can change your mind or otherwise squirm out of doing so."

"Squirm out of— Mr. Montvale, now I think you're just insulting me and—"

"And finally," Montvale went on, "vis-à-vis Lieutenant Colonel (Retired) Castillo and his Merry Band of Outlaw . . ."

"What about Castillo?" It was clear that even saying his name left a bad taste in Clendennen's mouth.

Montvale said: "I think the CIA's Distinguished Intelligence Cross would be appropriate for him. I know he's never actually been in the CIA, but as the attorney general has pointed out, he has been doing their work for them. So I think it's appropriate."

President Clendennen, white-faced and tight-lipped, glared at him, but said nothing.

"And for Colonel Torine, Colonel Hamilton, and Mr. Leverette, the CIA Distinguished Intelligence Medal seems fitting," Montvale went on. "And for everyone else in Castillo's Merry Band of Outlaws who played a role in this, the CIA Intelligence Star.

"Wouldn't you agree, Mr. President?"

For the rest of his life, neither the future Vice President of the United States nor any of the other people in the room would ever forget the kaleidoscope of emotions that passed over Clendennen's face before he finally opened his mouth and said the one word:

"Yes."